Praise for the Shadow Falls Series

"Hunter sucks you in . . . an amazing roller-coaster ride." —*RT Book Reviews*

"The Shadow Falls series belongs to my favorite YA series. It has everything I wish for in a YA paranormal series. A thrilling tale that moves with a great pace, where layers of secrets are revealed in a way that we are never bored. It continues a gripping story about self-discoveries, finding a place in the world, friendship, and love. So if you didn't start this series yet, I can only encourage you to do so." —*Bewitched Bookworms*

"Ms. Hunter handles this series with such deftness, crafting a wonderful tale that speaks to the adolescent in me. I highly recommend this series filled with darkness and light, hope and danger, friendship and romance."
—*Night Owl Reviews* (Top Pick)

"Jam-packed with action and romance from the very beginning . . . Hunter's lifelike characters and paranormal creatures populate a plot that will keep you guessing till the very end. A perfect mesh of mystery, thriller, and romance. Vampires, weres, and fae, oh my!" —*RT Book Reviews* on *Taken at Dusk*

"An emotional thrill ride full of suspense, action, laughter, multiple love stories, and an intriguing variety of paranormal species. I could not put this book down and can't wait to start the next book as soon as I finish this review."
—*Guilty Pleasures Book Reviews* on *Awake at Dawn*

"There are so many books in the young adult paranormal genre these days that it's hard to choose a good one. I was so very glad to discover *Born at Midnight*. If you like P. C. and Kristin Cast or Alyson Noël, I am sure you will enjoy *Born at Midnight*!" —*Night Owl Reviews*

"The evolving, not-always-easy relationships among Kylie and her cabin mates Della and Miranda are rendered as engagingly as Kylie's angst over dangerous Lucas and appealing Derek. Just enough plot threads are tied up to make a satisfying stand-alone tale while whetting appetites for sequels to come."
—*Publishers Weekly*

"With intricate plotting and characters so vivid you'd swear they are real, *Born at Midnight* is an addictive treat. Funny, poignant, romantic, and downright scary in places, it hits all the right notes. Highly recommended."
—*Houston Lifestyles & Homes*

"I laughed and cried so much while reading this. . . . I LOVED this book. I read it every chance I could get because I didn't want to put it down. The characters were well developed and I felt like I knew them from the beginning. The story line and mystery that went along with it kept me glued to my couch not wanting to do anything else but find out what the heck was going on."

—*Urban Fantasy Investigations Blog*

"This has everything a YA reader would want. . . . I read it over a week ago and I am still thinking about it. I can't get it out of my head. I can't wait to read more. This series is going to be a hit!"

—*Awesome Sauce Book Club* on *Born at Midnight*

"The newest in the super-popular teen paranormal genre, this book is one of the best. Kylie is funny and vulnerable, struggling to deal with her real-world life and her life in a fantastical world she's not sure she wants to be a part of. Peppered throughout with humor and teen angst, *Born at Midnight* is a laugh-out-loud page-turner. This one is going on the keeper shelf next to my Armstrong and Meyer collections!"

—*Fresh Fiction*

"Seriously loved this book! This is definitely a series you will want to watch out for. C. C. Hunter has created a world of hot paranormals that I didn't want to leave."

—*Looksie Lovitz Book Blog*

"*Born at Midnight* has a bit of everything . . . a strong unique voice from a feisty female lead, a myriad of supporting supernatural characters, a fiery romance with two intriguing guys—mixed all together with a bit of mystery—making *Born at Midnight* a surefire hit!"

—*A Life Bound by Books*

"Very exciting, taking twists and turns I never expected. The main character grows very well throughout the story, overcoming obstacles and realizing things she never thought possible. And the author masterfully ended it just right."

—*Flamingnet Book Reviews*

"I absolutely LOVED it. Wow, it blew me away."

—Nina Bangs, author of *Eternal Prey*

"Fun and compulsively readable, with a winning heroine and an intriguing cast of secondary characters."

—Jenna Black, author of *Glimmerglass*

— SHADOW FALLS ✦ AFTER DARK —

Reborn

C.C. HUNTER

ST. MARTIN'S GRIFFIN ⚓ NEW YORK

REBORN. Copyright © 2014 by Christie Craig. All rights reserved. Printed in the United States of America. For information, address St. Martin's Press, 175 Fifth Avenue, New York, N.Y. 10010.

www.stmartins.com

The Library of Congress Cataloging-in-Publication Data is available upon request.

ISBN 978-1-250-03591-2 (trade paperback)
ISBN 978-1-250-04745-8 (hardcover)
ISBN 978-1-250-03592-9 (e-book)

St. Martin's Griffin books may be purchased for educational, business, or promotional use. For information on bulk purchases, please contact Macmillan Corporate and Premium Sales Department at 1-800-221-7945, extension 5442, or write specialmarkets@macmillan.com.

First Edition: May 2014

10 9 8 7 6 5 4 3 2 1

To my friends and book pimps. To all those wonderful readers and friends out there who constantly hand-sell my books: Betty Hobbs, Susan and Ally Brittain, Shawna Stringer, and Lucero Guerrero. Thanks to Natasha Benway, the best children's librarian ever. And a special big thank-you to my street team. You guys rock.

Acknowledgments

To my hubby, you are my world, and my inspiration. Thank you for allowing me to chase a dream and for making me believe I could catch it. To my editor, Rose Hilliard, and agent, Kim Lionetti—we make a pretty darn good team. Thank you to my assistants who keep me on track: Kathleen Adey and Shawnna Perigo. Thanks to my friends and writing buddies who are there for all the woes, whines, wows, and walks: Lori Wilde, Susan C. Muller, Jody Payne, and R. M. Brand. You guys are to me like Kylie and Miranda are to Della—vital to my well-being. Thank you all.

Reborn

Chapter One

The monster charged down the moonlit alley, right at Della Tsang. Even in the dark, she could see its yellowed fangs, its stained claws, and its horns, sharp and deadly. The thing reminded her of a supersized, chubby gargoyle, but in all honesty, she didn't have a clue what it was.

Not vampire. Too ugly for that.

Maybe a rabid werewolf. She'd heard of them, but never seen one.

She tried to check its forehead to identify its pattern. Every species had one, and every supernatural could read them. This one, however, moved too fast.

One thing she did know: It hadn't come in peace. The blood-red eyes, along with the look of pure evil, warned Della of its malicious intent.

Two options. *Flight or fight,* her instincts screamed. Her heart pounded. Only cowards ran. Taking a deep breath, she tugged at the shirt hem of her Smurf pajamas and prepared herself for the attack.

Smurf pajamas?

What was she doing in an alley wearing . . . ?

The cobwebs in her mind cleared and she vaguely realized the third option. She could wake up.

A dream. Not real.

But even waking herself to escape felt cowardly. Della Tsang was no coward. So she allowed the nightmare to pull her in deeper, and watched and waited as the monster heaved closer. She had mere seconds.

One.

Two.

Three.

The creature smelled of death. The huge beast barely got within a foot of her when it leapt up, twisted in midair, and pounced down behind her. Della hadn't completed her turn when the creature latched on to her shoulders. She felt a pain in the base of her neck as if a claw or fang had punctured her spine. Grabbing behind her, she buried her fingers into a mass of loose-feeling skin, and with every ounce of strength she had, she hurled the creature over her shoulder. "Take that, you obnoxious lardass!"

A loud thud brought Della fully alert. Jackknifing out of bed, her heart pounding in her throat, she saw her pillow, the object she'd just mistaken as Obnoxious Lardass and thrown across her room, sticking half in and half out of her Sheetrock.

Correction. Not her Sheetrock. Her parents' Sheetrock!

She was home on a mandatory parent weekend. *Home?* The word sank into her mind like a splinter.

This wasn't her home anymore. Shadow Falls was home. The camp/boarding school that the outside world thought was a place troubled kids got sent to, but in reality was a place supernatural kids went to learn to deal with being . . . supernatural.

Kylie, Miranda, and all her friends were her family now. This place. . . . She glanced around her old room, filled with old memories. This was where she came to be reminded of everything she'd lost.

She glanced back at the pillow and the freaking hole in the wall.
Crap!

Catching her breath, she tried to think how she would explain this to her parents.

On the opposite wall stood her dresser with the attached mirror. When she looked at it, a plan emerged. A little furniture rearranging and the hole would be hidden. She glanced back at the pillow, and when she moved her head, a sharp pain pinched in the very top of her neck. Right where that damn monster had gotten her in her dream.

She reached up to rub the pain away and felt the cool stickiness. Pulling her hand around, she stared at the blood. *What the heck?*

Reaching back again, she felt a large pimple at the very base of her skull. Perhaps the pimple had simply been hurting and brought on the crazy dream. The smell of her own blood reminded her that she hadn't fed in two days. But bringing a bag of blood home with her was too risky.

The last time she'd come here, she'd caught her mom rummaging through her things. Her mom had looked up guiltily and said, "I'm sorry, I just wanted to make sure there wasn't any . . . I have to worry about your sister."

"You don't worry about me anymore?" Della had asked. It hadn't mattered that her mom thought she was doing drugs, it was that she didn't worry about her anymore that hurt the most. Then Della had left the room before she had to listen her mom's heart beat to the lie she was about to tell.

Pushing the past back, Della grabbed a tissue from her bedside table to stop the bleeding. In a few minutes, she tossed the tissue in the garbage, pulled the pillow out of the wall, and picked up the dresser and hauled it across the room to hide her dream-induced oops.

Standing back, eyeing the newly placed piece of furniture, she sighed in relief. They would never know—or wouldn't know now. Someday her dad would find it, and he'd probably call her and tell her again how disappointed he was in her. But hell and pain later was better than hell and pain now.

Glancing up, she saw herself in the mirror and had an epiphany. She might face monsters—in her dreams and even in her real life—but the thought of facing her parents, of seeing the sheer disappointment in their eyes again, turned her into a spineless little girl.

Every change that had happened to her since she'd been turned into a vampire had been seen by her parents as a form of rebellion. They believed her to be an unappreciative, uncaring teen—probably on drugs, possibly pregnant—and out to make their lives miserable. But better to let them believe that, than to believe her a monster.

Sometimes she wondered if it wouldn't have been better to take the easy way out and just fake her death like most teens in her situation did. Losing her family would hurt like hell, but wasn't she still losing them? Day by day, bit by bit, she felt them distancing themselves from her. They barely talked to her anymore, hadn't hugged her in so long, Della couldn't remember what it felt like. And there was a part of her that missed them so badly she wanted to scream that it wasn't her fault. She hadn't asked to be turned.

"What are you doing?" The voice shattered the somber silence.

Della swung around. With her supersensitive hearing, she could normally hear her younger sister turning over in her bed. How had she not heard her slip into the room?

"Uh, nothing," Della answered. "What are you doing up?"

"I heard you . . ." Marla's eyes widened. "You moved your dresser."

Della glanced back at the piece of furniture. "Yeah, I couldn't sleep and I just . . . thought I'd freshen things up in here."

"That thing's heavy!"

"Yeah, well, I've been eating all my veggies."

Marla frowned. "You barely ate anything at supper. Mom's worried about you."

No, she isn't, Della thought.

Marla looked around again. "Did you ask Mom if you could rearrange your room?"

"Why would she care?" Della asked.

Marla shrugged. "I don't know, but you probably should've asked."

Della bit the edge of her lip, realizing that before she'd been turned, she probably would have asked for permission for even something that mundane. Chalk up one positive thing for living at Shadow Falls. Holiday and Burnett, the camp leaders, ran a tight ship, but they gave the students enough rope to either swing on or hang themselves. So far, Della hadn't gotten hung. Well, not hung too bad. And in the past six months, she'd grown to like her independence.

Marla walked closer. Her pink nightshirt only came down to mid-thigh. Della realized her sister was changing—growing. Now fourteen, she'd lost the little-girl look. Her long dark hair was blacker than Della's. Of the two of them, Marla looked more like their father. More Asian. That should make Dad happy, Della thought.

"Are you okay?" Marla asked.

Before Della realized what Marla intended to do, she'd touched her. Della pulled away, but Marla held her arm. "I'm fine."

Marla made a face. "You're still so cold. And you don't act like yourself anymore. You're always frowning."

Because I'm hungry! "I'm fine. You should probably go back to bed."

Marla didn't move. "I want my ol' sister back."

Tears stung Della's eyes. A part of Della wanted her back, too. "It's late." She blinked, dispersing the watery weakness. At Shadow Falls, she seldom cried, but here, tears came easier. Was it because here, she felt more human? Or was it because here, she felt like the monster she knew they'd believe her to be if they knew the truth?

"Dad's so worried about you," Marla continued. "I heard him and Mom talking the other night. He said you reminded him of his brother. He said he got cold and became difficult. Then he died. You're not gonna die, are you?"

Della pushed her emotions aside to digest what Marla had said. "Dad didn't have a brother."

"I didn't know about him, either. So I asked Mom later, and she said Dad had a twin but he got killed in a car accident."

"Why doesn't he ever talk about him?" Della asked.

"You know how Dad is, he never talks about things that hurt him. Like he never talks about you anymore."

Della's chest clutched. She knew Marla hadn't said it to be mean, but damn if the words didn't slice right into her heart. She wanted to curl up into a pathetic little ball and just sob.

But she couldn't do that. Vampires weren't weak or pathetic.

Two hours later, the sun still hadn't risen, and Della lay there, head on her monster pillow, staring at the ceiling. Not sleeping wasn't unusual. But now it wasn't just the normal nocturnal tendencies keeping her burning the midnight oil. The pimple on her neck throbbed. She ignored it. It would take more than a pimple to bring her down.

She remembered an old saying her mom used to tell her: "Sticks and stones can break my bones, but words can never hurt me."

Her mom was so friggin' wrong.

You know how Dad is, he never talks about things that hurt him. Like he never talks about you anymore. Those words broke her heart.

She lay there feeling the night ease by, and then she remembered something else Marla had said. *He said you reminded him of his brother. He said he got cold and became difficult. Then he died.*

Marla's words kept flowing through her head as if they were important. Della suddenly bolted up when she realized why. Did he mean cold literally? Or cold as in distant? Could her uncle have been . . . a vampire? Did he fake his own death to save his family from knowing the truth?

The susceptibility to the vampire virus ran in families. And she knew her cousin, Chan, was a vampire. Only he bordered on being rogue, making it hard for her to have any kind of a relationship with him.

But her father's twin . . . if he was at all like her father, he would be a stern man, but a man with principles. He would be a rule follower to the point of being a hardass. He wouldn't be rogue. If . . . he was like her father.

But how would she know? How could she find out with nothing to go on? Obviously her dad wouldn't tell her. Nor her mom. And she suspected Marla had told her all she knew.

Questions started forming in her head. What was his name? Where had they been living when he went missing . . . or when he died? She accepted she could be wrong. Her uncle could have really died.

A memory from the past suddenly started tapping at her brain. A book. An old photo album. Her dad had pulled it out years ago to show them a picture of his great-grandmother. She remembered the old leather cover and she recalled that her father had put it in that drawer beneath the liquor cabinet in his study.

Was it still there? And if so, could it possibly contain a photo of her dad's twin? Maybe a photo with his name? She stood up, clenching her fists. She had to look. Glancing at the clock, she saw it was four. Her parents didn't wake up until six.

Taking a deep breath, she quietly walked out her bedroom door, went down the steps, and moved into her father's study. It was his room, his private space. Her father was a private man.

She hesitated and swallowed a lump of emotion. Violating his space felt wrong, but how else was she going to get answers?

She twisted the doorknob and stepped inside. The room smelled like her father. His aftershave, and maybe hot tea with special herbs with a hint of the expensive brandy he sipped on Sundays. Memories of them spending time in here together tiptoed across her heart. He'd helped her with calculus sitting at that desk. He'd taught her to play chess with his love of the game, and after that, at least once a week, he would bring her in here to play. He usually beat her. He was good. Though a couple of times she suspected he'd let her win just to make her happy. He might have been strict, and even a hard ass, but he'd loved her. Who knew his love had been so conditional?

There were no more games now. No more father-daughter time. But maybe, just maybe, if she was right, she might find a man who was as good as her father. A man who would understand the difficulties she faced. A man who might care about her now that her father had turned his back on her.

She knelt down in front of the cabinet. If she recalled correctly, the book was in the back behind her father's favorite brandy. She pulled the brandy out and reached deeper in the cabinet. When her hand touched the smooth, dry-feeling old leather, her heart beat a little faster.

She pulled it out, sat on the floor, and opened it up in her lap. She needed a light to make out the images. She remembered that her dad used to keep a flashlight in his desk for when the lights went out. She stood up, opening the drawer quietly.

She found the flashlight, but it was what else she found in the drawer that had her breath catching: the picture of her and her dad playing chess at a tournament. At one time he'd kept it on the shelf. She looked up at the bookcase where the image had once rested. The spot was as empty as she felt.

Suddenly more determined than ever to find her uncle, she went back to the floor.

She brought the book on her lap and opened it up. She turned on the flashlight and shined it at the book. The images were old, faded, and even with the light she had to squint to make them out.

Mixed into the book were some old photos of her mom's family. She continued to flip through the album, turning the pages carefully, seeing faces that somehow looked familiar even though she didn't know them. In the shapes of the faces, or cuts of chins, she saw bits of her parents and bits of herself in these people.

Almost to the end, she found a picture of her grandmother and her dad with another boy that looked just like him. She pulled back the plastic flap and carefully pulled the image out. Thin from age, it felt as if it might tear. She held her breath and gently peeled it off the album, praying that on the back she'd find names. When she turned it over she saw the writing. Her heart paused in mid-beat as she read: *Feng and Chao Tsang with mother.* Her father's name was Chao. Feng must have been her uncle's name. The image appeared to have been taken in Houston, which meant her uncle would have been here when he'd been turned . . . or killed. But if he truly had been turned, he could still be here. In Houston. Or at least in America.

She carefully tucked the image into her pajama pocket. As she went to put the book away, she saw another picture tucked behind the flap in the back. She pulled it out. It was a group of kids, two boys and two girls. The picture was grainy, but when she looked harder she thought it was her father and his twin and two girls. One of them looked like her aunt. She turned the photo over, but no names were written on this one. Slipping the picture back, she put the book up, and was replacing the brandy in the cabinet when the light in the room flashed on.

"Shit!" she muttered and turned, completely shocked that for the second time tonight, someone had walked up on her. What was up with her hearing? She expected, or maybe hoped, it would be Marla again, but her hopes were futile.

Her father, anger in his eyes, stared down at her. "So now you have resorted to stealing your father's brandy, have you?"

His anger, even his accusation, she could have handled. It was the disappointment in his eyes that had her wanting to take a running dive out the window. She longed to get far away from him and this life she'd once loved but had now lost.

She didn't. She did what she always did with her parents. She stood up and simply let them think the worst of her, because the truth would have hurt them more.

"You're here early," Burnett said, meeting her right after she stepped through the Shadow Falls front gate after being dropped off by her mother. Her mom, who'd not spoken once on the trip. Not that they hadn't said plenty before they'd left. And not that it was anything new. It was the same ol' litany.

"Yeah," she said, not wanting to talk. Or at least not wanting to talk to him. Not only was Burnett the camp leader, but he worked for the FRU—the Fallen Research Unit, a part of the FBI that oversaw the supernatural community. A job Della herself wanted. A job she knew she'd be good at, in spite of how vulnerable she felt right now. She'd already assisted on one job, and waited for another opportunity. So appearing weak in front of Burnett wouldn't be prudent. She knew who she wanted and needed to see right now—a certain shape-shifter who always said the right thing. But chances were, he wasn't here yet.

"Is something wrong?" Burnett asked, his steps matching her fast and furious pace.

"No," she lied, not caring if he could hear her heart race to the lie or not. Or hell, maybe her heart was too broken to read. It sure felt like it.

"Della, stop and talk to me," Burnett said, using his authoritative tone.

"About what?" Della asked, using her pissy tone. She'd kissed ass all weekend, she didn't have the patience to be interrogated by the camp leader right now.

All of a sudden, Holiday, the other camp leader and Burnett's wife, came wobbling up, her belly swollen with child. "What's wrong?"

"Nothing's wrong, I simply want to go to my cabin."

"You're here early," Holiday said.

"Is that a crime? Do you want me to leave and come back in about four hours? I can."

"No, what we want is for you to tell us what's wrong," Burnett seethed.

"There's not a damn thing wrong," Della insisted.

"Then why are you crying?" Holiday asked.

Was she crying? She reached up and felt her wet face. "Allergies," she blurted out.

Burnett moaned in pure frustration. "Don't lie to—"

"Let's calm down." Holiday touched the hard-ass vampire on his forearm. Amazing how one touch from the fae and Burnett cratered. Of course, a fae's touch could be ultra-persuasive, but Della figured it was more his love for Holiday that kept the man in line than her powers.

"Everything is fine." Della ground her back teeth when she saw Holiday's expression of pure empathy. Della hated that look.

"But," Holiday continued, "if you need anything you know you can call me." She reached out and rested a hand on Della's arm. The warmth, the calm flowing from the touch took the edge off Della's emotions. But not enough. Nothing would take this away.

"Thanks," she offered, and took off in a dead run before Burnett decided to argue with his pregnant wife. Before Burnett saw even more of Della's weakness and decided she wasn't capable of working FRU cases.

"Remember, we're here if you need . . ." Holiday's words became background music to Della as she lit out.

The only thing Della needed was to be left alone. She ran faster, feeling her blood rush as her feet slowly started pulling off the ground and she was half running, half flying. She purposely didn't speed up to full flight; the thump of her feet on the ground felt like a much-needed release. It didn't matter that with each slap of her foot to the earth, her head throbbed. And her heart ached more.

Arriving at the fork in the trail that led to her cabin, she chose not to take it. She wasn't finished expending the pent-up emotions humming inside her. She dropped her backpack beside a tree to claim it later and headed north through the woods, knocking branches and even some limbs away with the backs of her forearms.

She came to the end of the property, and almost jumped the fence, but knowing the alarm would blow and it would bring Burnett nipping at her heels, she turned and headed east. She made the lap around the property twice, and was just about to head back to the trail that led to her cabin when she heard it. The pounding of another set of footsteps. Footsteps that came toward her. Right toward her.

A minuscule amount of relief came with knowing that her hearing was back in working order. She focused in the direction the sound came. She couldn't see the owner of those footsteps due to the thicket of trees. She lifted her nose in the air ever so slightly. The scent was vampire. But not a Shadow Falls vampire. She would have recognized it if it was.

Had she happened upon an intruder? Some rogue vamp out to cause trouble for Shadow Falls? Instantly feeling territorial to protect the only home she had, she felt her fangs lower. The thought of facing some scumbag sent a thrill through her. In her mood, it would feel so good to kick someone's butt. Especially someone's butt she didn't have to feel guilty for kicking.

The sounds of the footsteps faltered. Had they heard her? Smelled her? When the sound of steps suddenly faded as if they ran from her instead of in her direction, she knew she'd been right.

"Run as fast you can," she muttered. "It'll just make it more fun. But I will catch you!" She went into full vamp mode, flying over the tops of the trees to catch her prey. While running used muscles, flying used a different kind of energy. Every muscle in her body had to be clenched and focused.

The terrain below her became a blur at the breakneck speed she moved.

All of a sudden, she realized the intruder had stopped running and had gone into hiding. Was the vamp stupid? Did the rogue not know she was vampire and could sniff him out? She landed at a clearing by the lake. The scent came from the woods, just behind the trees.

The thought occurred to her that Burnett should be storming in any second. The rogue had to have jumped the gate. The alarm was no doubt blaring.

She only hoped she got first dibs on the intruder, maybe even had the problem completely contained before the camp leader showed up. After being caught crying, she'd like to prove she wasn't a wimp to Burnett. Prove she was capable to assist with other cases.

"I can smell you," she called out. "Just come out and make it easy on yourself." See, she was fair. "Or don't come out. And I'll come in and get your ass."

She stepped closer to the line of trees, watching, waiting for an attack.

She could swear she heard a twig snap. She started forward, letting her nose guide her. The closer she got, the vamp's aroma became familiar. Not . . . a Shadow Falls member, but this wasn't the first time she'd inhaled this certain scent. She had his scent in her sensory bank. A feeling of leeriness pulled at her chest. A sensation that wherever, whenever, she'd come across this vampire before, it hadn't been good.

The hair stood up on the back of her neck. Her headache returned. She continued forward, seeing a thick patch of underbrush. Her instincts said the intruder hid there. A tad spooked by the negative déjà vu, she took a deep breath, giving Burnett one more second to show up.

Suddenly, realizing her pause to be a sure sign of weakness, she surged forward, landing in the middle of the brush, growling. Nothing scurried out. But she saw something in the midst of the thorns. A blue piece of cotton. A shirt. Had the scoundrel removed his shirt to throw her off the scent?

Yeah, he had. Unfortunately, it had worked. She lifted her face into the air to find another trace. The scent hit the same time the voice did. Coming right behind her.

"You looking for me?"

Chapter Two

Della turned, feeling her canines extend even more. A dark-haired boy with pale, pale green eyes stood a few feet away. He wore a pair of jeans and a T-shirt, probably an undershirt to the one he left in the brush. Her gaze whispered down the white cotton spread tight over a sinewy chest and wide shoulders. Not that his chest or his shoulders mattered, she reminded herself, and cut her eyes back up to his face.

She'd been certain of his vampire scent, but the facts that his fangs weren't extended and that the situation hadn't colored his eyes had her squinting at his forehead to check his pattern. Definitely vampire. She saw him checking out her pattern, too. But he still didn't react to the situation at hand.

Didn't he know enough to be afraid?

"You are trespassing on Shadow Falls property," she barked.

He quirked an eyebrow at her. "You think so?"

His smartass demeanor ticked her off and she bolted forward, giving his muscled chest a good push. He landed on his ass. Hard. Shock filled his expression.

Satisfied, she tilted her head to the side. "Yeah, I think so."

He popped up, flew across the few feet separating them, and landed inches from her. He leaned down and put his face right into hers. "You're feisty for a little thing, aren't you?"

She had to give him credit for his bravery. Or perhaps stupidity. Sure, he stood a head above her. Not that his size intimidated her.

And to prove it, she went to give him another shove, but he caught her. His fingers locked around her wrists like vise grips. She went to jerk away but he held her tight. His eyes brightened and she saw a touch of his canines appearing below his upper lips.

Good. At least now he knew she meant business. "Release me!" she seethed.

When he didn't do it instantly, she went into full attack mode. She swung her knee up to smash his balls. He released one of her hands to catch her rising knee. Which had been her hope all along. She didn't like being that close to anyone's genitals—especially someone she didn't know. She caught his free arm and slung him about twenty feet in the air. In spite of being caught off guard, he landed on his feet, his canines now fully extended, his eyes a bright yellow.

"What is it you are trying to prove?" he asked, moving toward her without an ounce of fear.

That I have what it takes to be an FRU agent. "That scum like you doesn't belong on Shadow Falls property," she said, and swayed from the balls of her feet to her heels, her plan to shoot forward again. Only this time she was going for blood.

"Stop, Della!" a deep voice commanded behind her.

She recognized the voice instantly.

"What took you so long? I found this rogue trespassing," she said, cutting Burnett a quick glance back, glad he'd gotten the chance to see her in action.

"Did you bother asking him if he was trespassing?" Burnett spat out the question.

"Sort of." Bullcrappy! Della flinched with the knowledge that it sounded like she'd screwed up.

Burnett's stern gaze shot to the other vamp. "Did you tell her you weren't trespassing?"

So was the guy like a new student? She didn't ask, because that would be the only thing that made sense.

"Did you?" Burnett repeated his question.

The nontrespassing piece of crap shrugged. "Sort of."

Burnett held out his hands as if exasperated. "Then I guess it's sort of both of your faults for starting this shit," he fumed. "Can I trust you enough to go back to what I was doing, or do I need to babysit you two?" His gaze flipped from the brown-haired boy to Della.

Della frowned, only willing to accept part of the blame for this. She stared right at the camp leader. "You should have told me you had someone new on the premises."

"I would have told you if you hadn't run off." And with that, Burnett flew away.

She turned and faced the newcomer. A half-assed apology sat on the tip of her tongue, but then she remembered that sensation, the feeling she'd come across him before. Inhaling, she knew now that his trace was definitely in her sensory bank. But from where? And why did his scent stir up negative feelings in her?

She almost asked him if they'd met, but she suddenly didn't feel like talking to the guy whose butt she'd wanted to kick a minute ago. Without a word, she turned and started back to her cabin.

"Nice to have met you," he called out in his smartass tone.

She didn't turn around, or say a word, but she shot her hand back and gave him the third-finger salute.

His laughter only managed to piss her off more.

Della went right to bed, her heart still hurting from the visit with her family. In spite of thinking she wouldn't, she managed to sleep. She'd still be asleep if Kylie and Miranda hadn't come in and started pounding on her door. What part about vampires sleeping better during the day didn't they get? Then again, she was eager to see them, too. As long as she had her friends, who cared what her parents thought about her. Right?

"Coming," she said when their pounding started up again.

She swung open the door and Kylie and Miranda rushed in for a hug. Not a hugger, she wanted to insist. Instead, she rolled her eyes and let them get it out of their systems. And damn it if she didn't draw some pleasure from it, too.

"Why didn't you call us?" Kylie asked, concern filling her eyes and voice. The blonde, a chameleon, was a rare supernatural who could transform into different species. On top of that, Kylie was a protector—meaning she couldn't protect herself, but if anyone tried to hurt someone she cared about, her powers were phenomenal. Majorly phenomenal.

"Because my phone died and I forgot to bring my charger," Della explained.

"You never forget anything," Miranda, the witch, said.

Miranda was right. Della didn't forget stuff. What was wrong with her? She'd felt off for the last week. She reached back and touched the pimple that had brought on the weird nightmares. It was almost gone. Good.

Realizing they were both staring at her, she made a face. "So shoot me for forgetting something just this once."

Kylie sighed. "We were just worried. How bad was it?"

"Did they make you take some more pregnancy tests?" Miranda asked.

"No." Della sighed. "But I'll need a Diet Coke if I'm going to spill my guts." She started toward the fridge. "How was y'all's weekend?"

"I'll need a Diet Coke, too," Miranda said. "I swear my mom's the biggest B with an itch in the world. All she talked about was her friend's daughter winning all the Wicca competitions. Please, I don't want to win those stupid contests. So what if Little Miss Suzie can turn a grasshopper into a firefly. I'm glad I'm dyslexic."

Della had just grabbed three sodas from the fridge when she heard the little witch's heart race to the untruth. Gritting her back teeth, Della fought the urge to squeeze one can until it exploded. It totally pissed her off that Miranda wanted to please her mom so badly. She wished Miranda would tell her mom to go climb up a broom's ass.

Heck, Della wouldn't even mind doing it for her. It was one thing having parents who were disappointed in you because they didn't know you were vampire, but another to have a mom who just thought you sucked for real. Della had listened in to the conversations between Miranda and her mom at almost every parent meeting, and sometimes Della wanted nothing more than to go vamp on the witch's ass and teach her a few lessons.

Couldn't Miranda's mom see how much her daughter wanted her approval? And considering Miranda was dyslexic, she was learning to manage her witch powers pretty well. Heck, she hadn't accidentally turned anyone into a kangaroo or a skunk in almost a month. And for Miranda, that was good.

Della passed Kylie a soda. "How was your weekend?"

"Not terrible." Kylie popped her can open.

The soft fizzing sound filled the room. Oddly enough, Della had started to equate that sound with their round-table discussions, which always eased any negative crap weighing on her shoulders. The bubbly popping sound meant stress relief. It meant friends who, though they might not know her sleeping or hugging habits, still cared.

"Have you told her you can turn invisible yet?" Della asked Kylie. The chameleon had actually told her mom she was only part human, she just hadn't told all the neat things she could do yet.

"No, I'm afraid she'd freak out," Kylie said. "It's sort of like telling a kid about where babies come from, you have to ease them into it."

Della laughed. "You know, I've actually seen a show on childbirth. It was like an accident where you didn't want to see it, but you couldn't look away." Della handed Miranda her can of soda, then popped the top on her own. Letting the sparkling sound fill her senses, she dropped into a chair as her two best friends did the same. The diet-soda round-table discussions were a normal part of their lives. A part Della needed more than she wished she did. She'd become attached to her roommates, big time. Which was dangerous, because face it, if your parents could turn their backs on you, your friends could do the same.

Kylie turned the can in her hand. "I missed you guys all weekend."

"She didn't miss Lucas." Miranda popped open her Coke and wiggled in her chair. The little witch always squirmed with excitement when she got to tell a piece of gossip. Not that Della didn't trust Miranda. The three of them had a pact. What happened at the Diet Soda Round Table stayed there.

"Her mom let Lucas come over," Miranda said, and squealed a little.

Della looked back at Kylie. "She did? Did she force you to read ten how-not-to-get-pregnant pamphlets before he showed up?"

Kylie grinned. "Only one. Did you know that only about fifty percent of teen mothers receive a high school diploma? And the children of teenaged mothers are more likely to have lower school achievement and drop out of high school, have more health problems, and be incarcerated at some time during their adolescence?" She grinned. "At least it wasn't about condoms this time."

They all laughed again, something they did a lot at these meetings. "Did she let you go out with him, on a date date?"

"No, we went out to eat with my mom and then Lucas and I just went up to my room to talk."

"I'll bet you talked. The language of the tongue," Della teased, and ran her tongue over her lips. Kylie and Lucas were a real couple, meaning they'd done the deed. Not that Kylie talked about it. Well, other than to say it was wonderful. Della could relate to her not wanting to share. Seriously, sex was . . . embarrassing.

And sometimes wonderful. For one second, she recalled how

things had been with her ex-boyfriend Lee. Then she recalled how close things had come to being wonderful with Steve, the sexy-as-sin Southern shape-shifter. Thank God, she'd wised up before she went down that road.

"Okay, you've avoided it long enough, give us the lowdown," Miranda said to Della.

Della frowned. Spilling guts wasn't her favorite thing to do. While it always ended up cathartic, it also felt a bit like whining, and a bit like being disloyal. Disloyal to her parents. Loyalty had been inbred in her by her father.

She recalled again the picture she'd found in the old photo album. And that's when she remembered she'd left her backpack with the photo in the fork of the woods.

"Crap!" Della jumped up.

"What?" Kylie asked.

"I left my backpack on the trail."

"No, you didn't," Miranda said. "It was on the front porch. I brought it in. It's on the sofa."

"Burnett must have found it and . . ." Then it occurred to Della. What if it wasn't Burnett? Could the no-good vamp have done it? He didn't know which cabin was hers, but he could have followed her scent.

Had he gone through her stuff? The possibility of him looking through her bag annoyed the hell out of her. And it wasn't just about her padded bras, but because of the picture. If he'd bent it or . . . Oh, hell, why had she been so careless with the backpack to start with? Oh, yeah, she'd been an emotional wreck.

"What is it?" Kylie asked, obviously reading Della's mood.

Suddenly extra leery, Della took a flying leap over the table into the living room and snatched up the bag. "There's a new guy here. He might have been the one who brought this to me."

"Yeah," Kylie said. "Lucas told me he showed up on Saturday right after we left. He's a vampire."

Della scowled. "He's a jerk!"

"Why's he a jerk?" Miranda asked. "If he found your bag and brought it to you, what's the problem?"

"He might've gone through my stuff," Della said, not believing they didn't understand. Who wanted a guy rummaging through your underwear or your Smurf pajamas?

She pulled the bag to her nose and sniffed it. "Damn it! His scent is all over it!"

"You met him already?" Kylie asked.

"Yeah, I met him. Burnett neglected to inform me we had a new student on board, and when I found him I thought he was a rogue trespasser."

"Oh, my!" Miranda giggled. "Did you kick his butt?"

"I was in the process of kicking it when Burnett showed up."

"Is he cute?" Miranda asked. "Not that I'm looking . . . Well, I might look, just not touch." She giggled again.

"I told you, he's a jerk." Right then the image of him wearing only a tight undershirt and walking toward her filled Della's mind. She opened her bag, looking for the photograph of her grandmother with her father and his brother.

"Is this whole bag thing a ploy just so you don't have to talk about your weekend?" Miranda asked.

"No," Della said. "I just want to make sure that . . ."

She unzipped the bag, looking for the little white envelope she'd carefully placed between her underwear and her PJs. It wasn't there! She started tossing everything out. She even turned the bag upside down and shook it, praying it would flutter out. Nothing fluttered. No picture.

"Nooo!" she muttered, thinking she might never get it back. It was probably the only picture her dad had of his brother, too. She couldn't have lost it. Her father would kill her.

No, he wouldn't, the thought hit. He'd just be disappointed in her even more than he was.

"This can't be happening," Della said.

"What can't be happening?" Kylie asked.

"He took it. Why the hell would he have taken it?"

"Took what?" Kylie asked.

Della didn't answer. She had to find that piece-of-shit vamp and find her father's picture. She flashed out of the room.

When she went into full fly mode she realized she wasn't alone. Kylie had transformed into a vampire and was chasing the wind beside her.

"What did he take?" she asked, her hair flipping around her face.

"A picture," Della said, searching the terrain below her for the dirty little thief. "An old picture that belongs to my dad. I swear, if he even dog-eared one corner of that photograph, I'm . . ."

"Why would he take your picture?"

"I don't know, but I'm gonna find out. And you might not want to be a part of this. Because if I have to, I'm beating the answer out of him."

"You can't . . ."

"Watch me," she snapped. Then her blood started firing into full-on vamp mode when she spotted the guy walking through the woods.

Chapter Three

Right before Della's feet slapped against the earth, the thieving vamp's gaze shot up. Della landed about five feet in front of him. Kylie, forever the peacemaker, landed between them.

"Where is it?" Della asked, gripping and ungripping her hands, leaning to the right to look over Kylie to see her potential victim.

The vamp focused on Kylie for a second, reading her pattern. Since she morphed into vampire, he didn't seem to worry. Right then, Della kind of hoped the bastard would lay a hand on her and then Kylie'd go into protective mode. Between the two of them, they'd be tossing his vamp butt around like a dead squirrel.

He cut his eyes back to Della. "Well, whatcha know, Smurf girl returns. At least your underwear doesn't have Disney characters on them."

Della's blood pressure shot up a few points, or maybe a lot of points. "What? You get a kick out of going through a girl's panties? Pervert," Della growled, low and deadly. Taking a step forward, trying but unable to get around Kylie, she glared at the boy. "Where is it?" she asked for the last time. He'd better decide to come clean, or she was gonna get dirty.

Kylie looked back at Della and held out her hand as if to say *calm down.* She couldn't calm down. The guy had stolen her dad's picture. The fact that Della had stolen it first was beside the point.

"Are you talking about this?" The smartass guy pulled the folded envelope from his back pocket.

She snatched it from his hand. "Why did you take it?" She opened it to make sure he hadn't ripped or damaged the photo. It looked unharmed. Relief filled her chest.

"I was bringing it to you now. When I found the backpack, I went through it to see whose it was. I left it on your porch. It wasn't until I was walking back that I saw the envelope on the ground right where I'd opened your bag, and when I looked, I realized it must have fallen out."

"Liar," she accused, even though his heart didn't claim his words as an untruth. She shot around Kylie.

"Slow down," Kylie said, moving between them again and giving Della a pleading look. "You got the picture back," Kylie said. "And I checked his heartbeat. He was telling the truth about bringing it to you."

Duh, Della knew that, but something wasn't adding up and she smelled a rat. "How did you even know it was my bag if you didn't see the picture with my last name—? Wait, how would you even know my name?"

The boy smiled at Kylie, then frowned over her shoulder at Della. "Mr. James referred to you by the name Della. And your mommy wrote your name on the tag inside the backpack. Probably when she was packing your Smurf pajamas for you."

Della ground her teeth. But oh Lordie, she wanted to go psycho on his butt. She couldn't recall seeing the tag with her name on it, but it did sound like something her mom would do. Or would have done when she cared about her. But he could bet she'd check.

"Okay, let's go," Kylie said. "We got what we came for."

No she hadn't gotten it. She wanted a pound of flesh. She shot around Kylie again, stood a few inches from the boy, and leaned in to take another long sniff. "Have we met before?"

He tucked his hands into his jeans and leaned back on the heels of his tennis shoes. "Gosh, you've forgotten already. I'm the guy you tried to start shit with back in the woods."

"I know that, you idiot! I mean before."

He took a big whiff of air, as if checking her scent. "I don't think so."

She listened to his heartbeat. It didn't race to a lie. But she'd heard about some vamps being able to control that, or about pathological liars, whose lies never even registered. He looked like a pathological liar. Tall, cocky, and those pale green eyes that didn't even look real.

She tucked the white envelope into the back pocket of her jeans. Turning and giving him her back, she spoke to Kylie. "Let's leave this Popsicle stand."

"Darn," he said. "And just when it was getting interesting, too."

Della swiveled around, and arched a brow at him. "Interesting? I'd rather watch toenails grow than hang out with you."

He laughed. And it pissed her off that she'd amused him. She let go of another deadly growl.

"Okay, we should go." Kylie touched Della's arm. But then, being Kylie and unable to leave on a bad note, she looked back at the new vamp. "Welcome to Shadow Falls. I'm Kylie."

Della rolled her eyes. Why did Kylie think she had to play nice?

"You're Kylie Galen?" he asked, looking in awe. "Wow, I've heard about you."

"Don't believe half of it," Kylie said, a bit bashful.

"I'm Chase Tallman," he said, totally trying to impress Kylie. He even puffed out his chest a little, like a damn bird doing some kind of mating dance. *Yeah, keep that up and I know a werewolf that'll be chomping on your ass!* Hell, she'd help Lucas get his revenge on . . . Chase Tallman. Della stored his name into her memory bank for future reference—and not in the good vault of references—then turned and took off.

She didn't like this guy.

Didn't trust this guy. And she wouldn't until she figured out where she knew him from and why and how he was lying.

"I hate it when you two skip out on me!" Miranda whined when Della, followed by Kylie, walked back into the cabin. "I want to come, too."

Della huffed out an exasperated breath. Was it her fault that witches couldn't fly? "What did you want us to do? Give you a piggyback ride?"

"You could have," the little witch whined. "I miss out on all the fun."

"That was not fun. The guy's a smartass, green-eyed panty pervert." Della went straight to the sofa and checked her backpack for her name on the inside tag. And sure as hell, it was there. Dad blast it, she'd wanted to catch that sorry vamp in a lie. She shot back to the kitchen, dropped the envelope on the table, and plopped back in her chair.

"Wow, don't hold back," Miranda said.

Della saw Miranda glance at Kylie with questions. Kylie shrugged as if to say, *beats the hell out of me.*

"That's odd," Miranda continued. "Word around camp is that he's a complete hottie. Not that he could be hotter than Perry." She smiled. The witch looked at Kylie. "Is the guy hot?"

Kylie shot Della an apologetic look. "Yeah, he kind of is. But he could still be a panty pervert."

"Aren't all guys panty perverts?" Miranda asked.

"No, this guy's creepy," Della snapped. "And egotistical. And his scent . . . It's familiar, and not in good way."

"Maybe he just smells like someone else?" Kylie said.

Della shook her head. "Obviously you haven't developed your vampire nose yet. We don't forget scents. And if something intense was happening when you smelled that scent, then there's an emotional trace."

"Wow. Lucas told me that werewolves do that, too," Kylie said.

"Not nearly as good as vampires," Della huffed. "I mean, I know they're wolves, but for a vampire, who doesn't go around putting their nose everywhere, an emotional trace is stronger."

"Wouldn't you know," Miranda said sarcastically. "Nothing is as good as vampires."

Della shot the witch a go-to-hell look that implied she should not just go to Hades, but go in a hurry.

Miranda snickered.

Obviously, Della's go-to-hell look wasn't in working order.

"So what emotion does he remind you of?" Kylie asked, and both she and Miranda eased up to the table and sat down.

"Danger," Della said, and pulled the photo closer to stare at the image. Her uncle really looked just like her father.

"Maybe it's the good kind of danger," Miranda offered. "You know, you're hot for him and worried about what you are feeling for Steve."

"I don't feel anything for Steve," Della snapped, and frowned when she heard her own heart pick up its pace. So what if she felt something, she wasn't going to let it lead anywhere. Swallowing, she focused on the photo again.

"We pretty much figured that out," Miranda said. "Or you'd be hooking up with him."

"That sounds so stupid. What does hooking up really mean? We're not dogs, you know!"

Kylie held up both hands as if requesting peace. "What's going on, Della?"

"Nothing's going on," Della insisted.

"Yes, it is," Kylie said. "You're grumpy."

"I'm always grumpy!" Della insisted.

"Then you're extra arrogant," Miranda snapped.

"There's a difference between arrogance and confidence," Della insisted.

Her friends weren't buying it. "What happened this weekend?" Kylie asked.

Della felt a wave of emotion swell inside her, but she pushed it back and locked it away so she wouldn't start blubbering like a little girl. Then, in a monotone voice, she told them about the weekend, about her nightmare, the hole in the wall, and her sister, Marla, saying her dad never talked about her. She told them what she learned about possibly having a vampire uncle. Oh, and she saved the best for last, getting caught in her father's study and practically being accused of being a thieving alcoholic.

Kylie sat there, her light blue eyes looking consumed with worry. Miranda sat there, expression tight, her fingers laced together, except for her pinkies, which she twirled in tight circles.

"I'm so sorry," Kylie said.

"Why? It's not as if you did anything," Della said, trying to make light of the whole thing.

"But I could do something," Miranda said. "I could put a curse on your dad. A bad case of athlete's foot. Or jock itch. I'm good at that curse. There was this football player at school that—"

"Leave my dad's feet and junk alone!"

"I just want to help," Miranda said.

"It wouldn't help," Della said in a calmer voice. "You can't even blame him. It looked like I was into his brandy."

"Why didn't you just tell him the truth?" The somberness of Kylie's words expressed empathy.

Della's chest tightened. Kylie's concern, and even Miranda's desire to zap her father with a foot or private-part fungus, was why Della loved her two best friends. They cared. Everyone needed someone to care. Thank God she'd found them. Her sinuses stung, but she swallowed hard to keep her eyes from watering. She reached for the envelope, remembering the possibility that she might have an actual family member who would understand her. Maybe even care.

"You could have told him Marla mentioned he had a brother and you were curious," Kylie continued. "Maybe he would have told you more about him."

"You don't know my dad. Anyway, Marla said she overheard him telling this to my mom, and while she asked my mom, my dad probably didn't know she heard it. The last thing I want to do is get him mad at Marla. He's already lost one daughter."

"I guess so," Kylie said.

"I still think he was an asshole," Miranda concluded.

"He was," Della said, "but if I'd done what he suspected me of doing, then he had a right to be an asshole."

"But you didn't do it," Miranda snapped.

"No, but I looked guilty, and I couldn't defend myself. So my only option is to just accept it."

"That sucks," Miranda said. "I'm so glad I don't have to deal with being a supernatural and having to keep it from my parents."

But that doesn't make Miranda's mom any less of an asswipe. Just before Della vocalized the thought, she decided it might be best to leave it unsaid.

How was it Holiday had put it? *Just because crap pops in here—* Holiday had tapped her temple—*doesn't mean crap has to pop out here.* She had touched her lips. The camp leader had also said that supernatural scientists were considering doing medical research to prove vampires were missing the thingamajig that filtered out inappropriate dialogue. Della wasn't sure if Holiday was joking or not.

But considering Holiday was married to Burnett, who was famous for speaking his mind, Della figured Holiday might be telling the truth.

Then again, Della had kind of spoken her mind even before she'd been turned.

She'd been suspended from kindergarten for telling the teacher she looked like Yoda in *Star Wars*—if Yoda was older, fatter, and smelled funny. That, of course, came after the teacher had asked Della why she had an Asian name, but didn't look more Asian. At the time, Della had a supercomplex about being of mixed race and not looking more like all her Asian cousins. Especially when she didn't even look like her mom, who was an all-American blonde.

Kylie leaned over and stared at the image. "So did you ask Burnett to see if he could help find out if your uncle is still alive?"

Della inhaled. "No, I don't want to get the FRU involved."

"You think your uncle could be rogue?" Kylie asked, sounding concerned.

"No, if he's anything like my dad, he's a rule follower. But if he isn't registered or something I don't want to be the person who gets him in trouble."

"Burnett didn't turn in my grandfather and aunt when he first discovered them," Kylie said.

"That's because they were chameleons. If they were anything else, he'd probably have done it. Being an agent, he's officially obligated to report them. He actually told me that once when he asked me about Chan, my cousin."

"So how are we going to find out?" Kylie asked.

The "we" in Kylie's question tugged at Della's emotional cords again. That was the kind of friends they were. When one of them was in trouble, they stuck together. But what wasn't normal was Della feeling those tugs on her emotions. Was something wrong with her?

Pushing the emotion aside again, this time with a little more force, she said, "I was thinking of asking Derek if he might help. You said he worked for that PI once, and I know he'd helped you figure out a couple of your ghost issues."

"That is a great idea. I think he and a bunch of guys were playing basketball when we headed up here," Kylie said. "Why don't we go see if we can find him?"

"Do we have to?" Miranda sighed. "There's nothing worse than watching a bunch of sweaty, good-looking guys playing ball. I mean, they might even be taking off their shirts." She grinned. "Not that any of them on the court could hold a candle to Perry. But eye candy is eye candy."

Giggling, they started out. Della, her heartache eased, ran back to the table to get the photograph in case Derek needed to see it. When she slipped it back into the envelope, she got another whiff of Chase Tallman, the panty pervert. The emotional ripples of danger, of fear, hit again and chased away her lighthearted mood.

She really needed to figure out when and where she could have come in contact with him before. And the sooner the better.

"Told you they might have their shirts off," Miranda whispered, and elbowed Della.

While it was October, fall had fallen behind and summer had snuck back in. At two in the afternoon, the sun beat down on the court. Della's gaze, of its own accord, shot across the court of guys looking for one chest in particular. The sexy shape-shifter, Steve.

She found him, the same time his light brown eyes found hers. He had his shirt on, but it molded to his damp chest. Sweaty, his brown hair looked darker, and flipped up on the ends. He had the basketball in his hands and he smiled at her. Her heart did a tumble, and she fought to keep from putting off any pheromones.

"Oh, my, Kylie's right, the panty pervert is cute," Miranda said. "No wonder he got to you."

Della panicked and her gaze zipped around until she found Chase. Chase without his shirt. His chest looked wider, and more muscled than it had with the white T-shirt on. She swallowed and remembered Miranda's remark about eye candy. Escorting that thought from her addled brain, she became determined not to show any appreciation at his . . . his lack of clothes. Then she realized it was too late. She'd stared a fraction of a second too long and he stood, one arm on his hip, looking right at her, relishing that fraction of a second. He smiled. Crap! Had he heard Miranda, too?

"Well, if it isn't Smurf girl!" He ran his hand though his dark hair. And no sooner had the words left his lips than the basketball whacked him in the head.

Everyone laughed. Even Della. Especially Della. She cut her gaze back to Steve and sent him an appreciative smile. And that's when she heard Chase's growl and saw him swing around toward Steve.

Chapter Four

Della's shoulders came back and she was prepared to get right in the middle of it. But before the guy took even a step, Derek and Kylie's boyfriend, Lucas, had moved between him and Steve.

"Rule number one, no trouble on the court," Lucas said. "A fight breaks out here, and we're all grounded from basketball for a week."

While Lucas took the more direct route, Derek moved in and placed a hand on Chase's shoulder. "It was just an accident," he said.

It wasn't an accident—Della knew Steve had done it on purpose—but let Chase believe it if he was that gullible.

Chase shook off Derek's fae touch, which no doubt had been to shed the tension. And while Chase did seem calmer, he still managed to shoot Steve a cold look. Steve didn't back down for a second, and Della worried the two would go at it. Not that she worried Steve couldn't hold his own. She'd seen him in action when they were on their mission. But she didn't want him getting into trouble because of her.

Steve wasn't the get-into-trouble kind of guy.

"Why don't we just call it a day," Lucas said, and Della noted he was looking at Kylie like he was parched and she was a cool drink of sweet tea. The two were so in love that they couldn't look at each other without getting that silly grin on their faces.

Another reason she was staying the heck away from love. Vampires didn't do silly grins.

Lucas came walking up, grabbing his shirt from the bench by the court. "Hey," he said, eyes and pheromones only for Kylie. "You want to go for a walk?"

"Yeah, but first I need to talk to Derek."

"About what?" Lucas asked, sounding a tad jealous.

"An issue for Della. Can I meet you in front of the office in about five minutes?" Kylie asked.

"Yeah," he said. He was frowning slightly, but he leaned down to kiss her.

Della looked the other way. Unfortunately, her eyes landed right on Miranda and Perry sucking face.

"We could kiss and show them how it's done," a deep Southern voice said at her ear. A voice belonging to a body that she hadn't heard approaching. What was with her on-and-off hearing?

She turned around and stared at Steve. He stood so close his scent filled the air; his eyes, brown with some gold highlights, filled her vision. Leaning in just a bit, she could feel his warm breath on her lips.

Her first thought was to give in, let him kiss her, let herself kiss him, and show these amateurs how a kiss was supposed to go. Butterflies filled her chest at the thought of how good it would be. They'd kissed the first time when they were on FRU camp business. And against her better judgment, several times since. She blamed the weird electricity that snapped and popped whenever they got close. He studied her expectantly and her instinct said to spout out something off-putting about him expecting a kiss when they weren't . . . an item. But she remembered he'd thrown the ball at the panty perv. Steve didn't deserve any lip. He probably deserved a kiss, but not now. Maybe she'd pay up when they were alone.

She pulled back. "Hey."

"Hey." He leaned in. "Are you okay?"

"Yeah, why?"

"Did that new guy do something that pissed you off?"

"Yeah . . . no, I mean, it was nothing."

Steve's expression soured. "Why was he mouthing off at you about Smurfs?"

She usually told Steve the truth, but suddenly she didn't want him to know she wore Smurf pajamas. "I thought he was trespassing and we bumped heads." She glanced up over Steve's shoulder and saw the panty perv staring at her and Steve.

"Funny," Steve said in a nonfunny voice. "The way you were looking at him wasn't the way you'd look at someone you'd butted heads with."

Della nipped her lip to keep from smiling. She should be embarrassed at Steve calling her out about appreciating the panty perv's body. And she was, but her pride took second to the excitement of knowing that Steve cared enough to get his boxer shorts in a bunch.

Leaning back on her heels, she stared up into his eyes. "It sounds like someone's jealous, but I can't see why. It's not like you and I are going out or anything. We're just friends, so . . ." Della shrugged, feigning innocence.

Steve quirked his lip in a cocky half smile and took a step closer. The electricity started to crackle. They stood less than an inch apart, but Della, aware only of him and the magic he brought on, refused to step back this time. They'd been playing this game for weeks—flirting and teasing each time they saw each other—and Della could give as well as he could take.

"Yup, we're just friends, but friends look after each other, and make sure they don't go goo-goo-eyed at new campers they don't know anything about."

Goo-goo-eyed? She bit the inside of her mouth to keep from chuckling. "I have no idea what you are talking about. You must be seeing things. Vampires never go goo-goo-eyed. Maybe a drop of sweat got in your eyes."

She reached up to and thumbed away a nonexistent drop from the corner of Steve's brow. She heard his heartbeat surge the second her skin touched his, and willed her own heart rate to stay calm.

He caught her wrist, and drew a tiny little heart on the tender skin above her veins. "You're looking a little gooey right now, Miss Priss."

She almost laughed. Almost. Instead she became instantly aware that they weren't alone, but still in the midst of nosy campers—some of them with super hearing. And this game, the flirting game she and Steve played, she insisted they only play it in private. What the heck had she been thinking. Oh, yeah, she wasn't thinking!

She took a step back, and when she did she saw Derek walking away. Derek, whom she'd come here to talk to about her missing uncle. "We'll talk later," she told Steve. "I need to see Derek about something."

"About what?" Steve asked as if he had all the right in the world to know.

Derek was almost to the trail. "I . . . I really gotta go. I'll talk to you later."

She glanced back at her two best friends, both looking . . . goo-goo-eyed at their boyfriends, and decided to talk to Derek without them.

Taking off, she caught up with Derek right as he entered the path back to his cabin. "Derek," she called, shaking off the warm, fuzzy feeling left over from her encounter with Steve. Damn that boy had a way of getting to her.

Derek stopped and turned around. "Yeah?" he asked.

"I. . . . Do you have a minute?"

He almost frowned. "Just a minute, I'm meeting someone. What do you need?"

Was he meeting Jenny? Probably. Everyone seemed to be in love or on their way to it. Except her, she told herself, not willing to accept that her and Steve's "thing" was more than a passing fancy. And it would pass, because that's what she wanted.

She looked at Derek. "I'm . . ." How did she explain it? She forced herself to just spit it out, and as she did, she realized how hard it was to ask anyone for help. "I'm looking for a missing person. I want you . . . I was hoping you would flex your PI muscles to help me find him."

"My PI muscles?"

"Your gift of doing investigation," she clarified. "I know you used to work at a PI agency and I wanted to ask for your help."

"Who is it you're looking for?"

"My uncle," she said.

"How long has he been missing?" Derek asked.

Della did the math in her head. "Around nineteen years."

Derek's mouth dropped open. "What?"

"My dad had a twin that he never talked about, and I just learned about him. Supposedly, he died in a car crash."

Derek's mouth dropped a little more and his brow pinched in confusion. "If he's dead, why . . ."

"I think maybe he was turned and faked his own death like most vampire teens do."

"Are you sure he was turned?"

"No, but the vampire virus runs in families and it would make sense that . . . that it was what happened."

"Not really. I'd say the odds of him being killed in a car crash are fifty times greater than him being turned. And the virus doesn't always run in families. That's only with about thirty percent of vampires," Derek said. "Chris and I were just talking about that."

"I know, but I have a cousin who's vampire, too. So . . . so that has to up the odds some. And my sister heard my dad say his brother got cold and then went off and got himself killed in a car crash."

"Cold as in physically cold?" Derek asked, for the first time seeming as if he believed her.

"I don't know. My sister just overheard him saying that, so I can't go ask my dad. But I was hoping you could research it. See if you find out anything on him."

Derek made a what-the-hell face, and Della feared he was about to tell her no.

"Please," she said. God, she hated begging.

He sighed. "I don't mind trying, but nineteen years is a long time ago. Normally, I find stuff on the Internet, and being that long ago, chances of finding anything there is slim to none." He paused as if to take everything in. "Wait, why don't you go to Burnett? He could probably . . ."

"I don't want Burnett involved until I know for sure he's registered, or as a last resort."

Derek frowned. "You think he could be rogue?"

"I don't think so, but I don't want to bring the FRU down on him."

Derek nodded and then looked at his watch as if he had to be somewhere. "Do you have his name and birthday, and the day he died?"

"Everything but the day he died," Della said. "Oh, and I have a picture." She went to pull it out of her pocket.

Derek held up his hand. "I have to . . . I'm supposed to meet Jenny. Can you scan the picture and e-mail it to me? And send any info you have on him. Where he was living. If he'd lived anywhere else recently. I can't promise you anything, but I'll try."

Hope welled up in Della. "I'll go home and send it to you right now."

He turned to go, but Della was suddenly so giddy with the possibility of this actually being true that she grabbed his arm and gave it a squeeze. "Thank you!" It only took a second for her to realize how odd that was—her initiating something that almost resembled a hug.

"You're welcome," he said, and pulled away, looking at her a little strangely. But for once, she didn't care. The thought that she honestly might find an uncle—a man who looked just like her father—and have a family member who understood the whole vampire life was like unfriggin' believable.

Maybe then she wouldn't grieve so much for her own family. Maybe she could go back to thinking life didn't suck so much.

That night Della couldn't sleep. She should be exhausted, since she'd been too busy allegedly stealing her dad's brandy the night before, and had only napped an hour during the day, but her mind kept running on the possibility of finding her uncle. She got out the picture and stared at his face. He looked so much like her dad. They must be identical twins.

She couldn't help but wonder if the man's approval would make her feel as proud as her father's.

It suddenly occurred to her that her cousin Chan might know something about him. Perhaps his mom had mentioned the uncle when her dad wouldn't? She jumped up and snagged her phone off her dresser and called. She didn't even worry about the time; considering he was vampire, and living on the edge of rogue, he didn't try to conform his sleeping habits to match the human ways.

His phone rang and rang. It finally went to voicemail. "Hey, it's Della. I have something I wanted to ask you. Can you give me a call?"

She hung up, but brought the phone to bed with her. Would he call her right back? She lay there staring at the phone for another hour, remembering he'd tried to call a week ago and she'd never called him back. Finally, feeling too antsy to just lie there, she decided to take a run. Maybe if she wore herself out, she might be able to sleep.

After donning a pair of jeans, she pulled on a top, and then the idea that she might run into Steve had her dashing to the bathroom to comb her hair and rinse out her mouth.

She popped her phone into her back pocket, then quietly opened the window and took off. The night held a chill, but it didn't bother her. The moon, a silver crescent, hung a little low. A few clouds flickered in the black sky as if begging for attention. She ran to the edge of the woods, looking for a certain bird watching her from above. She slowed down to check and see if her hearing was on or off.

She heard birds calling, a few fluttering feathers in their nests above in the trees. A few crickets sang from beneath the brush, and something, a rabbit or a possum, stirred in the grass about fifty feet away. Her hearing was on. But glancing up, she didn't see the particular bird she sought. Steve normally chose to shift into a peregrine falcon—because it was the fastest bird, he'd told her once.

As she started to move, her feet still hitting the ground, she maneuvered between the trees, dodging the branches, to spend some of the energy bubbling inside her. She recalled running earlier and finding Chase. Her mind flashed to the image of him playing ball without his shirt on.

She took a deep breath, tasting the air to make sure the panty perv wasn't out tonight. The only scents she drew in were natural scents: the damp forest ground, and the smell of fall—that earthly smell of the leaves losing the battle to hold on to life, and turning from green to golds, reds, and oranges. As pretty as some people thought fall was, it was about death. And that was kind of sad.

She made the lap through the woods twice—never going into full flight. The large gate to her right marked the edge of Shadow Falls's property. Her heart thumped in her chest. She inhaled, her nose picking up new scents . . . animals. A deer moved close by in the woods, its hooves stomping into wet earth as it darted between the trees with grace. Above, she sensed a bird. She heard the wings flying over her. Glancing up, she saw the falcon pass in front of the glimmer of light from the moon.

Steve?

She stopped. Watched the bird swing around and land in the tree.

"You following me?" she asked. But her tone lacked any conviction.

She squinted in the darkness and could barely make out the bird. "I know it's you, so just quit hiding."

She heard the bird fluttering its wings. Was he mad at her?

In the distance she heard the deer coming toward her, but she ignored that and stared up at Steve perched on the limb. She bent at the knees and leapt up into the tree. Steve bolted back and fluttered his wings as if threatening to fly away.

"Stop pretending," she said, and when bubbles of energy didn't start popping off around him as he changed, she remembered running off in the middle of their latest flirtation session on the basketball court.

"Look, I had to go ask Derek about something. I didn't mean to make you mad."

The bird lowered its head and made a slight noise.

"I'm sorry if it was rude. I didn't mean to be."

He still didn't say anything or start turning.

"Are you mad because I wouldn't kiss you? I told you I'm not the touchy-feely type. We're not even supposed to be kissing. We're not . . . together." The bird cocked its head and gawked at her. "Don't look at me like that. I know I've let you kiss me before, but . . . if you weren't such a good kisser, I wouldn't even be tempted." Suddenly a noise stirred below the tree.

"You and the bird have made out, huh?" a voice said from below.

Della stared at the deer on the ground looking up at her. The deer that sounded just like . . . Oh, shit! The moon spit out just enough light so that she could see the bubbles popping off around the big buck. Once the bubbles cleared, Steve appeared.

She looked back at the bird. "Who are you?" she demanded. The bird squawked at her.

"I'm pretty sure it's just a bird. But since you two have been having an intimate little conversation about kissing and all, maybe you should name him."

Growling, embarrassed she'd been duped by a bird, she dropped down to the ground. As soon as her feet hit, Steve caught her and pulled her into him. His hands, which fit perfectly, felt so firm and yet tender around the curve of her waist. What was it about his touch that just felt so darn right?

"So now you and the bird have a thing going, huh?" Humor twinkled in his eyes, and his brown hair, flipping up on the ends, looked a bit mussed. He wore a light brown T-shirt with some sport logo and a pair of jeans, and he wore them quite nicely.

She placed her hands on his chest with full intent to push him on his ass, but the feel of his skin against her palms sent her embarrassment packing. Suddenly, the desire to teach him a lesson was gone, and she simply wanted to touch him. His masculine chest, warm and with firm muscles, had her wanting to run her hands up to his neck and pull him down for a kiss.

Then the laughter in his eyes and his special spicy scent sealed the deal. It was so damn hard to be mad at him—even when he was poking fun at her. Or not really poking fun, but teasing, in a totally unhurtful way. He didn't tease to be mean; his teasing even made her feel special.

Too nice, she thought. Steve was too nice.

"You'd better not laugh," she said, trying to sound angry, but it didn't come out with any animosity.

"I can't help it," he said. "Being with you makes me happy. I waited up half the night to see if you'd come to me. I'm glad I wasn't wasting my time."

"I didn't come to see you," she said. His words vibrated in her head. *Being with you makes me happy.* A warm pool of goo went straight to her heart.

Her lying heart. "I was running because I couldn't sleep." That was true, she told herself, but she'd thought about him when she'd come out. She'd wanted to see him. And this wasn't the first time, far from it. At least three times a week she came out at night, and ninety percent of the time she ran into him. Oh, Lordie, she needed to stop counting on him.

He leaned his forehead down on hers. "I don't believe you."

"You're impossible," she said.

"You're beautiful," he countered. "Now what was it you said about the bird being a good kisser?"

She cut her eyes up at him. "Don't push your luck."

"I've always had to push with you," he said, sounding a little more serious. "If I didn't, you wouldn't have given me the time of day."

"I still won't give you the time of day," she snapped.

"Yeah, but you just admitted liking my kisses." His lips brushed against hers.

She pulled back. "I admitted to liking the bird's kisses." She couldn't stop herself from grinning. Damn, he made her happy. And that was dangerous.

"I'll remember that the next time I shift. Any kind of bird you like best?"

Then he kissed her—a soft, sweet kiss that pretty much made her putty in his hands.

She let herself get swept away for several seconds, maybe a minute; then she pulled back, gasped for air, and put her hand on his chest to stop him from coming back in for more.

"We shouldn't . . ."

"Why not?" he asked.

"Because I'm not . . ."

"Ready to commit." He frowned. "I know, you've told me that a dozen times. And I can accept that, but out here, it's just you and me. We're not committing, we're just . . . kissing."

"But you know where this will lead and I'm not ready for that either." She looked away, partly out of embarrassment, and partly because she thought she heard something in the woods.

He touched the side of her face and made her look back at him. "Look, I enjoy kissing you, and if that's all I can get, then that's what I'll take. At least until you're ready for more."

"What if I'm never ready and you're just wasting your time?" she said.

He pulled her against him again. "I think I can persuade you to change your mind."

"You think you're that good?"

"I know I am," he said, and chuckled. "A little birdie told me," he teased.

She punched him in the ribs.

And right then she heard that noise again. She swung around, lifted her nose up, and got a whiff of another vampire. A vampire and fresh blood. Lots of blood.

Chapter Five

"What is it?" Steve asked, obviously sensing her quick turn to mean trouble.

"Vampire?" she muttered, and took another deep breath, half expecting it to be Chase, the panty perv.

But nope. This scent was different, and she could tell that even with the tangy, fresh aroma of blood mixed in. Human blood. B negative and . . . another type.

Della felt her eyes grow brighter.

She stared up and barely made out the bloody vampire passing overhead. She half considered going after him or her.

Before she could decide, another vampire scent hit, and this one she recognized. Della pulled away from Steve.

Burnett dropped beside them. He wore only his jeans, and his hair looked sleep-mussed. The man was all muscle and brawn. "Are you okay?" he asked.

"Fine," Della and Steve said at the time.

"Someone jumped the north fence," Burnett said, giving them a suspicious look.

"I know," Della said, trying hard not to notice the man's chest. The camp leader might be old, or at least too old for her, but he could do Diet Coke commercials. "I heard and smelled them. They flew past. I think they're gone."

"Yeah," Burnett said.

"Did you catch the scent?"

"Yes," she said. "With blood. Two different types."

Burnett's jaw muscles tightened. "Human?"

She nodded.

He growled. "What are you two doing out at this time of night?"

Della internally flinched. "I couldn't sleep," she said, and since it was the truth, her heart didn't race.

Burnett glanced at Steve. "I was . . ." Steve's heart fluttered with a lie. He glanced at Della and said, "I was hoping she couldn't sleep."

Della cut him a cold look, but Steve shrugged. Burnett sighed.

Right then Burnett's phone rang. He yanked it out of his jeans pocket. "Shit," he said when he looked at the number. He turned around and took the call. "Agent James."

The way he answered told Della it was official. She tuned her hearing to listen to the caller.

"We've got two bodies right outside Fallen city limits. Looks as if our killer is vampire."

"Damn it," Burnett spouted out. "They passed by here. What's your exact location?" Burnett got the address. "I'll be right there." He hung up and faced Della and Steve.

"Do you want me to come?" The possibility of going on a live mission sent a shot of adrenaline through her. This was what she wanted to do, what she felt she was meant to do.

"No. Stay here and keep an eye out. Call Lucas, Derek, Perry, and Kylie and have them join you and Steve, and all of you be on guard. Call me first thing if anyone passes by again."

Disappointment spiraled through Della. "But I caught the scent, and only I'll know if it was the same person."

Burnett sighed. "It's not pretty, Della."

"I never was fond of pretty."

"Fine." He turned to Steve. "Call the others and you guys patrol the grounds."

Steve nodded.

"Meet me at the gate, I need to go grab a shirt." Burnett took off.

Della started to take flight behind him, but Steve caught her arm.

"Be safe," he said. Della could see the worry in his gaze. Before she knew his intent, he'd leaned down and kissed her again. She kept it brief. As good as it felt to know he cared, it was just another reminder that this thing between them had gone too far.

Nodding, she took off. She'd only gotten a few feet when she caught another scent. A familiar one—Chase. Glancing down, she spotted him in the trees. How long had he been there? Had he been spying on her and Steve? She almost went down to give him hell but knew Burnett wouldn't tolerate her being late. So she passed Chase by and went to meet Burnett by the front gate.

But later, she and the panty perv would have a chat, and she didn't expect it to go nicely.

Della told herself she could handle it. She wasn't a kid. Blood didn't bother her, it made her hungry. The second time she threw up, she wondered how she could have been so wrong.

But blood wasn't food when it came with dead bodies. It was ugly. It was emotional. It was death and murder. And that was so wrong.

She felt a touch on her shoulder. Her hearing must be going on the fritz again. Growling, she swung around, angry and embarrassed that someone had witnessed her weakness. Her growl came to a quick halt when her gaze landed on Burnett.

She'd fled from the scene under the bridge and hid behind some trees. Obviously, she hadn't hidden well enough.

"I'm okay." She jerked away from his touch. "I just ate too much human food when I was at my parents'."

He arched an eyebrow, leaving little doubt he'd heard her heart lie, but when she glanced up into his eyes, it wasn't condemnation she saw, but empathy. That pissed her off even more. "I'm fine," she snapped.

He leaned in and spoke quietly. "I puked every time my first year working cases like this." Honesty rang from his voice in the silent night. "Actually, if you hadn't gotten sick, I would have worried about you."

His words of comfort had her nose and throat stinging with tears that she'd be damned before she let fall. Unbidden, the image of what she'd just seen sprang to mind. Two victims right outside their car. Their throats torn. Their eyes open wide in horror. And all that blood—like they'd been bathed in it. What they must have felt as their lives were wrenched from them. "How could . . . how could anyone do that?"

He exhaled. "Sometimes it's hunger, a recently turned vampire not having someone to help them through the change. Other times it's a lack of respect for humankind."

Della inhaled deeply and fought the need to throw up again. "We're monsters," she said, not meaning to say the thought aloud.

"No, we're vampires. And we're no more monstrous than any other species. Humans included. Good, bad, and evil isn't species-specific. Don't you ever question that."

She blinked, hating that she'd expressed her insecurity to the one person she longed to impress more than the others.

He reached out and squeezed her shoulder. She nodded and looked away.

"Did you get a trace of his scent?" Burnett asked as if he sensed her need to change the subject. "Or was it too contaminated?"

Della looked back toward the bridge before facing the camp leader. The glow from the crescent moon reflected off his black hair.

His dark eyes still held a touch of empathy, but he was back to being a tough FRU agent.

"I can't be a hundred percent sure, with all the scents of the others, but I think it was the same vampire who passed over Shadow Falls. There're traces of what seems like the same scent."

He shrugged. "Which means you coming here was futile. I'm sorry I allowed you—"

"I'm not," she said. "I want this, Burnett. I want to be a part of the FRU. It's what I'm meant to do. I can handle it. I can. Even you said you got sick at first."

He nodded. "Yes, but . . . there are easier ways to make a living, Della."

"I don't want easy. I want to catch the bad guys. I want to make a difference." The words rolled off her tongue with honesty and sincerity.

He arched one brow. "You sure you just don't want to kick someone's ass?"

"Well, there's that, too," she admitted, and almost smiled, hoping that would ease the tension.

"That's what worries me," he said with a tone so dead serious that it wiped the half-assed smile from her face. "You're tough, Della, I know that. But you're going to run into bad guys who are tougher than you, and with your attitude you'll end up like our Jane Doe back there. Being willing and eager to fight doesn't make you a good agent. Knowing how to avoid a fight that you'll lose, and being able to set your pride aside are better qualities. Qualities you haven't developed yet."

She tilted her chin upward and bit back her urge to argue with his opinion of both her toughness and her character. "I'll learn."

"I hope so." He turned.

She reached out and touched his arm. "I want to help work this case. I want to get justice for . . . them." She motioned back to the crime scene.

He sighed. "We'll see."

"Please," she said.

"I said, we'll see. The case won't start until we get full reports back from the autopsies."

He left her and went back to join the other FRU agents. But the sting of his words *Qualities you haven't developed yet* stayed behind and cut her to the core. Burnett didn't think she had what it would take to make it into the FRU.

Somehow, someway, she'd prove him wrong.

And to start, she forced herself to go and face the gruesome murder scene again. With each step she took, she vowed to not throw up again. It didn't matter if Burnett had done it for a year, she wasn't going to do it again.

She'd prove to him that she had what it took. Then she'd catch the bastard who did it.

It was almost four in the morning when Della got back to her cabin. Kylie was sitting at the table, looking kind of eerie in the dark wearing a white gown. Her blond hair hung down around her shoulders and her expression told a story that was a cross between *The Exorcist* and *Friday the 13th*. Or maybe Della was just overreacting after seeing . . . real death.

"Hey, you okay?" Della asked.

Kylie blinked. "Yeah, just couldn't sleep."

Bullcrappy! Chances were, Kylie had company. The kind of company Della couldn't stand. "Are we alone?"

Kylie shrugged. Della moaned. The chameleon was a full-fledged, over-the-top ghost whisperer, and while Della hated to admit it, that scared the living shit out of her. If Kylie wasn't one of her best friends, Della would've kicked the spirit magnet out the door. But being mean to Kylie was like being mean to a hungry puppy with a hurt paw. And frankly, if anyone was mean to her, Della would kick their butt so fast they wouldn't know what hit 'em. But they sure as heck would know they'd been hit.

"Don't just shrug. Tell me the truth, are we alone?"

"Right now we are," she said with an apologetic voice.

"But someone just left?"

"Someone's playing with me."

"Playing with you? You make it sound like fun."

Kylie frowned. "It's not. But he/she keeps whizzing past, not saying anything and not slowing down long enough for me to get a good look." Kylie made a face. "Holiday would say that's a sign. Who do I know that zips past and doesn't slow down long enough to be recognized?" She tilted her head and then pointed her finger at Della. "You."

"Sorry, I'm not dead."

"I don't mean you exactly. I mean . . . a vampire. Maybe my new ghost is a vampire."

"Great. We've got a dead, pissed-off vamp hanging around."

Kylie made her frustrated face. "I didn't say he/she was pissed off."

Della walked up to the table. "So he/she wasn't pissed off?"

"Yeah, but I didn't say it." She grinned.

Della rolled her eyes. "I swear, you've been hanging around Miranda too long. You're using her logic."

"I sometimes like her logic," Kylie said.

Della did, too, but she wasn't in an agreeable enough mood to admit it. She glanced back at her bedroom door and considered going and falling into oblivion. Then she refocused on the empty chair across from Kylie and considered just spending a little time with her best friend.

The chair won. She sank into it and tried to stop her shoulders from drawing up from the tension.

"Where have you been?" Kylie asked.

Della's gut tightened. "I went for a run and we had an intruder that flew past. I picked up on his scent. Burnett showed up a second later and he got a call from the FRU. I went with him on the call." She bit her lip, unsure she could talk about it without making it hurt even more.

"What kind of a call?" Kylie asked.

Della hesitated, then decided that if she wanted to do this, to be an agent—and it was what she wanted more than anything—then she needed to learn to deal with it. "Two people right outside of Fallen were killed."

Kylie's expression went to pure empathy. "Was one of them vampire?"

Della understood what Kylie meant. She thought the ghost who'd shot by had been one of the victims. Della shook her head. "Human." She had even checked. As hard as it had been to look at them directly, she'd done it. "But it looks like a vampire killer," she forced herself to say.

Kylie frowned. "Does Burnett suspect rogues?"

"I don't know. They aren't suspecting anyone yet. They took the bodies in to be checked and then they're going to do a code red." Code red meaning they'd stage the deaths as an accident so the human world didn't catch on.

Kylie's eyes showed heartfelt emotion. "Was it . . . terrible to see?"

"No," Della lied. Then her breath shook, along with her lying heart. "Yeah, it was awful."

"Sorry." Kylie put her hand on Della's. "You want a diet soda?"

Della almost said yes, then sighed. "No, I need to try to get some sleep." She slipped her hand away from beneath Kylie's and stood. Dad blast it if she didn't feel the emptiness from the lack of Kylie's touch. If she were just a little weaker, she would ask Kylie for a hug. One of those long ones that helped heal the worst heartaches. But she wasn't that weak.

"Why don't you just sleep in tomorrow?" Kylie said as Della got to her bedroom door.

Della looked back and considered it. Then she remembered that Burnett already saw her as not tough enough. "No, I'll be fine." She needed to convince Burnett that she could handle this. Handle the murder, the mayhem, and the sleepless nights that came with it. Convince him that she had what it took to work for the FRU.

She walked through the door, then glanced back. "Thanks," she said.

"For what?" Kylie asked.

Della shrugged. "I don't know. For being awake."

Kylie grinned. "You'll have to thank the ghost for that."

"Not likely." Della glanced around. She wasn't sure what she was looking for, especially considering she couldn't see them, but sometimes when Kylie said they were here, she felt a cold chill. One that reminded Della of death.

And with death came the death angels—those who stood judgment over all supernaturals. Those whose punishment was swift and final. Who wanted their life splayed open and checked for mistakes. God knew she'd made plenty.

Realizing she was staring at nothing, she glanced back at her friend. "He/she's not here now, are they?"

"No," Kylie said.

"Good, keep it that way." Della walked into her bedroom. A silent room where she was alone with her thoughts. At least she hoped she was alone. She glanced around, trying to sense if Kylie's ghost had returned. There was no unnatural chill.

As soon as she plopped on the bed, her mind shot away from Kylie's possible visitor, to the terrible scene she'd witnessed tonight. Images flashed in her head again.

The woman had only been a few years older than Della, and the guy had looked like her boyfriend. It appeared as if they'd been parking in the moonlight, probably making out, high on kisses and sweet touches when they'd been attacked and fled their car. Two people having a romantic night and then brutally murdered. Maybe thoughts of the ghost were better.

Burnett's words from earlier filled her head. *We're no more monstrous than any other species.* Her heart throbbed and it felt raw. It didn't matter what he said. The fact that it was a vampire who had done this despicable act made her ashamed of her species. Ashamed that she needed blood to live.

Not monsters, my butt. If she weren't so afraid that her own parents would see her as just that, she'd tell them the truth. She could still be a part of her family. Still be her daddy's little girl. Instead, she was an outsider forced to visit, only to realize how much she'd lost. Forced to let them think she was probably doing drugs, might be pregnant, and would stoop so low as to steal from them.

She tried to chase away the images of the two dead bodies lying faceup on the wet ground, their necks mutilated from so many bites, their open eyes missing any sign of life. She tried, but couldn't get it out of her head.

"We are monsters," she whispered into the silent—with any luck—ghost-free room.

She felt a few tears slip down her cheek and she batted them away. Hopefully the fact that she wanted to catch the bloodsucker who murdered that innocent couple—that she wanted to make him pay—hopefully that made her a little less of a monster.

"I'm gonna catch you," Della said, vowing to never forget the scent of the killer who'd rushed by tonight. Someday, sooner or later, she would run into him again. "And when I do," she spoke into the dark room, "I don't care what Burnett says, I'm gonna enjoy kicking your ass."

"Della?"

The deep voice echoed in her mind and penetrated her dream. A familiar dream. She stood again in that dark alley in her Smurf pajamas. The monster, the supersized, chubby gargoyle, stood about five feet in front of her. His eyes glowed red and evil. His intent, to maul her, was made clear by the gooey-looking drool that dangled from his jowls.

What the hell did this ugly, loose-skinned, slobbery varmint want with her?

"Della, are you okay?" the voice came again, from behind the garbage can. Which was a shame, because that was exactly where she planned to toss the ugly monster, who commenced charging at her.

She flinched, prepared to fight, and instantly became more co-herent.

"Della?" This time the voice hadn't come from behind the gar-bage cans, but from the other side of the dark curtain in her mind. A side where real life existed. Where gargoyles didn't exist. Where the monsters walking the earth were simply vampires.

When she felt a touch brush across her brow, she became fully alert. With vampire speed and strength, and even before her eyes fluttered open, she caught the hand and held it away from her face.

Her vision hadn't completely cleared when she recognized the dark-haired, dark-eyed shape-shifter standing over her.

She dropped her tight hold of his wrist. "What are you doing in here?"

Steve frowned. "I tapped on your window and when you didn't stir it worried me."

"So you just decided to help yourself into my bedroom?" she snapped, coming to the pissy realization that her hearing must be off again. What the hell was up with this?

"I came in to check on you. You're usually awake by the time I get anywhere close to your window. I knocked for a whole five to ten seconds and you didn't even roll over. Are you feeling okay?"

He reached down to touch her brow again and she swatted his hand away.

"Don't touch me."

He scowled down at her. "I'm checking your temperature. You didn't feel right." He put his hand back on her brow.

She almost swatted his hand away again, but realized she was taking her frustration with the dream and her hearing problems out on him. "I'm vampire. I'm friggin' cold, remember?"

He grimaced as his hand tenderly moved across her brow. "I know, that's what's wrong. You don't feel . . . as cold. I think you might have a fever."

"I'm fine." She sat up. "I just didn't get any sleep." Her gaze shifted to the window. The sun hadn't completely chased the night away yet, but the little corner of the sky she could see through the glass panes had streaks of pink in it. "What time is it?"

"Five-thirty."

She flopped back onto her pillow. "That means I've slept a whole hour," she muttered.

"Sorry for waking you. I was worried. I told you to call and you didn't."

"When did you tell me to call?" She cut her eyes at him, now sitting on her bed, looking morning peppy. She hated morning people. Then she tried to remember their last encounter, when Burnett showed up. "You didn't tell me to call you."

"In the note, I told you to call me as soon as you got back."

"What note?" she asked.

He pulled a piece of notebook paper that rested half under her shoulder. "The one you're sleeping on. After you took off, I got worried, so I came here and left a note on your bed. I barely slept myself, I kept waking up every ten minutes checking my phone. All I could think was that something went wrong."

It had gone wrong, Della thought. Two innocent people were killed and then she learned Burnett didn't think she had what it took to be an FRU agent.

The images of the victims flashed in her head, making her chest feel like it had been filled with syrup. The really thick kind of syrup.

But there was nothing sweet about the weighty feeling. Just heavy empathy for two young lovers.

"I finally just decided to come over here and check for myself," Steve said. "Besides, I have to leave in ten minutes."

He'd been worried. He was leaving? Della's mind spun to keep up with him. It was Monday, he didn't go to play doctor on Mondays—not that it was really play. Just as she longed to be an FRU agent, Steve longed to be a doctor, a supernatural doctor. Because there weren't really schools to study supernatural medicine, someone wanting to go into this field had to get a degree in either regular medicine or veterinarian medicine, as well as work under another paranormal doctor. Steve, trying to get ahead of the game, assisted the only supernatural doctor in town. "I didn't see the note. I . . . was exhausted."

He ran his hand up and down her forearm. "Are you really okay?"

"I'm fine."

His eyes twinkled. "You are fine. I especially like the Smurf pajamas."

See, there was nothing wrong with Smurf pajamas! Crap! Why was she thinking about that low-life vamp?

"And if that new vamp mentions your pajamas again, I might have to teach him a lesson."

Why was he thinking about . . . ?

Steve straightened the collar of her PJ top and then leaned down. "I'm the only one who can tease you about what you sleep in, or don't sleep in." He wiggled his brows and then went in for a kiss.

She fully intended to push him away, but the moment his lips brushed against hers, she . . . well, she didn't do a dad-blasted thing. Hadn't this been how they'd gotten in trouble on the mission? She'd let him kiss her while in bed, and the next thing she knew their clothes started falling off.

Yup, that's what happened, and she was going to stop this right now. She put her palm on his chest to give him a good-bye shove. Not hard enough to hurt him, just . . . Then his hand slipped under her pajama top and his palm eased ever so softly over the naked curve of her waist. Well, maybe she wasn't going to stop it right *now*, but for sure before their clothes started . . .

Just when she really started feeling all tingly, he pulled away, his expression puzzled, his lips a little wet from their kiss. "Are you on your period?"

Her mouth dropped open and she gave his chest a hard thump with her palm. "A guy isn't supposed to ask a girl that. And if you thought I was going to—"

"No!" He shook his head and chuckled as he sat up. "I didn't mean . . . I'm asking as a doctor, not as your boyfriend."

"You're not my boyfriend."

"Right," he said, as if he didn't believe it.

Oh, Lordie, was he her boyfriend? Had she slipped up and let this thing between them get that out of hand?

"Seriously, are you on your period?" he asked.

She frowned at him. "You're not my doctor, either."

He shook his head as if she was silly. "Look, sometimes when a female vampire is on her cycle, she runs a slight temperature. You really do feel warmer." He put his hand on her forehead again.

"I just didn't get enough sleep," she said, but then remembered her headache and hearing problems. Could she have some kind of flu?

"Are you on your cycle?" he asked again.

She rolled her eyes and nodded. It wasn't exactly the truth; she wasn't due for about three days. She wondered if PMS could mess with her hearing as well.

She sat up and looked at him sitting on the edge of her bed as if he had every right in the world to be here. Then she remembered him saying he was leaving. "Where are you going?"

"To work with Dr. Whitman."

She shook her head. "But you don't go on Mondays."

"I do now. Dr. Whitman asked Holiday if I could come in four days a week instead of three and stay there at night. Half the super-natural clientele comes in after hours. He's got a room where I can sleep in the back of the clinic." He studied her expression. "I was going to tell you last night, if you hadn't run off to play FRU agent."

It hadn't been play, Della thought, and then her mind went to Steve and his new schedule.

"What about school?" Della didn't like the sound of this. She didn't like that he wouldn't be around at night when she went out for a run to clear her mind. Then she didn't like the fact that she didn't like it. Depending on people got you in trouble. Jeepers! Had she already started depending on him? Face it, with Miranda with Perry and Kylie with Lucas, she'd had some time to fill.

Not that she blamed them . . . well, she sort of did, but she also understood. When she'd gotten with Lee, she'd basically ignored her friends, too.

"School's not a big deal," Steve said. "Before I even came here I tested out of high school."

"I knew you were a smart . . . ass," she said, hoping to hide her emotional upheaval with humor. But bullcrappers if her heart didn't feel tight at the thought of him being gone.

"Like you're not smart." He grinned. "But Holiday is going to make me take some tests every Friday so on the record it shows I went here. It'll look better on my files when I start college." He brushed a strand of dark hair from her cheek tenderly. "Are you go-ing to miss me?"

She frowned. Could he read her mind? "No," she lied.

He made a face at her answer. "I'll miss you. But we'll see each other on Fridays and the weekends. Of course, if you'd stop pretend-ing that you don't like me, and would be seen in public with me, then we could spend more time together. I wouldn't have to wait until the middle of the night or early morning to steal a kiss."

He leaned in to steal one then, and she put her hand up and pressed her finger to his lips. "It's late, I should be getting dressed."

"Go ahead." He flopped back on her bed and rested his head on his hands as if he was going to enjoy watching her. His reclined position did wonders to showcase the muscles in his arms and chest. He grinned that sexy bedroom smile at her and she wanted to kick his ass.

"Out!" she ordered.

He sat up. "After you kiss me good-bye."

"No! You are incorrigible." She shook her finger at him. "Presumptuous. Arrogant."

"Call me all the names you want, but if you want me to leave, it'll cost you a kiss."

"And impossible," she growled. "You do know I could pick you up, twirl you around like a baton, then toss your ass out the window, don't you?"

"Could and would are two different things, sweetheart."

Friggin' frack! How did this guy know her so well? When had she opened up and invited him into her life? Into her heart?

He leaned in and collected a kiss. A short one, that's all she allowed. But it was a hell of a lot more than she should have permitted. Right then she knew his leaving was a good thing. She needed to put some distance between them. Needed a slowdown.

"I'll see you Friday. But promise me you'll call me."

"I don't make promises." She swallowed a slight lump in her throat at his expression. "I'll try." *Try not to,* she amended. She had to put on her emotional brakes. Stop these feelings before they got out of hand.

He put one leg out the window and then glanced back. "Stay away from that new vamp. I don't like him."

Me, either, she thought, but didn't say it.

Della sat there hugging her knees, staring out the opened window, trying not to care about the dad-blasted shape-shifter who'd left her feeling less than happy. A cold blast of wind snaked in her bedroom, and she shivered. She popped off the bed to go shut the window, and that's when it suddenly occurred to her. She felt cold.

Since she'd been turned, she'd been aware of temperature, but she hadn't really felt cold. She remembered Steve insinuating that she might have a fever. Placing a hand on her forehead, she moved to the window. She got there just in time to see Derek watching Steve walk away.

Great. Now Fairy Boy was going to think she and Steve were dirtying up the sheets. Derek looked toward the window, half smirked, and started walking over. Her first impulse was to offer him the third-finger salute and slam the window. Then she remembered he was assisting in looking for her uncle. Was he here for that? Did he already have something for her? She leaped out the window and met him halfway.

"I'm *not* sleeping with Steve," she said first thing, deciding to make that clear from the get-go.

He rolled his eyes. "I really don't care." Then his gaze moved over her. "Smurfs, huh?" He chuckled.

"Oh, please, give it a break. You guys just want to fantasize about us girls wearing sexy lingerie to bed every night. We wear what's comfortable. We wear what we like. So get over it!"

He scratched his jaw. "I'll try to wrap my brain around that."

She shook her head, her dark, straight hair flipping in front of her face. "Do you wear thongs and lingerie to bed?"

"Uhh, no."

"Well neither do women. So if you don't like to floss body parts that don't need flossing, why would we?"

"I . . ." he stuttered. "I didn't say anything about . . . I meant, I just didn't expect to see a vampire liking little blue people."

"Why not? I'm not prejudiced," she said. "I like people of all colors, nationalities, and species. I even like you. A little bit."

He looked taken aback. "You do know Smurfs don't exist, right?"

"Of course I do. And you know all women don't wear thongs or sexy lingerie. And wearing Smurf PJs isn't weird." Steve had even liked them.

Derek had the decency to blush, and held up one hand. "Forget I said anything."

She realized she was overreacting and being grumpy, especially considering he was probably here to help her. "Sorry. I didn't get enough sleep." And the new vamp's insult about her PJs had obviously stung more than it should have. "Did you find something out about my uncle?"

He nodded. "That's why I'm here."

Chapter Six

"What did you get?" Della asked, feeling as if his answer could change things. If her uncle was alive . . .

Derek shrugged as if he was about to disappoint her. "Not a lot, but I was able to dig up an obituary from some old newspapers that were accessible through the library Internet." He pulled out a piece of paper. "I went ahead and printed it out. Of course, this doesn't mean that he actually died. But it's a place to start checking if maybe it was falsified. And I'm not done searching the Internet. If I can find out what school he went to, sometimes if there's a reunion of that class, some classmates might have posted something."

Della took the folded paper and frowned. "I don't know what school he went to, but I'll see if I can find out."

He nodded. "Just remember, it's not overly promising with something that happened so long ago."

Disappointment whispered through her.

"Oh," he said. "Can I sort of ask for a favor in return?"

Well, duh, she couldn't say no, now could she? But what in the world could Derek want from her? "What is it?"

"I was hoping . . . maybe you could sort of be nice to Jenny."

So it was really true. Derek had a serious thing for Jenny.

"Be nice to her?" Della asked. "I haven't been rude to her."

Now, Della couldn't say that about everyone here at the school, but because Kylie liked Jenny and sort of took her under her wing like a little sister, Della had gone out of her way not to be rude.

"I didn't say 'not be rude' to her, I said 'be nice' to her. There's a difference, you know?"

Della shook her head. "Me not being rude *is* me being nice."

He cut his eyes at her in a frustrated manner. "Look, Jenny's really . . . insecure right now. She sees the kind of friendship that you and Kylie and Miranda have and she feels kind of left out."

"Left out? Kylie visits with her every other day and she sits with her almost every day at lunch."

"I know, but you guys don't sit with them."

"That's because they're sitting at the chameleon table, idiot!"

He frowned. "There's not enough chameleons to *be* a chameleon table. Jenny wants to feel like she's fitting in. And for some reason, she admires you. Thinks you're cool."

"I am cool," Della insisted.

"Yeah, well, can you be cool and a little nicer?"

Della exhaled. "Fine, I'll . . . try."

"Thank you," he said. "And I'll continue to see if I can find anything about your uncle. And let me know if you find out what high school he attended."

Della watched the fae walk away, glanced at the obituary in her hand, worrying how she might get the school information on her uncle, and worried how she was going to be nice to Jenny. She didn't dislike the girl, but she wasn't into making new friends. Her friend quota was full. Kylie and Miranda were all she needed.

She turned her Smurf-covered butt around and leaped back into her window. She turned to shut the door, and when she did, she got *his* scent again.

Chase.

Dad-blasted vamp! She growled into the wind that carried his spicy smell and remembered he'd been in the woods last night when she'd flown off to meet Burnett. Was the panty perv just walking past to get to breakfast now? Was last night just another coincidence? Or for some unknown reason was he keeping tabs on her? Somehow, someway, she needed to find out.

Five minutes later, dressed for breakfast, the folded and still unread piece of paper with her uncle's obituary in her hand, she glanced up at the door as someone knocked.

"Yeah," she called out.

Kylie pushed open the door, a worried look on her face. "You okay?"

"Fine, why?" she asked.

"Several reasons," Kylie said. "One, you're here. You didn't go to the vamp meeting."

Della shrugged. "I slept late." Bypassing the fact that Steve had woken her up. Bypassing the fact that after last night, the thought of drinking blood made her queasy.

"I figured that. Are you feeling better?"

The whole dead-bodies memory and disappointment over Burnett's lack of confidence in her came rolling over her again. "I'll live."

Kylie sent her a sympathetic smile. "Was that Derek you were talking to?"

"Yeah." She held up the folded piece of paper. "He found an obituary for my uncle."

"So . . . he's really dead?"

"Not necessarily. The families usually post an obituary of the person if they think they're dead."

"I see," she said, and nipped on her bottom lip. Kylie always nipped when she was nervous. But about what?

Della recalled Kylie's answer of "several reasons" to why she was worried about Della.

"What's the other reason. . . . The reason you're worried about me?"

Kylie rolled her top teeth over her lip again. "I. . . . It's about the ghost."

Okay, this couldn't be good. "What about the ghost?"

"Remember I told you I thought it was vampire?"

"Yeah."

"Well, I'm pretty sure I was right. Not that it's completely manifested yet, but . . . and I don't think it's looking for me. It's not hanging out in my room."

"Where's it hanging?" she asked . . . and while she was smart enough to guess, she really, really hoped she was wrong.

Kylie hesitated. "In your room."

"Oh, hell no. I have no desire, none, zilch, to have a ghost hanging around me. Tell it to go take a flying leap into the oblivion. "

Kylie sighed. "It doesn't work that way. And usually when a ghost appears, there's a reason. I was . . . I was wondering if maybe it was your uncle."

Della's stomach clenched. "Why do you say that?"

"I'm not sure, I just . . . You're looking for him and everyone says he's dead, I thought maybe . . ."

"He can't be dead. I need him to be alive." And she didn't realize how true it was until she'd said it. She needed someone, a family someone, in her life. Someone who wouldn't look at her like a monster. She shook her head. "No, it's not him."

Kylie nodded, but didn't look convinced. "I . . . I'm meeting Lucas for a picnic breakfast. So I'd better run. And Miranda had a Witch Council meeting this morning. I'm afraid you're on your own for breakfast."

"I don't care," Della said, feeling anxious about the whole ghost thing.

Kylie nodded and started to walk away.

"Hey," Della called to her. "It's not here now, is it? The ghost?"

"No." Kylie looked concerned. "You sure you're okay? Even Miranda is worried about you."

"Of course I am." Della didn't need anyone feeling sorry for her, she just needed a ghost-free environment. And she needed her uncle to be alive. Hence her hesitation to read the obituary.

The images of death from last night flashed in her head again.

"Go." She waved Kylie away. When the door closed, she looked around the silent cabin. She tucked the obituary in her pocket, deciding to face runny eggs and burnt bacon before she had to face the possibility that her uncle was really dead.

Della walked into the chatter of the crowded dining hall. She was all set to join a few other vampires who'd obviously bypassed this morning's early breakfast when she spotted Jenny. The girl sat alone and looked lonely. Knowing it was the right thing to do, she grabbed a tray and then dropped down in the seat beside the little chameleon.

"Hey," Della said, staring down at her eggs and the yellow goo they floated in. Ugg, she so wasn't going to eat those. Then she saw that her bacon was indeed burnt.

"Hi," Jenny said, sounding peppy, her hazel eyes lighting up with a smile.

Della had to tighten her face not to frown. It was just way too early to deal with peppy, but she owed Derek for his help.

"Have you seen Kylie this morning?" Jenny asked, almost as if she just needed something to say.

"Yeah," Della answered. "She and Lucas were having a breakfast picnic." Meaning they were off sucking face somewhere. And maybe getting naked. Though Della didn't think Kylie would take her clothes off in the woods; she was much too proper and smart for that. Being naked in the woods led to chiggers and bug bites in places you really didn't want them.

"That's nice." Jenny's gaze shifted across the room. Della followed it and saw she'd glanced at the fae table. Particularly at the end of the table where Derek sat. The brown-haired fae was laughing at something one of the new fae chicks was saying. He wasn't coming off as if he was actually flirting, but Della saw a touch of disappointment flash in Jenny's eyes.

"So what's up with you and Derek?" Della asked, stabbing her half-cooked eggs with her fork.

"Nothing's up," Jenny said.

"I thought you two were sort of an item. I mean, you slept with him when you first got here."

Jenny's face reddened. "No. We shared a bed, but we didn't . . . do anything. We're just friends."

The chameleon's heart did one light flutter with her last sentence, so it wasn't a complete lie, but it wasn't the complete truth, either. "Not that it's any of my business, but I think he'd like to be more than friends." Della saw that Jenny's bacon was practically raw. Just the way Della liked it. Her stomach growled.

"Yeah. He kind of hinted at that," Jenny said.

Della continued to eye Jenny's bacon. "You gonna eat that?"

"No." She wrinkled her nose. "It's barely cooked."

"I'll trade you my burnt one for your raw one?"

Jenny pushed her tray over and Della snagged the uncooked meat and took a bite. After her first swallow, she asked, "So Fairy Boy doesn't do it for you, huh? That surprises me. I mean, Kylie was all over him."

Jenny's peppy look vanished. "Yeah, I know."

Della suddenly realized how what she'd said sounded. "I didn't mean . . . all over him like . . . She was just into him for a while."

Jenny picked up her fork and moved her eggs around her plate. "Yeah, I heard she was back and forth between Lucas and Derek."

Della heard something in the girl's tone. "You do know Kylie and Lucas are a real thing now, don't you?"

She nodded, but didn't look convinced.

"Is that what's keeping you from going for Derek? You're worried about him and Kylie?"

"No," she said, but her heart raced to an all-out lie.

Della cut her a cold look. "Why do people try to lie to me?"

"Okay, maybe I'm worried a little. I like Kylie a lot and I don't want anything between me and Derek to cause issues."

"You need to talk to Kylie," Della said, and munched on another bite of bacon. "I know she'd tell you to go for it. Derek's a decent guy. If you like his type."

Jenny looked up again at the fae table and then back at Della. "He asked you to talk to me, didn't he?"

"No," she said, and didn't like how the answer felt on her tongue. "I mean, he didn't ask me to talk about him."

"What did he ask you to talk to me about?"

Okay, she'd really put her foot in her mouth now. So she stuffed the rest of the bacon in there with it. After swallowing, she said, "He didn't ask me to talk to you."

"Now who's lying?" Disbelief flashed in Jenny's green eyes, and for some reason Della thought about Chase's green eyes. "Just tell me the truth," Jenny said.

Della debated being completely honest, then realized what she'd said wasn't a lie. "I'm not lying. He didn't ask me to talk to you." Being nice and talking were two different things. The look on the girl's face said she still wasn't convinced. *Oh, what the hell.* "He asked me to be nice to you."

Her shoulders slumped a bit. "And that's why you sat next to me."

"No," Della said. "Okay, maybe, but it's not as if I don't like you."

"Yeah. I'm just different, chameleon, and it weirds you out?"

"Why would you say that? Kylie's my best friend and she's a chameleon. I don't give a toad's butt what you are."

Jenny glanced up. "Then why are you always so . . . distant?"

"Because . . . that's just me. I don't make friends easy."

Jenny glanced around the dining hall. "Everyone here just keeps staring at my pattern as if I'm a freak."

"Not everyone. But what can I say, there's a few idiots here." Della's gaze shifted around the room and found Chase. She still needed to find a way to have a powwow with him. He turned and looked at her. Was he listening to her conversation? She took another bite of bacon and looked back at Jenny staring down at her plate. "You really don't like it here?" Della asked, in almost a whisper.

"I don't fit in here. But I didn't fit in at home, either." Emotion filled the girl's voice.

Jenny's words did laps around Della's head and then dropped to her heart. Damn if Della didn't know how not fitting in at home felt—as if someone had taken a sledgehammer to your whole foundation of life. You simply felt broken.

"Give it some time," she offered, feeling empathy for the chameleon. "This place ain't all bad."

"I didn't say it was bad. I just don't fit in." Tears welled up in the girl's eyes. "I gotta go." Jenny stood up and left.

Della watched Jenny walk away, and the girl turned invisible right before she walked through the door. Gasps filled the lunchroom from those who'd seen her. The whole turning-invisible thing that chameleons did—which, like chameleons themselves, was super rare in the paranormal community—still freaked some people out.

Disappointment pulled at Della's mood. She wasn't sure this being-nice encounter had helped Jenny. She might have even made it worse. Someone stopped at the side of her table, and the fact that she didn't hear them walking up took her mood down another notch.

"I said be nice to her, not hurt her feelings," Derek said. "What did you say?"

Della exhaled and stared up at the guy. Being fae, he could reach out with his emotional fairy wand to pick up on the feelings of others. Had Della hurt Jenny's feelings? She hadn't meant to. She honestly felt bad for Jenny. *I don't fit in here. But I didn't fit in at home, either.* She reheard Jenny's words. "I didn't . . . I mean, all I . . . Oh, hell, I told you I wasn't good at being nice."

Derek shot out as if to find Jenny, and Della tossed her last bite of bacon on her untouched tray, her heart aching for the chameleon. But damn if she couldn't relate to how it felt to suddenly not fit in with your own family. To have the people you assumed would never turn their backs on you, turn away. But bloody hell, she had enough on her plate right now and didn't need to start worrying about someone else's problems.

See, that was the reason why she didn't want to start being nice to someone!

"Make sure you come to the campmate-hour announcement." The voice came out of nowhere. A voice belonging to another person standing beside her who she hadn't heard step up. What the frack was wrong with her hearing?

Della looked over at Chris, the blond vamp who ran Meet Your Campmate hour. Campmate hour basically being a tactic to encourage campers of different species to spend an hour together. Names were randomly drawn and paired together. The only way to secure an hour with someone of your choosing was to donate a pint of blood.

The tall, blue-eyed California-surfer-looking dude stood there smirking like a cat who'd just swallowed a bird. A very big bird.

"Why?" she asked the semi-hot-looking, overconfident vamp.

"Why? It's written in the rules that vampires have to attend campmate hour. It's our blood drive. Check your rule book, Miss Sass."

He said the words with honesty. Yes, it was a rule, but one that had never been enforced. Add the fact that his blue eyes twinkled mischievously, and she suspected he was leaving something out. Something that had to do with her.

Oh, bullcrappy! Had someone paid blood for her time?

Chapter Seven

"Curiosity killed the cat," Della muttered under her breath, standing in the midst of the other students and trying to ignore the low-grade headache throbbing at the back of her head. She'd been going to skip out on campmate hour, had even started toward the woods to take a long walk and read the obituary still tucked in her pocket. She didn't care about breaking the never-enforced rule, but at the last moment she turned around and came back to the dining hall.

Good thing she wasn't a cat.

Chris's little be-there request had to mean someone wanted to spend an hour with her, didn't it? And if so, who? Steve wasn't here. She considered it could possibly be Chase, but why? What would his objective be? Yes, she needed to have a powwow with him, but it wasn't one he should be looking forward to, or know about. She recalled thinking it was strange that he took the picture of her uncle. Sure, he claimed it had simply fallen out of her backpack, but that story lacked credibility. Especially when she was dang certain she'd crossed his path before.

Della heard two people walking up behind her. So her hearing was back, huh? And she recognized the footfalls, too.

"Hey," Kylie said, stopping on one side of her and Miranda on the other.

Della glanced at Kylie. "How was the picnic?"

"Good," Kylie said, always keeping it vague when it came to her and Lucas's relationship. "He's supposed to meet me here," she said, looking around.

"Have you seen Perry yet?" Miranda asked, tucking her loose blond hair with streaks of pink, green, and black behind her ear. Della never quite understood Miranda's crazy hair, but it seemed to be her trademark, and perhaps her desire to stand out a bit.

"No," Della said, thinking back on her morning. "I don't think I saw him at breakfast either. Did you cast a few spells at your witch meeting?"

"No." Miranda rolled her eyes. "We don't go around casting spells all the time."

"Why not?" Della asked. "If I could cast 'em, I'd be doing it all the time."

Miranda shook her head. "Our motto is to cause no harm."

"That doesn't sound like a lot of fun."

"Good thing you're not a witch," Miranda said. "Your attitude alone would bring you so much bad karma."

"There's nothing wrong with my attitude," Della insisted.

"Be nice, both of you," Kylie said, shooting them a stern look.

"Sorry, but I suck at being nice," Della said, remembering Jenny. She glanced around to see if the girl was there. She wasn't. But she did spot Chase, standing a few feet from the others looking out into the woods as if he wanted to disappear. As if he didn't exactly fit in. Della recalled her first week here. If it hadn't been for Miranda and Kylie, she would've been lost. All of a sudden, Chase looked back. His gaze locked with Della's and held.

She frowned.

He smiled.

Miranda bumped shoulders with Della. "I think he likes you."

"He shouldn't," Della snapped, and looked away.

"Why not?" Perry asked, moving in beside Miranda and slipping his hand around her waist. If the shape-shifter was within arm's reach of the little witch, he had his arms around her. "He seems like an all-right guy to me. Of course, Steve will kill the vamp if he starts liking you as in 'liking you.'"

"Steve and I aren't—" Della stopped talking and groaned when Miranda reached up on her tiptoes and started sucking face with the shape-shifter.

"That's sweet, isn't it?" Kylie whispered in her ear.

Della glanced at Kylie and copied Miranda's trademark overstated eye roll. Kylie snickered.

She had opened her mouth to tell Kylie she was leaving when Chris started talking. Inhaling, she looked up toward the front, and her curiosity returned.

"Welcome," he said, making it sound like a show. The guy really liked being in the limelight. Since he was from California, she wondered if he'd dipped his toe into acting. He had the looks and personality for it.

"Let's see what we have first?" His gaze shifted around the crowd.

Della held her breath, hoping she'd been wrong in her assumptions. *Don't let his gaze land on me. Don't let his gaze land on me.*

His gaze landed on her. *Damn! Damn! Damn!*

He pulled a piece of paper from his stupid hat. Unfolding the paper slowly, as if to add drama, he didn't even look down before starting to talk. He didn't have to; he obviously knew what it said. He smiled and paused, just to draw it out.

Good Lord, she wanted to go pinch his ears and make him spill it already.

He finally cleared his throat. "Della Tsang, I, Chris Whitmore, will have one pint of blood donated to our bank to spend an hour with you."

Chris? Her mouth dropped open. Everyone's eyes were on her. Oohs and aahs were spouted out of the crowd.

"Oh, shit," Perry said.

"Shit what?" Lucas asked, walking up beside Kylie.

"Chris just offered a donated pint for Della's time," Miranda answered Lucas's question.

Lucas looked at Della. "I'm not surprised. He's had a thing for you for like forever. And now that Steve's spending a lot of time helping the doctor, Chris's trying to move in."

"It's a little underhanded, if you ask me," Perry said.

"What do you expect?" Lucas added. "He's vampire."

Kylie elbowed Lucas in his ribs. He grumbled and met Della's gaze. "Sorry."

Normally, Della would have had a smartass comment, but she didn't say a word. She was . . . stunned. Sure, she recalled at one time there had been tension between Steve and Chris, and rumor had it that they both had a thing for her, but. . . . Well, she didn't completely buy it.

"I'll donate two pints to spend an hour with her," a voice in the crowd spoke up.

Della's gaze shot to the owner of the voice. Chase.

Della's breath caught and she tightened her hands at her sides.

Chris swerved around, finding Chase, and the blond vamp's expression hardened. His light blue eyes shined iridescent. "Maybe where you come from vamps drink each other's blood, but not here."

Della's mouth dropped open a bit more. This was not going to end well.

"I'm not offering *my* blood," he said. "I'm offering some from my personal stash. When I came here, I'd been on my own. I don't travel without rations. So I've got some extra."

"It doesn't matter," Chris spouted. "That's not how this works. This isn't an auction."

"I thought it was a blood drive," Chase added. "The more blood the better. Maybe you don't really need the blood."

Chris's eyes grew brighter. "Fine."

"Damn, Steve's gonna have to kill two people," Perry sputtered.

"You okay?" Kylie muttered close to Della's ear.

"Hell, no," she said. "This is ridiculous."

"I'll offer three," Kylie instantly spoke up.

Everyone turned and stared at Kylie. Including Della. Leave it to Kylie to come to her rescue.

"I'll up you one more," Chase said.

"Five," Kylie said, not backing down, and giving Chase a dirty look.

Chris grinned and shot Chase a smirk. But then Peter, Chris's assistant in the campmate hour, spoke up. "You can't donate five pints. It isn't allowed."

"I'm not going to donate all five," Kylie answered, and seemed to hesitate in thought. "I'll donate one, Miranda will donate one, and Lucas and . . . Perry and . . ."

"That's only four," said Chase.

Della saw Kylie look around as if searching for another person. One more person who would stand up for Della. "And Derek . . . he'll donate one," Kylie said with confidence.

Derek's eyes widened. Della waited for him to tell Kylie he wasn't in. He'd been pissed at her for upsetting Jenny, but a few pregnant seconds passed and he didn't pull out. As a matter of fact, his gaze briefly found hers and he nodded. "Count me in."

"And I'll donate a pint, too," a low feminine voice said behind them. Della swung around and her gaze met Jenny's.

The chameleon looked nervous with all eyes on her, but she didn't back down. And hadn't Della just hurt the girl's feelings? Not intentionally, but . . . Jenny didn't know that for sure.

"My blood is just as good as anyone else's here," she said, her shoulders tightening, showing she had spunk.

Chris glanced back at Chase. "Are you out of the bidding?" Everyone's gaze went to him to see if the new vamp would up his bid. The unasked question hung in the air: *Just how much extra blood does this newbie have?*

"I guess I lose. Or not. Looks like we'll have plenty of food for a while." He glanced at Chris and smiled as if that had been his plan all along. "By the way, that's how a blood drive should be run." Tucking his hands into his jeans pockets, he strolled away. Not as if he'd been beaten, but with confidence that bordered on cockiness.

Della watched him, still confused. Was that what he'd been doing? Just trying to secure food? Or . . . ?

"Okay, let's move on." Chris started matching names to spend the hour together.

Kylie moved closer to Della. "I don't know if we've been played, or not."

Della gritted her teeth. "Me, either. I'm sorry."

"Don't be. It's for a good cause. And . . . I didn't want you to have to do something you didn't want to do."

"Thanks," Della said, her head still spinning with what had happened. And not just Chase, but the blood donors who'd come to her rescue.

Jenny walked up. "Where do I need to go to donate?"

Kylie smiled at her. "I'll show you this afternoon."

Della met Jenny's hazel eyes. "Thanks."

"You're welcome," the girl said.

Della instantly felt bad, undeserving. She glanced around at the people standing in her circle. The people who'd all been willing to offer blood just to save her from having to spend time with someone she didn't want to be with.

Friends. All of them. She'd told herself she only had Kylie and Miranda, but she'd been fooling herself. Each one of these guys stood up for her, and by golly, if they needed her she'd do the same for them.

Completely unexpectedly, her sinuses started stinging and tears threatened to appear. She glanced away, blinking the watery weakness from her eyes. Okay, that confirmed it. She had to be sick; why else would she be so weepy?

. . .

Since her hour was paid for in blood, and yet no one actually expected her to spend it with them, Della started back to her cabin. She'd read the obituary and maybe take a short nap before classes started.

The idea to skip classes and call it a sick day tempted her, especially with her slight headache still hanging in there. But not wanting to appear weak in any way to Burnett, she mentally yanked up her big-girl panties and told herself she could make it.

She got halfway to her cabin when something caused her to stop. Water. Like a shower running. No, not a shower, a waterfall. Was it the falls, the spooky and eerie place for which the school was named? The place rumored to be the hangout of the death angels, aka the supernatural spirits who stood in judgment of the supernatural.

She tilted her head and listened. It couldn't be the falls. Even with her super hearing she couldn't hear that from here.

Compelled to go check it out, she started toward the woods, following the tinkling sound, which for some reason sounded peaceful. Several footfalls later, she left the bright sunshine and entered the woodsy dusk. The smell of rich dirt filled the thick air. A few shadows from the sun above danced on the forest floor. It wasn't actually cold, but under the umbrella of trees the chill of fall hung in the air. Looking up, she noted the fall colors: reds, oranges, and shades of murky browns painted on the leaves. The colors of death, she reminded herself.

She kept walking. Kept listening to the sound, feeling almost called, or lured, by the soft splashing noise. After several minutes, she realized it must be the falls she was hearing, because she was indeed heading toward it.

She'd only been there once. Kylie had begged her and Miranda to go with her. They'd refused to go, then felt bad and gone after her.

Della suddenly stopped walking. What the hell was she doing?

Why was she going to the falls? The place scared the bejeebies out of her.

Or it had.

Now . . . she didn't feel as afraid as she did . . . curious. She stood there digging the toe of her black boots into the dirt and trying to figure out what compelled her to continue forward. Oh, hell, death angels hung out at the falls. It was said they danced on the walls behind the falls. She had no need to see them dance, or be judged by them.

Della didn't think she'd committed any crimes serious enough for them to burn her alive—and according to Miranda that could really happen—but no way was her soul lily white. Hell, just this morning she'd brought Jenny to tears by saying the wrong thing. And her failure seemed even worse when Jenny'd spoken up and offered her blood for her.

Chills ran down her back. She really should just turn around and go back to her cabin. But then the sound grew louder. Like music being played off in the distance. Maybe she could just get a little closer to it, not actually go all the way there.

She continued moving, more frightened by her lack of fear than fear itself.

Something didn't feel right.

Suddenly anxious to get it over with, she started running—moving fast, so fast the trees became only a blur to her left and right. So fast her breathing seemed a bit labored and her hair flipping to and fro actually stung when it swiped across her face. But she continued. She kept waiting for that cumbersome feeling, that sense that she shouldn't draw any closer.

It didn't come.

She didn't even think about the direction to take, she simply followed the sound. The soft bubbly sound became hypnotic. She came to an abrupt stop at the water's edge. A thin sheet of water fell from about sixty feet above off the edge of the embankment, tossing tiny pin drops of water onto the variety of plant life and rocks.

Oddly, while a lot of the forest had changed with the season, here the color green thrived. It even smelled green. Fresh, clean. A little bit like spring. It smelled like life, new life.

The sun sprayed golden light through the trees, making all the tiny water droplets twinkle like Christmas lights. The view was like something out of a fairytale. A magical wonderland that didn't exist.

Della clearly remembered standing in almost the exact same spot months back and feeling nothing but terror. Where was her terror now?

Was this how Kylie saw this place? But wow, why did it feel so different now? What did this mean? Or did it mean anything at all?

She longed to move into the water, to step behind the sheet of water, to take it all in, but something held her back. Something inside her said, *Not yet and maybe never.*

Where the heck had that voice come from? she wondered, and then felt a bit insulted.

"Why not now? Why not ever?" The questions slipped from her lips, and as crazy as it sounded, she felt as if someone listened. But who? When no answer floated back, she tossed out another question. "Who are you?"

Still no answer. She felt it then, a feeling that she shouldn't be here. That she wasn't welcome. She took one step back, her whole being instantly filled with the terror that she'd felt the last time. The beauty of the place was suddenly lost to her, and only the creepiness remained. Poised to turn around and flee, she heard it. A subtle snap of a twig. Someone . . . or something . . . was behind her.

Pain exploded in the back of her head as if she'd been struck by . . . by . . .

She fell to her knees, black spots appeared in her vision, and the last thing she saw was a shadowy figure dancing behind the spray of water.

Chapter Eight

The smell was hideous. Her gag reflex started bouncing in her throat.

"Is she coming to?" a voice somewhere in the distance asked. She recognized the voice. Holiday.

Della felt a hand move under her nose, carrying the smell. Growling, she reached up and caught the hand and held it away from her nose. Only then did she open her eyes. Only then did she see the opened clove of garlic.

Only then did she find herself staring right at Steve.

"It's me," he said.

"That stinks!" she spouted out, shaking his hand until he dropped the clove.

He stared down at her with concern. "Garlic works as smelling salts on vampires." His gaze shot to his hand. "Would you mind *not* breaking my wrist?"

She released her tight grip and tried to get a grip on the situation. Tried to wrap her head around what she was doing . . . here. Tried to figure out where "here" was and how in Hades she had gotten . . . here.

"What happened?" A deep voice tossed out the question. The inquiry bounced around her sore brain.

Sore brain or sore head?

Her gaze shifted and she saw Burnett standing several feet away from the table that she was resting on.

Freaking great! Here she wanted to look capable to him, and this happened. But exactly what had happened, she still didn't know.

"Thank God you're okay." The very pregnant Holiday came rushing to the table.

"What happened?" Burnett asked again.

Della blinked and tried to find the answer to Burnett's question, as well as about a dozen more questions that zinged back and forth in her head.

The words *I don't know* formed on her tongue, but she knew how ill received they would be by Burnett, so she struggled to find a better answer.

Problem was, she didn't have a better one.

"I . . . I . . ." Bits and pieces of memory started rolling around her head. She'd gone on a run and ended up at the. . . . She went to sit up. Steve, standing close, tried to help her. She nudged him away. She didn't need any help, thank you very much.

Sitting up, dangling her feet off the table, she glanced around the room. Between the garlic smell and Steve's spicy scent, she caught the scent of . . . animals.

A poster of two kittens chasing a butterfly drew her attention, and then her gaze flipped back to Steve. A worried Steve.

She realized she was at the veterinarian's office. Which doubled as a doctor's office for supernaturals. At least one of her questions was answered. Now she just needed to figure out why.

Burnett cleared his throat, his gaze locked on her as if waiting for her to answer his question. And he didn't look too patient.

"I went for a run." She thought harder. "I ended up at the falls." She recalled hearing the sound of water running, but for some reason it sounded too crazy to say. "I . . . I was leaving but I heard something, or someone, behind me."

"That explains the lump on your head," Steve said. "Someone hit you with something."

Della's gaze shot to Holiday. "Would the death angels do that?"

Holiday's brows puckered. "Why would they hit you on the head?"

"Because they didn't want me there, because they're jerks, because their mamas dressed them funny. I don't know." Her gag reflex wiggled again when she got a whiff of the garlic still on the floor.

"I don't think it was the death angels," Burnett said. "The alarm went off about three minutes before Holiday found you."

Holiday leaned a little against Burnett. "It could have just been someone curious about the falls and they got spooked when Della showed up."

"Being spooked doesn't give anyone the right to hit her," Steve said, emotion tightening his voice.

Burnett scowled and looked at Steve. "Can you please get the garlic out of here?"

Steve nodded, then looked at Della. "Stay away from the falls from now on."

She cut him a hard look. It was bad enough having to deal with Holiday and Burnett. Steve didn't have a right to order her around. They weren't an item. The shape-shifter snatched the garlic cloves and left the room.

Holiday waddled closer. "Luckily, I was going to the falls, or you could still be there unconscious."

So Holiday had found her.

"Why would someone break in just to hit me on the head?" Just like that, Della's fury rose. "What kind of coward hits someone over the head? Why couldn't they face me and fight?"

"Maybe it has something to do with the person who killed the couple," Burnett said. "If you got a trace of his scent when he flew over, maybe he got yours, too. Did you smell the intruder before he hit you?"

Della tried to remember. "No, I . . . didn't." She wondered if her sense of smell was coming and going like her hearing. Since she was at the doctor, maybe she should mention it, but recalling Burnett's belief that she wasn't strong enough to be an FRU agent, she held her tongue. "I . . . think I was too weirded out about the falls." It wasn't a lie, but . . .

Burnett nodded as if he understood. Della wished she could buy it. Something was going on with her.

"But if it was the same guy who killed the couple, why would he stop at hitting me in the head? We've seen what he's capable of doing." She emotionally flinched as she recalled the bloody image of the couple.

"Maybe the death angels saved you," Holiday said, and being a ghost whisperer, Holiday was one of the few who had a connection to the death angels. "Maybe they scared him off." She set her hand on Della's arm. The fae's touch felt warm and chased away the emerging panic building in Della's chest. Panic that Holiday probably picked up on with her fae abilities.

Embarrassed that she was having difficulty, she brushed Holiday's touch off. "I'm fine."

"It had to be upsetting," Holiday said.

Upsetting? More like infuriating. "I'm fine," she muttered again. And she would be fine as soon as she caught the creep who hit her.

Burnett glanced at Holiday. "If the death angels protected her, do you think you could get them to tell us anything?"

The idea of actually trying to communicate with the death angels sent another shiver down Della's spine. "I wouldn't bother them," Della said. "They might have been the ones who did this and decide to come back and finish the job."

Holiday shook her head. "I don't think the death angels did this, Della." Then she looked at Burnett. "It's not as if I can just pick up the phone and ask them a question."

Burnett didn't look happy. "But you've gotten messages and visions from them."

"When they feel it's needed," Holiday said, and then paused. "Frankly, my level of communication isn't nearly as strong as someone else."

"Kylie," Burnett said, and nodded. "I'll talk to her about it as soon as I get back."

Steve walked back into the room, and this time Dr. Whitman was with him.

"Hello." The doctor wore a white coat and came with the scent of anesthetic and a trace of dog. No doubt he really tended to the animals in his practice as well. Of course, she should have guessed that by the jar of dog biscuits on the counter. Della snuck a peek at the man's pattern, half fae and half human.

The doctor's gaze fell on Holiday. "How are you feeling? You remember we have an appointment next week."

"We'll be there," Burnett said. For some reason it seemed out of his badass character to be a doting husband. Then again, she'd already come to the conclusion that he wasn't nearly the badass he pretended to be.

Holiday motioned to Della. "Is she going to be okay?"

"Ahh, this one." The doctor moved closer to Della. "I think she'll be fine," he said, but he looked puzzled as he tilted Della's chin up to look at her eyes. "You have a concussion. But . . . concussions are practically unheard of in vampires. The virus . . ."

"I have a virus?" Della asked, thinking that could be what was messing with her hearing.

"The vampire virus," Steve said.

"Oh," Della said, thinking the doctor had found something else.

The doctor continued, "The V-one virus actually strengthens all the blood vessels and they heal before any real swelling occurs and can cause concussions"

"So why do I have a concussion?"

The doctor shined a light in her eyes. "Well, there is an exception." His brows puckered as if puzzled again. "But I wouldn't have been aware of it if I hadn't . . ."

"Hadn't what?" Della asked, not liking that the man didn't finish his sentences.

Ignoring Della's question, he walked around the table and started parting Della's hair, touching a sore spot. She forced herself not to flinch at the pain.

"Does that hurt?" the doctor asked her.

"Not really," she lied.

"Yes, it did," Burnett, the walking, breathing lie detector, spit out, and frowned.

Della rolled her eyes at him.

The doctor continued to look at her bump. "You got a nice-size goose egg. And . . ."

"And what?" Della muttered, feeling like an idiot for being here.

"And I was right," the doctor said.

Della turned and looked at the man's hazel eyes. "Right about what?"

"Yesterday, there was an article written up in *Supernatural Medical* about how a blow delivered in an exact spot, a half an inch behind the right ear, can cause a slight cerebral hemorrhaging in the one weak spot of a V-one-affected brain. While the odds of it causing any real damage are slight, it can render a vampire unconscious."

"Which could be considered damaging," Burnett snapped.

"I don't like it," Steve added, looking at her, concern still pulling at his lips.

The doctor scratched his jaw. "It almost feels too coincidental."

"What's coincidental?" Della asked.

"That I read about it one day and see it the next. It's almost as if . . ."

"Are you suggesting someone read that article and did this on purpose?" Burnett asked, sounding annoyed at the man's unfinished dialogue with Della. "Why the hell would anyone publish it? Why tell the world of our weak spot?"

"The article was about a medical study," the doctor answered as if it made it okay. "And I'm not saying it was intentional, I . . . I'm just saying it feels coincidental."

"I don't believe in coincidences," Burnett said.

Neither did Della. But the kind of people reading medical journals weren't the type running around hitting people in the head. Were they? This didn't make a lick of sense.

Then again, not much in her life made sense, not since she'd caught the dang V1 virus. She should be used to craziness. What she wasn't used to was someone getting the upper hand on her. Someone making her look bad in front of Burnett. She'd never prove herself FRU-worthy like this.

But as soon as she figured out who that someone was, he'd have hell to pay. And she'd personally make sure he paid it, too. That might win her a few brownie points with Burnett. She even hoped he was the killer of the couple, because that would make her justice even sweeter.

A few minutes later, the doctor had just finished checking her blood pressure and instructing Della to take it easy for a while when a knock sounded at the door.

A girl, around seventeen, popped her head in the door. Her short blond hair bounced around her neck. Her big blue eyes shifted from the doctor to Steve, and just like that, her smile widened.

"There's some people here. Friends of the patient." She glanced at Della. Her smile faded. "Oh, and Dad, Mrs. Ledbetter is here with her cat. I put her in room two."

"Fine," the doctor said. "I'll be right out."

The girl took a small step back, and Della spotted Miranda and

Kylie behind her. Miranda, always the more impatient of the two, wiggled between the girl and the door and ran to Della.

"Are you okay?" Miranda asked, her green eyes teary.

"I'm fine," Della said, hating that she appeared like a sick little girl sitting on a doctor's table. A doctor's table that smelled like dog.

Miranda let go of a deep breath. "Lucas said he saw Burnett carrying you to the car and they were taking you to the doctor. Kylie and I both were panicking."

"She's going to be okay." Holiday moved in.

"We were worried." Kylie focused on Holiday as she moved inside. "Why didn't you call us?"

"Because I didn't want to worry you. I was just about to contact you guys."

"You should have gotten me. I could have . . . helped."

By "helped," Della got that Kylie meant to heal her. Among all of Kylie's talents, she was also a healer. The only problem was that every time Kylie healed someone she started glowing.

"I didn't need healing. I'm fine."

"Anytime there's a brain injury, it can be difficult," Holiday said. "My gut said I needed to get her to a doctor."

"Well, your gut was wrong. I'm fine," Della insisted again. She looked up and saw the blond chick, obviously the doctor's daughter, still poised in the door. The girl's gaze had slipped back to Steve. Della checked her pattern and saw she was part fae and shape-shifter. An ugly feeling stirred in Della's gut when she caught a scent of the girl's pheromones polluting the air. So the girl had a thing for Steve.

Not that Della had any hold on him. They weren't an item. And yet . . .

"What matters is you're okay," Steve said, sounding like someone who cared too much. Della also noted that he wasn't paying the blond girl any attention. However, the chick was paying him enough attention for the both of them.

Kylie moved to the table and squeezed Della's hand. "Don't scare me like this. What happened?"

"How about let's get out of this crowded room that still stinks and we can explain later." Burnett waved toward the door.

Following Burnett's orders, everyone started walking out like good little soldiers. Della slid her butt off the table.

Her feet hadn't hit the ground when Steve moved next to her and caught her arm as if he was afraid she might fall. "Stop it," she seethed in a low voice.

"Stop what?" he asked.

"Treating me like a weakling."

"I'm just treating you like someone who cares." His whisper came right at her ear. "Call me when you get home." He ran a hand down her forearm. His touch sent a sharp twinge of emotion right to her chest.

She managed to nod and then frowned when she realized Steve would be staying here. Here with the pheromone-polluting blonde.

They all stood in the Shadow Falls parking lot. After being force-fed a few more hugs from Miranda, Della watched her two friends head off. She stood between Burnett and Holiday, waiting to see if she was going to be read the riot act for going to the falls in the first place—waiting to get a chance to ask Burnett if any reports had come in on the murder case.

"You need to go to the cabin and rest," Holiday said.

"No, I'm fine," Della insisted.

"No, you are not fine," Holiday countered. "Go rest and I'm going to come by in a couple of hours and we're going to talk."

Oh, so the riot act is going to come later, huh? "But—"

Burnett growled. "Do not argue with her."

Della let out a deep frustrated breath. "Have you gotten anything back on the autopsy yet?"

"Not yet," he said.

"When you do, please call me."

"Don't worry about that right now," Burnett said. "You go do as Holiday said and rest."

"You are going to let me work the case, right?"

He growled again.

Knowing when to shut her trap, she swung around and started walking back to her cabin. She got past the first bend and then looked at the woods. Would her attacker's scent still be lingering at the falls? It was probably too late.

Or was it?

The memory of the terror she'd felt for those few seconds before she'd been hit had her gut knotting. Not fear of the intruder, she hadn't sensed them at all, but fear of the falls, the death angels, and what they stood for: judgment. Having your life picked apart and all your sins thrown at you like rocks.

Fear curled up in her gut, and vowing never to let fear stop her, she took off into the woods, right back to where trouble started this morning.

The ugly sensation of being unwelcome swelled in her chest as she drew closer, but she'd be damned if she let that stop her.

The death angels were going to have to deal with her visit.

Or they'd deal with her. Again. Could they have done this?

What confused her was why the hell she hadn't felt the cumbersome feeling coming here this morning. And why, for a little while, the falls looked like some kind of paradise instead of a creepy hangout for dead people.

Stopping a few feet from the edge of the woods, she inhaled deeply. The cascading sound of the falls echoed too loudly, as if to chase her away. Dampness seemed to make the trees heavy. Dark shadows swayed on the ground, adding to the haunted feel.

She pushed back the terror crawling up her spine like prickly-legged spiders, raised her face, and breathed in, hoping to find a scent.

Only the smell of wet dirt lingered in the air. But if someone touched something, the scent would hang around longer. She walked closer to a couple of trees, thinking someone might have touched the branches. Nothing. Her gaze shifted and fell to a rock on the ground. Wasn't that right where she'd been hit? Was that what had bashed her in the head? She picked it up. Bringing the stone to her face, she took a deep sniff.

When the scent filled her nose, her breath caught. Fury, raw and pure, started building, bubbling inside her chest. She dropped the rock, growled, and went to collect her pound of justice.

Chapter Nine

Della hid behind a shed outside the school building, checking her phone for the time every few minutes. Holiday hadn't said what time she planned on stopping by, but if she came and Della wasn't "resting," there'd be hell to pay.

Della didn't plan on paying hell, she planned on collecting it.

And from one person in particular.

Staring back at one of the three cabin classrooms, she couldn't get close enough to smell if he was there . . . well, not without being seen. But classes would end in a few minutes, and if he wasn't here, she'd have to. . . . The classroom door opened, the new vamp was the first one out, and she felt her fury inch up a degree or two.

He started strolling straight toward the woods.

Great. She preferred to do it without an audience.

Waiting a few minutes for the crowd to scatter, she followed.

Did he know she was here? Probably. Since she'd already picked up on his scent, he'd probably done the same.

But she didn't care what he knew. It was time for their powwow. And it wasn't going to be pretty. Hell seldom was.

She spotted his green T-shirt and faded jeans moving between the trees. She'd barely passed the first line of small trees when she realized he'd disappeared. She growled, felt her eyes brighten with anger, and lifted her face to the wind to catch his scent.

"You looking for me?" a voice came from above.

She looked up. He sat perched on a limb about fifty feet off the ground, casually shifting his legs back and forth as if he'd been hanging out there all day. Or as if he was showing off.

But for what? So he could climb trees. Climb trees fast. Did he think that made him special?

The sun peeked behind a cloud and caused her to blink. When she opened her eyes, he'd disappeared again.

What kind of game was he playing? "I'll find you," she growled. "And when I do—"

"You won't have to work hard. I'm right here." His voice came from behind a tree.

She shot over, ready to ring his neck, but found the space empty.

"Behind you," he said, so close she could feel his words on the back of her neck.

She swerved around, caught him by his shirt, and yanked him to her. "Stop it," she seethed, and tightened her fist with wads of green cotton between her fingers.

"Stop what?" he asked, his pale jade eyes so close she saw his pupils change size.

She twisted her hold on his shirt, almost to the point of ripping it, just to let him know she meant business. "You hit me and you're going to be sorry."

"Hit you? Where did you get that idea?" he asked.

"Your scent was all over the rock by the falls."

"Yeah, Mr. James, I mean Burnett, asked me to go there and see if there was any scent left behind when he took you to the doctor."

She listened as his heart thumped against his chest bone at a normal pace. Of course, he could still be lying, but . . . why would he when all she'd have to do is ask Burnett?

A slight smile appeared on his lips as if he knew just what conclusion she'd come to. He leaned in a bit. His breath stirred in her hair. "You're cute when you get mad."

She shoved him back.

He barely shifted, giving her only an inch, not enough. She could still feel his presence. Smell his skin. See humor dance in his eyes.

"That falls place was creepy, by the way," he said.

She almost asked if he'd gotten any scent, but didn't want to be beholden to him for anything.

Yeah, I'll bet the death angels were eager to put some fire to his egotistical ass. She recalled her other reason for needing a powwow with him. "Last night, were you following me?"

"Following you?"

Her canines came out a bit. "I saw you when I went to meet Burnett at the gate to go to . . ."

"The FRU case?" he finished.

She clenched her hands. "You were there."

"Yeah, but I wasn't following you. I couldn't sleep and was taking a run. Sorry, I didn't mean to interrupt your little rendezvous."

So he'd seen her and Steve together. Had she even tried to detect anyone? She growled at the vamp.

His smile widened as if he enjoyed knowing he got to her. Which meant from this moment on, she couldn't let him get to her. She had to ignore him. Pay him about as much attention as a bug stealthily sneaking across a piece of dead grass.

"Fine." She pivoted around to leave—to show disinterest—the heels of her black ankle-high boots leaving grooves in the dirt. *Adios, asswipe!*

"Hey, not so quick," he spouted out, and flashed in front of her, blocking her path.

Damn, he was fast. Almost as fast as Burnett. No wonder he'd been able to hide from her in the trees.

She crossed her arms over her chest and shot him her best go-to-hell look. He didn't go anywhere, he just stood there studying her as if she'd given him permission. But to call him on it would mean he was getting to her, so she lingered there as if his presence or his observation of her didn't affect her at all.

But it did. And that annoyed the hell out of her.

"Can't you give a guy a break?" he finally asked.

"Arm? Leg? Neck? You name it, I'll break it."

He chuckled. And she so hadn't meant it to be funny. But damn this guy was like a squeaky-voiced mosquito buzzing in her ear. All she wanted to do was smash him between her palms and wipe his remains on her jeans.

She moved around him and continued down the path.

"Can't we talk?" he asked, sounding as if he was right behind her.

About what? What the hell did they have to talk about?

"No," she snapped, and continued moving. She wanted to flash away, to put as much distance as she could between him and her as soon as possible, but that would tell him how much he aggravated her.

"Come on. I was even going to give up my stash of blood for you so you wouldn't have to go off for an hour with that crazy blond vamp."

She stopped and twisted around so fast he ran right into her. He caught her by her forearms and held her there. Their bodies came together. Her breasts pressed against his chest. And since her breasts weren't that big, that meant they were really close. She pulled away.

"I thought you did that to help the blood drive? Or just to annoy me."

He shrugged. "Maybe it was a little of all three."

"Why?" she asked, now more curious and even more leery. She was almost positive she'd run across him before. His scent, his trace, was in her memory bank. And it stirred up vague feelings of danger.

"Why what?"

"Why would you give up blood for me?"

"To talk." He shrugged. "I think we got off on the wrong foot."

She listened again to his heart, steady and honest.

"I'm new here," he continued. "And let me tell you, this place isn't exactly friendly. You're the only one I've clicked with."

What? When had they . . . "We have *not* clicked," she snapped. "If you'll recall, I was going to kick your butt."

He grinned. "But you didn't."

"I would have if Burnett hadn't showed up."

"You would have tried. But I'm going to overlook that."

She barely managed to stop a frustrated groan. "You know, if you weren't so damn arrogant, you might make a few friends around here."

"I'm not arrogant. I'm confident. I know they sometimes appear the same, but they aren't."

Della had a vague memory of saying almost the same thing to Miranda. But she didn't have to tell him she agreed. Frankly, having anything in common with this jerk pissed her off.

"Yeah, you just keep believing that." She swung around and started back down the path.

"What is it? You afraid your shifter friend wouldn't approve of us hanging out?"

She stopped and swung around again, but this time she put her hands out, prepared to stop him from touching her. Her plan backfired. Now he wasn't touching her, but she touched him. Her palms pressed solidly against his chest. His heart pumped against his breastbone and the vibration melted in her palms. She could feel his solid mass of muscle, feel the coolness of his vampire skin. She yanked her hands away.

"I'm not afraid of anything." It was a lie. She had fears, a lot of them—death angels, ghosts, losing people she loved, even an occasional spider—but she hoped he wasn't listening to the telltale rhythm of her lying heart.

"So you two aren't an item?" he asked, quirking one of his dark brows upward.

The phone in her back pocket buzzed. Using it as a reason not to respond to his question, and maybe not to even think about it, she snatched her pink cell out. Her mind immediately went to her unregistered vampire cousin Chan, who still hadn't returned her call. What was up with that? Sure she hadn't returned his call from the week before, but in his message, he'd said it wasn't important. Probably calling to try to talk her into leaving Shadow Falls again. He didn't seem to understand why she'd want to be here instead of living on the streets. And she couldn't understand how he saw it the other way.

Her gaze caught the number on the tiny screen. Shit!

It wasn't Chan.

It was Holiday. No doubt she was at Della's cabin and probably pissed Della wasn't following her instructions and resting. But dang it, she didn't need rest. Nor did she need Holiday or Burnett pissed.

"Gotta go!" she moaned, and took off.

"Let's do this again," he called out.

"Yeah, when Hell starts serving soft-serve ice cream with sprinkles," she yelled, and kept going, knowing she was probably going to catch hell when she caught up with Holiday. And then Holiday would tell Burnett and she'd catch double hell.

Della spotted Holiday before she dropped down. The red-haired, pregnant fae sat on Della's front porch, her feet swinging off the edge, her hand placed on her belly, her expression one of tenderness as she whispered sweet words of affection to the unborn child. Della had almost texted Holiday back, but it would have taken the same amount of time to get there.

She came to an abrupt stop on the steps. Holiday looked up. Her mouth tightened into a disapproving bow. Whatever sweet affection she offered the child wasn't going to be passed to Della.

"You were supposed to be resting," Holiday scolded.

Della stepped up on the porch. "Sorry, I . . . I was coming here and suddenly felt the need to go back to the falls and see if I could find a trace or a clue of who did this."

"Felt the need to disobey?" she reprimanded.

"No, I felt the need to catch the jerk who knocked me in the head."

Holiday sighed. "You were unconscious, Della. The doctor said for you to take it easy. I didn't want you running around."

Della knew Holiday argued because she cared, but . . . "It was important to me. I don't like . . ." Her throat tightened with frustration and she felt the sting of her sinuses as tears threatened. Ignoring the feeling, she tried to explain again. "I want to work for the FRU. I thought if I could figure this out, Burnett would see I'm not a weakling."

Holiday looked surprised. "Burnett doesn't think you're a weakling."

"Yes, he does. He told me he didn't think I have what it takes to work with the FRU."

She made a face. "I don't think. . . . He has a lot of respect for you, Della."

"Not enough that he thinks I'd be a good agent. He even said there were easier ways for me to make a living. And he knows how badly I want this."

Holiday's gaze filled with empathy. "If he was trying to discourage you, and I'm not saying he was, it's probably because he's a male chauvinist pig."

Della was shocked by Holiday's confession. She'd thought the fae would defend her husband. "That's what I thought," she said. "It's because I'm a girl, isn't it?"

"Don't get me wrong, I love that man more than life, and he is the way he is because he cares so deeply, but it's true, he's more protective over a female than a male. And if this baby is a girl, I have a feeling she and her father will be having a battle of wills from day one."

"It's not fair," Della said.

"I know it's not. But . . ." She pointed her finger at Della. ". . . if there's one thing Burnett looks for in an agent, it's obedience. If you can't follow orders, he'll never trust you on a mission. And that, young lady, is your issue. Lucky for you, I decided not to call him when I didn't find you here."

Della wanted to argue that her going to the falls hadn't been so much disobedience as a necessary slip of the rules. She had the words on the tip of her tongue, but swallowed them.

"I'll work on that," she finally said. Della even wondered if this hadn't been Holiday's plan all along to get her to see her own flaws. Yes, Holiday was that good at manipulation . . . well, maybe not manipulation, but with encouraging someone to see the error of their ways.

Holiday smiled. "Good, and I'll work on making sure he doesn't let his chauvinistic ways interfere with your goals."

"Thank you," Della said.

Holiday rested her palms behind her and leaned back. Her round belly was even more apparent with her back slightly arched. "Now that we got that out of the way, can we talk about what happened this weekend at your parents', and then about last night?"

Della pulled her legs to her chest and wrapped her arms around them tightly. "Do we have to?"

"Have to? No. But I would like it if you confided in me." She looked at Della. "I know you don't like talking about personal issues. I can respect that you're vampire and that makes you a little less open. I'm married to Burnett, who thinks he can solve his and the world's issues with no help from anyone. But even my big bad husband is learning that it's not a weakness to confide in someone." She glanced up to the sky and then back to Della. "I can feel your pain, and I wouldn't be doing my job as counselor if I didn't try to help."

For one second Della considered telling Holiday about her uncle, but the fear that if he was alive and not registered with the FRU had her reconsidering. Holiday would probably tell Burnett, and he might feel obligated to report it. "Nothing is going to help with my parents," Della said, deciding that, while she couldn't tell Holiday everything, maybe some things were safe.

"What happened?"

"Same ol' story. They see all the changes that being vampire has brought on as some kind of rebellion on my part. I'd tell them the truth if I didn't know it would be harder for them to accept than anything they suspect is wrong." Her chest grew heavy. "I hate disappointing them. I hate . . ." She swallowed. "I hate knowing that I'm hurting them." Tears filled her eyes and she glanced away. "I don't feel like I belong in my own family anymore."

She swiped the tears crawling down her cheeks.

Holiday placed a hand on Della's shoulder. The warmth of the fae's touch eased the pain in Della's chest. As much as she hated needing a reprieve, she savored the comfort. No wonder Burnett fell for Holiday. The woman's touch was magical.

"I know it's hard to live with a secret between you," Holiday said. "And it's so unfair. I also know it would be easier to do what most vampires do, to let them think you're dead. It takes courage to do it this way. I admire you for doing it. And as hard as it is, I've seen this work."

"How can it work when they . . . think I'm a lying drug addict."

Holiday sighed. "As soon as you're an adult, and they recognize that you are a functioning member of society, they'll assume that you just went through some tough teen years and outgrew it. This way, you can and will maintain a relationship with them. If you go the other route, you'll lose them forever."

"I'm not sure I won't lose them anyway," Della said. "I think they're already giving up on me." Her dad didn't even talk about her.

"No, they haven't," Holiday said. "They love you. If they didn't, they wouldn't care. Your mom calls me at least once a week just to check in."

"But not my dad," Della said, and in spite of knowing it wasn't so, she held her breath that Holiday would say differently.

"He's a man. Men deal with things differently."

Yeah, some men just stop loving you. For some reason, she remembered Steve and the doctor's daughter. Was Steve on his way to giving up on her?

Della hugged her legs and let the silence settle in. The fact that her mom was calling sent a wave of fresh emotion inside her . . . or was it relief knowing at least one of her parents still loved her?

"About last night and what you saw . . ." Holiday said.

"I'm okay," Della insisted. "If I want to work for the FRU, I'm going to have to learn to deal with it. And I can." At least the flashbacks had lessened.

"Yes, you will have to learn, but you don't have to deal with it alone. Della, don't tell Burnett I said this, but even he needs someone to lean on. If you really want to work for the FRU, you've got to accept that you're going to need other people. You have to counter the bad with the good. If not, you'll get lost in the evilness of it all. It can darken your soul and you'll lose all joy in life."

"The joy will be catching the mofo who did that," Della said, and right then the flashback hit again. Her heart filled with the need for justice. "I don't even know the couple, but they didn't deserve that."

"I know." Holiday grasped Della's hand. "But before you lose yourself in making things right for others, you need to work on making them right for yourself. I get this feeling you are searching for something. Something you long for. But I also get the feeling you're procrastinating."

The truth of the fae's words hit with a thud on her conscience. Her uncle. Finding something to replace the feeling of the family she felt she'd lost. And what was she was procrastinating about? Reading the obituary. Della glanced away, not liking that Holiday could read her so clearly.

"Don't worry, I'm not going to force you to tell me anything. But I will tell you this: Whatever it is you're looking for, make it your quest, but make sure you don't take too many risks. I know you, Della, and sometimes you act before you think."

"Maybe I just think fast." Della smiled, hoping to lighten the conversation.

Holiday rolled her eyes as if she knew exactly what Della was up to. "This trait is part of being vampire, but it's also part of your personality. You've got more raw gumption than anyone I've ever met. Gumption is to be admired. But I'm just afraid that if mishandled, it can do you more harm than good."

Della nodded. "I'll try to remember that."

"Make sure you do," Holiday said, and sighed. Then the fae sat up and placed a hand on her pregnant stomach.

Still wanting to change the conversation, Della asked, "Is the baby moving much?"

"All the time. I think it's going to be impatient like its daddy. You want to feel it?"

Della hesitated. "You don't mind?"

"Not at all." She took Della's hand and placed it on her stomach.

Della felt the movement. "Wow. I think your baby just kicked me. That's so cool," she said, meaning it. She couldn't imagine what it would feel like to have a person growing inside of you. "Weird, but cool." She grinned up at the camp leader. "And you're freaking huge. You sure there's not two of them in there?"

Holiday grimaced. "Freaking huge? Thanks."

Della frowned. "Sorry, I just meant . . ."

"Don't worry." Holiday leaned in and bumped her shoulder. "I *am* freaking huge. And no, it's not twins. But it appears my baby is going to be vampire dominant."

"You had one of those X-ray things? Does that tell you the baby's pattern?"

"A special sonogram can show it. But I asked not to be told. I want to be surprised."

"Then how do you know for sure it will be vampire dominant?"

"Supernaturals very seldom carry babies to full term. But the gestational cycle for a vampire can really vary. Sometimes it can happen as quickly as four or five months."

"Wow, so you could like have the baby really soon?"

"Yup."

"Are you scared? Of having it?" Della had seen a birth on some freaky documentary once and it was pretty darn terrifying. It had showed everything. Like the baby coming out. It had made Della extra careful about birth control.

The fae glanced down at her belly. "I'd be lying if I said I wasn't a little nervous. But I'm more worried about the baby than myself." She pulled her hair over her shoulder, her hand dropping to rest on her huge baby bump. Then she suddenly turned her head and looked behind her, then to the right. The quick movement reminded Della of Kylie when . . .

"What's wrong?" Della asked.

"Nothing," Holiday said, but her heart rate told Della it was a white lie.

"Is it the ghost?" Della pulled her knees closer to her chest.

Holiday fixed her green eyes on Della and her brow wrinkled. "Yes. How did you know?"

"Kylie said there was one hanging around. She thinks it might be vampire."

Holiday nodded. "I think she's right. It's traveling at high speeds."

Della also remembered Kylie suspecting that it might be her uncle. "Did you see it?"

"No." Holiday continued to look left to right. "It's moving so fast." She shrugged. "Has it made contact with Kylie? Does she know what it wants?"

Della shook her head. "Not unless she's seen it since this morning."

"It's odd," Holiday said.

"What's odd?"

"I don't understand why it's visiting both Kylie and me. Usually it only chooses one person to attach itself to. And it shouldn't be hanging around if Kylie's not here."

Della recalled Kylie saying she thought the ghost was there for Della. A chill ran down her backbone. No way did she want any ghost getting attached to her.

Stiffening her spine, Della looked around and then asked, "Can you tell it to leave?"

"Ghosts don't work that way."

"Why did I know you were going to say that?" Probably because Kylie had already said it.

Holiday pulled her phone out of her pocket. "Yikes, I'm supposed to meet Perry at the office right now."

Something about Holiday's tone caught her attention. "Is something wrong with him?"

Holiday hesitated. "No. Not really. I'd better go." She gave Della a stern look and pointed to the front door to the cabin. "You get some sleep and if I find you running around again, you'll have Burnett to deal with next time."

Holiday, belly huge, struggled to stand up. Della popped up and offered her a hand.

"Don't make it look so easy," Holiday mumbled, but she accepted Della's hand.

Della watched Holiday waddle down the steps, her round belly leading the way. Della suddenly remembered. "Hey, what about the ghost?"

"I'm sure it'll follow me," Holiday said. "A ghost usually only hangs around people who can detect it."

Della sure as heck hoped so. But as she walked inside the door, she could swear she felt a brush of cold air against her arm. Cold air as if someone flew past. As if a vampire flew past. She stopped and glanced around. No vampire, not even a blur of a really fast vampire.

But the feeling, the feeling she wasn't alone, didn't go away.

"Oh, crap," she muttered.

A ghost usually only hangs around people who can detect it. Holiday's words echoed in Della's head. If she'd felt something, wasn't that detecting it? Or had she imagined it? Right then, something vibrated against her hip. She nearly jumped out of her skin before she realized it was her phone. She must have accidentally put it on vibrate.

Glad for the interruption from her haunted thoughts, she snatched out her phone. Thinking and hoping it was Chan, she glanced at the number. It wasn't Chan.

Chapter Ten

"Why didn't you call me?" Steve asked first thing.

"I got caught up with a few things and was busy," Della said, knowing it wasn't the complete truth. The real reason she hadn't called him was fear. Fear she'd end up spouting out something about the cute little doctor's daughter who'd polluted the air with all kinds of pheromones when she'd shot him that toothpaste-ad smile.

Della couldn't be jealous. Well, she shouldn't be jealous. She had no hold on Steve. Had no right to insist he stay away from blond chicks with bigger boobs than she had and who wanted his body.

But telling herself that didn't make the feeling go away. It only made it worse. Because she hadn't really thought about the girl's boobs until now.

"Too busy to call me?" he asked, sounding ticked.

"Sorry," she offered, and went into her bedroom, shut the door, and fell on the bed. "I wanted to go back to the falls on the off chance I could still catch a scent of the person who knocked me in the head."

"Dr. Whitman said for you to rest."

She rolled her eyes. "Look, I've already been read the riot act by Holiday, I don't need you adding to it."

He huffed. "I'm not . . . I'm just worried. The doctor was looking over the paperwork I did on you after you left and he noticed your temperature was elevated. Remember I told you that you felt warm this morning. Anyway, he wanted to know if I'd asked if you were on your menstrual cycle. And I told him you'd said you were—but his concern just sort of worried me."

Della reached up and touched her brow. Did she have a fever?

"I especially don't like it that someone hit you on the head. Does Burnett have a clue who did this?"

"No, I don't think so." She almost told him about Chase's scent being on the rock, but decided against it. Steve had already expressed dislike for the guy and she didn't want to encourage it.

"Could it have anything to do with the case you helped Burnett with and the intruder at the falls that you caught a trace of?"

She frowned. "He mentioned it could be a possibility," she said.

"Is the young couple who died involved in this case?"

The image flashed in her head. "How did you know?"

"I read about an accident in the paper. I know they sometimes cover up the deaths when it involves supernaturals, so I just assumed . . ." He paused. "Shit, I don't like this. A murderer could be after you."

"We don't know it was him. And if he comes back again, he'll be the one who needs a doctor."

A pregnant pause lingered both on the line and in her bedroom. Della looked around. The door to the bedroom was open. Hadn't she shut it?

"Did you actually see it?" Steve asked. "See them dead?"

She inhaled, her mind shifting away from the door to death. "Yeah."

"Damn, I'm sorry, Della. I mean, it had to be tough."

"It was, but it just makes me more determined that this is what I want to do. Catch bastards like that. Make them pay for what they did. Keep them from doing it again."

"Yeah, but I don't like thinking about you looking for sick bastards like that."

I don't like you hanging out with blondie, either. Silence came to the line. "I'm sorry." The line went quiet again. She tried to think of something to say. *So tell me about the doctor's daughter and her thing for you.* She spit the words off her tongue and went with something else. Something that didn't sound so jealous. "So do you see all the patients who come in? Even the animals?"

"Yeah," he said, as if knowing she'd taken a conversational U-turn.

"Do you enjoy it?" she asked. *Enjoy being around the doctor's daughter?*

"Yeah. Dr. Whitman suggested I go to veterinarian school if I want to practice medicine for supernaturals. He said the few supernatural doctors he knows who went through regular medical school have a lot more trouble. And he said I could work for him while going to school. Besides, I like animals."

She couldn't help but wonder if the good doctor had his sights set on Steve for a son-in-law. "You don't have to work as a vet. Supernatural doctors work at regular hospitals. I know because when I was turned I ran into a nurse and doctor."

"Yeah, but how often do you think supernaturals come in to the emergency room? Which means I'd mostly be working on humans. I could open my own practice, but then it gets messy with insurance and all the regulations. Jessie said Dr. Whitman and his partner were talking about bringing in another partner in a few years, so when I graduate I wouldn't even have to set up a clinic and find clients."

"Who's Jessie?" she asked, but she was afraid she already knew.

"Dr. Whitman's daughter. I think you met her. The one with the big smile."

Big smile? "I see," Della said.

And she did see. Blond and big-smiling Jessie had her life all planned out. And Steve was part of it.

The question was if Della was ready to become the hiccup in the girl's plans. Or better put, was Della ready to put her heart on the chopping block?

An hour later, almost four in the afternoon, Holiday's "get some sleep" command was yet to be obeyed. However, not for lack of trying.

After getting off the phone with a certain shape-shifter, Della kept thinking about Jessie's big boobs and bigger smile.

Covers up to her chin, she kept practicing smiling. She wasn't sure she could smile as big as Jessie if someone paid her.

When she wasn't thinking about that, she was contemplating the ghost. Boobs, smiles, and ghosts . . . the crazy thoughts didn't mesh together. Add an occasional vision of last night's real-life horror flick, accompanied with the need to get justice for the couple, and Della's head was spinning and hurting. Right along with her heart.

She could even swear there was a chill in the room. She snuggled deeper into the covers and stared at the ceiling. A bug of some sort inched across the white plaster. Even the insect moved slow, as if it was cold.

When Kylie had a ghost show up, the room temperature dropped. Could it be that? Or was Della's fever going up? She preferred the fever. A flu she could deal with, a ghost, not so much.

I also get the feeling you're procrastinating. Holiday's words whispered in her head.

The obituary was still folded and tucked in her jeans pocket.

Sitting up, she pulled it out. Her gaze caught on the door again. Hadn't she closed it? She had. She could swear she had.

Looking around the room, ceiling to floor, she whispered, "Are you here? Is it you?"

"Who are you talking to?" a voice spoke at the door.

Startled, Della glared at Miranda and Kylie shoulder-to-shoulder standing in her door. "No one," Della insisted, and she saw Kylie frown and glance up as if . . . as if looking for an unwanted visitor. "Is it here?" Della asked, not even caring they knew she was frightened.

"Is what here?" Miranda asked.

Kylie frowned. "It was, but it's gone."

"What's gone?" Miranda snapped.

Kylie looked at Miranda. "A ghost."

Miranda eyes widened. "You've got another ghost?"

Kylie shrugged. "I don't think this one's mine."

Miranda's mouth dropped open and she looked at Della. "You've got a ghost? You can't have a ghost. You're not a ghost whisperer."

"Nor do I ever aspire to be one," Della said, and looked back at Kylie. "So how the hell is this happening?"

Kylie moved in and sat on the edge of the bed. "I . . . I remember Holiday said that some ghosts contain so much energy that they can appear to normal people."

"Yeah, but I'm not normal. I've been called a lot of things, but never normal."

"You're normal enough for us to like you." Miranda bounced down on the bed. Then her gaze shifted to Kylie. "It is gone, right?"

Kylie nodded and her gaze shifted back to Della. "Do you know who it is now?"

"No," Della said, and hugged her legs.

"It didn't appear to you?" Kylie asked.

"No," Della repeated.

"It didn't talk to you?"

"No," Della said again.

"Then how did you know it was here?"

"Because . . . because it was cold and . . . and I thought I felt something brush up against my shoulder. Oh . . . and I'm almost positive it opened my door."

"Opened your door?" Kylie's brows puckered.

"Yeah," Della said.

Kylie shook her head. "That's unlikely. Ghosts usually only have enough power to move tiny objects, like a cell phone."

"Well, explain how I closed my door and then it came open?"

Kylie glanced eerily at the door, but disbelief flashed in her blue eyes. "Maybe you just thought you shut it."

"So now I'm crazy?"

Kylie shook her head. "I didn't say that."

"I didn't just imagine it." Della pushed her hands against her eyes. "This is so wrong. So very, very wrong. Frankly, I don't get why you can't tell a ghost to leave. What makes them so special?"

Miranda giggled. "I guess they feel as if being dead should give them some rights. Maybe it's in their death contract. You know, you die, you don't have to follow rules anymore. Do whatever the frack you want."

"I'm not joking," Della said. "I don't like this."

"Sorry," Miranda said. "That hit on your head made you even grumpier."

Della growled at the witch. "If you had a ghost hanging around you, I'd like to see you be Miss Cheery!"

"No fighting," Kylie said, and right then her phone rang. She checked it. "It's Holiday." She took the call. "Hey."

Della continued to frown at Miranda and focused on trying to hear Holiday's voice, but she couldn't. Her damn hearing was off again.

"Yeah," Kylie said, and looked at Della. "No, but she's in bed. Okay." Kylie hung up.

Della stared. "Was she checking on me?"

"Yeah. She said you needed to stay in bed and she'd bring you supper."

"She told me you went back to the falls again," Miranda said. "And you were supposed to be sleeping. Why would you go to the falls to start with? That place is over-the-top eerie. You might have run into a death angel."

When Della didn't answer, Miranda's eyes went wide. "Did you see a death angel?"

"I . . . not really," Della huffed. "I saw some shadows, that's all. And it happened like the second I was hit on the head, so I probably just . . . imagined it." And that was what Della kept telling herself.

"What kind of shadows?" Miranda asked. "Did they look like monsters or . . . what?"

Della saw Kylie's eyes light up with interest. Kylie being another ghost whisperer, she shared Holiday's connection with the death angels.

"No," Della said. "Just shadows." When the witch didn't look happy with Della's answer, she added, "Hell, ask Kylie about them. She's like their best buddy."

With all eyes now on Kylie, she spoke up, "They aren't monsters. Imagine a spiritual being."

Miranda shook her head. "They still scare the crap out of me." Her gaze went back to Della. "I still don't get why you'd go there."

Della growled. "The second time I went, I wanted to find out who hit me. The first . . . I . . . I don't know why I went the first time, I was running and I sort of just ended up there."

"Then you turn your butt around and run the other away," Miranda said.

"I was going to, but I was hit before I could." Then Della remembered. "Did Burnett ask you to see if the death angels saw who hit me?"

Kylie nodded. "I put the question out there, but haven't gotten an answer. Maybe they weren't there."

"It felt like they were there," Della said. "I . . . I felt like I was trespassing. Like someone there was making me feel that way." She shivered ever so slightly. "I still halfway think they're the ones who hit me."

"And yet you went back the second time?" Miranda snagged one of Della's pillows to rest on. "And here I thought you were smart."

Della scowled at the annoying witch. "I told you, I was hoping to find a trace of the piece of shit who hit me."

"Did you get anything?" Kylie asked.

Della nodded. "Chase."

Kylie's mouth dropped open. "What?"

Miranda's popped up from her reclined position. "Chase is the one who knocked you out?" Her eyes got wide. "And I thought he liked you. Oh, hell, Burnett's going to kick his ass out of here for messing with his favorite vamp."

Della shook her head. "First, I'm not Burnett's favorite vamp."

"Yeah, you are," Miranda said.

Della looked at Kylie, who nodded her head as if agreeing with the witch. If Della was his favorite anything, why would he want to stop her from going into the FRU? She pushed that thought away to ponder later. "Second, I said I found Chase's scent there, but then I found him. He told me Burnett sent him there to see if he could find a trace after I was hit."

Kylie pulled one knee up to her chest. "Did you ask Burnett?"

"No, but I don't think he would lie about something that I could so easily check on."

Miranda crossed her legs. "Maybe he figured you'd think that and not ask."

"Maybe," Della said, and tried to think how she could pose the question to Burnett.

Kylie leaned back against the headboard. "Is that the obituary?" She nodded to the folded paper now resting beside her on the bed.

"Yeah," Della answered.

"Whose obituary?" Miranda asked.

"My uncle's." Della pushed the covers off, noting that the cold had left. "Derek found it in some old newspaper files."

Miranda put on a pout. "Why is it that Kylie always knows stuff before I do?"

Della cut her gaze at Miranda and made a face. "Because you're always away with Perry getting your earlobes sucked."

Miranda snatched a pillow and threw it at Della.

Frustrated, Della caught it with two hands and accidentally pulled it apart. Duck feathers exploded in the air like snow and then rained down from the ceiling.

Miranda started giggling. Kylie joined in. Eventually, Della couldn't help herself. The giggles were contagious.

They laughed for a good five minutes, tossing handfuls of feathers at each other until they had them in each other's hair, stuck to each other's faces. Miranda even pulled a couple out of her bra. When the giggles stopped, Kylie found the folded-up obituary under a thick pile of feathers.

The chameleon looked at Della with empathy. "Do you want me to read it to you?"

Della almost said no, not wanting them to think she was too chicken to read it on her own. Part of her even felt guilty. Wasn't wanting her uncle to be alive so badly saying her family at Shadow Falls wasn't enough? But if anyone could understand and make this easier, it was Kylie and Miranda.

"Yeah. But I think I might need a Diet Coke."

They went to get up, but they all froze when the bedroom door slammed. The air in the room became instantly frigid. The feathers, mostly on the bed, rose up and started swirling.

Cold air caught in Della's lungs. She looked at Kylie. "You still think I'm crazy?"

"Shit," Kylie said. "This can't be good."

Chapter Eleven

The feathers flew around the room for another few seconds. Huddling on the bed, their fear hanging in the cold air, they didn't say anything until the last feather dropped and the room warmed up.

"Is it gone?" Miranda pulled her knees up to her chest, her eyes wide with panic.

Kylie nodded. They all cautiously stood up and moved into the kitchen, got drinks, and settled around the table. No one talked, as if afraid it would bring the dang ghost back.

"Is he still here?" Della finally asked Kylie.

"No." Kylie turned the Coke can in her hand, then looked at Della. "Him? Do you think it's a him?"

"I don't know. You said you thought it might be my uncle."

"I was just guessing." Kylie bit down on her lip. "I think we should call Holiday."

"No," Della said.

"Why not?" Miranda and Kylie asked at the same time.

"Because she'd want to know who we thought it was and then we'd end up telling about my uncle, and then if this isn't him then she'd tell Burnett and then if he's not registered . . ."

"You don't know she'd tell Burnett," Kylie said.

Della made a face. "They're married. They tell each other every-thing. I bet you tell Lucas everything."

Kylie sighed and nodded. "I see your point. But—"

"Aren't you the one who says no buts?" Della asked.

"Yes. But . . ." She closed her mouth for a second and then continued, "However, Holiday might know better how to handle this."

"No," Della insisted. "Look, Holiday told me that she felt I had a quest and she understood that I didn't want to talk about it. She told me to work on it, but not to take any stupid risks. And that's what I want to do. Remember when you were dealing with that creep that was after you? Well, you handled it yourself. Both of you have dealt with your own problems instead of running for help." She saw some understanding in her friends' eyes.

Miranda slumped in her chair. "She's right. We all kind of want to take care of our own issues sometimes."

"Okay," Kylie said. "But let's just make sure we do as Holiday said, and watch out for stupid risks."

"We?" Della said? "You two don't—"

"Please," Miranda snapped. "To quote someone I know, 'Bull-crappers!' We're a team. We work together."

"She's right," Kylie said. "That's what we do. Help each other."

A tightness filled Della's chest again. "Okay, here's to no stupid risks." Della raised her Diet Coke. As they all clicked cans, Della added, "And to good friends." She didn't want to sound too senti-mental, but for the life of her, she didn't know what she would do without her best buddies.

"Now, how do we go about finding out if your uncle is alive?" Miranda asked. "We need a plan."

Yup, without them she would be lost. Completely lost.

"I think we start by reading the obituary," Kylie said, still hold-ing the piece of paper.

Della nodded. "Derek also asked me to see if I could find out where he went to school when he died. I'm sure it's the same place my dad went. I guess I could ask my mom. If she'll talk to me."

"Why wouldn't she talk to you?" Miranda asked.

"She was pretty mad at me when she dropped me off. I'm not sure she said one word to me the whole trip." The memory of it still sent pain rolling around Della's chest.

"Yeah, but she's your mom," Miranda said. "She can't stay mad at you forever."

Della shrugged. She wished she could believe that. Then again, she recalled Holiday saying her mom called about once a week. That meant she cared, even though she didn't always show it.

"Do you want me to read it now?" Kylie asked, holding up the folded paper.

"Do you think it's safe?" Della asked, squeezing her soda can. The coolness of the drink felt odd in her hands, reminding her that she still might have a fever. "It almost seemed like the obituary is what got the ghost stirred up before."

Kylie glanced around the room as if searching for ghosts. "It's not here now." Kylie's words hadn't completely left her lips when a lone feather came twirling down from the ceiling and landed slowly, eerily, in the center of the table.

"Are you sure?" Miranda asked.

They sat there in silence for a few minutes, waiting for the feather to get up and dance again. When it didn't, Kylie spoke up in a low voice, as if afraid they weren't alone. "Jenny's called me twice to check on you. I think she really likes you for some reason."

"Why do you act like that surprises you?" Della asked.

Miranda snorted.

Della shot Miranda a go-to-hell look and then went back to watching the feather to make sure it didn't start moving.

"I didn't mean it like that," Kylie said. "I just meant she seems to admire you."

"Poor girl's confused." Miranda laughed. "I'm joking," she said when Della shot her the third-finger salute.

Della sighed and looked back at Kylie. "I like Jenny, too. She . . . she reminds me of you a little when you first came here."

"I haven't changed," Kylie said.

Both Miranda and Della made faces at Kylie.

"You changed for the better," Miranda said. "You're . . . bolder."

"Bold is good," Della said, and they all went back to watching the feather. Finally, Kylie picked up the paper with the obituary. "You ready?"

Della and Miranda nodded.

Kylie started to read. " 'Feng Tsang was lost to us on December 23rd. Feng, a dedicated young man, already had his life planned. He was to become a doctor and marry his childhood sweetheart, Jing Chen. Loyal to his family, he walked a path to make his family proud. Now his path leads him another way. Loved by so—' "

"Wait," Della said. "What did that say? That last sentence."

Kylie looked at the paper. " 'Now his path leads him another way.' "

Della shook her head. "Isn't that strange for an obituary?"

"What?" Miranda asked.

"The whole 'his path led him' crap. They don't say he's dead. It's as if whoever wrote the obituary knew he wasn't dead."

"Do they use the word 'dead' in obituaries?" Kylie asked. "It seems harsh."

"Harsh?" Della shook her head. "They're dead, why would that be harsh?"

"I think they might say something else, like passed, or gone to meet their maker."

"Yeah, but they didn't even use the word 'passed.' " She sighed. "Just finish reading it."

Kylie glanced back at the paper. " 'Loved by so many, his presence will be missed by all. Feng left behind his parents, Wei and Xui Tsang, his sisters Miao and Bao Yu Tsang . . .'"

"Wait," Della said. "My father only has one sister."

Kylie shrugged. "I'm just reading what it says."

Della recalled the picture with four kids that she'd seen in the old photo album.

"Hey, if you think your uncle is a vampire, maybe your aunt is too," Miranda said.

Was that possible? Della's mind spun.

Kylie looked down again and started reading where she'd left off. "'. . . and his twin brother, Chao Tsang, whose bond with his brother was inseparable.'" Kylie gazed up and frowned, as if knowing the words had been difficult to hear, and then she continued, "'While gone to us, the person he was will remain in our hearts. A memorial will be held in his honor at Rosemount Funeral Home.'"

"There it is again," Della said. "'Gone to us.' '*Us*' as if he's not really gone to everyone."

Kylie shrugged. "I don't know. It could just be obituary lingo or just a coincidence."

Della recalled Burnett saying he didn't believe in coincidences. Questions ran around her brain like scared mice. Was her uncle really dead? What happened to her dad's other sister?

But damn! Did Della have another aunt who'd been turned as well? Kylie's words floated through her head again. *His twin brother, Chao Tsang, whose bond with his brother was inseparable.*

Her throat tightened as she thought how it would be to lose her sister. Marla was a pain in the butt sometimes, but Della would do anything for her. She could only imagine how hard it had been on her father to lose his twin, especially as a teenager. And what happened to his other sister? The grief must have been immense. It didn't even matter if that loss had just meant that her uncle, and possibly even her aunt, had been turned and faked their own deaths. The pain would have been the same.

Could the person who'd written the obituary have known that her uncle hadn't really died? How could she find out who wrote it?

She took the paper from Kylie's hands and reread it herself. Something else bothered her, too. But she couldn't put her finger on it.

Emotion hitting all sides of her heart, she remembered considering faking her own death, and right then she knew she could never do it. It might hurt like hell letting them believe the worst of her, to feel as if she disappointed them at every turn, but Holiday was right. Death was final—be it a faked death or real. She'd take this pain to the one of knowing she'd never see them again.

Glancing down at the paper, she reread the words, waiting for that something that bothered her to become known.

Kylie took a sip of diet soda. "You need to ask Derek to see if he can find anything out on the aunt you didn't know about."

Della nodded and went back to reading. Her eyes landed on the name of the funeral home. *Rosemount.* It listed a Houston address. She wasn't positive, but she thought her dad had lived way over on the opposite side of the city. Why would her dad's family choose a funeral home so far from where they lived?

Rosemount Funeral Home. Her gaze went back to the name and a lightbulb came on. "That's it," she said.

"What's it?" Miranda asked.

"Rosemount Funeral Home was where my cousin Chan's memorial service was held. His fake memorial service. That funeral home must work with the vampires who do this." Della inhaled and something akin to excitement filled her chest. "My uncle is alive. He faked his own death just like Chan did."

"You don't know that for sure," Miranda said.

Della closed her eyes. As much as she wanted to deny it, she couldn't. She needed proof.

"Then who's the ghost?" Kylie asked.

Della shrugged. "Maybe you're wrong. Maybe it's not here for me, but for you. Or maybe it's just a random dead person hanging out."

Kylie lifted her left shoulder in a nonconvinced shrug. "I don't think so."

Miranda leaned an elbow on the table. "Okay, let's say you're right. If your cousin used the same funeral home as your uncle, how did he know about it? Did he just stumble across it? Do vampires set up their own services? You'd think the family would do it. But maybe vampires somehow have it set up."

"I don't know." Della's mind rushed to where she could go to get this info. She couldn't ask Burnett or Holiday without them thinking she wanted to fake her own death. Or without them asking questions. And none of the vampires here had faked their own deaths. Only a few had been turned as a teen; most of them here had been born with the live virus—meaning both their parents were vampires at the time they were conceived.

Kylie sat staring at Miranda. "But that's a good question." Kylie pulled the paper over and studied it. "You know, if Chan somehow arranged it and had the memorial service set up, then maybe he knows your uncle? Hey, wait!" Kylie's eyes lit up as if she'd just come to some conclusion. "If Chan was the one who caused you to be turned, then maybe your uncle is the one who turned Chan. That could be how he knew about the funeral home."

"Chan didn't mean to turn me," Della said. "I had an open wound and—"

"I know," Kylie said, "but maybe the same thing happened to Chan and your uncle."

Everything Kylie and Miranda said stirred inside Della's head, causing a whirlwind of thoughts that twisted into questions. And there was only one person who could answer them, if he'd take her darn call. She snagged her cell from her pocket and dialed Chan.

Chapter Twelve

Chan's phone rang. And rang. Then it went to voicemail. "Call me, damn it!" Della muttered; then she set the phone down. Frustration building inside her, she picked up her soda can, drank the last sip, then crunched the thing in her hand and wadded it up into a small aluminum ball.

Was Chan mad because she hadn't returned his call last week? No, he'd said it wasn't important.

"Wow!" Miranda said, staring at Della's new version of a stress ball. "That looks badass!"

Della didn't care how it looked. "I want answers."

"Then let's get them," Kylie said. "I've got an idea. My mom's been begging me to bring you two home with me for a weekend. The funeral home is only about ten miles from my house. If we go there and see it's run by supernaturals, then chances are you're right. Plus, it'll just be fun to have you guys hang out at my old house. Before my mom sells it."

Hope started filling Della's chest. "If they're supernaturals, I'm having a little powwow with the owner."

Kylie looked unsure. "Remember Holiday's rule. No stupid risks."

Della got an idea. "Let's look it up online." She stood and went to the computer desk on the other side of the kitchen. The funeral home came right up. There was even a "meet the owner" page. A photo of a Tomas Ayala, a Hispanic man who looked older than dirt, appeared.

"Okay, come take a peek at this guy." Della looked back at her two friends still sitting at the table. "You gonna tell me he's a risk? He's an old geezer."

"Okay," Kylie said. "Now the question is, do you think your parents would let you come to my house?"

"Mine would," Miranda answered.

Della squeezed the aluminum ball down to a smaller, tighter orb. "I don't know if my mom will agree to it," Della said. "Maybe if I beg."

"You beg?" Miranda mouthed off. "I'd love to witness that."

Della growled at the witch then glanced back at Kylie. "I'll talk to my mom tomorrow."

"Good," Kylie said.

Good? Not really. Della hated the idea of begging. She hated the idea of waiting until the weekend to get answers, but she didn't have a choice. At least she now had a plan.

Holiday showed up at the cabin around six that evening and brought Della a glass of blood and some chicken-and-stars soup. Tray in hand, the camp leader ushered her back to bed. Thank goodness, Della had cleaned up the pillow guts.

Della grumbled about the in-bed rule, but she really hadn't meant to. The sound came from her stomach . . . her completely empty stomach. She hadn't realized she'd been starving until she smelled the blood. Leaning against three pillows, she enjoyed every sip, but at one point had to push the thought of the murder scene from her mind.

Deep down she knew drinking blood didn't make her evil; killing to get that blood made one immoral and wicked. Which she would never have to consider doing, thanks to the camp's reserves of donor blood. As Kylie had once told her, people donate blood to help save lives, what's the difference in donating blood to keep a vampire healthy?

Yup, leave it to Kylie's words of wisdom, even months after she'd said them, to help Della through a rough patch.

With Holiday hovering over her, Della even ate the soup. It tasted like crap, but there was something nostalgic about watching the star-shaped pasta swim circles in the chicken broth. Her mom had always served her chicken-and-stars when she was sick.

But Della wasn't sick. Or was she?

"I'm glad to see you eating," Holiday said, and she paused as if she needed to say something. The fae had a gift of reading other's emotions, but she couldn't seem to hide her own worth a flip.

"What is it?" Della asked.

"I had to call your mom about your little accident."

"Oh, frack! Why?"

"Because they are still your parents," the camp leader said. "I didn't tell her you were unconscious, I just said you'd fallen and bumped your head. I assured her you were okay."

"And?" Della asked, worried her mom said she didn't care. In spite of what Holiday said about her mom calling once a week, Della could still remember how quiet and how disappointed her mom had seemed to be with Della on the drive up here on Sunday.

"She's worried. She asked for you to call her."

Della exhaled. "I needed to talk to her anyway."

"About what?"

"Kylie asked Miranda and me to go to her house this weekend."

Holiday smiled. "That sounds like fun. But we'll also have to clear it with Burnett."

"Why?" Della asked.

"If he thinks the attack on you was personal, he might worry about you leaving."

"Why would he worry about me? I'll be fine. Besides, I'm with Kylie, the protector. What more do I need?"

Holiday shrugged. "I agree, but we'll still have to check with Burnett. I don't know if I've ever seen him so scared as when he carried you out of the woods."

Della rolled her eyes. "I'm fine. And I'll be fine at Kylie's."

"I know you think you're okay. But this morning you were unconscious. And the doctor called me a while ago wanting to confirm you are on your cycle. You apparently had a little raised temperature. You are on your period, aren't you?"

"Geez, what's with the entire camp wanting to know about my menstrual cycle? Can't some things just be private?"

"This isn't about invading your privacy, it's about looking after your health."

"Fine," Della sighed. "Yes, I'm on my period—practically."

"Practically?" Holiday questioned.

"It should be here anytime. Like clockwork. Aunt Flo never lets me down." No way was Della going to tell Holiday about possibly having a flu. She'd never agree to let Della go to Kylie's then.

Holiday left shortly after that, but not without leaving orders. Della was to call her mom, then go to bed early. She wasn't allowed to go out for a run until she got some sleep. How Holiday knew about Della's nightly runs was a mystery. Then again, Holiday probably knew a hell of a lot more than she let on.

Sitting in the quiet room, Della reached for her phone on the bedside table. Her stomach hurt at the thought of talking to her mom. And how she was going to convince her to say yes to going to Kylie's.

She was still staring down at the cell and coming up short with convincing methods when her cell rang. *Please be Chan?* She looked at her phone. No. Ready or not, she had to talk to her mom.

Della came up with one idea: Channel the old Della, the one who wasn't insecure in her mother's love. The one who used to know exactly how to persuade her mom to give in. The one who hadn't been vampire.

"Hey, Mom!" Della grimaced at the false cheeriness in her tone.

"Are you okay?"

"I'm fine. Really."

"Holiday said you took a blow to the head."

"It was nothing. Holiday's pregnant, and she's a worrywart these days. Seriously, I can't even find where I was hit." She reached up and flinched when she found the large lump, making it a whopper of a lie.

"You do sound good," her mom said, and Della congratulated herself on pretending everything was okay. Maybe her mom would pretend then, too. Wasn't a pretend relationship better than what they had lately?

"I am good." Della bit down on her lip, debating if she should bring it up. "I'm sorry," she blurted out. "Sorry about . . . what happened."

"You were getting into your dad's liquor, weren't you?"

Frigging hell. Why had she said anything? Should she just say yes, admit to something she wasn't guilty of doing? She opened her mouth to say yes, but instead said, "I didn't touch his precious brandy. I wouldn't do that. I was . . . I was thinking about Chan and wanted to see a picture of him. I remembered Dad kept his photo albums in there."

Silence filled the line. Oh, crap! She'd really flubbed things up now. Her mom would probably go look at the album and see the missing picture.

"Why . . . why didn't you say that? Why didn't you tell your dad that's what you were doing?"

"Dad just started accusing me. He's . . . he's so disappointed in me, I just . . . It hurt." Still hurt.

"You should have spoken up," her mom said.

"I'll try to remember that." Della realized it sounded like the conversation was winding down, and she still needed two things. "Oh, Mom. I . . . I was wondering if you would mind if I went to see a friend next weekend? Kylie, my roommate, you've met her before, she's invited me and Miranda, my other roommate, to her house."

"To do what?" her mom asked, suspicious.

"To hang out. You know, like I used to do with Chelsea. To go over some homework." Her mom used to be a sucker for anything involving group study. Every date with her ex-boyfriend, Della used to bring her schoolbooks, and she'd actually open them at least once, so she didn't have to lie when she said they'd spent "some" time with their nose in a book.

"Can't you do that at school?"

"It's not as fun."

Her mom was quiet. "Can I talk with her parents?"

"I'm sure her mom would be happy to talk to you." Della hoped.

"If her mom will talk with me, then . . . then . . ."

"Thanks," Della said, not wanting to give her mom a chance to back out. "Oh, one more thing. We're writing essays, and one of the things we have to discuss is where our parents went to school. Where did Dad go to high school?"

"Klein High. You don't want to know where I went?" her mom asked, reminding Della that there had been a day her mom had been a little jealous of her relationship with her dad.

"I know where you went," Della said. "You went to Freemont High. You told me." And Della did remember. She remembered they used to talk a lot. She used to talk a lot with both her parents. Though, she just now realized how little her dad talked about his past. Her father was always focused on the future.

The line went silent again. "I remember the story about how you and two other girls got caught letting the frogs go before the school used them as lab experiments."

Her mom chuckled. "I haven't thought about that in a while." She exhaled. "I miss you, Della."

Tears filled Della's eyes. Was her mom pretending, too? Or were they being real? "I miss you, too." God, what was she saying? The last thing she needed was for her mom to try to make her come home. "Not that I don't like it here." Della swiped a lone tear that had escaped her lashes. "I'll text you Ms. Galen's number later."

"Okay," her mom said.

Della was about to hang up.

"Della?" her mom said in a rush.

"Yeah?"

"I know your dad is hard on you, but he . . ."

You're both hard on me, Della thought, remembering when she caught her mom going through her bags, afraid she'd brought home drugs and might pass them to her sister. But Della didn't say it.

"He what?" Della asked.

"He loves you."

"Yeah," Della said. Part of her almost believed it.

Almost.

By eight o'clock that night, Miranda had taken off to meet Perry. Kylie had given Della her mom's number so Della could text it and then she had skipped out to meet Lucas. Alone, and exhausted, Della turned the lights off. Surprisingly, she did sleep. Well, until four that morning. She wasn't sure what woke her up. She tucked her feet under the blankets to keep her toes from freezing. Okay, so maybe she did know what had woken her, and just didn't want to admit it.

She stayed in bed, covers up to her chin, leery of the cold. Cold she hadn't felt in a long time. Was it the ghost or was it the fever?

She feared it was the ghost. Trying to push that thought away, one equally disturbing hit and this one came with images. She saw the dead girl. Then her mind created images of her fighting a shadowy attacker. Fighting and losing.

The temptation to wake up her friends bit hard. But Della's fear of cowardice bit harder.

Crawling out of bed, she slipped on a pair of jeans and a long-sleeved T-shirt and jumped out the window. Since she'd slept some, she wasn't breaking Holiday's rules. The only downside was she couldn't expect to run into Steve. Thoughts of him had her thinking about Jessie, the doctor's daughter, and she ran faster.

Wanting to feel the rhythm of her feet hitting the ground, she never went to full flight. But it was fast enough. The cold wind swept away most of her negative feelings. Moving at this speed offered a sense of freedom and an escape from the humdrum stresses. No, it didn't solve problems, but Della would take the reprieve.

In a matter of minutes, she'd made it around the Shadow Falls property twice. Her heart thumped against her chest bone, her skin tingled from the October air, and she drew in fast and hard gulps of oxygen.

Slowing down, she bent at the waist and waited for her heart to slow down. When she went to rise up, she saw a figure fall behind the trees right outside the fence. Her first thought was of Steve. In spite of her leeriness of the doctor's daughter, in spite of her insisting she needed a slowdown between them, a warm smile filled her chest.

She lifted her face to catch some air, hoping to identify his scent. No scent came. But she saw the person shift again. This time, it didn't remind her of Steve.

She inhaled again. The scent of woods and trees, adorned in fall colors and preparing to shed their leaves, filled her nose. Yet no other aroma.

So her smelling was acting out like her hearing, huh? But not her eyes. Through the trees she could make out the figure. Not enough to see the face, but enough to know it was male.

Was it Chase?

She started running again, got almost to the fence, and took another breath. Still no scent. "Show yourself!" she demanded, not knowing if he was friend or foe.

She considered it could be the vamp who killed the couple, or perhaps the culprit who'd hit her on the head. Her muscles tensed. She debated leaping over the fence and facing the scoundrel. But knowing it would piss off Burnett, she forced herself not to act.

"So you hide like a coward, do you?" she spit out, gripping the fence and shaking it.

The intruder darted deeper into the woods, hid for one second, and then took off. Fast. But not so fast that she didn't recognize him.

Chapter Thirteen

His gait. His jet black Asian hair. His skinny legs.

"Chan stop. I need to talk to you," Della called out

He didn't stop; he ran into the woods and became nothing more than a speck in the night. "Call me!" she yelled. "I need to—"

Why the hell would he run from her? Better question, why had he come here? She'd told him numerous times that Burnett had installed an alarm. Then again, he wasn't on the property. Not yet, but no doubt he'd been about to jump it. He had to be here to see her, right? So why hadn't he?

Right then, she heard the telltale sound of someone flying close by. Company. So that's why Chan had skipped out. She turned her head and breathed in the scent. This time her nose worked. Damn Chase for preventing her from getting information.

"Who's Chan?" the panty perv's deep, rich voice asked behind her.

No one, she longed to say, but that would have been a lie. And he would know.

"My cousin." She turned to face him. "I thought I saw him, but he disappeared, so there's a possibility that I could have been mistaken." She posed the answer so it wouldn't sound like a lie. The fact that she didn't believe that possibility was another matter.

Chase raised his face in the air, searching for a scent. Della's gut knotted.

"I don't get a trace of anyone," he said.

"Yeah, I told you, I think I was mistaken." She formed her words so he couldn't read her untruths, but she cut her gaze back to the woods, relieved Chan had escaped and taken his scent with him.

"Did you get a trace?" Chase asked.

"No," she said, another truth. The fact that her ability to pick up scents had failed her again should concern her, but it worked in her favor now. But whatever this was interfering with her senses had better pass quickly . . . smell and hearing were part of her defense mechanism. She needed them if she was going to work for the FRU.

"Did you get a visual?" he asked.

On the inside Della grimaced. Was he testing her, trying to see if she was lying? "I did, but it came and went so fast. And since it's not on our property, it could have been anyone." She stared out the fence and prayed Chan wouldn't come back. Jeepers, why had he come here to start with? Yes, she'd called him, but not once had she told him to come here.

Feeling Chase standing behind her, she wished the vamp would go. His presence annoyed her. His scent annoyed her. For some reason, she recalled their encounter earlier: *You're cute when you get mad.* She continued to stare out into the dark woods. In the distance she could hear the animals at the wildlife park. An elephant. A lion.

He actually moved closer. She could sense him only a few inches from her. She could hear the sound of his heart thumping rather fast. His scent became stronger.

"Are you sure it wasn't the same vampire who attacked and killed that couple?"

She did an about-face and stared at him through tight eyes. Standing too close, she took a step back. "How do you know about that?"

"I'm working with Burnett and the FRU on the case."

He was working with Burnett? Hadn't she told the camp leader she wanted to do this? "Burnett wouldn't allow that. He barely knows you." Besides, this was her case. She was already invested in it. She'd gotten a trace. She'd lived with the images of the dead for days.

"I guess some people around here are more trustworthy than others."

She glared at him and lit out. It was almost five now. If Burnett wasn't up, he was about to be.

Della landed on the front porch of Holiday and Burnett's cabin. The front door swung open, and Burnett, hair a little mussed and looking sleepy, stood there wearing only his boxers. He did have a pair of jeans in his hands as if he'd been planning on getting dressed and had run out of time.

"What is it?" he asked, his tone tight and his voice morning raspy. Then, in one swift move, he donned the jeans. Della watched his toned legs disappear into the denim.

"Have you assigned Chase to the recent FRU case?" she asked.

Burnett ran a palm over his face as if still trying to wake up. "You . . . you came here at this time to ask me about that?"

"Did you?"

He exhaled. "You couldn't have waited another hour?"

She could have, but she didn't want to. "It's almost five, I thought you'd be up. Are you avoiding my question?" She tilted up her chin, hurt and determined to make him see his mistake. She wanted to work this case. After seeing the ugliness of what that creep did, she wanted to help bring him down.

"No, I'm choosing not to answer *any* questions at this time."

"What's wrong?" Holiday walked out wearing a robe and a sleepy expression.

Della hadn't minded waking up Burnett, but a pregnant Holiday, looking extra tired, dinged her conscience. "Sorry, but I . . . ran into Chase and he told me that Burnett had assigned him to work on the new case. The case I told Burnett I wanted to work on. Now he won't even tell me if it's true."

Holiday looked at Burnett as if waiting for him to answer the accusation.

"You were out sick," Burnett said.

"I got hit in the head. But I was fine, I told you I was fine. I remember the doctor had to come here once to take care of you when you were knocked on your ass by a ghost. Nobody took away your right to work a case."

"I don't assign cases just because someone wants to work it. And I was not knocked on my ass."

"I got a trace of the guy."

"So did Chase, he was out the night when the vampire set off the alarm."

"I went with you to the scene and I saw what he did to that couple. I told you I wanted to work it. And besides, you barely know Chase. He hasn't even been here a week. You trust him more than you trust me?"

"I never said I don't trust you. He has certain gifts that make him an asset."

"What, like a penis?" Della crossed her arms.

"Excuse me?" Burnett asked, shock widening his eyes.

"I've done everything you've told me I had to do to make the FRU. And you've sent me only on one case. One!" Della tried to keep her voice from cracking with emotion. "You are constantly bypassing me and sending either Lucas or Derek. And now it's Chase. Why are you trying to stop me?"

Burnett glanced at Holiday almost as if expecting her to help him.

She didn't speak up and that reminded Della of what Holiday had said earlier. "Is it because I'm a woman? You think I can't do this because I've got breasts? Well, let me tell you, my breasts aren't that big and what I lack in upper-body strength, I make up for in smarts and spunk."

"It's not because you're a woman." He glanced at Holiday again, and when she didn't jump to his defense, he growled. "It's not!"

Della heard his heart flutter to a slight mistruth. Not a whole lie, but . . . "Your heart just skipped a few beats, buddy!"

Burnett glanced at Holiday again, as if asking for her to intervene, but she remained silent. She obviously knew Della was right. Burnett wasn't being fair. He'd been passing her over and choosing guys to do the job.

"Why don't you think I can do this?" she asked again. "If not because you're a male chauvinist pig, then tell me what it is. Tell me what I need to do to meet up to your standards!"

"I'm not . . . It's because I don't want to see you hurt."

"And you think I'll end up hurt because I'm a woman," she said.

He raked another hand through his hair. "I care, damn it. I care about everyone here, but you're . . . different. You're special. And maybe, just maybe, there's a tiny part of it because you are a woman, but that's not really it. I just care."

His words went right to her heart. Her chest felt tight. A weak part of her wanted to hug him. But more than his affection, she wanted his respect. "But that's not right."

"And you're stubborn," he said. "I'm scared that stubbornness can backfire on you. And I know it can backfire because I was just like you when I was young."

Holiday rocked back on her heels and smiled as if completely content with the way this worked out.

Della had to swallow to keep the emotion from her throat. Everyone had always said Burnett was partial to her, but all she'd seen was him being a hardass. Then again, maybe that was just tough love. But he was still being a hardass and she didn't like that!

"I'm not nearly as stubborn as you," she told him. "And caring about me isn't a good enough reason to stop me from accomplishing my dream. Don't you think Holiday cares about you? She hasn't made you stop working for the FRU."

Burnett laced his hands behind his neck and squeezed. And without a shirt, the motion showcased a fine set of muscles and chest. Holiday was a lucky gal to have him. Of course, Della also knew he was lucky to snag Holiday.

"Let's compromise," he said. "You work on your stubbornness and I'll work on my issues. How's that?"

She nodded. "But I want to be on this case. I keep seeing her, the victim, in my head. Dead. I need to find who did this to her."

He frowned. "Victims, there were two of them."

"I know," Della said. "But for some reason I keep seeing her. Let me help work this case, please."

"I'll consider it."

She wanted to say that wasn't good enough, but a warning look from Holiday changed her mind. Della turned to leave and then she swung back around. "Thank you for " . . . *caring* . . . "compromising."

Holiday rubbed her hands together, a smile shining from her green eyes. "Why don't you two just hug and get it over with? The moment's begging for it. The emotion is right."

"That's okay." Burnett and Della answered at the same time.

They both laughed, and while they didn't hug, Burnett reached and grasped her shoulder. *It was,* Della thought as she walked off, *as comforting as a hug.*

As she approached her cabin, the sky clung to a hovering darkness. Only a few stars flickered above as if the hour had already chased them away. In the distance the sounds of the new day rang out. A few crickets chirping, a bird fluttering its wings, getting ready to do its morning flight. The warm feeling of affection she'd gotten from the visit to see Burnett filled her chest. Or it did until the dad-blasted panty perv flew down and landed right in front of her.

"So do you believe me now?" he asked, his confident smile downright infuriating.

She took a step back, realizing he stood a little too close. "I believe that you are more annoying than a mosquito trying to drink my dinner."

"Ah, come on. You like me a little bit. I can tell."

"You're nuts. Loco. Living in la-la land. I don't like you, not even a little bit!"

"Then give me a chance to change your mind."

She felt her mouth drop open. "Why?"

"Because I'm not all bad. Because I think we have more in common than you think."

"What do we have common? Oh, wait . . . do you think you're a pain in the butt, too?"

He grinned, his teeth showing white beneath his lips. "You see, that's part of what we have in common."

"I don't see shit," she insisted, and tried not to stare at his mouth.

"I meant, we're both smartasses," he said. "We're both vampire. We're both tough as nails."

His compliment caught her off guard and she didn't have another smartass comment to offer him.

He took advantage of that momentary befuddlement. He stepped closer and let his gaze whisper over her. She felt it, too. Slow and an easy like a soft breath against one's skin. "We're both kind of hot," he said, his voice deep and low.

"I don't think . . ." *you're hot.* She stopped in midsentence, knowing it would have been a lie and he would have heard it. She had to think fast. "You think you're hot. Why am I not surprised? And for the record, I don't consider myself—"

He pressed a finger to her lips. "You are hot. You got that whole 'don't mess with me' attitude going. Which just makes a guy want to mess with you."

"I wouldn't recommend it." She moved his finger from her lips and released it before she was tempted to snap it in two. What kind of game was he playing? And why had she let him play it at all?

"Hey." He reached for her.

She held up one hand. "Do me a favor and just stay out of my way or I'm gonna squish you like that pestering bug you remind me of." She slapped her hands together. "And I'm gonna enjoy it."

Della got another headache during math class. Aunt Flo finally decided to drop by for her monthly visit. Between classes, her temples throbbing, Della went back to her cabin to get her tampons. While she walked, she thought about seeing Chan the night before. Had she imagined it? If not, what was he doing here in Texas? Yeah, he came here often, but he usually called her when he did. She thought about his reasons for not calling her back. Too busy? In trouble? But why would he have come here if he didn't want to talk to her? She pulled out her phone. Finding his message from last week, she listened to it again.

Hey . . . just thought I'd call you. Hadn't heard from you in a while. You tired of that prison yet? Wanna come join me and have some fun? Anyway, it's not important, but call me when you get a chance.

Deciding to try again, she dialed his number.

It went to voicemail. All of a sudden, she remembered a message Chan had sent her months ago on a friend's phone. She did a few swipes and found the text and the number. Angry at herself for not remembering earlier, she called it.

It rang twice. "Yeah," a deep voice answered.

"Hi, I'm Della Tsang, Chan Hon's cousin. Is this Kevin?"

"I don't know anyone named Chan Hon."

Yes, he did. She could hear his lie. And he hadn't denied being Kevin. "This is his vampire cousin," Della said, thinking he might think she was human. "Are you Kevin Miller? He used your phone once to send me a text."

Silence filled the line. Finally he spoke. "You're the one who goes to that fancy school. I was there with Chan in Texas when you got the virus and Chan took care of your ass. You're the half-white one, aren't you?"

He sounded like he was going to hold it against her. With a name like Kevin Miller, wasn't he white? "Yeah, I'm trying to contact Chan and can't reach him."

"He moved to Texas."

So it was Chan at the gate. She knew it.

"There's a whole group of them who joined the Crimson Blood gang. Up in the Houston area."

Della groaned inwardly. Chan had joined a gang? So far, he'd avoided joining one because he knew they could get him in a whole lot of trouble.

Della hadn't heard of the Crimson Blood. Not all gangs were bad, but most of them were. And with a name like Crimson Blood, it didn't sound good.

"Do you know exactly where this gang is?" Della asked, wondering if that was what Chan had called her about last week. Guilt wiggled through her chest. If she'd called him back then, maybe she could have talked him out of it.

"No, since I'm already with a gang, I didn't pay attention."

"Could you ask around?" Della asked. "I'd be grateful," she added, realizing how stupid that sounded the moment she said it. Vampires didn't care about grateful—especially those in a gang.

He chuckled. "What does grateful do for me?"

Okay, so maybe she could spin this her way. "It never hurts to have someone who owes you a favor. If you're ever in Texas."

He hesitated. "I do get to Texas a lot."

"Then it could be a win-win."

"You do know paybacks can be hell," he said.

"Yeah." But if she could find Chan she'd gladly pay hell.

He exhaled. "I'll see if I can't find the time."

"Thanks." She hung up, now more confused than ever. Since Chan had come here last night, he'd obviously wanted to see her. So why wasn't he answering her calls?

All sorts of answers formed in her head. He'd lost his phone. He couldn't afford to pay the phone bill. She'd have to find a way to see him. But how?

Wednesday morning at campmate hour, everyone stood in front of the dining hall. Della had actually slept. The flashes of the dead girl popping in her head had lessened and there had been no more feathers or feeling of ghosts. Which made Della certain that the whole thing hadn't been connected to her, but to Kylie. She was, after all, the ghost whisperer.

Maybe Della just wanted to believe that, but until something proved her wrong she was going to let herself believe it.

Chris walked up with his silly-looking hat. "Well, today we have no special meet-ups."

Which meant no one was paying blood to choose someone special.

"Surprising." Chris shot Chase a cold stare. Chase just stared back, as if he didn't give a flip how Chris felt. Both being vampire, you'd think they would have found enough common ground for a truce.

That thought reminded Della what Chase had said about them having a lot in common. Not that it was true.

The blond vamp cleared his throat and pulled two bags from his hat. Then he pulled one name out of each. He started pairing up campers. Della tensed, waiting to see who she'd be joined at the hip with for the next hour. Sixty minutes could seem really long if you were stuck with someone totally lame. Chris's gaze went to her.

Chris exhaled, adding a bit of drama to the moment. "Della, you get to spend an hour with Jenny Yates. Our new chameleon chick."

Della relaxed. She hadn't really gotten a chance to talk to Jenny since the girl had donated a pint of blood along with the others to get her out of meeting Chase.

As she started over to Jenny, Derek stepped beside her. "Be nice, could you?" he muttered.

Della scowled up. Lately, the fact that everyone seemed to think she was a rude bitch bothered her.

"Damn," Della snapped. "I guess that means I can't suck all her blood and give her to the weres to use as a chew toy."

Derek shook his head. "You know what I mean."

She'd spent a good hour talking to Derek yesterday about her uncle, and her aunt. And getting pissy with him wouldn't help her cause, but Della couldn't help it.

"Yeah, I do know," she said. "You think I'm such a bitch that I'd hurt her on purpose." She left Derek and walked over to Jenny, trying not to let others' opinions annoy her. She recalled again that old saying her mom taught her? "Sticks and stones can break my bones, but words can never hurt me."

Her mom was wrong. Words did hurt. And you couldn't take words back.

"Did Derek rig this?" Jenny asked as Della approached her.

"Rig what?" Della asked.

"Us being together?"

"No," Della said. "You just got unlucky." She started walking away from the crowd, Derek's comment still stinging.

Jenny just arched a brow and followed.

"You okay?" Jenny asked when Della didn't speak.

"Fine. You want to just go to my cabin?" Della asked.

"Sure." Jenny looked back at Derek. "What did he say to you?"

Della frowned. "For me to be nice."

Jenny made a face. "I don't get why he thinks it's his job to take care of me."

"He likes you," Della said. *And he thinks I'm a rude bitch.*

They got to the trail, away from the crowd. The morning air felt fresh and crisp. Jenny kicked a rock and watched it bounce into the brush. "Steve likes you and I don't see him going around making people be nice to you," Jenny said.

"I'm not here because Derek made me." All of a sudden, Della caught what else Jenny had said. She stopped walking. "How do you know Steve likes me?"

Jenny shrugged. "Everyone knows Steve likes you. It's super obvious by the way he looks at you. Like everything about you is the most fascinating, amazing thing he's ever witnessed. I've seen him just hear your voice across the room and he completely tunes everything else out and looks for you. It's so sweet."

Della exhaled and wished she didn't think it was sweet.

"Don't you like him?" Jenny asked.

"Don't you like Derek?" Della countered, thinking the girl would get the message that some things were too personal to ask.

"I do, but I'm sort of scared. And you?"

Della hadn't expected her to answer, and now to be nice she had to reciprocate. "Ditto."

"Wow, I didn't think you were scared of anything."

Della wanted to take the confession back. But it was too late. She arrived at her cabin and dropped down on the porch. "I guess I'm not a tough as you think."

"No, you're just human. Oh, well, not human, but just . . . normal."

Della cut her eyes at Jenny. "Normal is boring. I want to be successful. Accomplished." *I want to show Burnett that I'm good enough to be in the FRU.*

"I'd love to be normal." Jenny sat beside Della. "Then everyone wouldn't stare at me all the time."

"You'll get used to it. Kylie did." Della reclined back on the porch. "But I agree, it totally sucks, but we don't get to choose what we are or what we look like."

"What is it you *don't* want to be?" Jenny asked.

"I wasn't talking about me." But the word "vampire" popped into Della's mind. And how many times had she wished she looked more like her dad—just thinking it would have made him happier? But that was only part of it.

"Right," Jenny said in disbelief.

Della huffed. Then for unknown reasons she decided to let her guard down a little. "I don't want to be weak, and I don't want to depend on people. I want to be able to take care of myself, and to be totally fine on my own." A slight wind blew and a few leaves from a silver maple fluttered to the ground. "But it's not all that easy. Sometimes it's really hard to be so distant from my parents, and I'm not talking about physical distance either."

Another wind stirred a few more leaves free. "Derek told me that he's helping you look for an uncle and maybe an aunt. Is that the reason you're looking for them?"

Della frowned at the thought of Derek talking about that, but she supposed she couldn't complain. "Part of it, but don't mention it to anyone else."

"Oh, don't worry." Jenny paused. "What are you going to do if you find them? Will you leave here and live with them?"

"No," Della said. "It would just be nice to have family who understands me."

"I know what you mean," Jenny said, and it had Della remembering there were still issues between Jenny and her real parents. She supposed she and Jenny had a lot in common.

Silence hung in the air.

"Derek kissed me," Jenny blurted out.

Della looked at her, happy to move her thoughts away from Steve, and her parents. "And?"

"And what?"

"A kiss always comes with a story. A kiss is never just a kiss. Did you like it? Did you slap the crap out of him? Did it come with tongue? Did it make your toes curl? Did it stop at just a kiss?"

Jenny grinned. "Isn't there a rule about not kissing and telling?"

"That only counts with guys," Della said. "Girls can tell things." She grinned back. "And don't worry, I wouldn't tell anyone."

Jenny paused. "I told him he shouldn't have done it, but then I didn't stop him while he was doing it. So I guess I liked it." She sighed. "And when he kissed me, it was as if . . . everything looked different. Beautiful."

Della had heard that before, from Kylie, but she didn't think Jenny would like hearing that.

"If you liked it, why did you tell him he shouldn't have done it?"

"I don't know . . . it feels weird. I wonder if he liked kissing Kylie more. I wonder if he just likes me because I remind him of Kylie because I'm a chameleon. But I'm not special like she is."

"Why don't you just ask him?"

"If I start asking questions, he'll think I'm jealous."

Now, that was something Della could relate to. And it was the exact reason she didn't ask Steve about his little nurse assistant. "Are you jealous?"

"No. Maybe. But it's wrong."

Ditto, Della thought. It was wrong of her to be jealous, too. Especially when she had no ties to Steve.

Jenny pushed her brown hair from her eyes. "I think she's over him, but is he really over her?"

"You should talk to him. And Kylie, too. I think she could help you deal with this."

Jenny made a face. "It would feel weird."

Della rolled over on her belly on the porch, kicked her legs up behind her, and looked at Jenny. "Sometimes you gotta pull your big-girl panties up and just do it." But when Della considered asking Steve about Jessie, it didn't seem so easy. She had a feeling she'd be walking around with her panties around her ankles for a while.

Jenny looked at Della. "What are you doing about you and Chase?"

Della's mouth dropped. "What?"

"He offered blood to spend an hour with you and he looks at you when you aren't looking. Not as sweet as Steve does, but you can tell he has something for you."

"He offered blood just to get people to donate more. And he's not looking at me like that."

"Has he tried to kiss you?" Jenny asked.

"No." But Della recalled him telling her she was hot and touching her lips. He'd probably just been trying to annoy her. And it had worked. "I don't like him like that."

"Because you like Steve?"

"I just don't like him." She didn't want to go into how his scent felt familiar. Didn't want to admit that she found him . . . attractive. Or that she'd thought about how his finger had felt against her lips. Nope, she didn't want to go there, because it didn't mean anything.

"I think you're right to be leery of him."

It was how Jenny said it that had Della sitting up. "Why? What do you know?"

Jenny's pause told Della the girl knew something.

"What is it, Jenny? Spill it! Before I have to choke it out of you." And there went Della's playing-nice promise.

Chapter Fourteen

"Please," Della said.

Jenny frowned. "If you promise not to tell anyone."

"My lips are sealed."

"I take walks. I don't leave the property, but I still have to sneak out because my brother doesn't think I should go out alone. But I'm not doing anything, I just walk around the woods. To think."

"I go out most nights," Della said. "I've never seen you."

"You wouldn't. I turn invisible. I just feel better knowing no one is staring at me. But I saw you once. I was going to show myself, but you were gone too fast."

Della pulled one leg up to her chest to fight an unnatural chill. She cut her eyes around, praying she wouldn't see a duck feather, then focused back on Jenny. "What does this have to do with Chase?"

"A couple of times I've seen him out at night, too. It's always late. And one time I heard him talking to someone. A person who was on the other side of the gate. They were talking really low. I don't know why, but it just felt . . . secretive."

Della remembered seeing Chan outside the gate last night. Could Chan know Chase? Was that where she'd met Chase before? Why Della remembered his scent? "Was the guy he was speaking to Asian?" Della asked.

"I never really saw him. Chase was in front of him."

Della tried to wrap her head around this. "Was this last night?"

"No. Tuesday night."

So it wasn't the same night, but wasn't it too big of a coincidence not to be connected? Della's mind raced. What in the world would Chase have to do with Chan? And if Chase did know Chan, why wouldn't he tell Della?

"Wait," Della said. "You couldn't see him, but you heard them. What were Chase and this guy talking about?"

"I don't know, I forced myself not to listen. That would have been eavesdropping, and Burnett has warned me, several times, that it would be wrong for me to use my invisibility powers for that. So I left. But as I was walking away, Chase kept looking around as if he was afraid someone would see him. I think he was doing something he shouldn't. He acted as if he was afraid he'd get caught."

After school Della lay in her bed, fighting a mild headache and feeling as if she was getting nowhere fast on any of her quests. She was coming up empty-handed on her search for her uncle. She still didn't have a clue who had knocked her out. Burnett still hadn't agreed to let her work the murder case. Her cousin was still unreachable, and now she had the mystery about Chase and his visitor to figure out.

Not that she'd confronted the panty perv.

Yet.

She wanted to talk to Chan first. The next time she accused Chase of something, she didn't want him to have an easy out. She wanted proof. If only Chan would call her back.

Her frustration over Chase turned on a dime to frustration over her cousin. Or maybe not just frustration, but concern. If Chan was already entrenched in a gang, they might not let him return calls. She'd heard that some gangs forced you to give up everyone from your old life. Was that what was happening with Chan? She hoped like hell he hadn't completely gone rogue. Rogues did bad things. A lot of rogue gangs fed off humans. Could Chan do that?

Closing her eyes, she recalled Chan helping her through the toughest part of the change. The only time he'd left her side was when her mom or someone would come in. Or when they took her to the hospital. And even then he'd come to the hospital to check on her. He could have just abandoned her. Left her. Let her fend for herself. She could have ended up killing someone. Supposedly a lot of fresh turns did.

But Chan hadn't left her. He wasn't bad. He might join a gang, but surely it wasn't one that condoned killing humans.

Once again she regretted not calling him back. Regretted not trying harder to be a bigger part of his life. God, not only was she a bitch, she was a bad cousin.

But not so bad that she believed Chan could kill innocent people. The image of the dead girl popped in her head again. She pushed it out of her head, and went back to her cousin.

"Call me, Chan, please," she muttered, as if he might magically hear her.

Her phone rang. Della popped up and snagged the phone, and stared at the number. Again, not Chan. But it was her mom.

"Hey mom," Della said, trying to sound cheery.

"I spoke with Ms. Galen. I think it's okay you go, but . . . don't mention it to your dad."

Why? Della wanted to ask, but then she knew: Her father would have objected. Just on the principle of *not* making Della happy, because he probably still thought she was stealing from him.

"Thanks," Della said, and then, because the conversation felt awkward, she asked, "How was your day?"

"Fine."

All of a sudden Della's curiosity got the best of her. "Mom, can I ask you something?"

"I guess," her mom said.

"Why doesn't Dad ever talk about his past? His childhood?" *His dead brother and missing sister?*

"That's a strange question," her mom said.

"I know," Della admitted. "But it's just odd that he doesn't talk about his life like you do. You talk about being in high school." Feeling brave, she added, "And you even talk about your brother who died of cancer. But Dad says nothing about . . . anything."

"He . . . he didn't have an easy childhood," her mom said, but Della could hear in her mom's voice that she felt she was betraying her father by even saying that much.

"What made it so hard?" Della asked. Voices sounded in the background of her mom's line. Her dad's voice. "Gotta go." The line died.

The lonely sound echoed in Della's chest.

Well, that little conversation didn't get her anywhere. Except more depressed. How sad was it that her mom felt she had to hide the fact that she was talking to her.

Not wanting to just wallow in self-pity, she decided it was time to face Burnett about going to Kylie's. Hopefully that would go smooth.

Why did Della ever expect anything to go smooth?

"Why can't I go?" she insisted. "Even my mom said I could." Della looked first to Holiday and then Burnett.

Holiday took a step back as if wanting to stay out of the discussion. But how could she when Burnett was being completely unreasonable? He hadn't let her finish asking when he'd given the idea a thumbs-down. "Have you forgotten that there's a chance you could still be the target of a murderer?"

"How can you say that? If the guy had wanted to kill me he could have done it. I was unconscious for God's sake. How hard would it have been to finish me off?" She ran a finger across her neck.

Burnett's eyes grew a tad brighter with aggravation. "It's just like Holiday said, the death angels could have scared him off."

"Scared him off, my ass. I still suspect the death angels are the ones who hit me. And frankly, I don't think you even believe it was the murderer or you'd be all up in arms about it."

Burnett's expression told Della she'd hit the nail on the head with that remark. "I didn't say I believed it, I said there was a chance."

"And there's a chance an asteroid is going to hit the earth and kill us all tomorrow!"

"I'm responsible for your safety," he seethed. "And I can't look out for you when you're not on camp grounds."

"But I'm not going alone. Miranda and Kylie will be there, and I don't know if you forgot but Kylie just happens to be a protector and could probably kick an asteroid's ass if it tried to land on me."

When the expression of stern disapproval didn't waver on Burnett's face, she took off the kid gloves and told him what she really thought. It was an old argument, but the best one she had. "I know what this is about. It's because we're girls, right? If it was Lucas and Derek and Perry wanting to go somewhere, you wouldn't have questioned it. You are nothing but a male chauvinist pig. Oh, and that's why you don't want me working with this case, isn't it? I'm a girl."

"That's not it!" Burnett snapped back and looked at Holiday as if pleading for her to intervene, but once again, his wife didn't say a word.

Which meant she still agreed with Della. And that upped the fire in Della's belly.

"So you are going to let me work on the case?" she asked, deciding she'd already pissed him off, she might as well go for gold.

"We haven't moved forward on the case yet."

"You didn't answer my question," she pointed out.

Apparently, the big bad vampire didn't like being put on the spot.

He growled. "You are an unreasonable stubborn little vamp and you need to learn to respect authority."

"I will respect the authority, when the authority respects me! And that includes my breasts!"

Burnett looked again at Holiday. "Can't you do something with her?"

Holiday shrugged. "I think you both have good points."

Now Burnett looked mad at Holiday. "She's not being reasonable."

"I think she just accused you of the same thing," Holiday said.

Yup, the warm and cozy, almost hug-worthy emotional place Della and Burnett had found the other night was nothing more than a memory. They were back to butting heads.

Della continued, because Burnett wasn't the only one with hard head. "If you can tell me without your heart jumping beats that if it was Lucas, or Chase, asking for a weekend away you'd tell them no, I'll shut up."

He couldn't tell her that. He didn't even try lying. So she didn't shut up. And after several more minutes of ranting and a few touches of Holiday's hand, the obstinate vampire agreed to let her go to Kylie's.

She was walking back to her cabin when she realized he'd never agreed to let her work the case. The temptation to go back bit, but her gut said she should fight that battle another day.

What mattered was that come Saturday, Della would be making a trip to the funeral home that had helped fake both her uncle's and Chan's deaths. And while she was out and about, she hoped to possibly get a lead on the Crimson Blood gang. If the funeral-home director worked with vampires to plan fake deaths, he might know something about the local gangs. Hell, maybe the old man had kept in touch with Chan.

But if she found out where the Crimson Bloods were located, she didn't know if she could find a way to get there. She recalled Holiday's "no risks" rule.

Della exhaled. She'd just wait and see what she got from the funeral home, and then she'd make the decision if it was too risky.

But feeling rather productive after winning the argument with Burnett, she decided not to stop just yet. Instead she went to find Derek and see if he'd found anything else out about her aunt and uncle. She'd given him the school name, earlier, and he'd said he was back online.

Answers, Della thought. It would really feel good to at least learn something. Something that at least told her that her uncle and aunt were really alive.

Zilch. Nothing. That's what she got from Derek. Well, almost nothing. He'd found an old classmate from Klein High who was considering selling his yearbook. Della had gladly agreed to hand over her fifty dollars of allowance to pay for the damn thing. Derek went online right then to tell the guy they had the money, but then the guy started wavering. Maybe he wanted to sell it, or maybe he didn't.

Frankly, Della wasn't certain why the damn book was so important. She already had a picture of her uncle, but Derek explained that a yearbook could give them names of who he'd hung out with, his interests outside of the school, and that might offer them more leads. Della didn't want more leads, she wanted answers.

Chan would have answers. Now back in her cabin, and in bed, she looked at her phone resting on her bedside table and willed it to ring.

When it rang, she nearly jumped out of her skin.

Heart thumping, she grabbed the phone, thinking it could be Chan, and looked at the number.

Not Chan.

Steve. She'd spoken with him last night and barely managed to get off the phone without pummeling him with questions about big-smile-big-boobs Jessie. The last thing she wanted to do was come off like a jealous girlfriend.

She stared at the ringing phone. And gave in.

"Hey," she said.

"Hi, I thought you weren't going to answer."

"Sorry, I was caught up in . . . something." *The decision to take or not to take your call.*

"Is everything okay?" he asked.

"Yeah, fine. How are things with you?" *You having fun with Jessie?*

"Missing you," he said. "I wake up at night and you're all I can think about."

But not during the day when you have Jessie around, huh? She bit her lip to keep from saying her thoughts out loud. "I'm sorry," she said instead.

"Why? I like thinking about you."

She closed her eyes. "It's unhealthy. Not sleeping like that." She hadn't been sleeping too well herself.

He paused. "You don't think about me sometimes? About how it feels when we kiss. How it feels when we almost—"

"Sometimes," she admitted abruptly, not wanting to be reminded of things.

"What exactly do you think about?"

"Stop it," she said.

"Stop what?" he asked.

"Stop sounding like you want to have phone sex."

He burst out laughing. "I never said anything about phone sex."

She smiled. Della liked his laugh—liked knowing she made him laugh. Did Jessie make him laugh? "Well, you sounded like it. Using that deep Southern sexy voice."

"Do you think my voice is sexy?"

"Stop talking about sex," she snipped.

"You're the one who started it."

"Well, I'm finishing it, then!"

"Just one more question," he pleaded. "And then I'll shut up."

"Okay," she said, knowing Steve wasn't easy to persuade. Sometimes the guy came off more vampire than shape-shifter. Not that he really had any vampire in him. He was just stubborn sometimes. As crazy as it sounded, she admired that streak in him.

"Have you ever had phone sex?"

"No, I just saw it in a movie."

"What kind of movie?" he asked, sounding intrigued.

"Not the kind you think. It was a romantic comedy. A chick flick."

"Hmm," he said. "How did they do it?"

"Nope. You said one question," she reminded him.

"Okay." He paused. "Oh, I remembered something you said that you never explained. You said you had something you wanted to talk to Derek about. What's up with that?"

She hadn't told Steve about her weekend discoveries, and part of her didn't know if she should, but suddenly she wanted to tell him.

"I . . . I think I might have an uncle who is a vampire. And maybe even an aunt."

"What? How . . . what makes you think that?"

She told him about what her sister had said and then taking the picture. And about Derek finding the obituary. And reading about an aunt she didn't know she had.

"Damn," Steve said. "So now what? Are you going to ask Burnett to help you?"

"No, I don't want to get them in trouble if they aren't registered."

"But if they aren't registered, then they could be rogue."

"Or they could just be part of the group of vampires who don't trust the FRU. Just because someone isn't registered doesn't mean they're bad. My cousin Chan isn't bad. He's just a nonconformist."

"I know, it's just . . . I worry."

Me, too. About you and Jessie. "You shouldn't worry. I can take care of myself." The residuals of anger left over from Burnett popped up. "Is it because I'm a girl and you think I can't take care of myself?"

"No. It's . . . because when a guy likes a girl as much as I do, he sort of wants to protect her."

"Then stop liking me so much!" she said, and rubbed her aching temple.

"It's a little late for that." Silence filled the line. "Do you need me to do anything?" he asked.

"No, I think I've got it under control." She'd already accepted Miranda's and Kylie's help. That was already two people she could get into trouble if things didn't go smoothly. She didn't want to add a third person to the equation.

"Are you sure?" he asked.

"Sure," she said, hoping by Saturday she'd at least have some answers.

A knock sounded on Steve's side of the line.

"Hang on a second," Steve said. "Jessie's at the door."

Jessie was at his bedroom door? For what?

Della could guess what she wanted. Clenching her hands, she listened.

"I'll put her in room two," the feminine voice said. Della could almost hear the adoration in the girl's soft flirty voice.

"I'll be right there," Steve answered.

"You might want to put a shirt on first," Jessie said with a tease in her voice. "You might give her a heart attack looking like that."

Della growled, remembering distinctly how good Steve looked without a shirt. Right then her dislike for the doctor's daughter inched up a few degrees. Okay, more than a few.

"Then again, she'd probably die happy," Jessie added.

Steve laughed. "Don't worry, I'll get dressed."

So Jessie did make him laugh. And she knew how to flirt. Jessie was flirting with her boyfri—with Steve, who didn't even see it. Or did he?

"Hey, Della, I gotta run. We've got a patient. But I can't wait to see you tomorrow. We need to talk."

"Talk about what?" she asked.

"About us," he said.

"What about us?" she asked.

"I'm sorry, but I have to go," he said. "I'll see you tomorrow, okay? Maybe you'll tell me about the phone-sex movie."

Della growled again.

Steve laughed.

She frowned. And it wasn't until he hung up that she realized she hadn't told him she was leaving this weekend. Chances were he wasn't going to be happy. But he could join her in the unhappy wagon. The thought of him off playing doctor with Jessie didn't exactly fill her with joy.

Was it better to ask for permission, or to ask for forgiveness? The question hung in Della's thoughts, bumping against her conscience.

She sat at her computer Thursday morning, dressed in black, missing her first class and staring at the face on the screen. Lorraine Baker's brown hair hung in loose curls around her shoulders. Her smile was . . . magnetic. Her green eyes bright with . . . life. That light wasn't there anymore.

Dead.

Della hadn't been able to sleep last night after Steve's call, so she'd gotten up and started surfing the Internet for something boring enough to put her to sleep. Instead, she'd found a story about Lorraine in the local online paper. A nineteen-year-old college student with a promising future who'd died tragically in an automobile accident with her fiancé.

Lies, Della thought. Lorraine and her fiancé had died horrifically at the hands of a vampire.

And today was her funeral. Della didn't have a clue why she felt compelled to go. But the compulsion breathed inside her.

In the back of her mind she could already hear Burnett listing reasons why she shouldn't go. Reasons that didn't mean diddly-squat to Della.

Permission or forgiveness?

She looked at her phone to check the time. She had to make up her mind.

Chapter Fifteen

"Is Burnett here?" Della stuck her head into Holiday's office.

"No, he was called away for the day."

"The FRU?" Della took another step inside the doorway when Holiday nodded. "Is it about the recent murder case?" Della asked, ready to get mad that he hadn't taken her with him.

"No, it's a case in Dallas." Holiday rose belly-first from the chair. Her belly bump was getting bigger by the day. Della couldn't help but wonder how that would feel. To have a life growing inside you.

All of a sudden, Della noticed Holiday's black dress. Unlike Della, the fae never wore black. Bright colors were her trademark.

"Is there a problem?" Holiday asked, noting Della staring.

"No, I just . . . you're dressed in black."

Holiday nodded. "I'm going to a funeral."

So am I. "Whose?" Della asked.

Holiday's brow wrinkled as if concerned. "Aren't you supposed to be in class?"

And just like that, Della instinctively knew. "You're going to Lorraine Baker's funeral, aren't you?"

Holiday leaned against her desk and nodded. "She's stopped in for a visit, but isn't communicating yet. I thought if I went to the funeral, I might be able to help her."

"Help her do what?" Della asked. "What does she want from you?"

"I don't know. They usually want something. But in some cases, especially in unexpected deaths, the spirit just needs to be consoled and told that it's okay to cross over."

"Or maybe she knows something about the killer. Maybe she wants you to help catch this creep."

"That's a possibility, too," Holiday said.

Della hesitated one second. "I want to go," she said.

Holiday pulled her hair around her shoulder and twisted it. "I don't know if that's protocol for an agent to—"

"I don't give a flip about protocol. Look, here's the truth. I was going," Della said. "I was just going to sneak out and then I decided to try to reason with Burnett to let me go. That's what I wanted to talk to him about. I stumbled across the article about her online last night, and I . . . I want to go."

"I know it was upsetting for you to see the crime scene, but—"

"I need to do this, Holiday. I don't know why, but I just need to say I'm sorry. Please don't try to stop me."

Empathy filled Holiday's green eyes. "Sorry? How is this your fault, Della?"

"It's not, but . . . it was a vampire and . . . I want to make it right." Even as she said it, she knew she couldn't make it right. There was no bringing back Lorraine. But something inside her said attending that funeral was the best she could do.

The grief was so thick in the air, Della could hardly breathe. In spite of the fact that Della didn't know the victim, the heavy feeling of loss lodged in her chest.

Men in dark suits kept moving bouquets and wreaths around the casket. The smell of too-sweet flowers clogged the air. While they were still colorful cut from their vines, the scent of their upcoming death made Della question the custom of floral arrangements.

She and Holiday had arrived ten minutes earlier and sat in the last pew in the back of the church, taking the last seats. The crowd kept getting bigger. People shifted closer until everyone practically sat shoulder-to-shoulder. Della fought the need to cry out for more room. But she knew the crowding sensation was as much internal as physical.

Too many emotions—emotions from all her issues. Though right now, the one foremost on her mind was the one in the casket. The guilt she somehow felt for the couple's death . . . guilt for just being vampire.

The echo of the crowd seemed to vibrate the ceilings. Obviously, Lorraine had a lot of friends and loved ones.

Della sat listening to the sorrowful mourners. Some people cried. Other just sighed—sympathy lacing that low sound. Others talked about her, little things. *She loved chocolate mint ice cream. She hated algebra. She sort of snorted when she laughed really loud.* They said things as if saying them would somehow keep Lorraine alive.

"Is she here?" Della leaned into Holiday's shoulder and asked. She should have felt frightened at the thought of a ghost around, but oddly she didn't. If Holiday could get any clues to the girl's death, Della could find the bastard who did this. She really wanted to find him.

"I haven't seen or felt her," Holiday whispered back. "But there's another spirit here. I think it might be the same one that's hanging around Kylie. It keeps flashing past. Definitely vampire."

Della closed her eyes for a second, not wanting to believe the spirit was her own uncle or aunt, but it did make sense.

"And I was really hoping Lorraine would be here," Holiday whispered.

"If she does show up, make sure you ask her about her killer." Della let her gaze shift around the room, and it landed on the casket centered in front of the pews, surrounded by people.

"She looks good," a woman at the front told the other woman

accompanying her. "You can't even tell she was in such a bad accident."

Good? She's dead! Della wanted to scream out.

Then a vision of Lorraine, bloody and mauled, flashed in Della's mind. The vision kept showing the girl's fingers drenched in more blood. Della blinked and inwardly flinched.

"Are you okay?" Holiday asked, no doubt reading Della's wayward emotions.

"Fine," she lied.

Holiday rested her hand on top of Della's. Some of the weightiness crowding her lungs lightened.

The pieces of dialogue echoed around the church.

So sad. She was just starting her life. Did you know she got a puppy?

Della closed her eyes. Why had she felt driven to be here? How was paying respect going to help the poor dead girl or her fiancé? How would it help Della find their killer?

It wouldn't, Della realized. In some crazy way she was here out of guilt. Guilt because one of her own kind had done this.

Funerals aren't for the dead, they are for the living. Della recalled her father's words when she begged him not to make her attend Chan's funeral. She hadn't wanted to see her aunt cry, or to see them drop her cousin's coffin in the earth. In a way, she'd felt that if she hadn't been forced to go to the funeral she could have pretended he was still alive. Little did she know, he had been alive after all.

A sob escaped from someone standing beside the casket.

"Are you going to Jake's funeral tomorrow?" a young girl asked another girl sitting two rows up. Their dialogue played like distant music. Music about a life lost. Della forced herself to listen.

"Probably. I just keep wondering if this wouldn't have happened if Phillip hadn't run off like he did."

"She loved Jake."

"I think she loved Phillip more."

"Phillip broke her heart, leaving her like that."

So Loraine had boy troubles like everyone else, Della thought.

"At least she and Jake went together."

How did that make it better? Della wondered, not wanting to think how terrifying those last few moments of Lorraine's life had been. Facing a monster. Fearing for her life, and fearing for someone she loved.

Music started playing. The pastor moved to the podium and talked about Lorraine's love of life, and helping others. After his ten-minute memorial service finished, the crowd stood and everyone walked past the casket. Della almost broke the human chain to escape having to see the body. Then, realizing it might be insulting, she slowly, with Holiday behind her, made the trek to the casket.

She told herself she wouldn't look, that it wasn't necessary. But once she got to the front, her gaze fell to the too-still girl, wearing a pink dress. Her dark hair was the only thing about her that didn't look dead. Her hands—no longer bloody like they appeared in the flashes of Della's mind—were folded together. Her eyes closed. Her throat no longer mangled.

Della paused by the polished wooden casket just long enough to leave a promise.

I'll catch him. I'll catch the monster who did this to you.

Right before Della walked away, a tiny feather floated from above and landed softly on the girl's cheek, almost looking like a tear. Della fought the need to brush it away, but hesitant to touch the body, she followed the crowd out of the church.

"So you never saw her?" Della asked Holiday as the fae drove back to Shadow Falls.

"No," Holiday said, "but maybe she'll come back later. Sometimes . . ." Holiday's phone rang and she pulled it out of her purse and checked the number. Frowning, she took the call. "Is everything okay?"

Della tried to listen to the call but she couldn't pick up the voice on the line. Her hearing was out again, but she studied the camp leader's expression. And knew whatever was being said on the other end wasn't good.

"We're about two minutes out," Holiday said. "Set him up in the conference room. Tell him his daughter's at her cabin and that you'll bring her right up." When Holiday hung up, she glanced at Della, her eyes filled with concern.

"What?" Della asked, worried that one of her friends' parents were causing problems. Both Kylie and Miranda had home issues. Oh, heck, it could even be Jenny.

Holiday's expression tightened with empathy. "It's your dad, Della. Hayden says that he is really upset. He claims you took something of his from the house and he wants it back immediately."

Della's heart sank to the pit of her stomach, and the organ proceeded to knot.

Holiday stared at her with questions. "Do you have any idea what he's talking about?"

Della went straight to the cabin to get the picture. Careful not to bend it, she tucked it into a pristine white envelope and started to the office. The only thing she'd told Holiday was she'd taken an old photograph of his family. While the fae waited for Della to explain her reasons, she didn't offer any. She'd just stared out the window. They'd driven the next few miles in total silence while the chaotic noise of hurt in Della's heart rang far too loud.

Now, as she walked toward the office, the picture in her hands, her entire body shook with nerves at the thought of facing her father. Or rather, at facing the disappointment she knew he'd have in his eyes. The memory of the look in his eyes when he'd caught her in his cabinet hurt like a burn. His accusation of her stealing his brandy vibrated in her ears.

She made it up the steps up to the office, but paused at the door.

What the hell was she going to tell him? She couldn't tell him the truth about Marla overhearing his conversation about his twin. Her father valued privacy; he'd be furious. And Della wouldn't throw her sister under the bus. She'd rather take the blame and be run over by the bus herself. Besides, where her parents were concerned, she was already under that bus—had been plowed over several times.

Questions bounced around her head as she made those last steps inside. How had her father discovered the missing picture? Did he regularly go through the album? Suddenly, Della recalled the phone conversation with her mom where she'd denied drinking her father's brandy and telling her mom that she'd been looking for Chan's picture. It had been a lie, but closer to the real truth.

Her mom must have told her dad this, and that had him going through the album. She could almost imagine him angrily flipping pages, suspecting she'd taken something. And wouldn't you know, she'd proved him right. At least this time, she was actually guilty of the crime he accused her of.

She walked into the meeting room, her stomach a quiver of nerves. Her father sat at the back of the table, facing the door. He frowned when she appeared in the doorway. Not that Della expected any differently, but it still stung—the deep kind of sting that hurt all the way to the bone.

There had been a time when his eyes would have lit up with love. Now all she got were frowns, disapproval, and disappointment.

Where was the love he'd held for her? Had it died so quickly? *It's not my fault, Daddy. I caught a virus, I didn't want it.*

She inhaled and felt her breath sputter.

His brows pinched in what appeared to be anger, with a hint of disappointment. She preferred the anger. He pointed a finger at her. "Can I assume that's my picture?"

She moved in and set the envelope on the table. The huge ass lump in her throat made talking difficult. "I . . . I stumbled across it and it looked like . . . you had a twin brother. I was curious."

"You had no right to go through my personal things."

Why do you hate me daddy? She breathed in deep to keep the sting of tears from her eyes and nodded. "I'm sorry," she said, knowing arguing wouldn't help.

"You told your mom you weren't drinking," he said. "Why didn't you tell me that?"

"You were so angry. I didn't think you'd believe me."

"What were you looking for?" he asked, his tone still hostile. She suspected her mom had already told him what she said, so she repeated that lie. "I've been thinking about Chan and thought maybe you'd have a picture of him."

He stood up. "Chan is dead. Let him rest in peace."

But he wasn't dead, Della thought. And perhaps her uncle wasn't either. She watched her father start to walk away. He hadn't hugged her since right after she'd been turned.

"Daddy?" she said.

He turned and glanced back. For one second, one heartbeat of time, she could swear she saw regret in his eyes. Regret for all they had lost.

"What?" he asked.

She hurried to him, wanting to feel his protective arms around her. Wanting to know he didn't hate her.

Before she got all the way to his side, he held out his hand to stop her. Her heart tightened into one big knot of pain.

She inhaled and swallowed. If she wasn't going to get a hug, maybe she'd at least get answers.

"Is that your twin brother in the picture?"

His lips thinned and tightened. She thought he was simply going to leave without answering, but he finally spoke. "I came to get what was mine, not to give answers."

"Why haven't you ever talked about him?" Della asked, not willing to give up so easily.

"Why bring up painful memories? Some things are best forgotten."

Like me, Della thought. He was working on forgetting her.

He turned to leave.

"I still love you," she said, her voice low and filled with hurt.

His steps faltered for one, maybe two, seconds. Then he continued on. He didn't look back. He didn't say he loved her back. Why would he? She didn't matter anymore. She was just another painful memory.

"Are you ready to go?" Kylie asked as she and Miranda came running to Della Friday after their classes were dismissed. Kylie was smiling. Since she and Lucas had gotten together, the chameleon smiled a lot. "Mom said she'd be here around four."

"I'm all packed, but I need to do one thing first." One thing, yet Della felt pulled in ten different directions. The funeral had left her feeling determined to convince Burnett she was worthy of working for the FRU. Her father's visit had left her determined to find her uncle and aunt. And somehow she had to find Chan and talk him out of the gang. And then there was Steve.

"What?" Miranda asked. "What do you have to do?" The witch refused to let anything be a mystery. Last night when Burnett got home and summoned Della down for a visit, the witch had gone bonkers until Della explained everything. She told them that Burnett hadn't been happy about her attending Lorraine's funeral.

Della could still hear the vamp's words ringing in her ears. *An agent has to keep some emotional distance.* Yeah, she'd try to remember that as soon as her heart stopped breaking.

He'd also asked her about her father's visit. Della told him what she'd told Holiday when her father had left. She'd taken an old photograph of him and his siblings and he'd discovered it missing. Unlike Miranda, Holiday and Burnett didn't pry. Oh, Della suspected the two camp leaders knew there was more to the story, but they obviously respected her right to privacy.

Something Miranda needed to learn to do. It wasn't as if Della kept that many secrets from her two best friends. She'd even told them about her dad's visit.

"What could be more important than our trip?" Miranda asked. But holy moly, did the girl ever give up?

Della let out a low growl. She almost smarted off that it wasn't any of the witch's friggin' business. But right before the words left her lips, she realized she wasn't really annoyed at Miranda, or her questions. She was annoyed at the situation. And while Della had a lot of situations going on, the one crowding her plate at this minute was her Steve situation.

He'd shown up for classes today as he said he would. And because he knew she didn't want everyone assuming they were together, he hadn't been overly friendly. But dad blast it if every time she looked his way, he wasn't watching her through his thick dark lashes with a sexy smile on his face. She'd bet her best bra that he was thinking about them kissing. About what it would be like to do more than make out.

And seeing him and that heart-stopping smile made her think about it, too. It was as if her brain needed an escape from her other problems, so it took her there. It took her back to Steve's lips on hers, to feeling his touch.

But damn it, she didn't want to go there. Especially in the middle of math, with several students able to smell her pheromones.

Nor did she want to think about having to tell him she was leaving shortly after classes were over. But she had to tell him. She couldn't just leave. That would be rude. Della might not excel at being nice, but she worked at not being rude. Well, most of the time.

Miranda cleared her throat and brought her back to the problem at hand: the nosy little witch problem.

"I won't be long," Della huffed.

"What is it that you have to do?" Miranda asked, her tone filled with impatience.

Della almost broke her anti-rude rule. "I have to talk to Steve," she bellowed out.

"Now see, was that so hard to just tell us?" Miranda's eyes grew round. "Oh, wait. Are you going to confront him about the doctor's daughter?"

Kylie gave Miranda a sharp elbow in her ribs.

Della frowned. "What do you know about that?"

Miranda's expression went forcibly innocent. "I don't know anything." She looked at Kylie and then shifted to stand behind her as if Della might attack.

Della was considering it, too. "Spill it!" Della rubbed her head when the throbbing pain in her right temple inched up a degree.

Kylie exhaled. "She . . . we don't know anything." She pulled Miranda from behind her. "Look, we both noticed the girl didn't seem to be able to look away from Steve. She seemed to have a thing for him."

They weren't saying anything Della hadn't already concluded, but it hurt to know she wasn't the only one to notice.

"I . . . I gotta go. I'll be back here before four." She took off, not even sure where she was going, except to find Steve. Heck, she didn't know what she was going to say to him, except to tell him she was leaving. But the hurt and jealously radiating through her stung deep. It reminded her of how she felt when her dad walked out yesterday.

Chapter Sixteen

Della ended up at Steve's cabin. Instead of knocking on the door, she peered into his window. Heart still hurting, she studied him. Looking comfortable, he stretched across his bed. His orange T-shirt lay on the corner of his nightstand. All that golden skin covering his chest and back looked so touchable. The muscles in his shoulders and arms had her remembering what it felt like to lean against him. His faded jeans fit nicely—not tight, tight would have looked gross—but snug enough to showcase the firm body below.

Holy moly, she wanted to pull that window up and crawl into that bed with him. To feel all of him, against all of her. She wanted to forget her problems and just let him make her feel . . . alive and cared about.

It wasn't just how much she liked how Steve looked. She liked how he made her feel about herself. He made her feel normal. And sexy. The smile pulled at her lips again as she let herself enjoy the view a little longer.

Instantly, she recalled their conversation when Jessie had knocked on his door and mentioned him being shirtless. The fact that she wasn't the only one enjoying the half-naked Steve had her chest tightening with jealousy. And that feeling confirmed her fear.

She was too damn close to falling smack-dab in the middle of love with the sweet, hot shape-shifter lying on that bed. Did she really want to go there again? Hadn't love already let her down once?

Steve glanced up, a sexy bedroom smile spread across his expression. Then he bounced off the mattress and opened the window.

"I was hoping you'd drop by." He offered her a hand.

She debated telling him to come outside, not wanting to stir up any rumors by getting caught in his bedroom. Then again, he'd already been caught leaving her bedroom. Sure, Derek wasn't the type to start rumors, but according to Jenny, everyone already knew Della and Steve had a "thing."

Define "thing," her heart screamed out as she placed her hand in his. His warm palm came against hers. That touch was all it took to make her whole body zing with electricity. Steve's touch was like a live wire, and yet despite its intensity, she still wanted more.

Her breath caught. Was she going to let this continue? Or was she going nip this thing in the bud before . . . before it was too late?

It might already be too late, a voice inside her head whispered.

She let him help her up even though she didn't need his help.

Her feet weren't flat on the floor when he pulled her against him and kissed her.

She put her hands on his chest to protest, but nothing inside her wanted to object. So she didn't. She let it happen, like she'd let all his kisses happen. Had she successfully stopped even one of his kisses? She didn't think so. When it came to him, she was a weakling. Was it wrong not to hate that?

He tasted a little like mint. He tasted like Steve.

And she loved that taste.

His tongue slowly glided over hers. His warm hands found her waist and pulled her against him. Of all the places in the world, right here, in his arms, was her favorite.

She let herself lean into him, just a little, and only for a moment.

Ever since she'd been turned, she'd sworn she didn't need anyone.

Not her parents, not Lee, not even her friends from her old life. But when Steve held her, she wasn't so sure it was true anymore.

"I missed you," he said, pulling back just a bit.

I missed you, too. The words perched on the tip of her tongue, but she didn't say them. Looking up, she saw that his pupils were large. His warm breath brushed across her cheek.

She swallowed and tried to figure out how to tell him she was leaving. Tried to figure out if she had the right to ask him about Jessie.

He moved in to kiss her again and she put her fingers on his lips. "Steve, I . . . I need . . . we need to talk."

"I know." He smiled. "My mom and dad are coming tomorrow and I wanted you to go out with us for dinner. They want to meet you."

Meet his parents? They wanted to meet her? Bad feelings started going off like fireworks in her head. Feelings that took her back to her and Lee's relationship and how his parents hadn't liked her. "Why?"

"Why what?"

"Why would your parents want to meet me?"

"Because I've mentioned you and they're curious. Because I think they know you're important to me."

Important to him? She shook her head. "That's not a good idea."

"Why?"

Because if I meet your parents, it's official. I'll officially be your girlfriend. And they may not like me. "Because I'm not going to be here." It wasn't a complete lie. She took some comfort in knowing that.

His brow pinched. "This isn't a parent weekend."

"I know, but I'm going to Kylie's house. Miranda and I both. That's what I came to tell you."

He frowned. "My parents hardly ever get off on the weekend. Can't you go to Kylie's later?"

She shook her head. "No, because I'm . . . I'm not just going to visit, I'm going to check out the funeral home where my uncle's funeral services were held. I realized that my cousin Chan's funeral services were held at the same place. So maybe they can give me something about my uncle and my aunt."

Looking unhappy, he shook his head. "How did you find this out?"

"The obituary. Remember I told you that Derek found it?"

"Yeah, but you didn't tell me about the funeral home. Or your plans." His frown tightened and pulled at the corner of his eyes. "Going into a funeral home that fakes people's deaths could be dangerous. Have you cleared it with Burnett?"

"He's agreed to me going to Kylie's," she answered. "And Kylie's a protector." Steve didn't need to know the approval only came with Holiday's persuasion. Or that they didn't know anything about . . .

Steve paced across the room and then confronted her again. "Della, I don't like this."

"I'm going to be fine," she said, knowing he really cared, but realizing having people care about her came with a price. Like her ex-boyfriend. Like her dad.

She met Steve's gaze. He looked upset again, his jaw muscles tightening. "Why didn't you tell me this before?"

She'd expected him to be upset, but not this much. "Since when do I have to get permission from you to—"

"I didn't say get permission, I just meant—"

"I know exactly what you mean," she said. "Look, I . . ." She tried to stop the swarm of emotions zipping through her brain. But after everything that was happening, the funeral, her father's little drop-in visit, learning Chan might be involved with a gang, she was on edge. "I probably would have told you when we were talking, but you were summoned by . . . Jessie and—"

"What? Summoned by Jessie?" he asked, obviously picking up on her pent-up emotion about the big-boobed girl with the big smile.

"We were interrupted on the phone by her," Della explained, trying not to let her emotions leak out. *When you didn't have your shirt on, by the way, and she made sure to comment about it, too!* Right then, Della wondered if Jessie had known that Steve had been talking to Della. Had Jessie made the comment on purpose? Damn it, Della hadn't even thought about that angle, and now it made it even worse.

Steve stood there with a funny expression on his face as if trying to follow the conversation. "There was a patient," he said. "It's not like it was something personal."

"You're right. You didn't do anything wrong." At least Della hoped not. "It doesn't matter." She looked out the window, really wanting to leave before she said something else. Something like: *Forget me ever meeting your parents. It's not happening. Anyway, I'll bet they'd like the doctor's daughter better.* "Look, the reason I came here was to tell you I was leaving. Kylie's mom should be here anytime. I should go."

"Damn it, Della! Why are you acting this way? Are you mad because I'm working with Dr. Whitman? This is my education. It's important."

"So is finding my family," she said.

She turned to leave through the window.

He caught her. "Wait." She could hear in his voice that he was trying to hold back his frustration.

"Wait for what?" she asked, and his eyes tightened with anger.

"I can't believe you didn't tell me this earlier," he blurted out, his tone now tighter, deeper.

"Well, if you'd told me about your parents coming, I would have told you a lot sooner that I couldn't do it." *Wouldn't have done it even if I hadn't been leaving.*

He let go of her arm and laced his fingers together behind his neck. His soft brown eyes brightened to an amber color. "I'm not just talking about that. I'm talking about the whole uncle thing. And the funeral-home thing. And someone mentioned that you went to that murdered girl's funeral. And you were already talking to Derek about your uncle, asking him for help, and you hadn't even told me. You don't tell me things. Don't you trust me?"

"I didn't get a chance to tell you because you were busy."

"So you *are* mad that I'm working with Dr. Whitman?"

It's the doctor's daughter I have problems with. "I'm just saying you weren't here."

"Don't give me that, Della. I was here all day Sunday and Monday morning. I saw you at the clinic, and we've talked on the phone most nights." He made a low growling sound and stared up at the ceiling. Then he looked back at her. "It's happening again, just like it always does. Whenever I get a little bit closer to you, you start pulling back. Why the hell is that?"

She felt her throat tighten. She opened her mouth, but no words would form.

Her phone rang. She yanked it out of her pocket, thankful for a reason to look away from the hurt in Steve's expression. Kylie's name filled her phone's screen, and then she saw the time. It was five minutes after four. She was late.

"I have to go," she said.

"Fine, go!" he snapped.

She got one leg out the window and looked back. "I'm sorry," she said. Then she took off before he saw the sheen of tears in her eyes.

But what the hell was she apologizing for? Pushing him away? Not wanting to push him away? For going to Kylie's? For not wanting to meet his parents? For being afraid to love? Damn it! She was so screwed up!

"Are you okay?" Kylie asked Della thirty minutes into their drive.

"Yeah," Della lied. Later, she might tell her and Miranda the truth. Though she wasn't sure what the truth really was, except that she and Steve had their first fight. Sure, they'd bickered before, but this felt different. It felt . . . it felt like it could be the end.

"Are you still upset about your dad? Or is it about you and Steve?" Kylie asked.

"I'm okay," she insisted, thinking Miranda's pushiness was rubbing off on Kylie. Couldn't she just drop it? Couldn't she see it hurt too much to talk about?

The pain sitting like a lump of dough in her chest was a not-so-subtle reminder of why she shouldn't have let her and Steve's little "thing" go this far. Why she shouldn't let it go any farther.

Maybe it was best that it ended. Her chest gripped and a big *"hell no"* seemed to come from her heart. She didn't want it to end. But she didn't want it to go further either, did she? She didn't want to meet his parents, or let herself completely start relying on him.

She tightened her hands in her lap. Confusion bounced around her sore heart and aching head.

Swallowing the tears before they crawled up her nose and filled her eyes, she glanced forward at Miranda, sitting shotgun in the front seat, jabbering away with Kylie's mom about being a witch. Kylie's mom had just learned about Kylie's supernatural talents—about supernaturals in general—and it was clear the woman was still processing the details of her daughter's life.

"We don't actually fly around on brooms," Miranda said to Ms. Galen, "that is such an old wives' tale. And the first rule we learn is to do no harm. Not that all witches follow that rule. But if they get caught . . . well, let's just say it's not pretty. And if you screw up really bad, the death angels will torch your butt."

Kylie's mom looked into the rearview mirror and her green eyes locked on Della. This was like the sixth time Della had caught the woman gaping at her with . . . suspicion or mistrust. What was up with that?

A possible reason for those wary looks slammed against Della's brain.

She leaned into Kylie and whispered, "Does your mom know I'm vampire now?"

The chameleon's expression answered the question before she did. "She came right out and asked me. I had to tell her. I hope that's okay."

"Great," Della said. "She's freaking afraid of me."

"No, she's not," Kylie whispered. "She's just . . . trying to deal with it. I personally think she's doing really well. I was afraid she'd rescind the invitation." Kylie flinched as if realizing she'd said the wrong thing. "It'll be fine, I promise. Remember, I was leery of you at first, too."

Because I'm a monster. Because my kind go around feeding on people.

"Give my mom a chance, please," Kylie whispered.

Della let go of a deep emotional sigh. "You sure she's not going to run a stake through my heart while I'm sleeping?"

Kylie chuckled. "No, but she might take a bath in garlic." When Della didn't find the comment humorous, Kylie asked, "Did you and Steve have a fight?"

Della decided denying it wouldn't do any good. She'd end up telling them, she always did. "Yeah."

"Was he mad because you were coming here?"

"He was mad about a bunch of stuff." Della stared out the window at the trees passing by, her heart heavy.

"What kind of stuff?" Kylie asked.

Della glanced up and spotted Kylie's mom staring at her. Again. "We'll talk later, okay?"

"Okay." Kylie squeezed Della hand. The chameleon must have turned herself into a fae, because her touch was extra warm and comforting.

Della felt the ache in her chest lessen, but no sooner had she relaxed than another chest-tensing thought hit. Chan. Was he involved with a gang? If so, was Chase involved? She needed to figure things out. And quickly.

"Crap," Kylie muttered under her breath.

"Crap what?" Della muttered back.

Kylie reached up in Della's hair and pulled something out. It took her a second to realize what it was. Another feather.

Oh, fracking hell! The ghost was back.

Della swallowed a lump of panic down her throat. "I still think it's here for you or Holiday," she whispered to Kylie. "It showed up when Holiday and I were at the funeral."

"Yeah, but you were there," Kylie whispered back. "And I've only seen it hanging out by your room, and I don't think Holiday has seen it unless you're around. So I still think it's your uncle, or maybe your aunt."

Almost as if the ghost heard her, two more tiny white feathers spiraled past Della's nose and landed on her lap—her lap and not Kylie's.

Della knocked them on the floorboard. Didn't she have enough to deal with already?

Chapter Seventeen

The dang ghost still never showed himself or herself, but Kylie said it was in the car with them most of the ride. Ms. Galen kept turning the heat up and complaining about the weather getting cold too early. About five miles from Kylie's house, the car warmed up and stayed warm as they pulled into the driveway.

"Does this mean it won't know where we are?" Della asked as they piled out of Kylie's car.

"Sorry, when a ghost's attached to you they seem to have internal GPS. They want you; they find you."

"That sounds like stalking," Della said.

"It sort of is," Kylie said. "Sorry."

"I love your house," Miranda said to Ms. Galen as she bounced up the sidewalk in front of them.

As Della admired the two-story home, she reached up and rubbed her temple. She'd been doing that a lot lately. The tiny but persistent headache wouldn't go away. She wanted to blame it on Aunt Flo, but she had taken leave for the month already.

"Thank you," Ms. Galen answered. "I'm trying to sell it, but haven't had any luck." She glanced at Kylie. "I know she doesn't want me to move, but it's too big for me."

"It's not that I don't want you to move," Kylie said. "I just . . . I'll miss it."

Della considered how she'd feel if her parents sold their house. It would hurt, but nothing compared to how she felt losing the family who still lived there. And after her father's visit, it really felt as if she'd lost them. For one second, she wondered if faking her death wouldn't have been easier. Then that little spark of hope that she might have an uncle and even an aunt somewhere flickered to life.

She started walking up the sidewalk to the front porch. The sun hung low, painting the western sky in an array of colors, while darkness worked at chasing it away. A cool wind brushed past and stirred the trees. A few dead leaves cascaded to the ground, reminding Della of feathers.

She leaned back into Kylie. "How long does it usually take before a ghost appears, or tells you what it wants?" Della asked, hanging on to that hope that her uncle or aunt was alive.

"That depends on the ghost," Kylie said.

Della sighed. She hated waiting. But maybe she wouldn't have to wait long. The trip to the funeral home could shed some light on things. She looked up at the darkening sky, which seemed to match her mood. She could use some light.

Light that didn't come with any kind of trouble. If she got Kylie and Miranda in trouble, or God forbid, if they got hurt, she was going to feel bad. Really, really bad.

An hour later, Miranda, Della, and Kylie were on the sofa, delivered pizza on the coffee table, surfing through Netflix looking for a good movie. Della had managed to eat one slice of pepperoni, and was trying to let go of her concern about tomorrow's visit to the funeral home. But the prickle of worry stayed with her.

Popping off the sofa, she went to the kitchen to grab another soda, hoping to get the aftertaste of the pizza from her mouth. She'd consumed a big glass of blood for lunch today so she wouldn't need any more until she was back at Shadow Falls on Sunday. The last thing she wanted was for Kylie's mom to see her drinking it. Who wanted to be looked at with disgust?

Almost as if her thoughts had conjured her, Ms. Galen walked into the kitchen from the opposite hall. She came to an abrupt halt when she saw Della.

"Oh . . . uh, did you need something?" Ms. Galen said, stumbling over her words.

Fear brightened her eyes, and seeing it hurt. *A couple pints of your blood*, Della almost blurted out, because Della could tell from her expression that that was what the woman expected her to say. Forcing herself to play nice, she told the truth. "I was just grabbing another soda."

"They're right there." She motioned downward, her feet firmly planted in the doorway, as if she was frightened to get any closer. "In the bottom drawer."

Della grabbed a diet drink, then looked back at Kylie's mom. The fear in her eyes seemed stronger, and before she could stop herself she said, "You know I'm not going to hurt you, don't you?"

Ms. Galen's face brightened to a nice shade of embarrassed pink. "I'm sorry. I guess I'm being pretty transparent, aren't I?"

"Afraid so." Della popped the top, the fizzing sound filled her ears, and she found herself regretting her bluntness. "But I understand it's hard to accept. And I appreciate you trusting me enough to invite me here." With her point made, she started out.

"Your mom sounded nice," Ms. Galen blurted out, as if trying to make peace.

Della turned around. If the woman was willing to try, why shouldn't she? "Thanks. And thank you for talking to her."

Ms. Galen toyed with the bottom of her blouse, obviously still nervous. "She doesn't know, does she? I mean about you being vampire."

Della flinched. "You didn't say anything, did you?"

"Oh, no. Burnett made it very clear I was never to speak with anyone about any of this unless it was cleared by him. I . . . I was just curious, I guess."

"Curious about what?" Della asked.

"How it happens. . . . Did you get bit by another vampire?"

"No. I mean, a few people are turned that way. Most vampires who aren't born with the live virus, meaning both parents are already vampires, are turned when they have an open wound and they come in contact with another vampire."

"How does a regular person know if they are a carrier of the virus?" she asked, as if frightened she might be one of them.

"They usually don't. But the FRU released statistics that less than one percent of the population are carriers. So I don't think you have to worry."

Ms. Galen nodded as if embarrassed again. "So I guess that makes you kind of special," she offered with a smile. This one actually looked genuine.

"That's one way of looking at it," Della said, but she wasn't sure she'd agree. Being "special," as Ms. Galen put it, had cost her a lot. Her family. Her life as she'd known it.

Right then, Della wondered, if Kylie's mom could accept this, why couldn't her parents? Was it possible that someday she could tell her parents the truth?

Ms. Galen walked closer and rested her hand on Della's shoulder as if to show she wasn't afraid anymore. But Della still felt the slight tremble in the touch. Not that she didn't appreciate the gesture; she did. So much so, her heart tightened with unwanted emotion.

"Kylie's told me how much you and Miranda mean to her," Ms. Galen continued. "She said you two were her friends when no one else wanted to accept her. I want you to know that I appreciate that."

"She's been a good friend to me, too," Della said.

The woman shifted a bit closer, as if to hug Della. To avoid it, to avoid seeing the shock in her eyes when she felt Della's cold temperature, she took a step back. "Thanks for the drink." *Thanks for trying to accept me.*

"The refrigerator is yours. Take anything you like."

When Della stepped back into the living room, Kylie looked concerned, as if she'd heard them talking. "Is everything okay?"

"Yeah," Della said. "I don't think she's gonna stake me in the heart tonight now."

"I wouldn't have let her do that," Miranda said, and they both giggled.

"I told you it was going to be okay," Kylie said. "My mom has her flaws, but she's not all bad."

"You're lucky." Della plopped on the sofa on the other side of Kylie.

Miranda leaned forward and grinned at Della. "Why is she lucky? Because she has two of the coolest friends ever?"

"No." Della rolled her eyes. "Because she has a cool mom." Della recalled the look on her father's face when she'd tried to hug him. He'd never accept her. She was kidding herself to think he ever would.

"Well, that, too." Miranda glanced at Kylie. "Your mom is pretty hip."

"I think I'm lucky to have all of you." The chameleon smiled. "I love it that you're here at my house. It's like I finally get to bring you into this part of my life." Kylie reached out and squeezed both Della's and Miranda's arms.

"Group hug, group hug." Miranda bounced off the sofa, stood in front of them, and wrapped her arms around both her and Kylie. Della sighed and tolerated it. Then again, it wasn't so hard to tolerate. Every day the bond between the three of them felt even more special. The warm mushy feeling swelling in her chest made Della reconsider bringing them with her to the funeral home.

What if something went bad? "You know what, guys," Della said, pulling out of the hug. "I think tomorrow I should go in the funeral home alone. Just let me—"

"No," both Kylie and Miranda said at the same time.

Kylie frowned. "You promised Holiday you wouldn't do any-thing risky. And while I don't see this as dangerous, going alone is a risk. And that would mean you weren't keeping your promise. Seri-ously, what if something crazy happens and it becomes dangerous?"

Which was exactly why Della didn't want them there. "I think they'd be more likely to talk to me, a vampire, if I'm alone."

"I can become a vampire," Kylie said.

"But if two of us go in there they might feel threatened. Let me go in by myself."

"No," Kylie said again, and her voice rang firm like it did when she turned into a protector.

Yet, protector or not, she could still be hurt. And Miranda was as defenseless as a puppy. Plus it wasn't just about them getting hurt. It was about them getting caught and getting their asses put in slings by Burnett. If Della got caught and landed in the lap of trouble, so be it, but she didn't want to bring her friends with her.

Della let go of a frustrated gulp of air. "I thought about this. If I go in alone, I have two choices. If the old man sounds cooperative, I'll just ask questions. If I sense he won't talk, I can pretend I'm there to plan my own fake funeral. If he goes for it, then at least we'll know for sure that he does the fake funerals and he was behind Chan's, and probably my uncle's, which would confirm my uncle might still be alive."

"You're not going in alone," Miranda said.

"Wait. She can go in alone." Kylie smiled. "Or at least that's what everyone will assume. I'll go invisible and I'll hold Miranda's hand and then they won't know we're there. That way, if trouble starts up, I'll go badass on them. And Miranda will . . ." Kylie looked at Miranda as if she knew the witch didn't want to feel as if she didn't contribute. "She'll turn them into kangaroos," Kylie finished, and grinned.

"I could do that with just a twitch of my pinkie," Miranda said, and held up her hand.

"That just might work," Della said, liking Kylie's plan. Liking it a lot. If Della was careful not to start trouble, then no one would even know Kylie and Miranda were there. And Della would work really hard to avoid any chaos.

"Or I could give them pimples," Miranda blurted out. "And some nasty jock-itch rash on their boys. And we know how seriously guys worry about their boys."

Della couldn't help it: She laughed. How had she gotten so lucky to find these two?

Chapter Eighteen

"Drive safe!" Kylie's mom waved from the doorway the next morning as the three of them got into Kylie's car.

Safe was the key word, Della thought, and got into the backseat. She still thought Kylie's plan was great, but it hadn't stopped her from imagining the worst-case scenario.

Miranda climbed into the front seat. She had called shotgun last night before they'd gone to bed. The three of them had piled into Kylie's queen-size bed, and talked about life and boys. Kylie had tried to get Della to talk about Steve, but the pain from their argument just felt too raw, so she avoided tiptoeing down that path of thorns.

Della hadn't slept well last night, worrying about those thorns and the word "safety." And occasionally worrying about feathers showing up again.

But no feathers appeared. Instead, she'd gone over things in her mind time and time again, rationalizing that this wasn't too risky. All they were doing was going to a funeral home to ask some old geezer who put makeup on dead people a few questions.

"And have fun," Ms. Galen added as Kylie inched the car out of the driveway.

A geezer and dead people. We're gonna have a blast. Della waved back, her thoughts going back to the safety issue. The old geezer was probably vampire, and if he didn't like her questions, it could mean trouble. But, the rational side of her brain countered, he was helping vampires, so he couldn't be all bad. Just how risky could this be?

"Call me and check in," Kylie's mom yelled louder.

They'd told Kylie's mom they were going shopping. And because Kylie didn't want it to be a lie, she insisted they actually go to one store. Leave it to Kylie to worry about lying when there was so much more at stake.

While Kylie drove, she had Miranda poke the funeral home's address into her GPS. The witch kept misspelling the name of the street or getting the street numbers backwards. Being dyslexic, she had problems with stuff like that. As tempting as it was to tell her to just pass the dang thing back, Della didn't. For Miranda, being dyslexic was as touchy a subject as being cold was to Della.

Della waited until the GPS spit out directions to start going over the plan. "Park down the street a couple of blocks and we'll walk up. You can't open doors when you're invisible, right?"

"No," Kylie said.

"Then when you two go invisible, stay close behind me. I don't want to have to worry about you while I'm trying to get information."

"You don't worry. We'll be right behind you."

The GPS announced they were arriving at their destination. Kylie pulled past the funeral home and then parked a half a block up the street.

They got out of the car. The morning sun was bright, the October air crisp. The feel of the cold on her skin reminded Della that she still might have a slight temperature. Just how long was this flu thing gonna last?

Kylie moved and stood behind the car, looking around as if checking whether it was clear to go invisible.

Della did the same. One car whizzed past, a block down, a few people strolled down the street, but no one was around who could actually spot what was going on.

"All set?" Kylie looked at Della.

Della nodded, and her heart raced at the thought of finding answers. In a few minutes, she actually might know for sure if she had an uncle and aunt out there.

Kylie took Miranda's hand and asked, "You ready?"

"Yup," Miranda said. "Let's do it. I've been practicing my jock-itch curse." She wiggled her pinkie. And right before Della's eyes they went invisible.

Della started down the sidewalk toward the funeral home. Because of Burnett's insistence that Kylie use her invisibility talent with extreme caution and never to invade anyone's privacy, Kylie hadn't practiced this gift very often. It felt odd knowing that Kylie and Miranda were behind her when she couldn't hear, see, or smell them. She sniffed again, but got nothing. Then again, with the craziness of her senses lately, she might not have known they were there. The temptation to talk to them rose, but she decided she'd better not.

With each step she told herself it was silly to worry. All she was doing was asking a few questions.

Tension still pulled at her stomach as she glanced around. Less than half a block up, a couple of rough-looking men ran across the four-lane road. Even from a distance, she felt them eyeing her. She inhaled to catch any scent. Her nose worked now.

"Only humans," she whispered, letting Kylie and Miranda know.

The two men darted across the road and started her way. One of the men swayed on his feet as if drunk. She moved to the side, giving them plenty of room. She ignored them, but did check their foreheads to make sure her nose hadn't fooled her. For sure humans. Lowlife humans, she amended when she saw the way the two men seemed to undress her with their eyes.

Not wanting trouble, she moved over and walked in the grass, hoping they'd just pass her by.

Her hopes were futile. They stepped off the sidewalk, blocking her path.

"Hey, babe, you want to earn a few bucks?" asked the first drunk-looking guy, sporting a dirty ponytail. He rotated his pelvis.

She fought the urge to grab the slimeball by his dirty ponytail and give him a couple of root-pulling whirls, then toss his ass back across the street. Instead, she moved to the other side of the sidewalk.

See, Burnett, she thought, *I can control myself.*

It wasn't just about kicking butt.

"I'm ignoring this," Della muttered, assuring herself and Kylie, in case the protector felt the need to kick ass.

The two thugs made a few more rude comments, but they didn't follow her. Or touch her. For which she was grateful, because their sour smell still polluted the air.

She passed a liquor store and pawnshop before getting to the funeral home. The white brick building looked tired, and the sign reading ROSEMOUNT FUNERAL HOME needed a fresh coat of paint. Gazing around, she realized the whole neighborhood needed a makeover.

As she neared the front door, she recalled her daddy complaining that his sister had chosen this place to have Chan's funeral service. But had her aunt chosen it? Della didn't have a clue how it worked when someone faked their own death.

Hopefully in a matter of minutes she'd have answers. She pushed open the door, holding it wide a second so Kylie and Miranda could walk in, too.

The smell in the funeral home stung her nose. Formaldehyde? Wasn't that what they used on bodies? She took another deep sniff to see who might be here, but the first odor prohibited her from catching any other traces.

Could that be intentional? She pushed that thought aside and glanced around.

The light was low, making everything appear gray and heavy. She cut her eyes left and right, noting the not-so-polished wood floors and unmanned desk, adorned with a vase of wilted flowers.

Tension pulled at her shoulders. She tried not to focus on the drab interior. What she sought was a geezer vampire. She didn't spot one. She didn't spot anyone.

She did a complete turn, noting two doors leading out of the entry. Was anyone here? Realizing there were probably dead people tucked away in coffins in the back made her skin prickle. She recalled the funeral of the murdered girl she'd attended just a few days ago. Her vow to find Loraine's killer wasn't null, just . . .

"Can I help you?" The deep, annoyed-sounding voice came out of nowhere, and she almost jumped.

Damn it. Why hadn't she heard him approach? Her hearing must be on the fritz again. She turned and tried to mask the panic on her face. The figure loomed in one of the doorways. And there was a lot of figure to loom.

The giant of a man, or giant of a vampire, wasn't anywhere near geezer status. Dark-haired and olive-skinned, he reminded her of Burnett, a little older but just as menacing.

She saw him checking her pattern. His left brow arched slightly and he almost smiled as if happy to see her. The tension in her stomach kicked up a notch.

"Actually, I was looking for the owner."

"And you've found him."

"I thought . . . The website showed—"

"My stepfather recently died." He didn't sound upset.

"Then in that case . . . Yes. You can help me." Her heart raced. It was decision time. Ask him outright for information, or ask questions as if interested in faking her own death.

"I was . . . my cousin's funeral service was held here."

"Was it?" he asked.

He didn't look like the type to hand over information.

"My cousin wasn't really dead," she said.

The six-foot-plus vamp nodded. "I'm assuming you're looking to follow in his footsteps? How long have you been turned?"

"I've considered faking my own death," she answered, thankful it was the truth. But she neglected answering his second question.

"I also had an uncle whose service you held . . . years ago."

"The strand of virus you carry must be strong," he stated.

"I was hoping to find my family. Do you . . . do you keep records?"

"Me? Not so much. But my stepfather—God rest his weak do-gooder soul—was a stickler for such." His cold smile told her just how much he cared about his stepfather. "Of course, this is no longer his business. The rules and such have changed."

"Do you still have his records?" she asked.

"Lucky for you I haven't gotten around to tossing them out yet. But, as I said, this isn't my stepfather's business anymore. I . . . don't offer my services for free. I offer fresh turns at a new life. And in return I ask for a few years of their service to either myself or one of my clients who are in need of various domestics."

"Domestics?" she asked, thinking "slavery" sounded like a better term. Or hadn't this kind of thing happened in the past and they called them indentured servants?

His gaze moved over her with the same kind of disgusting look as the drunk creeps on the street. She had a feeling she knew what kind of services he'd expect.

"If you'd like, we can go back to my office and discuss the legalities of the contract." He waved for her to follow him.

"There's a contract?" She didn't move, unsure going back with him was wise. Then again, she did need to see those files. Decisions, decisions.

"Oh, yes. We are careful not to break any laws that might bring us trouble. Being a fresh turn, you may not know it, but there are officials who monitor supernaturals. Idiots who think we should be registered and regulated."

Yeah, I kinda help those idiots out. "Really?" she asked, not lying again. But too bad about him not wanting trouble. As soon as she left here, she was contacting Burnett and the FRU about this little operation. He'd read her the riot act for coming here, but she had a feeling the riot act would be worth it. Her gut told her this guy needed to be stopped.

She felt someone walk behind her. And not Kylie or Miranda. The heavy footsteps told her it was someone big. She really needed her hearing to stop going out on her so she'd be better prepared to deal with heavy-footed surprises.

"Why don't we do as Mr. Anthony suggested and follow him?" The guy behind gave Della a nudge—a strong one. One that left a strong suspicion that signing that contract wasn't really a choice.

She took the next few steps, then hesitated, praying Kylie and Miranda would move with her. When the big dude poked her again, she continued following Mr. Anthony.

He led her to a huge office, with a whole wall lined with file cabinets. She nodded to them. "Are those your father's records?"

He glanced back. "As a matter of fact, they are." He smiled. "Let me explain to you how this works." He motioned for her to take a seat in the straight-backed chair in front of the big oak desk.

"Why don't you sweeten the deal first and let me peek at my cousin's and uncle's files?"

He propped his butt on the side of his desk and chuckled. "You are a bit obstinate. But I have several clients who actually prefer a little spunk in their servants."

He had no idea how much spunk she had.

"Sit," he ordered.

She debated whether doing as he said would win her anything, then decided to try. She lowered herself into the chair. Her elbow touched something sticky. Glancing down, she noted the duct tape hanging from the arm of the chair as if someone had been confined there.

Trying not to show any emotion, especially any trace of the fear that curled up inside her chest, she faced him again.

"Now what?" she asked. Her gaze shifted behind the man to where about six rolls of duct tape sat on top of the file cabinet. Taping people up must be his thing.

He stood up, reached into his desk, and handed her a piece of paper. "The contract is simple. You agree to work for two years, exclusively for the person I assign as your guardian. Your title and the type of work required of you will depend upon your guardian's . . . needs."

The way he said "needs" made her skin crawl. "And if I don't like the work?"

"If you choose not to complete the tasks that are assigned to you, your guardian will try to persuade you otherwise."

"Persuade? As in beat me?"

He arched an eyebrow. "Your guardian is much like your parent. If you follow the rules, there should be no reason for punishment."

Yeah, she believed that.

"I'm sure having been recently turned, you know the hardships of securing food. Have you killed yet?"

He said it coldly, as if to get a reaction from her. She decided not to answer and let him assume the worst.

"So you have. You need help, Miss . . . ?"

"Tsang," she answered.

"Asian?" he asked, studying her as if she didn't fit that bill.

"Half." The word tasted bad on her tongue.

"Many of my clients like Asian."

She was sure he didn't mean for the sleaze to leak out of his voice, but it did. She tightened her hands until her fingernails cut into her palms.

"For their loyalty of course," he added.

Oh, she was loyal all right. And right now her loyalties were on taking this guy's ass down.

"Statistics prove that without help, you will kill ten people within six months. It's not your fault, you simply can't help yourself. Of course, that is if you make it six months. You see, other supernaturals exist, like werewolves. They make finding and killing fresh turns a sport."

Della knew most of what he said was bullshit, but she couldn't help but wonder if she hadn't had Chan, if she hadn't found Shadow Falls, if she might have bought into all his lies. And how many new vampires were right now servants to this creep and his clients? The thought turned her stomach.

He pulled a pen out from his pocket and handed it to her. "All I need is for you to sign on the dotted line and then we'll see about finding those files you'd like and preparing your burial service."

When she didn't immediately start scribbling her name, he continued, "Believe me, if your parents knew what you are, they would be grateful that you have chosen to fake your own death so they don't have to see you like this."

She glanced down at the paper, trying to figure out when to put a stop to this nonsense. "Two years seems like an awful long time."

"It's nothing. As a matter of fact, I've been doing this at my other funeral home for years. There are many servants who choose not to leave their guardians. Once you learn to meet their expectations, it's easy to live the life your keeper has set out for you. You get food and care. It's not a bad life."

And I bet slave owners said the same thing in the eighteen hundreds. She shook her head. "I hate to bother you, but I think I might like to see those files before making up my mind."

The hand of the brute standing behind her fell to her shoulder. "Let's not upset Mr. Anthony. He's not a pleasant man when he's annoyed." He started to squeeze, hard, then harder. The pain became almost unbearable.

"Is that really necessary?" Della asked through gritted teeth, trying not to look relieved when his grip lessened. She glanced back at Mr. Anthony, who reached for the duct tape.

She'd heard that duct tape was good for everything, but would it really hold a vampire? She didn't want to test it.

She dropped her pen. "Oops." She leaned down, and whispered to Kylie, "I think I can handle this on my own."

"What did you say?" Mr. Anthony asked.

When Della rose to her feet, the brute behind her grabbed her arm. She didn't hesitate, turning, and with everything she had, she buried the pen into his forearm. He roared.

Mr. Anthony, roll of tape in hand, lunged across the desk. As he started to unroll the tape, Della buried her shoe in his face. He fell back against the desk. She grinned with pride. Or she did until the door swung open and three more hulky-looking vampires stormed in.

"Now it gets interesting," Della seethed.

Kylie appeared, standing in front of them in all her glory. Everything about her glowed with power. Her hair, her eyes, even her skin. She grabbed one big guy, and using him like bowling ball, she knocked down the other two goons.

But one of them popped right back up, his eyes green with fury and his fangs lengthened.

Della was about to move in to help her take down this brute when Mr. Anthony recovered from his foot-to-the-face incident and leapt at her.

She ducked as his fist came at her jaw, and at the same time honored him with another well-placed kick to his ribs.

Kylie bounced around the room, kicking, hitting, and outshining the two other vampires. Della continued to take on Mr. Anthony.

"What the hell are you?" one of the thugs fighting Kylie screamed out.

"Your worst nightmare," Kylie bit out.

"Look what I found," the goon who still had a pen buried in his arm yelled out.

Della, still taking on Mr. Anthony, didn't want to look, but when she heard Miranda's squeal she couldn't help it.

The pen-stabbed vamp had Miranda by the throat. Della's chest nearly exploded with fury. She felt her fangs grow, and she heard and felt Kylie's roar fill the room.

"One more move from either of you and I'll snap the little witch's neck! And I'll enjoy doing it."

Chapter Nineteen

Della saw the look in the big brute's eyes. He meant it. He'd kill Miranda.

Della shot Kylie one quick glance. Their eyes met briefly and the decision was made. Kylie held up her hands, as if not willing to chance it. Della did the same thing. Fear and panic built in her chest. She had to find a way out of this.

She glanced back at Miranda, expecting to see complete terror in the girl's eyes. Instead, the little witch was looking down at her hands. Della followed Miranda's gaze and saw her wiggle her right pinkie.

The realization of what the witch was doing hadn't completely set in when it happened. The five supersized vampires in the room all turned into kangaroos. Very pissed off and huge, but befuddled kangaroos.

And befuddled was good. It gave Della and Kylie the upper hand.

The kangaroo goon who'd had Miranda by the throat started flapping his short arms as if trying to reach Miranda's neck. Della did a flying leap into the air and planted both of her feet right in the animal's face. He wavered on his big kangaroo feet, then fell to the ground, knocked out cold.

Wasting no time, she turned to help Kylie. Much to her disappointment, the chameleon stood above four unconscious kangaroos.

"Everyone okay?" Kylie asked, her voice deepened by her protective mode.

"Yep." Della glanced at Miranda, who stood with her arms wrapped around her middle, looking panicked.

"You okay?" Della asked Miranda.

The girl nodded.

Della grinned at the witch. "I never thought I'd say this, but you saved our butts."

Miranda glanced up, and her panicked expression faded. Her shoulders came up and a slight smile appeared in her eyes. "I did, didn't I?"

The kangaroo still sporting a pen buried in his arm woke up and bolted to his feet as if ready to go another round. Della, not missing a beat, coldcocked him right in his ugly pink nose. Then she looked back at Kylie and motioned to the top of the file cabinets. "The duct tape. Let's wrap up this problem."

Della hauled one reddish-furred kangaroo over to Kylie's four, and tossed him into the pile. Yeah, it was a little embarrassing that Kylie had taken down four to her one, but then again, Kylie was a protector. Della could still hold up her head.

Kylie tossed Della two rolls of tape. They stuck the end pieces of the tape to the pile of marsupials, and then they both zipped around, circling the animals and taping all five of them in one big, eight-by-eight-foot duct-tape ball. When those four rolls ended, Miranda handed them four more she'd found in the corner of the room.

"It was nice of them to leave us the tape, wasn't it?" Miranda grinned.

Della glanced back at the chair with duct tape still hanging from one arm. She couldn't help but wonder about the fate of the fresh turn who'd last sat there.

"Yeah, very nice."

They finished all eight rolls. As a matter of fact, other than one twitching snout sticking out, you could barely see any kangaroo fur through the crisscrossed tape.

When the huge ball started jiggling, Miranda grinned. "They're probably trying to scratch their balls. I gave them jock itch, too."

Della cracked up laughing. When the moment of humor ended, she pulled out her phone. "I have to call Burnett."

Kylie nodded. "I was just about to say that. But what are you going to tell him? Are you going to tell him about your uncle and aunt?"

Della hesitated. Would she have to tell Burnett everything? "You're right. First, I should check the files." As fast as she could, she started thumbing through files. She found Chan's file first. The duct-tape ball jiggled even more, and she hurried to the T file for Tsang.

Her finger stopped on the file with the name Feng Tsang. "Found my uncle's," Della said, and continued thumbing through folders. "But not my aunt." She picked up her uncle's file and read just enough to know it was true. Her uncle hadn't died. He'd been turned and faked his own death.

Unexpected emotion filled her chest. Tears filled her eyes. She had a vampire uncle. Well, she did if he wasn't the ghost.

"This ball is moving quite a bit," Kylie said. "I think—"

"I know," Della said. "Here's my plan. I'm going to tell Burnett part of the truth. I came here to see if I could find Chan. He won't know I'm lying if I tell that truth." She grabbed the phone to call him.

But before she punched in the first number, she heard a loud crash from the front, and then came footsteps, as if someone, or more than someone, was heading right toward them.

"Shit." Della dropped the files on the desk, her skin prickling with a sense of danger. She took a flying leap forward to the door. Kylie beat her there.

Della inhaled, prepared to fight as the sound of footfalls moved closer. Then three figures came hauling ass down the hallway. She met the lead guy's gaze and her fear subsided. The stubborn shape-shifter with beautiful brown eyes stopped running. Relief flashed across Steve's face. Then the relief turned to anger.

Behind Steve, Perry and Lucas came to a sudden stop. Then all of them moved into the room, looking angry.

"What are y'all doing here?" Della demanded.

"What the hell is that?" Perry asked, motioning to the large duct-tape ball moving on the floor.

"Just a few marsupials," Miranda said, and ran up to Perry and put her hands on his chest. "I saved Della and Kylie by turning those creeps into kangaroos."

"I told you this could be dangerous," Steve growled.

Della frowned at him. "And I told you I'd be fine. And I am, we all are."

"And we caught the bad guys." Miranda's smile came with a ton of pride. "And he's really bad."

"You shouldn't have tried to do this alone," Lucas snapped, his eyes still glowing orange, but he was looking at Kylie, not Della.

Kylie stepped closer to him. "We weren't trying to do anything. We didn't think it would be dangerous, but it doesn't matter, because we handled it."

"You could have been hurt," Lucas said. "All of you could have been hurt. Why didn't you tell us about this and we could have handled it?"

Della frowned at Steve. What all had he told them? Shit, he had to have told them almost everything for them to be here.

"This was stupid," Lucas snapped.

For some reason, Lucas's words reminded her of Burnett's chauvinistic attitude, and the residual anger lingering in her chest swelled.

"Why was it stupid?" Della asked. "Why would we run to you instead of taking care of it ourselves? Is it because we're girls? Do you think having a penis makes you superior?"

Perry laughed. "It's not the penis, it's the strength."

"Strength?" Della asked, fuming. "You want me to show you who's stronger?"

Perry laughed at her as if she wasn't serious. And okay, maybe the twerp could transform into a giant dragon and do more pushups, or pick up an automobile easier than her, but she had speed.

"Strength isn't everything," Miranda said, pride in her voice, as she frowned at her beloved shape-shifter. "I'm not very strong, but I saved the day."

"It could have gone badly." Lucas glared at Della.

Della glared right back.

Lucas looked at Kylie as if expecting her to defend him. "You all could have been hurt."

"We could have," Kylie said, her words not angry, but confident and firm. "Just like you could have on any of your missions for the Were Council."

"My missions are completely different." Lucas gestured at the mass of duct tape inching across the floor. "We would have been more capable to handle this."

Kylie's chin came up a notch, telling Della that the chameleon wasn't about to back down. "I hate to admit it, but I think Della's right. You," her gaze shifted to Steve and Perry, "all of you think because we're girls, we're weak. But we aren't. And we weren't doing anything that was dangerous. We came to ask an old vampire a few questions. An old vampire who we knew was into helping vampires. We didn't know we were going to stumble across a vampire-trafficking organization."

"Damn, is that what this is?" Perry asked.

Miranda nodded, again looking proud of herself. Not that Della begrudged her. She'd really saved their asses.

Kylie continued, "That said, we dealt with it. And with class, I might add." She waved at the wrapped ball of kangaroos. "And if that isn't being capable, I don't know what is."

"It's not about who's more capable, damn it!" Steve growled out.

"It's the fact that we care what happens to you. Of course, you," he pointed at Della, "are more afraid of someone caring about you than any situation you could find yourself in." He stormed out.

Della stood there, embarrassed that Steve had blurted out something so personal. The bad thing was that she couldn't deny it. She'd take on bad guys any day of the week before putting her heart on the chopping block.

Kylie, looking a little miffed, spoke up. "Look, we're about to call Burnett to resolve the rest of this. If he's gets upset about this, you shouldn't be a part of it."

A deep frustrated sigh came from Lucas. But when Kylie motioned for the door, he didn't argue. He left. Perry cut Miranda an almost apologetic look and followed Lucas.

"Male chauvinistic pigs!" Della fumed, her anger still boiling, her heart still aching.

"They can't help it," Kylie said. "Holiday says it's in their DNA. They think they were put on earth to protect us. But that doesn't mean we have to like it, or accept it."

"I don't like it either," Miranda said, then smiled. "That's a lie. I do like it a little. I love it when he worries about me. I guess that makes me weak, huh?"

"No, it doesn't," Kylie said. "I like that Lucas wants to take care of me, I just don't like it when he acts like I can't take care of myself."

They both looked at Della as if to get her opinion, but all she offered was a nod. *Of course, you are more afraid of someone caring about you than any situation you could find yourself in.* Steve's words rolled around her head, bumping against her heart. And God help her, all she could think was that if Steve was so worried about her, maybe it wasn't really over. Then another unsettling thought hit. Like Miranda, she kind of liked Steve being protective. But contrary to what Kylie said, she did see that as a weakness. One she needed to work on.

Kylie glanced at the moving duct-tape ball of kangaroos. "You'd better call Burnett before they work their way out of there."

"I'd love to see them try," Della muttered. She started to dial Burnett and then stopped again. "Why don't you two leave, too? I'll tell Burnett I snuck off and did this alone."

Kylie made a face. "Do you think he'll believe you managed to do this all on your own?"

Della frowned. Kylie was right. She might have taken on two of the goons, but five would have been too much.

"Yeah, and how are you going to explain that they're kangaroos?" Miranda asked.

Della grinned. "Well, I was thinking you could change them back before you left, but now that I think about it, when one of them says something about being hopping mad, Burnett will see your mark all over it."

Della paused and looked back at the wiggling mass of slimeballs. "But you two know he's going to be spitting mad. I hate that you two will get in trouble."

"He can't get any madder than he did when I turned *him* into a kangaroo," Miranda said.

"He can't be *that* mad," Kylie said. "We got some bad guys. And we don't have a scratch on us."

Kylie was wrong. Burnett seemed mad from the moment he answered the phone. Della had given him the bit of truth that she'd decided to tell. She'd come here to see if she could find anything about her cousin Chan and accidentally stumbled across an organization that was forcing newly turned vampires into becoming indentured servants. Since the whole Chan bit wasn't a lie, Burnett wouldn't know she was withholding.

He calmed down a little when she assured him they were all fine, not a scratch on them. While still on the phone with her, he used his office phone and called some FRU authorities in Houston and had them coming there within five minutes. He would be there in about half an hour. The fact that Burnett could do that amazed her. Just how fast was he?

When she hung up, she went outside quickly to hide her uncle's file in Kylie's car. She'd just hidden the file in the trunk and slammed it shut when a peregrine falcon landed on it.

Della stared at the bird. "The FRU are due here any minute. You should leave or you might get your ass in a sling."

She saw the bird turn its little head first left, and then right, as if checking whether anyone was watching. Then magical electro-charged bubbles started popping off. "I don't care if I get in trouble," Steve said, and hopped down to the ground, landing only a few feet in front of her.

Della shook her head. "Well, I don't want you to get in trouble, so leave."

He closed his eyes a second, then opened them. "I just wanted . . . I'm sorry, okay? I'm sorry I overreacted yesterday, and then just now in there. I just . . . worry about you." Honesty and emotion sounded in his deep voice.

Her chest gripped. "I'm fine. Look, I'm not hurt."

"Then why are you bleeding?" he asked.

"I'm not bleeding," she said.

"Your nose." He grabbed the hem of his shirttail and brought it up to her nose.

When he pulled back, she saw the red stain. She touched her nose. "I don't even remember being hit."

"You wouldn't remember," he said. "I'm sure you were more worried about your friends than yourself." He dropped the hem of his shirt and glided his finger across her cheek. "Am I forgiven?"

The soft touch sent currents of breath-catching emotion right to her heart. "I wasn't the one who was angry," she said.

"I know, but you weren't the one who lost their cool, either. And the only reason I came here today was because . . . I just freaked out about you being hurt and all I could think was I'd been ugly to you."

She swallowed the lump of emotion down her throat. "I can't make you any promises, Steve."

"We'll see about that," he said, and smiled.

That was his way of saying he'd prove her wrong. And part of her almost wished he would.

"Did you find anything out about your cousin and uncle?"

She nodded. "It's true, my uncle was turned into a vampire."

"Do you know where to look for him?"

"No, but at least I know for sure now." It was a start, Della told herself, and she knew she wouldn't stop without finding all the answers. But now she needed to find out about her aunt.

"I'll help any way I can." He leaned in and kissed her cheek. A soft, sweet kiss. Her eyelids fluttered closed and she longed to lean closer. She ached to be held, to feel his strength around her.

When he pulled back, he had a frown on his face. "You're still warm." He reached up to touch her brow.

She caught his arm. "I might have a little cold or something. Now go before you get caught here."

"A cold?"

"Go," she insisted.

"Fine. But call me as soon as you can."

She nodded, and the bubbles appeared around him as he returned to bird form. Then, not wanting to leave Kylie and Miranda with the ball of kangaroos too long, she took off toward the door.

But before she got inside, two dark sedans squealed up in front of the funeral home, and six FRU agents hauled ass out of the car, charging right at her. Before Della could say anything, they had her circled. Two vamps, a were, a warlock, and two shape-shifters. And from the looks of them, they didn't know if she was friend or foe.

One of them grabbed one arm and another caught her other. Freaking fantastic. First she was confronted by the bad guys, and now it was the good guys.

"Let me go," she seethed. "I'm the one who called you."

A snarky-looking shape-shifter moved directly in front of her. Reaching over Della's shoulder, he grabbed her by her hair and yanked her head back. "You speak when you're spoken to!" he said in a threatening voice.

Before she questioned the wisdom of it, her kneefoot shot up and caught the jerk in the balls.

Chapter Twenty

The FRU agents calmed down as soon as Della told them her name and repeated that she'd been the one to call Burnett. Well, all of them calmed down except the lead agent, whose boys she'd offended. When he was able to stand, he moved in as if to confront her. The lone female agent, a were, stepped between her and the ball-busted shape-shifter.

"Move," the angry agent seethed, his hand still fisted between his legs.

The agent looked back at Della as if she was considering it, then refocused on the angry agent. "She's one of Burnett James's students, and the last person who affronted one of them is doing desk work in some unknown town in Montana. Do you really want to do this?"

"I don't give a flying—"

"What's the problem?" Burnett landed with a thud beside the group.

"She attacked me!" the shape-shifter bit out.

In a clipped voice, and very few words, Della gave her side of the story. The female were nodded when Burnett asked if that was correct. Burnett's eyes went red with fury at all the agents for coming in hostile when he'd informed them of the situation.

Unfortunately, he saved some wrath for Della, Miranda, and Kylie. Or, at least that's the way it appeared three minutes later when he set them down on the sofa in the back of the office and threatened their lives if either of them did more than breathe. He didn't say another word, didn't even ask one question. He and the six other agents stood around the duct-taped orb of kangaroos, each of them looking more puzzled than the other.

"What kind of animal is that?" one asked, pointing to the snout protruding from one little open spot in the ball.

The female were turned her head and studied the nose. "It looks like . . ."

"Kangaroo." Burnett shot Miranda a look.

Miranda smiled, but then she frowned when she saw Burnett's expression. "How can he be mad?"

"Being mad, for Burnett, is like blinking. It's a natural reflex," Kylie said. Burnett turned his head and glared at Kylie. "But don't worry, he always comes around," she added in a confident voice.

"I hope so," Della whispered, studying the team and thinking that one day she'd be doing this. Well, she hoped she didn't run into a ball of kangaroos, but she'd be working cases. Dealing with bad guys. Heck, it felt damn good knowing she'd helped stop Mr. Anthony from practically enslaving newly turned vamps. Would Burnett see this as a plus on her part? Or would he accuse her of doing something stupid? Knowing Burnett, it would be the latter.

The group of agents started talking about if they wanted the criminals turned back into vamps before unrolling them. The agent who drew Della's attention the most was the woman. She seemed savvy, but tough as nails. No makeup, not a piece of jewelry. Nothing about her said feminine. Even her hair was cut short.

Was that what it took to be a female and work for the FRU? You had to let go of anything feminine and put on a don't-mess-with-me attitude? Were all the male agents like Burnett, and a female agent had to constantly be on guard, afraid she might be viewed as weak?

Burnett and the warlock agent walked over to the sofa. "Please tell me you can change them back." Burnett spoke directly to Miranda.

She nodded.

"What kind of spell is this? Blood or herb?" the warlock asked.

Miranda looked worried. "Mind to pinkie. It wasn't preplanned or ordained."

The agent's brow puckered and he looked back at Burnett. "She's lying. It would take a high priestess to pull off a five-part transformation curse off the cuff."

"She is a high priestess," Della said, refraining from calling the man an asshole. How dare he question Miranda when the evidence was wrapped in duct tape.

"I'm not a high priestess," Miranda said, sounding embarrassed. She touched Della's arm as if to say it was okay. "My mother is, or was. She's since stepped down."

Burnett stared at Miranda. "Are you lying about the spell?" he asked, listening to her heart. Della tuned in as well. Not because she doubted Miranda but to check her hearing.

"No," she said. The little witch's heart didn't flutter.

Burnett refocused on the agent.

"But she couldn't—"

"You heard her," Burnett snapped.

The warlock didn't look convinced. "But to do a curse like that would take one of the highest degrees of power."

"Then I wouldn't recommend you piss her off by calling her a liar," Della spouted out. "Sometimes she has trouble controlling herself. Ask Burnett."

Burnett let out a low growl and motioned for the agent to leave. Then he glanced back at Miranda. "How were you able to pull this off?"

Miranda shrugged. "I don't know." The girl's green eyes grew a sheen of tears. "They were going to hurt Della and Kylie. I panicked and just did it."

Della found her chest filling up with warmth. Kylie reached over and held Miranda's hand.

"And you did a great job," Kylie said. "I'm so proud of you."

"Me, too," Della added.

"Group hug," Miranda said, holding out her arms.

"No damn hugs!" Burnett snapped. "You can undo it, right?" he asked.

"I'm pretty sure I can."

"Oh, hell!" He raked a hand over his face. "Try to do it. Try really hard. I don't think our jail is set up to house kangaroos."

Ten minutes later, the six agents—seven counting Burnett—had the five vampires handcuffed and at the door, waiting for the bus to transport them to the FRU jail. They'd get their day in court, but the evidence they'd found in Mr. Anthony's phone pretty much condemned them.

Miranda had managed to change them back, no issues. And Della, Miranda, and Kylie stayed on the sofa that Burnett had assigned them to, watching it all go down.

The warlock kept eyeing Miranda. Della wasn't sure if he was impressed or scared of the witch. Either way, it did Miranda's ego good.

The bus must have arrived, because the five thugs were being led out.

"Oh, crap." Miranda giggled.

"Crap what?" Della and Kylie asked at the same time.

"I just noticed they're walking funny. I didn't remove the jock-itch spell."

"Oh, darn," said Della. And they all laughed.

The humor was sucked right out of the air when Burnett came to a quick halt in front of them. "Now to deal with you three."

"No, to deal with me," Della said. "I practically forced them to help me. They didn't want to do it." It was an out-and-out lie, but she had to try.

"She did not!" Kylie looked up from her phone, where she seemed to be checking e-mails.

"Nope," Miranda said. "You punish one of us, you have to punish all of us."

Della shot the little witch a cold look. Why the heck was she encouraging Burnett to punish them?

"Who the hell do you girls think you are? Charlie's Angels? Why would—?"

"We do kind of look like Charlie's Angels, don't we?" Miranda grinned.

"Charlie's what?" Kylie asked.

"The movie." Miranda looked at Della. "You're Lucy Liu and I'm Drew Barrymore and you're," she glanced at Kylie, "that Cameron chick . . . what's her last name again?"

"Stop!" Burnett growled. "Do you three have any idea how badly this could have turned out?"

"Yes, we do," Kylie said. "But we didn't know going into it. So it isn't our fault."

"How the hell can you think it was okay to come here—?"

"Look!" Kylie held up her phone. "Here's a picture of the funeral-home owner. Tomas Ayala is at least ninety. We had no idea he'd died and his evil stepson had taken over."

Burnett glanced at the phone's screen, but didn't look convinced. "You came to an unregistered vampire-run business—"

"And that's wrong, how?" Della asked. "In a year, we'll all be leaving Shadow Falls and we're going to live in the normal world. In a world where other supernaturals live. And surprise, not everyone is registered. What do you expect us to do? Never leave our homes? The whole point of Shadow Falls is to teach us to survive in the normal world. And what's really nuts is that not only did we survive, we caught some bad guys."

"You should have come to me with your concerns about your cousin," Burnett said.

Della shook her head. "The last time I even mentioned him, you asked me how old he was. And I know why you did it, too. Because if he was eighteen, you'd have had to turn his name in as a possible rogue."

Burnett's mouth tightened before he spoke. "If he's an adult, he needs to be registered."

"In a perfect world, yes, but this world isn't perfect."

"I know that, damn it, which is why I worry about you three running around poking your noses in things that could get you killed."

Della shot up off the sofa. "I know you care about us. But you take it too far. And you're not nearly as hard on any of the male students. We're not weaklings. We just proved it to you, and yet you refuse to see the ball of kangaroo as evidence."

He gritted his teeth, his jaw muscles twitching. But Della saw something in his eyes. Understanding. She might not have won the war with him, but she'd won this battle. And considering she was up against Burnett, that was something to be proud of.

He sighed. "Let's get you three back to Shadow Falls."

"No," Della said. "We're staying at Kylie's for the weekend. You've already agreed to it."

His eyes grew bright, but he let out a deep puff of frustrated air. "Fine. But be careful for God's sake."

"We will." Della smiled, feeling rather victorious. "Thank you," she said, and Miranda and Kylie stood up.

They were almost to the door when Burnett added, "You did good. All of you. This guy, Craig Anthony, has been on the FRU's radar for several years, but we haven't been able to connect him with any of the crimes."

They all turned around and looked at Burnett. He looked as if it cost him to say this. Cost him to admit that three girls had done something the regular FRU agents hadn't been able to accomplish. And yet he said it anyway. Like Kylie said, Burnett generally came around.

"Thank you," Della said.

"I love you, man." Miranda ran up and hugged him. Burnett stiffened, but didn't stop her.

"Please be safe," he said to all of them when Miranda finally let him go.

Della started to walk out with Kylie and Miranda, but Burnett said, "Della, can I speak with you a second?"

Oh frack. Was she still in trouble? He motioned for Kylie and Miranda to leave. "Yeah?" Della asked.

"I got some information on the couple who was murdered. Next week, I'll send you out to do some legwork on the case."

Della nodded. Pride made her smile. "I appreciate it. Should I come on back now?"

"No, it can wait until tomorrow."

She stood there smiling, realizing that today had not only given her some information about her uncle, but gained back Burnett's confidence in her.

"You can go now."

"Yes." She started out, but looked back. "Thank you."

He nodded.

As Della got in Kylie's car, Burnett stood at the curb, watching them like a worried father.

When they stopped at the first red light, Miranda, who'd taken the backseat this time, leaned forward. "Do you know any more bad guys we could take out? I think I could get into this whole catching-criminals routine. Did you see how shocked that warlock was that I turned all five of those guys at the same time? Am I good or what?"

Della shot the witch a smile. She deserved to gloat a little. "You were," Della said.

"Your mother would have been proud," Kylie added.

Miranda gleamed. "She would, wouldn't she? I wish I could do this at the competitions."

As Kylie started talking about running by the mall Della's thoughts turned to getting a second chance to work on the FRU case. To get Lorraine justice.

While Della mentally mulled over the details of the case, Kylie turned to her. "Here."

"What?" Della asked, looking at the chameleon driving one-handed and holding something out.

"You've got a bloody nose. Take the tissue."

Before Della got the paper to her nose, a couple of feathers floated in front of her face and stuck on her upper lip.

When she pulled them off, they were bloody. And that looked extra freaky.

A chill ran up her spine.

All of a sudden, Kylie slammed on the brakes. The car swerved, then came to a jolting stop.

"What?" Della said, looking up, not seeing a car or any other reason for her to brake.

"The ghost." Kylie sounded panicked.

"You saw it?" Della held her breath.

"I . . . ran over it." Kylie bit down on her lip. "I don't like running over things, even ghosts."

They all turned in their seats and looked back. Nothing was in the road. Of course nothing was in the road. A blue car pulled up behind them.

"But you saw it?" Della turned back to Kylie.

"I didn't get a good look, it appeared right before . . . I ran over it." Kylie started driving, but her hands shook on the wheel.

The chameleon took a deep breath, then glanced at Della. "I don't know if it was male or female, but . . . I saw black."

"Black?"

"Black hair. Really black. And shiny."

"Like they might be Asian?"

Kylie nodded. "I'm sorry, Della, but it has to be either your aunt or your uncle."

Della stared out the window, watching the businesses pass in a blur, her emotions as distorted. Was it stupid to feel grief for someone she didn't know?

"How do we get the ghost to talk to us?"

"You don't," Kylie said. "They talk when they're ready. You can talk to them when you feel them, or in your case, when feathers show up, but this one isn't hanging around long enough to let you talk."

"So I can't do shit to find out what the hell it wants or who it is?"

"Pretty much," Kylie said. "Sorry."

Chapter Twenty-one

That night, Della lay in Kylie's bed sandwiched between Miranda and Kylie.

Earlier, they'd stopped by a mall and walked in and out, so Kylie could tell her mom they'd gone. When they got home, Kylie's mom took them out to eat. Della ordered French onion soup, her favorite human food. While they ate, Ms. Galen peppered Miranda and Della with questions about their parents. The woman's intent wasn't to be hurtful, but talking about her mom and dad and her sister made it hard to even swallow the soup past the lump in her throat.

"I'm surprised your mom hasn't called to check in," she'd told Della. "I mean, since I spoke with her that once."

Della wasn't surprised.

When they'd gotten home, Ms. Galen retired to her room. "Sorry about the interrogation," Kylie had said.

"All parents do that," Miranda said.

"It's nothing," Della lied, and then they grabbed sodas and went to Kylie's room and watched an old movie, *How to Lose a Guy in Ten Days*. A movie with some advice Della should probably pay attention to. Then again, she didn't want to lose Steve, did she?

They cut off the light a little after eleven, but none of them could sleep. No doubt the day they'd had left them all with lots to think about.

Della especially.

Ignoring the still present headache, she stared at the ceiling fan. Della's mind spun with questions. The biggest question being how the hell was she going to find Chan? She wanted to know if he knew anything about their uncle and aunt. She wanted to know if he was okay. She'd even tried to call his friend, Kevin Miller, again. He hadn't answered, so she'd left a message. Told him she was in Houston and asked if he'd found out anything about where the Crimson Blood hangout was. He hadn't called back.

Della's gaze shifted to the window. She could go out tonight and do her own search for the Crimson Blood gang. It wasn't that hard to sniff out another vampire. Surely, a stray vamp would know something about the gang. But then she'd really be breaking the promise to Holiday to not take any risks. It was one thing to go try to talk to some old geezer vamp . . . another to go in search of a gang—one she didn't know much about.

Was she desperate enough to break that promise to Holiday? To chance thoroughly pissing off Burnett and having him reconsider her working on the case? She really wanted to work on that case. Her mind conjured up the image of Lorraine again, lying in her casket—so cold, so dead. The thought gave Della a chill. She pulled the cover up a bit to fight the cold and tried to think about something pleasant.

Unfortunately her thoughts turned back to Chan and how he'd helped her through the turn. And she hadn't even taken his damn call. Maybe pissing off Holiday and Burnett would be worth the chance to help her cousin. But alone this time. She didn't want to drag Kylie and Miranda into this.

Closing her eyes, she heard her two friends' heartbeats. They weren't asleep yet. She'd have to wait to sneak out.

Miranda shifted on the mattress. She let out a big sigh and sat up. "Can I ask you guys something?"

Della blinked when she turned the lamp on. "If we said no would it stop you?"

Kylie elbowed her.

"I wasn't serious," Della said.

"Ask away," Kylie said.

The witch pulled her knees to her chest. "What's it like?"

"What's what like?" Della asked, but she was afraid she knew.

"You know, sex."

Yup, that's what Della was afraid she meant. "Not the sex talk, please?" Della dropped her arm over her eyes. And that earned her another poke in the ribs by Kylie.

Kylie sat up. "I have a whole drawer of pamphlets if you'd like to read them."

"I don't want to read about it. I want you to tell me about it."

Della sat up. "Okay, here's the basics. You get naked and tab A goes into slot B."

Kylie chuckled and Miranda grunted. "I'm serious. It's going to happen soon and I just want to be prepared."

"What do you want to know?" Kylie asked.

"Is it true it hurts at first?"

"It did the first time," Kylie said.

Miranda looked at Della as if needing both of their input. Della nodded.

"Was it worth it?" Miranda asked.

"Yeah," Kylie said. "It's amazing. When we're together, it's exciting and romantic and I feel so close to him." She sighed. "I'll admit it, it was embarrassing at first. And sometimes it still is." She grinned. "I still blush when he sees me naked, but it feels right. I really think it's the purest form of sharing your love. But I was sure that he was the right guy before it happened."

Was it worth it? The question rolled around Della's brain, and she knew Miranda was going to expect Della to answer it. It was a question she'd asked herself recently. A question she had yet to answer.

Miranda looked at Della.

Emotion swelled in her chest. She'd given her all to her ex-boyfriend, Lee, and he'd given up on her. In less than three months, he was engaged to someone else. How could giving her heart and body to him have been worth it?

"No, it wasn't worth it," Della said. "Don't get me wrong. I'm not saying don't sleep with Perry. I just think you need to be really sure that the guy you are giving this part of yourself to is the right guy."

"I think Perry is right," Miranda said. "I love him."

"I thought Lee was right, too," Della said. "And I'm not saying that the right guy has to be the only one, or the guy you marry. But it shouldn't be someone who could just walk away so easily. It makes me feel like I wasn't nearly as special to him as he was to me. I still feel cheated and angry. I wish I could take it back." Emotion sounded in her voice and she swallowed hard.

Kylie touched Della's arm and the warm comfort stemming from her touch told her that the chameleon had turned to fae.

"Holiday sort of said the same thing," Kylie added. "She said she'd slept with several guys, and a couple of those memories were like tattoos that she can't get removed. So I think Della's advice is good. Just make sure that no matter what happens, Perry is special enough to you that you won't regret it. Even if the worst thing happens and you don't stay together."

"How do you know you won't regret it?" Miranda asked.

"I . . . I just felt it," Kylie said. "I knew Lucas was the one. But . . . if you are questioning it, I would say you aren't sure."

"That's not what I wanted to hear." Miranda dropped back on the bed.

"I'm sorry," Della said. "I probably should have kept my mouth shut."

"No, you're being honest," Miranda said.

Della sighed. "Sometimes the truth sucks." And she wasn't just thinking about Lee, but about the ghost being her uncle or her aunt. And about not having a clue how to find Chan.

"Yeah," Kylie said. "That's why we have each other."

The slight buzzing noise sent Della on full alert. She hadn't slept yet, going back and forth over the pros and cons of going out looking for a gang.

Carefully, she slipped out of bed, snatched the phone, and headed to the bathroom. As she closed the door, she saw it was two a.m.

She checked the number. Her first choice was for it to be Chan. Her second was . . . Kevin Miller. Kevin it was.

"Hello," she answered, hopeful.

"Della?"

"Yeah."

"It's Kevin."

"I know, did you find Chan?"

"Where are you?"

"I told you in the message, I'm in Houston." No way would she tell him Kylie's address. Della would bet one vampire under Ms. Galen's roof at a time was all the woman could handle.

"Houston's big. What part?"

"Why?"

"I'm here myself. And I . . . sort of have news."

"What?"

"I think we should meet."

"Why?"

"Do you want the info or not?" he snapped.

Decision time. Shit. Shit. Shit. She remembered Chan taking care of her when she turned, wiping her brow with a wet washcloth, telling her she couldn't die. She had to do it.

"Where do you want to meet?"

. . .

Della landed in the park in northwest Houston where Kevin had suggested. It was only about ten miles from Kylie's home, but she was already late. Miranda had stirred when she went in to change clothes, so she'd waited a few minutes to let the witch fall back into slumber.

It was dark in the park. Lots of pine trees hid the sliver of the moon. She inhaled deeply, seeing if he was here. She didn't catch a scent. Looking around, she reconfirmed her goal: Get information about Chan and get the hell out. Hopefully, without Kylie or Miranda even knowing she'd left—especially without Holiday or Burnett learning about her little trip.

She pulled out her phone and checked the time. Had he already shown up and left? She listened to the night. Silence. Too silent.

She was giving him five minutes to show and then she was out of here.

"It took you a while." The voice came from behind her and echoed in the night's darkness.

Her breath caught. Damn it! Her senses were off again. She'd considered circling the park to see if she could see anyone. But because she'd been late, she'd ended up trusting her senses. A mistake.

What was it going to cost her?

Wiping all shock from her expression, she turned, the heels of her boots cutting grooves into the wet dirt beneath a layer of pine straw. She stared in the direction she'd heard the voice. She saw nothing but a clump of pine trees standing tall, looming over the earth as if keeping watch.

From now on she had to be extra careful. She could have walked right into an ambush. Or maybe she did. With at least eight pines in the brush, and more surrounding her, rogues could be hiding. She took in another breath, checking the night air for scents.

Just one. Or so her senses told her. But could she trust them?

Hell, no. She tensed, ready to fight if needed.

A sudden snap of a twig filled the darkness. A cloud must have shifted, because the moon's glow came out to play and touched the straw-covered ground.

Another, almost silent footfall came from the same direction.

Thankfully, only one guy walked out from behind a tree. And with the moon's glow she made him out. Blond, light eyes. He reminded her of Chris at Shadow Falls. On the small side. Probably only five-eight, and sort of slim. She could take him if she had to.

Just as she checked him out, she noticed him doing the same. Chances were, however, he underestimated her. She was stronger than she looked.

"You don't remember me, do you?" he asked.

Della took another deep noseful of air, and this time she recognized his scent. "Vaguely. It must have been right after I was turned."

He continued to stare. "Chan brought you by. You were still pretty out of it." His gaze shifted down her, this time checking her out in a different way. A male kind of way.

Had she acted inappropriately when she'd first met him? God, she hoped not.

He took a couple of steps closer.

She lifted her chin a notch. "I'm not out of it anymore."

"You can relax, I'm not here to cause trouble."

"Right," she said, as if she'd take his word. "You're here to give me information on Chan. Where is he?"

He glanced down at the ground and kicked at some clump of pine straw. The green earthy smell rose up into her nose. In the distance she heard a bird call. The lonely sound seemed to bounce against the trees, and Della felt the cold October air seep beneath her long black T-shirt.

"That's why I brought you here," he said.

"What's that supposed to mean?" she asked, trying to ignore the cold and what it meant—that her temperature was still running high.

"I knew you wouldn't believe it. I didn't want to believe it."

She started getting a really bad feeling. "Believe what?"

"I knew you'd have to see him, so I . . ."

"What?" She took a threatening step forward.

He didn't retreat. He looked right at her, not with challenge or menace. Empathy flashed in his blue eyes.

"Chan's dead."

"No," Della seethed. "I saw him, just the other night."

"No you didn't. It couldn't have been him. He died ten days ago. I just found out tonight."

"That can't be right. I . . ." Pain, raw bitter pain, scraped against her heart; then something brushed against her cheek. She reached up to catch the mosquito in her fist. But when she opened her hand, instead, she'd caught a feather.

The pain throbbing inside her swelled and made it hard to breathe.

Chan was dead.

Chan was gone.

She'd let him down. He'd helped her when she'd needed him, and she'd failed him.

Chapter Twenty-two

"I knew you wouldn't believe me, so I had them dig him up." Kevin took a step and then looked back. "You do want to see him, don't you?"

No. I don't want to see him. Della followed anyway. Maybe to punish herself. Maybe because there was still a little disbelief inside her.

He led her behind the trees to a clearing. Moonlight hit on a tarp covering up something. Something that looked like it could be a body. Beside the tarp was a hole in the ground.

Della's chest gripped tighter and her vision blurred.

Kevin reached down and pulled back the piece of plastic.

She expected to be assaulted by the smell of death. But no scent touched her nose. Not even Chan's scent. She expected to see a swollen and decayed body. Maybe a wound telling her how he'd died. Wrong.

She blinked the tears from her eyes. It was Chan. Chan, not swollen. Chan with no decay. Chan with no open wounds or sign of how he'd died. But it was his body lying there, not breathing. Dirt on his face. Dirt on his clothes.

Chan . . . dead.

"How . . . who did this? What happened?" She barely managed to speak, emotion thickening her tonsils.

"No one did it," he said. "When he left for Texas, he wasn't feeling right. They said he got sicker, and then he got a weird rash, and then about ten days ago he died. Just died. It's crazy. Vampires hardly ever get sick."

"But how . . ." She couldn't finish the question.

"The gang buried him here," Kevin finished. "They knew he'd faked his death, so they didn't think they had to let anyone know."

The knot in Della's throat doubled in size right along with the pain in her heart. Chan had been sick. He'd called her and she hadn't returned his call. What kind of cousin did that?

Her mind created the pristine vision of Lorraine's body in the casket. She fell to her knees and brushed some dirt from her cousin's face; then she dropped her chin on her chest and sobbed. She didn't care if Kevin saw her, or thought she was weak. Her heart was breaking and she didn't give a flying flip how she looked.

Della had stopped crying, but she hadn't moved from Chan's side when Burnett showed up. She'd sent Kevin away and called Burnett to tell him she'd found her cousin and he was dead. She wanted Chan buried in the grave with his gravestone—the one where his parents thought they'd put their son almost two years ago. And since she didn't think she could pull that off, she called someone who could.

Sure, Burnett would probably give her hell for being here, he might even stop her from ever working for the FRU, but right now she didn't care. She'd let Chan down, but the least she could do was put his body where it really belonged.

Burnett didn't speak; he simply walked up and knelt down beside her. He put his hand on her shoulder and her breath hitched.

"What happened?" he asked, no anger in his tone, just concern.

It took a second to swallow the unshed tears from her throat to answer. "He came here and joined the gang, the Crimson Blood. They say he died. Just died." She blinked. "They said it was ten days ago, but it couldn't have been. He doesn't look . . . like he's been dead ten days." And she'd seen him. Seen him at the fence. Was it possible that . . . ?

"They could be telling the truth. The V-one virus delays any form of decay in us. It can take as much as two weeks before our bodies start to break down. But we will do an autopsy. If there's any foul play involved, you know I'll do my best to catch those responsible."

She nodded. And suddenly she couldn't stop the tears. "He called me. He called me a couple of weeks ago and I didn't call him back."

"You couldn't have known this was going to happen," he said, and then stood. "Come on, I'll get you back to Shadow Falls. Holiday's concerned about you."

She stood as well and then stopped. "No, I . . . Kylie and Miranda don't even know I'm gone."

"I'll call them and let them know what happened and that you're okay. I have a team showing up any minute to take the body. We need to do it before light."

Della looked one last time at Chan, knowing she'd never see his face again. Never see him smile that silly quirky grin again.

But when she started walking with Burnett, she realized she was wrong. Chan stood peering at her behind a tree. And he wasn't alone. Someone was with him, half hidden. Chan waved. He had a sad smile on his face. Della's steps faltered.

Sorry. I'm so sorry, Chan.

"You okay?" Burnett asked.

"Yeah," she said, "I just thought . . ." When she looked back, Chan was gone.

"Thought what?"

Thought I saw a ghost. "Nothing, I'm just tired."

But she wasn't that tired. She was seeing ghosts. How the hell was that possible?

• • •

At ten that morning, Della sat alone at the kitchen table in her cabin. Sleep-deprived and feeling like she was dying inside, she found that even breathing hurt. Earlier, she'd spoken to Kylie and Miranda briefly, and told them she'd explain more later. They would be there after lunch, which gave her a few hours to prepare herself to tell the story again.

She'd also learned that Steve had gone back yesterday to the vet's office. Which explained why he wasn't here when she showed up. She'd bet Jessie was happy.

Holiday had spent several hours here commiserating and offering warm, comforting touches. But her comfort didn't last. Even Holiday said that grief was the one emotion a fae's touch had less effect on.

But Della wasn't sure which emotion she felt most. Grief or guilt.

And the camp leader sensed this, too. If she'd told Della once, she'd told her a dozen times . . . it wasn't Della's fault for not talking to Chan.

Della didn't buy it. Maybe Steve and his doctor buddy could have done something. Or perhaps she could have gotten Kylie to heal Chan. If she'd called him back.

If? If? If? Why the hell hadn't she called him back?

She'd almost told Holiday about seeing Chan at the gate and again tonight, but at the last minute decided to wait and ask Kylie about it. The fact that she could see ghosts should have scared the shit out of her, and maybe it would when she wasn't drowning in other emotions.

After Holiday left, Jenny came by. She'd wanted to come in and offer her condolences, but Della blocked the door. "I just need to be by myself."

The girl nodded, looking rejected, and turned to go.

Guilt pricked Della's conscience. "Jenny?"

She turned around as if hoping Della had changed her mind. Of course, she hadn't. "Thanks for understanding."

The girl nodded again, ran up the stairs, and hugged her. "I know

I'm not as cool as Kylie, but I think of you as my friend. And I know you must be hurting and I want you to know I care. I wish I could turn myself into fae like Kylie could, and take away some of your pain. But I haven't mastered that yet."

"I'm fine, but thanks." Della forced herself to say the right thing. Not just because it would have been rude to do otherwise, but because she did like Jenny. And through unwanted tears, she watched the girl leave. Finally alone again, Della went back in and plopped back at the kitchen table. She listened to Chan's message about a dozen times, and each time it hurt more than the last.

She looked at her phone on the table. Part of her said she should call Steve. She'd told him yesterday that she would. But if she called him now she might start crying. She didn't want to cry anymore.

What she wanted was to reach into her chest and yank out the pain. She wanted to go back in time and do things differently. Call Chan back. Never sleep with Lee. Make her daddy love her a little more so he wouldn't turn his back on her.

She heard footsteps moving toward her cabin. Had Steve heard the news and come? Her heart ached to have him here.

She inhaled. Not Steve.

Chase's scent filled her nose—a scent that again tickled her memory. She sure as hell didn't want to deal with him. Right then she remembered her theory that Chase had been meeting Chan. She'd obviously been wrong.

A knock sounded on her cabin door. Why had he come here?

"Go away," she said, head down, staring at her hands laced together. She could hear the carbonation fizzling from a Diet Coke she'd opened but hadn't drunk. She almost felt the same fizzing inside her head, inside her heart.

The cabin door opened and she smelled and heard the dark-haired vampire take a few steps inside.

She didn't look up. "I said—"

"I know, I heard what you said."

She finally glanced up. He stood there staring at her, his arms crossed over his chest, his posture making a statement of defiance.

And yet you came inside anyway. This was why the guy infuriated her. "Leave," she seethed. She had too much on her plate to have to deal with him.

"I heard about your cousin. I just wanted to say . . . I'm sorry."

Her chest gripped. "Fine, you said it. Now leave."

He took a few more steps inside. "You don't need to just sit here. You need to go run, move. Spend some energy. It'll help with . . . everything," he added.

"You don't know what I need!" she snapped, and it felt good to have a target other than herself to aim her anger at.

"Yes, I do. I know . . ." He paused. "I know how you . . ."

"How I what? Don't you dare tell me you know how I feel. You don't have a clue what I feel. You don't know me, you are just . . ." *A crazy, lying vampire who I know I've met, but don't remember.* "Leave, damn it!" She growled and showed him her canines.

He still didn't budge. Was she going to have to throw his ass out?

"Look, I lost my whole family in one day. My father, my mother, my sister. Hell, all I had left was Baxter, my dog. So I do know how you feel. And I know that just sitting at that table letting grief consume you isn't going to help. What *will* help is to move. Spend some of the energy. It'll help deal with the pain. So let's go for a run. Come on."

She didn't move. Her mind chewed on what he'd said. He'd lost his entire family. Was that a lie?

She didn't think so.

"Don't make me have to drag you out of here," he said.

She frowned. "You couldn't drag me."

"Oh, yes, I could." He half smiled as if he'd enjoy the challenge. "Come on. I promise it'll help."

Swallowing her pride, she nodded. "Fine." She lit out. He was right behind her.

At first, she kept her feet on the ground. The hard footfalls against the solid earth felt good. She pushed herself, fast and then faster, until she was in full flight. But the stamina it took to keep moving, and moving fast, was extreme. Her intent wasn't for it to be a race, but it turned into one. She would get ahead of him, and he would move faster. Energy from being emotionally overloaded fueled her speed.

But no matter how fast she went, she never got more than a few feet in front of him. Each time he'd pass her, he would glance back as if baiting her. She took the bait, each and every time.

How fast was this guy? As fast as Burnett?

They never left the Shadow Falls property. She lost count of how many times they circled it. The tops of the trees appeared in a blur as she moved. She wasn't even sure how long they'd been at this, she just kept going. All her focus went on flying, and the ache in her heart, the grief and regret, finally lessened.

Damn it, Chase had been right. This was helping.

But how long could she keep it up? How long could she push herself to the extreme? *As long as he could,* she thought. But after another five minutes, she cratered and admitted he'd won. Slowing down, she landed by the lake. Her descent wasn't pretty. She hit the ground, lost her footing, and rolled.

Before she could come to a complete stop, he caught her and stood her up. "I'm fine," she tried to say, but couldn't push the words out while still trying to draw in air.

She bent at the waist, her lungs working overtime to pull in much-needed oxygen. Just when she finally caught her breath, her stomach roiled. Unable to stop it, she heaved and lost the contents of her stomach. Lost it all over Chase's feet.

For reasons she didn't understand, she found it funny. She wiped her mouth, and rose. The expression on his face, staring down at his puke-covered boots, made it funnier. Laughter spilled from her mouth before she could stop it.

His gaze lifted. "Now that's gross," he said. His green eyes danced with humor as his lips gave way to a smile. "You feel better?" he asked, sounding genuinely concerned.

"Yeah," she admitted, giving him the credit he deserved. Oh, she still didn't like him, or trust him, but she was a big enough person to admit he'd been right.

He started cleaning the tops of his shoes by wiping them on the grass. When he stopped, he looked up. "You should run like that twice a day. Run until you get sick. It's what you need right now."

All the humor was sucked right out of the moment. She recalled what he'd told her about his family.

"What happened?" she asked before she could stop herself.

"When you push yourself over the limit, you often lose your cookies." He grinned, but it came off forced. "You just happened to lose yours all over my boots."

"No, about your family," she said, but had a sneaking suspicion he knew what she'd meant all along and just wasn't willing to talk about it.

She should understand that. It wasn't as if she didn't have her own Pandora's box of secrets. But if he hadn't wanted her to ask, he should have never said anything. So why had he told her?

Oh, yeah, to get her to go run. But why? Why did he care? It didn't make a lick of sense.

"I told you," he said, and glanced toward the lake. "They died."

"How?" she asked.

"Take thirty more laps with me and I'll tell you."

"That's okay," she said, realizing she shouldn't have asked. Not only should she respect his need for privacy, but she didn't want to know more about him. Knowing more about a person just opened doors to friendships and relationships. Look at Jenny. Della hadn't wanted to form any ties, and yet somehow they'd been formed anyway. She'd even let the little chameleon hug her. Della didn't have room in her life for one more person. Not another hugger and especially not a person she didn't trust.

All of a sudden the sound of water filled her ears. She glanced toward the woods. Was she hearing the rush of the spring, or was it . . . the falls again? She shouldn't hear the falls from here.

"I need to get back to the cabin," she said, and started to take off.

"So you can go back to mourning and feeling sorry for yourself?"

Angry that he made her grief sound so self-indulgent, she turned around, took two steps closer, and growled.

He didn't budge, his lack of fear a statement. Not that it mattered a flying flip. She wasn't afraid of him either.

"No," she seethed. "I'm going back because Kylie and Miranda will be back any minute."

"Good, then you won't be alone."

What was it to him? Since when had she become his concern?

She continued to stare at him as if the paradox of who he really was would suddenly become clear. Nothing became clear. Except that this close, his scent filled her nose. And his trace registered again as one that had been familiar—one somehow tied to fear. But damn it, she wanted to know where she'd run across this panty perv before. Wanted to know why her gut said he was up to something.

"Do you want to run again tonight?" he asked.

"No." *Not with you. Where the hell do I know you from? Who were you meeting at the fence in the middle of the night?* A bunch of questions rested on the tip of her tongue, but she'd already asked most of them, so why bother? Not that she'd stop looking for answers. Sooner or later, she'd get to the bottom of this.

"Come on, we'll just run together. Say around three in the morning."

"Why would I do that?"

"Because, like I said, you need to run, to push yourself so you can . . . deal with things?"

"Why do you care how I deal with this?"

He leaned back on the heels of his feet and hooked his thumbs in his belt loops. "You haven't figured that one out yet? And here I thought you were smart."

"Figured what out?" Was he finally going to tell her the truth?

"That I kind of like you, Della Tsang."

"I'm not that likable," she said.

He grinned. "I have to admit, you do make it hard."

Chapter Twenty-three

When she stepped out of the woods, Della saw Steve sitting on the porch. He started toward her, and from the empathy on his face, she could tell he knew about Chan.

For one second, a very short second, she felt guilty for running with Chase. She pushed that aside. She hadn't done anything wrong. And if he did have a thing for her, she'd basically told him to take a hike.

Once Steve got within arm's reach he pulled her against him.

She leaned against him, hoping no one was around to see them. "I thought you already went to Dr. Whitman's," she said, and drew back. But right before she moved her nose from his shoulder, she smelled it. A feminine perfume. Some girl had gotten awfully close to Steve. And she'd bet she knew which girl, too. As the jealously started to form, she smashed it like a mosquito. She had so much to deal with, she just couldn't deal with that now. And besides, Jessie could have accidentally brushed up against him. She wanted to believe that.

"I did, but I planned to come back to see you this afternoon. Then I called, and when you didn't answer—"

"I didn't get the call." She reached into her back pocket. Crap. Her phone? "I must have left it here." But she always put it in her pocket.

"When you didn't answer, I called Kylie's phone. She told me what happened." He raised her chin an inch to look her in the eyes. "Why didn't you call me? I would have come immediately."

She saw disappointment in his gaze. It seemed she was always disappointing him. Only not as bad as she'd disappointed Chan. "I . . . I knew if I called you I'd start crying again." Why did Steve bring out her weak side? She didn't know. Didn't like it.

As if to prove her right, tears stung her eyes. She started walking to the cabin. He followed at her side, so close she felt his heat against her hip.

When she shut the door, he reached for her again. "Maybe you need to cry."

"No." She pulled out of his embrace and wiped her eyes. "I've already cried. And it's not going to change a damn thing." She went to the table to check and see if her phone was there. It wasn't. She'd probably lost it when she'd been flying like a maniac trying to keep up with Chase.

Her parents would kill her if she couldn't find it. No, they wouldn't kill her, they'd just be disappointed in her. Again.

Steve frowned. "Tell me what happened."

It hit her then that her phone was the least of her problems. She'd look for it later, and she'd either find it or she wouldn't.

She dropped onto the sofa. The overstuffed piece of furniture sighed, a soft sad sound. Or maybe everything sounded sad to her today.

Steve sat beside her and put his arm around her. The smell of perfume clinging to his shirt filled her nose again. Was she going to lose Steve to the perky blonde?

Della sent that thought packing and told him what happened with Chan. In spite of not wanting to, when she got to the part about seeing Chan, his face partially covered in dirt, she felt a few tears slip down her cheeks.

"I've been so fixated on trying to find my uncle and aunt, that I didn't stop and realize that I'd been neglecting the one vampire family member I did have. How the hell could I have been so blind?"

His arm tightened around her. "First, you weren't neglecting Chan. You've told me dozens of times that you begged him to come to Shadow Falls. You tried, Della. Plus, you just said he told you it wasn't important. And looking for your uncle, who was your father's twin, is . . . well, that's you wanting to reconnect with your father. It's understandable that you feel stronger about connecting with him."

His words made sense. She wanted to find her uncle to fill the void she felt with her father. But making sense didn't make it right. "He shouldn't have been more important than Chan. I could have tried harder. I could have called him back. Five minutes. That's all it would have taken."

Steve's fingers moved in her hair as if to soothe her. "This isn't your fault."

"It sure as hell feels like it is."

"That's because you care and because you're angry about his death. Crazy thing is that usually when you're guilty you tend to shift the blame to other people. When you're not guilty you blame yourself."

She rested her head on his shoulder, listening to his heartbeat. Another rhythmic sound filled the background. Footsteps. Someone was moving toward the cabin. She heard the footsteps stop, then start moving again. She inhaled.

Oh, hell, it was Chase.

His knock sounded on the door. She stood up and went to answer it, ready to send him packing and worried that Steve would be upset.

"Yeah?"

He looked at her and then his gaze lifted over her shoulder. To Steve. Not that Chase could be surprised Steve was here. He had to have smelled him. Had the vamp come just to cause trouble? She could feel Steve staring at her from behind.

"Hey," Chase said, acknowledging Steve.

"Hey," Steve replied, but somehow that one word came out as *Go to hell*.

Chase's gaze dropped back to her. "I hope I'm not interrupting anything."

She scowled up at him.

He didn't seem to be affected at all. "You dropped this when we were at the lake." He held out her phone.

"Thank you." A whisper of relief had her chest lightening for one second. But the tension she felt radiating from the two guys sent that relief packing. She took her cell from his hand and closed the door.

She turned to face Steve, sensing he wasn't happy. He sat, cupping his knees with his hands and looking at her. His expression had shifted to disappointment. Again.

Standing in the same spot, she listened as Chase's footsteps moved away from the cabin.

"You were with him?" Steve stood up.

"I was running," she said.

"With him?"

The word "no" formed on her tongue. But damn it, she wasn't going to lie. She hadn't been doing anything wrong. "Yes. He heard about Chan and he came by and suggested a run to make me feel better. So we ran around the property."

"So you're running buddies, huh?" His eyes turned a gold color, a telltale sign of his mood.

"We're not buddies," she said tightly.

Steve stared down at the floor as if he found something there fascinating, but she knew he was lost in thought. He finally looked up. "I came rushing over here thinking you might need a shoulder to lean on, but it looks as if you've already found one."

"It's not like that," she assured him.

He exhaled. "To borrow your earlier words, 'it sure as hell feels like it.'"

"Don't make this into something it's not," she said.

"Chase likes you," he accused, as if that was her fault.

"All we did was run. We spent less than three minutes talking. Nothing happened."

"Don't lie to me," he said.

"I'm not." It wasn't like Steve to be so accusing. Why was he so certain she'd done something? Then the answer, the one he'd just given her, became painfully clear. *Crazy thing is that usually when you're guilty you tend to shift the blame to other people.*

"And Jessie likes you, right?" she asked.

A flash of guilt crossed his expression. A new wave of pain washed over her. Exactly what was he feeling guilty for? Had something really transpired between them?

He shut his eyes a second, then opened them. "I told her it wasn't going to happen."

"Before or after you two kissed?" Della asked, now knowing that the perfume on Steve's shirt hadn't been from an accidental touch. Jessie had been in his arms, probably rested her head on that spot by his shoulder that Della loved so much. The pain she felt had the memory of losing Lee returning to haunt her.

Steve passed a hand over his face as if trying to wipe away the blame.

More pain swelled up inside her, crowding her chest with the guilt and pain from losing Chan. She shook her head. "You know what? I can't handle this right now. I've got too much on my plate. Just go."

"Look, Della, I'm sorry," he said. "She kissed me. I didn't . . . I know I probably should have . . . Damn it! I'm sorry."

She heard his remorse and knew it was heartfelt, and for some reason it only hurt more. "Why are you sorry? What do you have to be sorry about? You and I aren't going out."

And she needed to remember that, too. How many times had she told herself she needed to put the brakes on this? Well, the brakes were on now. "I don't have any claim on you. We're not together."

She heard voices and footsteps outside. Familiar voices. "Miranda and Kylie are coming," she said. "You need to go."

"No, we need to talk."

"No can do," she said. "Just go. I can't handle this on top of everything else."

He stood there and just stared at her.

"Please," she said.

"Della, I didn't mean . . . I'm not giving up on us."

She gripped her hands into fists. "There is no us, Steve. There never has been an us."

Disappointment flashed in his eyes again, and she realized how much she hated disappointing people. Chan, her parents, and now Steve. The knot in her throat doubled. "Leave."

Kylie and Miranda showed up minutes after Steve left. Della had three diet drinks set out on the table. They forced condolence hugs on her, and then they sat down at the table to hear what happened. The last thing Della wanted was to go through Chan's death again, but she'd told them she would explain. She wasn't going back on her word—not even if it hurt.

She told them about getting the phone call from Chan's friend. She barely managed to tell them about finding Chan's body. She didn't tell them about Steve. Frankly, she felt stupid letting something as trivial as a breakup, not that it was even really a breakup, hurt her when she had her cousin's death to think about.

But it did hurt. Her heart burned with the knowledge that she'd lost someone else. It didn't even matter that, logically, he'd never really been hers to lose.

"Have you seen him again?" Kylie asked.

Della hesitated, half thinking Kylie knew about Steve. "Seen who?"

"Chan? Have any more feathers appeared? I mean, it seems that he might be the ghost. Don't you think?"

Della nodded. "Yeah, I've seen him. Remember I told you I saw him at the gate last week? And then when Burnett and I were leaving the park, I saw him again."

Miranda's eyes widened. "You actually saw a ghost? Isn't that un-heard of for vampires?"

"Not all vampires," Kylie answered Miranda. "Burnett sees them sometimes." Then the chameleon looked back at Della. "So, he's shown himself. Did he say what he wants?"

She shook her head, feeling the emotion tighten her throat. "No. He was like there one second and gone the next. And someone was with him." And he'd looked at Della with the saddest eyes.

"Maybe he just wanted to say good-bye," Miranda said. "Not that it makes it okay. It's spookier than hell."

"It is okay." Kylie placed her hand over Della's. "But chances are it's more than just him saying good-bye. So he didn't say anything at all?"

Della shook her head. "He probably wants to tell me I let him down." And it was going to hurt like hell hearing it, but she deserved it. She had let him down.

"I can't believe that," Kylie said. "You didn't let him down."

"Yeah, well everyone keeps saying that, but I don't see it that way."

"Then you're not seeing it right," Miranda said in a stern voice. "Della Tsang doesn't let people down. I mean, look at us. We fight all the time. I know you can't stand me sometimes, and yet you've never let me down. Even when you're mad at me, you always come through. That's why I love you." Tears filled the witch's eyes.

The emotion in Della's chest made it hard to breathe. "Thanks." But she wasn't sure Chan would see it that way.

Miranda wiped the tears from her face. "Maybe your cousin knows about your uncle and wanted to tell you."

"That could be it," Kylie said, and then she looked at Della. "Did you tell Holiday about seeing Chan?"

"No," Della said. "I haven't told her anything about the ghost. Not yet."

"You should," Kylie said. "She can help you deal with the whole ghost thing."

"First I have to deal with Chan's death," Della said.

"I know," Kylie said, and reached over and put her hand over Della's. "I know how hard it is. When I lost Nana, it nearly killed me."

"I haven't lost anyone, but I can imagine how it hurts," Miranda said. "And both Kylie and I are here for you. I won't even get mad at you when you get pissy. You've got an it's-okay-to-be-pissy pass from me."

"A pissy pass?" Della repeated, and while it sounded so funny she felt the air in her lungs shudder with emotion.

"Yes," Miranda said with conviction.

"Oh," Kylie said. "I brought you your uncle's file." She pulled it out of her bag sitting beside the table and handed it to Della. "Have you told Derek about this? It might help him find something."

"No, not yet." *I've been too busy breaking up with Steve.* Della opened it and stared down at the writing. Guilt for worrying more about finding her uncle than staying in touch with her cousin did another tug on her heart.

"You look exhausted," Kylie said. "Have you slept any?"

"Not yet." Della massaged her temple again. Her headache returning like a bad penny. Boy was she a mess. Her life falling apart piece by piece. Her dad hated her. She was getting clobbered on the head by either a murderer or the death angels. Steve was kissing Jessie. Her cousin was dead. And she was seeing ghosts. Could anything else happen?

Yup, it could. She found out Monday afternoon. Burnett had called and asked Della to meet him at his office. He started out telling her that Chan's autopsy had been delayed and it would be a week before they could place Chan in the grave site that held his marker from when he faked his death.

"Why so long?" The thought of Chan's body being in some cold morgue hurt.

"Because there were no signs of foul play, the autopsy is going to take a little longer than I'd hoped."

Della nodded. "I want to be there." Her chest grew heavy.

"At the autopsy?" he asked, confused.

"No, at the burial," she said.

He exhaled as if in disagreement. "It's going to be done in the middle of the night and quickly."

"I don't care. I don't want him to be buried alone." She hadn't seen Chan's ghost again, and thought maybe he'd passed on, but at the very least, she was going to be there when his body was put in the earth. She could remember the crowd that had been at Lorraine's funeral. The people who had been there to show their love for her. Della couldn't live with the thought that Chan would be dropped in a grave and not have anyone—not one person there to mourn for him.

Burnett stared at her with defiance and she suspected what he was about to say. "With all you have been through, don't you think it would be wise to forgo working on the recent murder case?"

Her suspicions were on the mark. "No! And don't use this as an excuse to stop me."

He held up his hand, his eyes tightening. "I just think you've had too much on your plate."

Of course it was too much. She felt like she was dying inside, but not doing anything would make it worse. "It doesn't matter. Not only do I want to do this, I need something else to think about other than my cousin's death." Other than her father's hatred of her and losing all hope of her and Steve. "Please. Didn't I, with Kylie and Miranda's help, do well at the funeral home yesterday? We caught that guy."

"You did. But I still don't think you three going to the funeral home alone was a good idea."

"And yet it turned out okay," she insisted.

She saw in the way his shoulders slumped that he'd given in. "Fine. Then you start tonight. I've got some information about a local gang hangout. I want you and Chase there to see if you—"

"Chase?" Della asked, panic forming in a tight ball in the pit of her stomach. "I'm working with Chase?"

Burnett nodded. "You have a problem with Chase?"

"Maybe," she said. Hell, yes, she had a problem. She knew when Chase brought over her phone that he'd done it with the intent to start trouble. And he'd succeeded, too.

Not that it was his fault Steve had swapped spit with Jessie, but Chase's part in the problem still irked her. She was so angry she'd even avoided eye contact with him during the two classes they shared. Oh, she felt him staring at her, but she'd never given him one glance.

And the phone issue was only part of the problem. There was her knowing she'd run across him before and then what Jenny had told her about him meeting someone at the gate. She almost told Burnett about Jenny's discovery, but then she recalled Jenny asking her not to say anything.

"What is your problem with Chase?" Burnett asked.

She couldn't out and out lie, but avoiding telling the truth was no sin. "Why not send Lucas?"

Burnett's brow wrinkled. "You'd rather work with a werewolf than another vampire? That's odd."

"Not really. I know Lucas. I trust Lucas. Besides, isn't that part of what Shadow Falls is all about? Getting along and playing nice with other species? I can deal with Lucas."

Burnett leaned back in his chair, and the piece of furniture groaned with his new position. "Why don't you like Chase?" he asked directly, as if he knew she was skipping around the truth.

Chapter Twenty-four

Della wasn't finished skipping over the truth. "He seems to be full of secrets."

"What kind of secrets?" Burnett asked.

"If I knew, they wouldn't be secrets." Yup, she could skip with the best of them.

Burnett frowned. "Chase's already working this case."

Della leaned forward in her seat. It was her turn to put Burnett in the hot seat. "Why do you trust Chase? He's not here a week and you recruit him. That's not like you. Did you know him before?"

"No," he answered, and while Della tried to listen to his heart, she couldn't. Her hearing was out. What the frack was wrong with her senses?

Burnett continued, "I think I mentioned that he has impressed me with his abilities."

"What abilities?" Della had noted Chase's speed, but . . .

"All of them," he answered, but looked unhappy about her inquisitiveness.

She suspected there were things he wasn't telling her, but if she continued to pursue this line of questioning, he might decide she shouldn't work the case at all. The last thing she wanted was to get this yanked from her.

He leaned forward, putting his elbows on his desk. "If you're not comfortable—"

"I'm fine," she said before he could say it.

"But if you don't trust him—"

"The best way for me to start trusting him is to work with him, right?" Her gut knotted at the thought of Burnett pulling her from the case.

He continued to stare at her. Hard. He didn't say anything. She could see the debate going on in his eyes. To give her this case or pull her off. And it didn't look as if it was going in her favor.

"I want to catch this creep," she said. "It's the least I can do."

Burnett's frown deepened. "Della, there is a fine line agents have to follow. It lies between wanting justice and somehow feeling responsible for the horrible things we see. There are cases that never get solved. People die. People we love die, like Chan, and I know you feel responsible, but . . ."

"I know I didn't cause his death," Della said.

"But you still feel responsible, don't you?" he said adamantly.

It was a direct question. She couldn't lie. "If I'd answered his call, or called him back, I might have been able to prevent it. But Chan's death doesn't have anything to do with me working this case."

"The emotional state of an agent always affects their ability to work a case."

"I can do this, Burnett."

He set his hands on his desk. The light from the window shined through and made his black hair look almost blue. He picked up a pen and rolled it in his hands.

He continued to study her. "When I was fourteen, there was a girl I liked. Half human, half fae. We used to go to the lake and swim all the time."

He paused and set the pen down as if the memory took him back to the past. "One afternoon she called and wanted me to go to the lake with her. I had another friend ask me to go running with him earlier, and I didn't want to let him down. She went to the lake with a few other friends. She drowned that day. I was horrified, and for about a year I blamed myself. If I'd been there, I could have saved her. It took a long time to realize that sometimes bad things happen, and it's not anyone's fault."

Della glanced up at him. "Maybe in time I'll come to the same conclusion. But only if I stay busy with other things." Like catching a killer.

"Fine. You can work the case with Chase, but don't make me regret this decision."

"I won't. I promise."

His gaze filled with empathy. "Time is always our friend," he said. "But in the meantime, try to ease up on yourself. Our hearts get too heavy if we carry too much guilt and grief around all the time."

She felt the weight in her chest right now. She nodded. "You're beginning to sound like Holiday."

"She does have a way of rubbing off on me." His concerned expression changed to something softer.

Love, Della thought. Burnett and Holiday were still crazy about each other. Just like Kylie and Lucas, Miranda and Perry. Even her parents. Would she ever be able to let herself go there again?

Della's thoughts jumped from love to the case. "Do you suspect the vampire gang of the murders?"

"We don't have a firm lead, yet," he said. "The morgue report is a bit confusing. The killer fed on the victims, was more physically violent than normal, which almost says the killer had motive, anger issues. The male victim was worse than the female."

"You think the vampire knew them?"

"It's a possibility, but it's more likely that he was a fresh turn and he was simply overzealous."

"He?" she asked, wondering how he knew it wasn't a female.

"Usually males will go easier on a female. And the size of the bite marks puts the jaw size more consistent with a male. There was also a hair found. DNA hasn't come back yet, but it was black and short. "

"Could it have been some random hair?"

"It had both victims' blood on it," he said matter-of-factly. "So it's unlikely. But still possible."

She almost shivered at the thought. "So a male with short, dark hair."

Burnett nodded. "Perhaps a fresh turn." He hesitated. "We're hoping if you and Chase hang out with a few gang members you will hear something that could help. And since both you and Chase got a trace of the killer, if he's there, you'll know. That said, my main concern is that if you got *his* trace, he might have gotten both of yours."

"I don't think so," Della said, having already thought about it. "He was escaping, running. I don't think his senses were on alert. The only reason I got his scent was because it was late and I knew he had to be an intruder."

"Maybe," he said. "But I still want you to be on high alert. And while you're out in the field, under no circumstances are you to leave Chase's side." He pointed a finger at her, and his expression went stern. "If you disobey this rule, your chances of ever working another case for the FRU are nil. Is that clear?"

Oh, it was clear, but she didn't like it. The last thing she wanted was to be attached to the hip of the panty perv. But if that's what it took to find the dirty vamp who'd killed Lorraine and her boyfriend, her hip had better just get used to the idea of having company.

"Is that clear, Della?"

"Crystal," she said. Like it or not, she and Chase were a team. And in the back of her mind, she thought about how Steve was going to feel when he heard about it.

Not that she should worry. Whatever they had was history. She had to accept that.

· · ·

When Della walked into the cabin, Miranda and Kylie were sitting at the kitchen table with three unopened Diet Cokes out. A sure sign someone had a problem and they needed to hold a powwow. In the back of her mind, she recalled Miranda asking questions about to do the deed or not to do the deed with Perry. Were there problems in paradise?

"What's wrong?" Della asked, looking at the little witch, hoping that she and her shape-shifter weren't having issues. The last time they'd broken up, Miranda had cried constantly, and ate a truckload of ice cream. It drove Della nuts.

"This is an intervention," Miranda said. "Sit down." She picked up a pencil and pulled over a pad.

"An intervention? Whose intervention?"

Miranda continued to stare at her.

Double damn! "My intervention? What, do you want me to pee on drug-test and pregnancy sticks like my parents now?"

"It's not that kind of intervention," Miranda said, all serious like.

Della made a face and looked at Kylie, the reasonable friend. "What's going on?"

"Miranda's dramatizing it," Kylie said. "But . . . Perry told her that Steve told him that you two had a fight."

"A big fight and it involved that girl at the vet's office," Miranda added.

Della dropped down in her chair. "Oh, hell! Isn't anything private around this place?"

"It shouldn't be private," Miranda said. "We're your best friends and we're supposed to tell each other everything. You needed us and didn't even let us help you. So we need to come up with a list of things that will help you deal with this." She pulled the paper closer. "I've already come up with a few ideas."

Della groaned. "Right now, Steve's the least of my problems." She'd told herself this ever since he walked out her door, and maybe if she said it enough times it would feel like the truth. Sure, it didn't compare to Chan's death, or the murderer she wanted to hunt down and teach a lesson, but it still hurt like the devil.

"That's why we're concerned," Kylie said. "You've had a tough time lately. The FRU case, your dad, Chan, trying to find your aunt and uncle, and now Steve. We just want to help."

"Help how?" Della asked. "There's nothing you can do. Nothing anyone can do." Her chest instantly felt heavy. "Besides, the break up's probably best. We weren't really together. I didn't want to be together. I don't even know why I let it go as far as it did."

"You like him, that's why," Miranda said. "You should see your eyes light up when you see him. He makes you happy. Now you're not happy. And for the last week, your aura has been really dark. It's a weird murky color, too. I told Kylie a couple of days ago that something was wrong. Now, it looks even worse."

"My aura is always kind of dark. I'm vampire, remember? You told me that once," Della remarked.

"Yeah, but not this dark. It's scary-looking."

"Then do some magic mojo and paint it a different color," Della said. And while the witch was at it, maybe she could fix her hearing problems. Della had tried to tune in to the distant sounds on the way here and couldn't.

"If I could fix your aura I would. Only you can fix it. But we can come up with ideas. Things you can do to make yourself happy and that are aura-cleansing. I've already listed several." She started reading from the list: "Enjoy a sunset. Take a slow walk in nature. And the best one, bird watching. Something about birds always lightens up an aura." Miranda smiled as if so proud of herself.

Della snagged the pen and paper from Miranda. "Here, I've got a few better ones." She started scribbling and reading it off as she did: "Find my uncle and aunt, find a killer, get my cousin buried, forget that my dad hates me, stop missing Steve. Damn, it looks as if I won't have time to watch any friggin' birds!" Della tossed down the pencil and shot across the kitchen to her bedroom.

. . .

Ten minutes later the knock came at Della's door. Ten entire slow minutes that Della had used to realize she was taking her problems out on her friends.

"Come in." She sat up, ready to take the blame.

Kylie stepped in. "Hey."

"Let me save you the trouble. I know I was a bitch and I'll apologize to the witch." She made a face. "But bird watching?"

Kylie chuckled. "Personally, I thought watching the sunset would have set you off. But . . ." Kylie's smile faded. "Miranda's seriously worried. This aura thing has her freaked out."

Della exhaled. "Aren't auras connected to our moods?"

"I think," Kylie said. "I skipped Auras 101."

"Well, I've been in a really dark, pissy mood. So it's understandable."

"But Miranda thinks a really dark aura can bring on more darkness, sort of like bad attracts bad. That's why she wants you to . . . find your happy place."

"My happy place is going to be finding a killer and getting Chan in his proper grave."

Kylie dropped on the bed. "Is that what Burnett wanted with you just now?"

"Yeah," Della said. "It's going to be a week before they can do Chan's autopsy, so they won't be burying him until after that. And I start on the case in . . . less than an hour."

"Less than an hour? Doing what?"

"Hanging out someplace that vampire gangs are known to be. Oh, and the real pisser is that I'll be working with Chase."

Kylie grimaced. "And you still don't like him."

"Do bears shit in the woods?"

Kylie made a face. "I don't know, I've never seen one."

Della shook her head. "I don't like him. I don't trust him."

"He's awfully cute," Kylie said, her voice laced with humor. "Might that be why you don't want to spend too much time with him?"

Della shook her head. "I don't like him that way. He's too . . . irritating."

Kylie's brow, now quirked with suspicion, didn't go down. Della finally blurted out the truth. "Fine, I find him attractive. But that doesn't mean anything. It's not as if he's . . ."

"Steve?" Kylie asked.

"Yeah," Della admitted, but hated doing it.

They sat silently for a second, and then Kylie asked, "Why didn't you tell us about Steve?"

Della shrugged. "It seems all I've been doing is whining about things. And it hurts to talk about it."

"But we're best friends. We just want to help."

"I know," Della said.

"Is it really over?" Kylie asked.

"I think so." Della bit down on her lip and suddenly wanted to talk. "He kissed Jessie. Or I should say, she kissed him. And he was all guilt-ridden so I know he enjoyed it. It makes me furious, but . . . last weekend he wanted me to meet his parents, and I totally freaked. I don't want to meet his parents. I don't want whatever we have to become . . . official. So is it fair for me to let this 'thing' we have keep going, when I don't know if I'll let it go anywhere?"

"Has he called you since then?" Kylie asked.

"No. And it's probably best." But Della had been checking her phone constantly. She wasn't sure if it was relief or disappointment she felt when she found he hadn't tried to contact her.

Kylie dropped back on the bed and stared up at the ceiling. "Holiday once told me that women who have daddy issues usually find a way to have issues with guys. We project our problems with our daddies onto other guys. It sounded like a bunch of crap at first, but then was it a coincidence that I finally gave in to Lucas after I resolved the issues with my stepdad."

Della reclined on the bed beside Kylie. "So, you're saying I need to fix my relationship with my dad before I can ever have a boyfriend?" She slapped her forehead. "Damn, looks like I might be going lesbian, because I don't think that will happen."

Kylie chuckled. "Sorry, I'm taken."

Socks, Kylie's cat, jumped up on the bed and rubbed against Della's side. She grinned. "Yeah, you and your hottie werewolf. You know, Socks here doesn't approve of the dog at all. I think Socks is afraid Lucas will give him fleas. "

Kylie frowned as she petted her cat. "Lucas doesn't have fleas. And besides, I approve of Lucas." Her eyes widened with affection. "I love him so much. Even when he's overbearing and a bit macho like he was at the funeral home. He makes me . . . feel complete. And I think you deserve to have that, too. Someone who just makes you feel so good inside. They touch you and you melt. They look at you all sexy like and you feel gooey inside. They hold you and whatever problems you've got going on, they just seem smaller."

"Maybe I'm not meant to have that." Della looked at Socks. "I'll get old and get a bunch of cats. That seems to be what women do who don't get married." But Della couldn't help but think about how Steve made her feel. And no cat would ever do that.

"I don't believe that," Kylie insisted. "And maybe all this crap happening right now is messing with your head. If none of this other stuff would have happened, you might not have panicked about meeting Steve's parents."

"What about him kissing Jessie and enjoying it?" Della asked.

"Did he tell you he enjoyed it?" Kylie asked. "Because I've seen the way he looks at you, and I find it hard to believe he enjoyed kissing anyone besides you."

"He didn't say it, but he's a guy. Of course he enjoyed it."

Kylie made a face. "Okay, I won't argue with that, but it sounds to me like you're looking for a reason to distance yourself from him.

Maybe what's really going on is that you know how much you like him and you're just afraid?"

Della opened her mouth to deny it, but she couldn't push the damn words out. Was Kylie right? "I still can't stand that he kissed her—even if she started it," Della muttered, and then, wanting to change the subject, she popped up. "Is Miranda still here? I should go eat crow now and apologize. I hate cold crow."

Kylie smiled. "Nope, Perry called her and asked her to meet him."

"So they're off sucking face, huh," Della said, hoping to take the conversation off her own boy issues by focusing on someone else's romance.

Kylie pursed her lips as if all too aware of Della's ploy. That chick was just way too smart. "Look, you don't have to like that Steve kissed her. It's natural that you're pissed, believe me, I know, but it doesn't have to be a deal breaker. Look at Miranda and Perry's and my and Lucas's relationships. We both had some similar rough spots. And don't think I'm looking out for Steve's interest here, I'm looking out for yours. Take my advice and give this thing with Steve a chance. Don't give up on him."

Della looked at the clock on the bedside table. She had to meet Chase. "Crap, I've gotta go."

"You know we should at least talk," Chase said, his words not even a whisper.

At least her hearing wasn't out. "About what?" Oh, she knew what she'd like to tell him, but she wasn't sure now was the time.

Della looked across the table, wishing it were someone else sitting there. Wishing she didn't appreciate the width of his shoulders, the daredevil way he carried himself, or the sharp cut of his jawline that made him look more like a man than a boy. They'd met and flown to this old abandoned house in the middle of the woods that the local gang had turned into a blood bar. Not a nice bar, but there were at least six vampires here. Supposedly, with the local gang in the area the owners thought they had enough traffic through the place to make a go of the business.

Della did another causal visual around the room and took a sip of the blood Chase had ordered her. It was A positive, and it wasn't fresh, but she hadn't had dinner, so she drank it without complaint.

"I don't know. We could talk about the weather, sports, or maybe what's got you so pissed at me," he said, obviously deciding he didn't need to whisper anymore.

"I hear it's supposed to rain tomorrow?" she said sarcastically.

He laughed.

Della glanced at a couple of guys sitting across the room. Rough-looking vamps with a bottle of whiskey that they kept adding to their blood. One was blond, one dark-haired, but it was long and hung in a ponytail.

For the first fifteen minutes all the patrons, even the bartender, had stared daggers at them, but now they seemed to have lost interest. Della remained on guard. She had to. Her sense of smell still hadn't come back. So she was studying people, looking for anyone suspicious. Anyone with short dark hair, or who looked like a killer. Not that she knew what one looked like, but damn it, she could still try.

"Come on. What did I do to tick you off?"

She met Chase's eyes, her fury still equivalent to that of a wet hen with PMS, but her need for vengeance would have to wait. They had a case to work on.

"Funny, I didn't take you as the type to hold your tongue," he taunted.

He'd gotten that right. She'd never been one to believe silence was golden. Oh, what the hell, they could talk as long as they didn't say anything about their assignment.

"You meant to cause trouble when you brought my phone back."

He pursed his lips as if debating his answer. "Maybe."

She scowled.

"Okay, probably. But I thought the guy needed to know he had some competition. While you were away on Friday, some chick—the same chick—called him three times. And she was flirting with him. I don't know what you two have going on, but I didn't think it was right."

Della's heart nosedived to her stomach. Jessie had been calling Steve? Ahh, but now wasn't the time to get caught up in that heartache. She cut Chase a cold look. "It's none of your business. You shouldn't have been listening to his calls."

"True, but I'm making it my business. Like I said, I like you. I think this thing we've got going might lead somewhere. So I want to look out for you."

"I don't need you to look out for me. And for this to lead anywhere, I'd have to reciprocate in the liking."

"You like me," he said with a confident smile, and damn if her stomach didn't flutter at the sight of his sexy grin. "You just don't realize it yet. I'm an acquired taste. Like one of those strange beers from other countries. It takes a while for a person to get used to me."

"I don't like beer. And I don't like—"

"But you're here."

"Only because . . ." She caught herself. "There's a dozen other people I'd prefer to be with right now."

"Only twelve? You care to tell me their names? I'll start knocking them off."

She showed him her fangs.

He laughed and picked up his blood, staring at her over the rim of the plastic cup. "How are you doing with . . . the whole cousin thing?" The lightness had vanished from his tone.

She recalled his story about losing his whole family. He'd probably made it up. "How are you doing with *your* whole family thing?" she said with accusation.

Something flashed in his eyes . . . anger, grief. Maybe he hadn't
made it up.

"So you weren't lying?" she asked.

"No." He cut his gaze around, lifting his nose up to check for
familiar scents.

"Anything?" she asked.

He looked back at her, almost too fast. "No. You?"

No way was she going to tell him her sense of smell was out. She
lifted her face as if testing the air. "No."

Footsteps heading their way sounded in the background. Della
prepared herself for company and possible trouble. One of the rough-
looking guys drinking whiskey dropped in the chair beside her and
leaned close.

"Hey beautiful," he said, his mouth way too close.

Chapter Twenty-five

"You two are new around these parts."

Della backed up. He looked to be in his early twenties, but it also seemed as if he'd had a rough life. He looked her up and down and then glanced at Chase.

"Since you don't seem to be her type, I thought she might like me better."

So the creep had been listening. Not that she hadn't been eavesdropping on him and his friend. But their talk about how they'd played football in high school hadn't been all that interesting.

"We're just having a bit of a tiff," Chase said, his voice deepening. "She's with me."

"Is that right, Sweetie?" he asked Della. "You know, at first, I thought you worked here. You know, as a professional girl."

Had he just told her she looked like a prostitute? She frowned. "First, I don't work here. Second, my name's not Sweetie. And third, if I'm anyone's girlfriend, I'm his." She turned to Chase, and when he tilted up his mouth in a wicked almost grin, she rolled her eyes. "Which I'm not," she added quickly.

"A shame," the half-drunk vamp said, his gaze shifting back to Chase. "You see, I'm not an acquired taste, I'm delicious from the first bite."

He showed his canines—which could use a good brushing—and Della suspected the pun was intended.

She pulled back, but that didn't stop him from stretching his arm across the back of Della's chair and touching her hair. She'd like to play with his hair—as in grab ahold of his ponytail and give him a good swing across the room.

"Where are you two from?" he asked. His touch stirred at her neck and she suppressed a shiver. And not the good kind!

Della debated breaking the guy's fingers. She could reach back and crack his bones before he could say uncle. But she didn't know if playing along for a few minutes might get some information.

"I'm from California," Chase said. "She's from the Houston area."

"What brings you from California?" Ponytail asked Chase, tilting his head to the side as if listening for an untruth. Della tried listening, too, but couldn't tune in. Instead of worrying, she studied Chase's expression.

"My mother moved here," Chase said.

The jerk sitting beside her appeared satisfied that Chase spoke the truth. Yet, hadn't Chase told her his mom was dead? Yes, he had, and she'd listened to his heart beat to the truth then, too. Della recalled how Chase's eyes shifted to the left when he'd just answered the half-drunk vamp. She'd heard that eyes shifting to the left was a small sign of someone lying.

She'd been right not to trust him. She tucked that info away to concentrate on the problem at hand. "Hand" being the key word. The creep's palm was slipping under the collar of her shirt to touch her lower neck right now.

She shifted her shoulder, as if to shoo away a pest, hoping he'd take a hint.

He didn't.

Chase's gaze shifted to her collar. His eyes brightened with discontent. But if anyone was going to teach this jerk a lesson, she was. She cut Chase a glare that said *stand down*.

"I'm looking for someone," Della said, struggling to ignore the man's touch. "I think he was newly turned. Short dark hair."

"Is he one of those twelve guys you just told this boy you'd prefer to be with right now?" The man nodded at Chase, but didn't look at him. Good thing, too, because the quick glance she got wasn't pretty. Fangs out, eyes a neon green.

"Yeah, I'd rather be with that guy." She focused on the jerk, knowing her heart sang to the truth. She'd rather be with Lorraine's killer right now. She even hoped he'd give her a fight, so she could give some fight back. Teach him a few lessons before she turned him over to Burnett.

The jerk nodded. "I heard a fresh turn was in the area last week. The Juggler gang was trying to recruit him." The jerk's fingers slipped farther inside her collar, all the way to her shoulder. Her skin crawled, but she wanted answers more than she hated his touch.

"Where can we find the Juggler gang?"

"Don't know. I don't belong to any gang. Don't need 'em. I can take care of myself. Of course, every now and then I like to take care of some pretty young thing like you." He shifted his chair closer, and his hand slipped a little farther inside her shirt. His whole cold palm rested on her bare shoulder. And she no longer wanted to break his fingers. His neck would do just nicely.

"Do you know any of the gang members?" she asked between clenched teeth.

"Nah, I've only been here a week. But I noticed one or two hanging around."

She lowered her voice. "Any here now?"

"Don't know. Since you walked in, all I've noticed is you. Young. Soft." He wiggled his fingers.

"Why don't you take a look around and see if any of them are here?"

He didn't answer. His fingers shifted beneath the bra strap on her shoulder. She adjusted her lips to hide her lowering fangs, and from the corner of her eye she saw Chase watching, his face a mask of fury.

Why was he so upset? The creep wasn't fingering *his* underwear. She had to clench her hands to keep from coldcocking the half-drunk jerk.

"Glance around," she said again. "Please." She wiggled her brow in what she hoped would appear to be a flirty gesture.

He shifted his gaze round the room, his finger moving back and forth under her bra strap, each stroke a little closer to her left breast. Each stroke bringing her closer to going apeshit on his ass.

"Nope, none are here now." Ponytail's eyes found hers again. "How about you and I go take a walk?"

"How about you telling me what you heard about the fresh turn?" It took effort to keep her voice soft. "Did he have short dark hair?"

"How about we talk after we walk?"

A growl, deep and sinister, sounded across the table. "How about you get your dirty hands off her?" Chase leaned into the table, his fangs fully extended, his eyes now such a bright lime green, you needed sunglasses to look at him.

The jerk glared back. For one second, he reacted to the brightness of Chase's eyes; then he seemed to toss the worry aside. Della wasn't so sure that was a good idea.

"Now, buddy," Ponytail said. "I don't hear Sweetie complaining."

The name was the straw that broke the camel's back. And would probably wind up being the straw that broke this freak's wrist. "I told you, my name's not Sweetie!" She yanked the guy's arm from around her and twisted it almost to the point of breaking it.

He growled, almost reached for her with his other hand, but she gave the limb another tight twist, letting him know one move and his arm would be dangling at an odd angle. And she'd make certain it wasn't at a pretty angle. Sure, vamps healed quickly, but she'd heard a broken bone still hurt like hell.

The scoundrel glared at her.

She glared right back, then cut her gaze around the room. All the bar patrons watched with malicious intent. And she had a feeling it wasn't aimed at Mr. Ponytail. She and Chase could probably take on four, but if they all teamed up, she might be testing the broken-bone theory herself. They had to get out of here. She glanced at Chase, and cut her eyes to the exit. Then she dropped her tight hold of the guy's arm and shot toward the door, assuming Chase would follow, and follow fast.

She'd assumed wrong.

She stopped at the last table on the way out.

Chase, taking his time, stood from his chair, but never stepped away from the table. He glared down at Ponytail. Chase's posture and hostile expression practically begged the jerk to try something. Was Chase nuts? Didn't he feel the glares from the crowd?

Did he not realize how outnumbered they were?

"Let's go," Della said.

She no more got the words out than she knew that had been a mistake.

"You always do what your whore tells you to?" the jerk, rubbing his arm, asked Chase.

"Did you just call her a whore?" Chase clenched his fist.

Every muscle in Della's body tightened, prepared to fight. But before she took one step, Chase had the asshole against the wall. And not the wall beside the table where they'd sat, but the one on the other side of the bar. How? She hadn't even seen him move. Holy crap! Just how fast was the panty perv?

He held the guy by the throat, pressing him against the faded paneling. The jerk's feet dangled a foot off the floor. He should have been kicking, but from the color of the lowlife's face, he wasn't getting air, and probably knew one wrong move and his windpipe would be crushed.

"Tell her you're sorry," Chase demanded.

"You wreck this place, you pay for it!" the bartender, leaning against the bar, yelled out. "You wanna kill each other, do it outside. We'll join you and take bets on who'll make it."

Chase, obviously ignoring the bartender, didn't move. "I said, tell her you're sorry!"

The jerk, his face now blood-red, couldn't talk, but he moved his lips.

"I didn't hear you," Chase seethed. "Try that again."

The man's friend shot up from his chair. Della flew toward him, but before she got there, he'd slung a table at Chase.

Chase never looked back, but with his free hand he caught the table by one leg and held it up in midair like some kind of circus performer.

"Sit your ass back down," Chase growled, and while he never looked at the table thrower, there was no doubt who he was talking to.

Della gazed around the room, watching for the next attack, prepared to intervene, if needed. Oddly enough, only the man's friend who'd thrown the furniture seemed to be a threat. Everyone else just seemed entertained.

Chase set the table down. Almost gently, not breaking it. He turned his head, giving the room a quick glance. "I said sit down!"

The man's friend remained standing, as if still debating his next move.

"I have a free hand," Chase seethed, and waved his left arm. "Put your butt in that chair or you'll be up against the wall with this guy and I'll choke the life out of both of you! And if anyone else tries anything, I'll do the same to them the second I'm finished crushing the windpipes of these lowlifes."

The friend of Mr. Ponytail flopped back in his seat. "I never really liked his ass that much anyway."

The bartender and the few other patrons laughed.

Chase didn't seem to appreciate the humor. He stared back up at the red-faced, bulging-eyed vamp he held against the wall. "Now, you want to apologize? Or do I break your freaking neck?"

The guy croaked out a sound. Chase must have been happy, because he moved his hand from the guy's neck, allowing him to fall to a heap on the floor.

The vamp coughed and rubbed his throat. Chase stood there for several long seconds, watching the guy try to draw air through his bruised throat, as if giving the creep a chance to get up and start more trouble. When he didn't, Chase started for the door. He moved slow and with confidence. Not a bit worried anyone would attack.

He stopped beside her, and motioned for her to go first.

Unfortunately, Della didn't follow orders. She waved him ahead.

He rolled his eyes, but then he walked out. As she moved through the door, she heard someone say, "I don't know what kind of blood that kid was drinking, but I want some of that."

Della stepped out into the cool October air. The night had grown darker. But the moon, almost full, cast silver light down on the woody terrain. She glanced around for threats, spotting only a couple leaning against the back of the building, their clothes half off.

Looking away, she studied Chase's back moving in front of her. She didn't want to be impressed. But, damn it! Color her impressed. She wanted some of whatever Chase was drinking, too.

Ten minutes later, she followed him in a fast run, or tried to follow him. He kept going faster and faster. His only comment to her when she'd stepped beside him outside the bar had been, "Keep up if you can."

The one thing Della hated more than taking a challenge she thought she'd lose was walking away from one without trying. Her feet pounded the cold dirt. She kept her focus on Chase, who seemed to run without effort. His feet left the ground and he went into full flight. Della did the same, but the energy it took her to fly at that speed caused her gut to ache.

Midflight, Chase turned and looked at her. Checking on her. As if noting her condition, he shifted and started down, navigating between the trees to solid ground. He came to an easy stop, not even breathing hard, and looked up at her descending.

She hit the ground with a thud, but thankfully managed to stay on her feet. She tried to hide the fact that her lungs wouldn't take air. Then, like the other night when they'd gone running, her stomach cramped. Swinging around, she lost the contents of her stomach in the brush.

When she rose up and wiped her mouth on the back of her hand, he stood beside her. "At least it wasn't on my shoes this time."

She glared up at him. She normally didn't puke after her runs, but then again, she didn't push herself like this either.

"Okay, you're faster than me," she snapped. "Don't rub it in." Admitting it cost her a bit of pride.

"I'm not trying to rub it in." For a flicker of a second she saw what looked like concern in his eyes. "Running is good for you, come on. It will help." He turned and took off again.

She didn't.

He got about fifty feet, stopped, and shot back to stand in front of her. "Don't wimp out on me."

She ignored his insult. "Help with what?"

He hesitated before answering. "The grief."

"I'm dealing with it." And as much as she hated admitting it, it was true. Focusing on finding Lorraine's killer held the grief at bay.

"Not very well." He started walking, fast. She moved beside him. They didn't speak for a few minutes.

"You ready to go?" he asked.

"To look for the Jugglers?" she asked, setting aside her angst with him.

"No," he said. "To run. We're done with the case for the night."

"Done? How could—?"

"Someone will tell the gang we were looking for them and they'll be here tomorrow when we come back."

"What makes you think someone will tell them?"

"Because establishments like that are loyal to the local gangs. They depend on them for protection and business."

"How do you know so much about gangs and establishments like that?" she asked, her mind going to her original beef with this guy. Where the hell did she know him from? Had he been a part of the gang that had been fighting when she first saw Chan?

"I've been on the streets a long time," he said.

"How long? When were you turned?" She stopped to see if he'd answer.

He took a couple more steps, then faced her again. "I was fourteen." He started jogging, but not at a breakneck speed.

She joined him. "How did you survive?" The muscles in her legs stung from her previous exertion.

"Race me back to Shadow Falls. If you win, I'll answer the question."

Temptation had her pulse racing, but she wasn't stupid. "I've already admitted you're faster."

He stopped. "Race me, and I'll tell you for trying."

She didn't like losing or consolation prizes. "Maybe I don't want to know that badly." She did, but her interest in him grated on her more than anything else.

"Sure you do," he said confidently. "You wouldn't have asked if you didn't want to know."

She frowned and tried to find a way to make this work for her. "I tell you what, I'll race you if . . . win or lose, you tell me where I know you from. And this time, don't lie to me."

He blinked. "I don't know what you're talking about."

"I think you do." She glared up at him.

"Can't you hear my heartbeat? I'm not lying."

"You're forgetting, I heard what you told our friend back there. You told me your parents were killed and you told him your mother lived here. So I know you lied to one of us, and your heart never skipped a beat." At least she assumed it hadn't skipped when he'd told this to the creep at the bar.

Chase appeared caught. "I lie when I have to."

"Or when it's convenient." *Maybe you're a pathological liar.*

"I wish it'd been that easy. Controlling my heartbeat is something I worked at for a long time."

She remembered seeing his expression twitch when she thought he'd lied earlier. She moved in front of him and studied his face, but tilted her head to the side so he'd assume she was listening. "Does your mother live here?"

"I told you they died." His eyes didn't shift.

"Where have we met before?" She tossed the question out there and didn't breathe, waiting.

"I don't think we've ever crossed paths." He didn't blink, but his left brow twitched. Was that enough to call it a lie?

And if he was lying, why? What wasn't he telling her?

He started walking again. She followed, trying to figure out her next move.

After a few minutes of silence, he spoke. "You should have never let him touch you."

When she didn't respond, he jumped in front of her and started walking backwards, making it hard to ignore him.

"He was answering my questions," she said. "More than you've done."

"I could have gotten those answers myself."

She tilted her chin up. "I don't think you were his type."

Chase's laugh caught her off guard. It sounded so deep and honest. She remembered how he'd handled himself in the bar. It irked her that she was still impressed. Impressed with a liar.

"You ready to run again?" he asked, as if thinking they'd found some kind of a truce. There was no truce. Not until she knew what he was up to. She recalled her conversation with Jenny. Who the hell was Chase secretly meeting with late at night at the Shadow Falls fence?

"Come on a short run," he prodded.

"I'm done running." What was it with this guy and racing? Was he training for the Olympics?

She darted around him, walking in the direction of Shadow Falls.

"Come on. It's good for you," he said, falling beside her again.

"The truth is good for me." She felt him, too close. As if they were old friends.

They walked in silence. The night seemed extra quiet. Only the sound of their footfalls on the soft earth and dead leaves filled the night.

They were almost to the gate when he spoke. "My father was a doctor. He owned a small plane. We were all in it. It went down."

She looked at him. Nothing about his expression said he lied. Quite the opposite. Grief touched his eyes.

"I was the only one to survive. But I was hurt pretty badly. The guy who found me was vampire. I was a carrier of the virus and when he helped me, I turned."

"So he took you in?"

"Yeah."

"Was he rogue?" She couldn't help but try to see his angle for being at Shadow Falls. Was he helping some rogue organization or gang who wanted to shut down the school because of its affiliation with the FRU?

This wouldn't be the first time.

"Depends on what you call rogue. He's a decent guy but not registered."

Of all the things he could have said, this was the one she could relate to the most. Wasn't this the very reason she'd kept information about Chan from Burnett? Why she wasn't mentioning her uncle or aunt?

"So why come to Shadow Falls?" she asked.

"I heard about it. Thought it'd be interesting." His pupil in his left eye dilated slightly.

So he was here for a reason, but what? She almost called him on the lie, but now that she had a better handle on detecting his untruths, maybe it was wise to see what she could learn. Let the guy lie himself into a corner he couldn't get out of.

Looking up, she saw the Shadow Falls fence ahead. She pulled out her phone to dial Burnett. She had missed two calls. But no voice messages.

She checked the numbers. One was unfamiliar for a second, but then she recognized it. Kevin, Chan's friend. The grief that had been pocketed away slipped out.

What did Kevin want with her? *Paybacks can be hell.* She did owe him a favor.

The second number flashed across the screen and she felt her heartstrings being yanked in another direction. Steve.

She tucked all those emotions away to deal with later and started to dial Burnett. But her phone rang first. Burnett's number lit up her cell screen.

"We're back. At the fence on the north side," she said in lieu of hello.

"Is everything okay?" The camp leader's tone came off short. Tense.

"Fine."

"Come to the office. Now," he insisted.

Oh, hell, Della thought. Sounded like some more shit had hit the fan.

"We'll be right there."

"No," Burnett clipped out. "Alone. I just want to see you right now. I'll contact Chase when I need him." The camp leader hung up.

Obviously listening, Chase's brow instantly creased with worry, and she didn't know who was in trouble. Her or the panty perv.

Chapter Twenty-six

Burnett stood silently on the office porch, waiting for her to arrive. When she landed right in front of the steps, he stood there, nose in the air and head slightly tilted as if checking to make sure they didn't have company.

When his gaze landed on her and he didn't scowl in the way he usually did when her butt was in trouble—which happened to be a look she was accustomed to seeing—she suspected the person on the camp leader's shit list was Chase and not her.

"How did things go?" he finally asked after leading her back into his office and motioning for her to sit down. As she followed his instructions, he dropped into the chair behind his huge mahogany desk. Somehow he still managed to make the desk look small.

She started spilling the details of the night, and he held up his hand. "I know what happened. I had another agent there and they've already reported back."

She frowned. "You didn't trust—"

Burnett dropped his palms on his desk with a thump. "Don't even go there. This isn't about trust. Generally speaking there is always a backup agent working any case with younger unpolished agents."

She resented the "unpolished" remark, but kept her mouth shut.

"What I need to know is how things went between you and Chase. Do you still mistrust him?"

"I . . ." She remembered Chase giving the guy hell for calling her a whore. She met Burnett's gaze. "Why?"

"Just answer me, please."

She had to stop for another second to know the answer. "Yes. I'm still leery. But probably not as much as before."

"And you still won't tell me why you have misgivings for this guy?"

Della chewed on that question for another second. She couldn't tell Burnett what Jenny had seen, but . . . "I recognized his scent when I first met him. I don't know from where. But it almost feels as if it has a negative vibe attached to it."

"And you chose not to tell me this earlier?" Burnett's brows pinched.

"I wanted to make sure I was right." She stood a little squarer, prepared for him to get miffed.

"And have you?"

She hesitated, something Burnett didn't like.

"Della, do you trust him or not?"

"Not completely, but I can't actually recall meeting him."

"Have you confronted him?"

"I have, and he tells me I'm wrong."

"But you still don't believe him." Burnett leaned against his desk, concern continuing to tighten his expression. "Did you not listen—?"

"The heart lies sometimes. Wasn't it you who told me that?" It suddenly occurred to her that Burnett had to suspect that Chase could lie, or he'd have him in here interrogating him instead of Della. Frankly, she wanted to find out how one went about training to do that, too. It could be quite useful while working for the FRU.

Burnett folded his hands together on the desk. "At any point during this operation did you fear for your safety? Or think Chase would hurt you? Or betray you?"

Della considered it, and all she could recall was how angry he'd gotten when the creep had taken liberties and touched her. "No."

"But you still don't trust him."

"Not wholeheartedly." She told the truth and then countered. "And neither do you. What's changed?"

"I didn't—"

"You trusted him this morning and now . . . not so much."

Burnett unfolded his hands. "Right before you called, some of the information he gave me came back . . . iffy."

So she and Burnett shared the same concern. "He told me his parents were killed in a plane wreck. He was turned then, at fourteen years old, when a vampire found him."

"I've confirmed his parents died in a plane crash," Burnett said.

Della couldn't help but imagine how hard it must have been on a young Chase, losing his family and being turned in the same day. Not that this actually meant she could trust him. Bad things happened to people and sometimes that was what twisted them into being bad.

"Then what's iffy?" she asked Burnett.

"Where he lived. Basic stuff."

"He said California," Della said, and then asked, "What other basic stuff?" She recalled Chase telling her the man who rescued her wasn't registered. If that was what he was hiding, she sure as hell couldn't blame him.

"I'm looking into it," Burnett said, and that was the camp leader's way of saying *back off*. Della hesitated to say anything more, but then . . . "You know there could be reasons he's keeping things from you. Reasons that don't necessarily mean he's bad."

God knew she kept some things to herself. Most of them painful things.

Burnett's brow pinched tighter. "True, but I need to make sure those secrets aren't anything that would cause the school or the FRU harm. And unfortunately I've also learned that when people hide things, it's usually not good." He leaned in. "Do you trust him or not? Why am I getting mixed feelings from you?"

You like me. You just don't realize it yet. Chase's words played in her head and she even saw his sexy smile. "I . . . don't know. I mean, I don't trust him like I would someone else from here, Lucas or Derek, or . . . Steve, but I . . . don't think he's all bad either." The truth tasted funny on her tongue.

"Fine." Burnett slapped his hands on the desk. "Meanwhile, let me know if you learn anything new?"

Feeling the meeting was over, she stood up.

"Any news on Chan's autopsy?"

"Not yet. Sorry."

She nodded, feeling the frustration of that issue still heavy on her heart, and then she walked away. Only a few feet out the door, she heard the stoic vampire say, "Good job tonight, Della. Between Craig Anthony's arrest and now this, I'm proud of you."

She didn't look back, but whispered, "Thanks." A sense of pride swelled up inside her, and she latched on to the feeling with a hungry heart. She would need any good emotion to counter the negative crap on her plate right now.

As she walked out, her phone dinged with a text. For some reason she suspected it was Steve. The negative crap had arrived.

Della's walk back to her cabin seemed too quiet, and thoughts of Steve became second to the eeriness of the night. She pulled out her phone and checked the text. She'd been wrong. The last ding hadn't been a text from Steve. It was from Kevin, Chan's friend.

Call me.

She hit a few buttons to return his call. It went to voicemail. "What's up? It's Della." She hung up, and right then a cold chill sent goose bumps chasing more goose bumps up her spine.

A few clouds kept passing over the moon and ridding the path of any silver glow. She didn't know which was creepier, the silver glow, the smothering blackness, or the cold silence.

All of a sudden, she didn't feel alone. She lifted her face to catch a scent, only to remember her nose wasn't working properly. She cut her eyes left and right. A pair of yellow possum eyes stared back. It wasn't a possum she felt.

She remembered Chan's ghost. Her heart grew instantly heavy. Was he here? She thought he'd passed on, but maybe she'd thought wrong.

"Chan, is that you?" The cold wind seemed to suck the question into the night's darkness.

The clouds shifted again, offering her enough glow to see the path. She heard the slightest rustle in the air and looked up, half expecting to see feathers. But only an orange leaf rained down. A dead leaf.

Had Chan shifted from feathers to leaves? Or was she simply over-reacting? "If you're here, I want you to know that I'm sorry. I didn't mean to ignore you."

The moon slipped away again. Out of the blackness came a sound. Footsteps trailing behind her. Chan?

Did a ghost's steps make sound? A current of fear ran through her. She fought the need to run. But she reminded herself it was Chan. Even dead, he was her cousin. A cousin she'd let down.

She turned. Her heart jolted when she saw the figure behind her. Because she was unable to smell who it could be, panic had her fangs extending.

"It's just me," a soft voice said. A soft, recognizable voice.

"Damn it, Jenny. Never sneak up on a vampire. I could have attacked."

"I'm sorry," Jenny said, not coming any closer. "I didn't mean to . . ." She glanced around nervously. ". . . intrude. Is there a ghost here?"

"Do you feel one?" Della asked, her voice almost resonating the same shaky tremble as Jenny's.

"No, I don't feel ghosts." Jenny stayed where she was. "But you were talking to . . . your cousin. The one that died. Do you feel ghosts?"

"No . . . not really." She wasn't even sure that was a lie. She'd seen Chan, but she wasn't so sure she'd felt him. At least not in the way Kylie felt ghosts.

"So, no one's here? You're sure?" Jenny asked.

"No one is here." And Della wanted to believe it.

"Good." Jenny caught up with her. "Has Derek called you?"

"Was he supposed to?" Della continued walking, and while she hated admitting it, she felt better not being alone.

"He got the yearbook with your uncle in it. He found both of your aunts, your uncle, and your dad in there."

Something akin to hope filled Della's chest. She might find herself with a real family after all. She pulled out her phone to call Derek.

"He's at your cabin now. With Kylie. Just Kylie," Jenny muttered. "I saw Miranda leaving with Perry." Her tone sounded accusing.

Della, eager to see the book, tucked her phone back in her pocket and started moving a little faster. She got several feet before she realized that Jenny had stayed behind.

Della glanced over her shoulder. "Come on."

"Nah," Jenny said, and scuffed her tennis shoe in the dirt.

Della knew what was going on in Jenny's mind, and sighed. Della pushed aside her own urgency. "Look, Jenny. Nothing's happening between Kylie and Derek."

"You don't know that for sure."

"The hell I don't. Kylie's so in love with Lucas, she wouldn't touch Derek with a ten-foot pole. And as for Derek, Kylie is last year's news. Look, a vampire can smell pheromones, and he's not stinking up any air when he's around her." At least he hadn't been when her nose had been working. "On the other hand, when he's around you, I can hardly breathe, he pollutes the air so much."

"But he admires Kylie."

"So? She's a protector. I admire her, and I'm not fooling around with her."

Jenny made a face. "How can I compete with Kylie? She's so great."

"That's my whole damn point. You aren't competing." Della got an idea. "You aren't going to believe it until you see it, are you?"

"See what?"

"See them. See them not doing anything. Let me prove it to you. Turn both of us invisible and let's go to the cabin."

"I . . . I don't think that's a good idea."

"Why not? You'd finally know the truth. Maybe then you'd get past this thing."

Jenny frowned. "But . . . but I don't know if I can turn you invisible. I'm not nearly as advanced as Kylie. And . . . Burnett told me that I wasn't to ever eavesdrop."

"Yeah, but you're not eavesdropping, you're proving something. There's a difference."

"Burnett made the rule very clear."

"Sometimes the rules have to be broken. Besides, aren't you breaking the rules running around invisible?"

"Yeah, but—"

"And how do you know you can't turn me invisible if you don't try?" Della saw temptation in the chameleon's eyes. The girl did have gumption. Maybe that's why Della liked her. "Come on. Give it a shot." She caught ahold of Jenny's hand. "Do it."

"This is cool, yet so fracking weird," Della said. She could feel herself but not see herself. She couldn't see Jenny either. They stood on her porch looking into the window and listening to Kylie and Derek talk about his mom.

"Shh," Jenny said, holding her hand extra tight.

Kylie offered Derek a drink and they sat down at the table. "Do you want me to call Burnett and find out how late Della will be?"

"Nah, I'll wait a few more minutes and then I'll leave the book. We can talk tomorrow. I know she'll want to see this, but unfortunately it really doesn't tell us much right now. But hopefully it will give us more leads."

Kylie nodded. "So how are things with you and Jenny?"

Jenny's grip tightened.

Della worried this whole thing might backfire on her. Not that Kylie and Derek still had a thing for each other, but if he said something about Jenny she shouldn't hear . . . Oh, shit. Maybe Burnett's rule was right.

"Slow." Derek sounded disappointed.

"Have you talked to her?" Kylie asked. "Told her how you feel?"

Della relaxed a bit.

"Sort of," Derek said. "I kissed her."

"Kissing her isn't talking to her. If you really like her, speak up."

"And if she says she's not interested, she'll pull back. I don't want to scare her off."

"I think the only one scared is you," Kylie said. "To quote Della on this one, 'For God's sake, grow a pair.'"

"She quotes me." Della giggled.

"Shh," Jenny said.

"What am I supposed to say to her?" Derek asked.

"I don't know. Why don't you start by telling her how you feel?" Kylie paused. "How *do* you feel about her?"

"I like her, *really* like her. I can feel her emotions clearer than anyone. I mean, even right now I feel her somewhere out there, feeling unsure of something."

"Stop feeling," Della whispered.

"I can't," Jenny snapped back. "And they can't hear us when we're invisible, so you don't have to whisper."

"But I'm trying to listen," Della shot back.

Derek shook his head as if thinking. "She's caring and yet amazingly spunky. Even though she's new and everyone's always looking at her funny for being a chameleon, she handles it with courage and poise." He paused. "She's beautiful, but not like one of those girls who knows it. She's innocent, but at the same time she's eager to experience things. She's smart and sometimes a bit of a smartass." He grinned, then sighed. "I love how she looks at life. And I want to be there to . . . well, to share in those experiences, and of course to make sure she doesn't get hurt."

"That's so sweet," Jenny said, her tone sounding like Miranda when she talked about Perry sucking her earlobes.

Della wondered if the chameleon knew that some of the experiences Derek meant were probably X-rated. But then again, it didn't matter. Jenny was right. It was sweet.

Just because Della wasn't ready to bask in all the gooeyness of romance didn't mean she couldn't admit it had its good sides. Someday she might even get her life straightened out enough that she could enjoy some of it, too.

"He really likes me," Jenny said.

"Told you," Della said. "Now can I go talk to Derek and check out the book that cost me a month's allowance?"

At ten that night Della lay in bed flipping through the high-school yearbook. She stared at the faces of all the Tsangs, but especially those of her missing aunt and uncle. Before leaving, Derek had taken note of who her uncle and aunt had been seen with in photos and planned to contact them via Facebook to see if they had any more information.

"It's amazing how many PI and police cases are solved using social media," he'd said.

Della started feeling bad about depending on him and offered, "I could do that."

"If you want," he'd answered, "but you need to be sly how you ask, or it could backfire."

In the end, she'd agreed to let him handle it. Besides, it wasn't as if she didn't have enough to worry about.

Her phone dinged again, reminding her she'd gotten another text when she'd been talking to Derek. She'd glanced earlier. It was from Steve. She hadn't read it. Didn't want to read it. Didn't think she could read it without getting drowned in missing him, in getting super pissed at him for kissing Jessie, and even more pissed for allowing Jessie to call him. Three times!

Turning the page of the yearbook, she released a deep gulp of emotionally charged air. Nope. She wasn't ready to deal with Steve. Maybe in a couple of years. Groaning, she buried her head in her pillow for a few minutes before returning to flipping through the book.

In one picture of the debate club, she noted a familiar face. There were too many in the photo to list names, so she wasn't sure if it was her uncle or her dad. They had to be identical twins. She traced the face with her fingernail, wondering if she would feel the connection to her uncle she used to feel with her dad.

Or still felt. He'd been the one to give up on her, not the other way around.

She closed her eyes again, emotion tightening her throat.

Swallowing back the hurt, she heard someone walking in front of her cabin. Shit! What if it was Steve? She inhaled to see if she could catch a scent. Nope. Her nose still wasn't working.

Her heart did a tumble. She wasn't ready to face him.

Chapter Twenty-seven

Della concentrated on the cadence of the steps. Not Steve. Too light. The footsteps sounded like . . . The cabin door opened.

"Anyone home?"

"In here." Della headed to the door, remembering she still needed to apologize to the witch for getting pissy this afternoon about the whole bird-watching/aura issue.

"Hey," Miranda said, and she didn't even look upset.

Della considered letting the apology slide—she hated eating crow—but she owed it to the little witch. "I'm sorry about earlier, I was a bitch."

"Yeah, you were. But that's okay," Miranda said. "I told you, I'm overlooking your pissiness due to all the crap you've got going on. I figure you've got a week or two of me overlooking your attitude. Then I bring my pinkie out."

What attitude? Della bit back the words and forced herself to play nice. "I appreciate it, but I'm still sorry."

"I accept." She smiled. "Is Kylie here?"

"No, she and Lucas took a late-night stroll to suck face."

Miranda walked to the fridge and pulled out two sodas. Della dropped in her chair. The witch handed her a can and studied Della a little hard.

Della figured out what the witch was up to: aura inspection. "How is it?"

"Still dangerously dark." Looking concerned, Miranda opened her drink, but kept looking at Della as the fizzing sound filled the room. Finally she asked, "What happened with you and Steve?"

"Jessie kissed him." Della didn't like talking about it . . . again. But if the witch found out she'd told Kylie and not her, she'd get her nose out of joint. Or perhaps her pinkie out of joint. And that could be dangerous.

"So he's dumping you for her?"

"No," Della said. "We had an argument and I told him I couldn't deal with it." Then again, she hadn't read his text. He might be telling her he was in love with Jessie now. But even pissed, she didn't think that was the case.

"Did he apologize?" Miranda asked.

"Yes, but . . ."

"But you're still furious, right?"

Della slunk deeper into the chair. "Yeah, but it's not like we're going out."

"That's nonsense. You two were going out. You just didn't tell anyone you were going out."

Della wanted to deny it, but couldn't.

Miranda sipped her soda. "Do you believe Steve when he said Jessie kissed him? Or do you think he kissed her?"

"I believe him," Della said, "but that's not the point."

"The point is you're still hurt, right?"

Della exhaled. "Maybe. I guess. Yeah. Shit, it hurts."

Miranda nodded with empathy. They sat in comfortable silence for a moment, the way friends do, the witch twirling a strand of pink hair around her finger. Her eyes suddenly widened. "I have an idea, but you're going to think I'm crazy."

"Since I already think you're crazy, you might as well tell me."

"It worked for Perry when he got mad about me kissing Jacob."

Miranda paused as if for dramatic effect. "He kissed Mandy, we got in a big fight, then we both forgave each other."

Della shook her head, not quite following Miranda. "Are you saying you want me to kiss Perry?"

"No. Not Perry. But you need to go kiss some other guy so you can get over being mad at Steve."

Della rolled her eyes. "I know math isn't your subject, but hasn't anyone told you that two wrongs don't make a right?"

"It does if it fixes things. You really like Steve. I know you do. And he likes you. So go kiss someone else. Hey, how about that Chase guy? Just walk up to him and plant one on him hard and heavy, and then the score'll be even, and you'll be able to move past this. You and Steve can get back together, your aura will lighten up, and everyone will be happy. I mean, it's that or go bird watching, which would you prefer?"

Della couldn't help but laugh. "Sorry, I know you're just trying to help, but that is probably the worst piece of advice I've ever been given."

"Bird watching?"

"No! Kissing Chase!"

Della ignored Chase all morning. Or she tried to. As she walked to lunch, Miranda, Kylie, and Jenny all chatting as they went, Chase stepped beside her and caught her by the arm. "Give me a minute, please." He tugged her into the woods. "She'll be right back," he said to her friends.

Della might have yanked free, but all she could think about was how cold his touch felt. Did that mean she still had a fever? Damn, she hadn't noticed the headache lately, and she'd just assumed the virus was improving. Well, minus her missing sense of smell.

It hit her then. Like a drop of mental bird crap. Chan had died after getting sick. What if . . . ?

Oh, hell, what was she thinking? She had a cold, a tiny bug. Kevin had said Chan had gotten really sick. Della wasn't really sick. And she wasn't a dad-blasted hypochondriac.

Snapping out of that train of thought, she looked back at her group of friends, and Miranda shot her a big smile. Della shot a frown right back, knowing what the little witch was thinking. No friggin' way was Della going to plaster a big smooch on the panty perv. Not happening!

He kept pulling her, and for reasons she didn't quite understand she allowed him to. "What?" Della finally spouted out the moment they got in the mix of trees.

"Three things. One: What time are we meeting tonight?"

"I think Burnett said to meet at the office at eight. Next?"

He frowned. "Do you know why the big bad camp leader suddenly lost trust in me?"

"Next?" Della said, not wanting to talk about Burnett's lack of confidence in Chase. Or her lack of distrust. She still hadn't gotten her head around the fact that she'd practically defended him to Burnett.

"He had me meet him at his office last night and interrogated me for over an hour."

"Well, get used to it. He does that to everyone," she said.

"I don't think so. Did he say anything to you about not trusting me?"

For one second she almost told him. Told him Burnett had figured out he'd lied about a few things. She opened her mouth, then thought better of it, and slammed it shut.

Chase's bright eyes tightened. "So something is up?"

"You'll have to ask Burnett. And you should."

"Should what?" he asked.

"Talk to him. He's not . . . I know he comes across like a hardass, but at least sixty percent of the time he's fair."

"So you confide in him about everything?" he asked, sounding almost suspicious.

Not about my uncle. "Almost." Right then the sound of the falls echoed in her ears. "Do you hear that?" she asked.

"Hear what?"

Regretting asking him, she snapped: "Nothing." She started tapping her foot against the cold dirt. "Is there something else? What else do you want?"

"Dangerous question," he said, in a sexy voice full of tease.

She crossed her arms and glared at him. "My friends are waiting on me."

He pulled out his phone. "What's your number?" When she didn't start spitting it out, he said, "So next time I have a question I can just call, and won't have to interrupt your little Chase-doesn't-exist game."

"I wasn't—"

"You've been ignoring me all day. You've worked hard at it."

She stomped her foot a little firmer and felt childish for her game, or rather, she felt childish being caught at it. But what choice did she have? Since he'd expressed an interest in her, the last thing she wanted to do was encourage him.

"Your number?" Impatience rang in his tone as he looked up from his phone. And damn if he didn't look hurt.

And damn if she didn't feel a little bad. Then the fact that she cared what he felt sent a wave of panic through her.

"Just give me your number," he said.

Deciding that getting a call from him would be better than being pulled off in the woods by him, she gave it to him.

"Thank you," he said. "I'll call you later so you'll have mine."

I don't need yours, she almost said, but bit it back. They were working together, so she might need his number. She just wished she really had his number, as in knowing for sure what he was up to. Or knowing if he was up to something.

Before she could turn to leave, he reached out and brushed a strand of hair from her cheek.

She slapped his hand.

He laughed, and then the humor left his expression. "How are you feeling?" He tucked his hand in his jeans pocket.

"Why?" she asked, wondering if he'd noticed her temperature.

He hesitated. "I mean dealing with your cousin's death," he said, sounding sincere.

"I'm okay." She softened her tone, wishing he would stop the nice crap. So she could stop the bitch crap. However, she wasn't sure how to project disinterest without ignoring him or giving him a 'tude. Not that her behavior was uncalled for.

She didn't trust him, but she was working with him and she'd practically defended him to Burnett.

She didn't like him, but felt empathy for him losing his family the way he did.

She knew he was keeping things from her and Burnett, but wasn't she keeping things from Burnett, too?

Where the heck had she picked up his scent? Why would he lie about it? What if she was wrong about him lying? Was it possible that she'd gotten his scent but he hadn't picked up on hers?

It was possible.

And you're impressed with his abilities, a little voice in her head said. She tuned the voice out, accepting that her feelings about this guy were black and white, yin and then yang. Problem was the black was quickly fading to gray and yin was shifting more to yang.

Not that there was anything romantic going on. *Hey, how about that Chase guy? Just walk up to him and plant one on him hard and heavy.*

Hard and heavy. Her gaze shifted to his lips, and she wondered what it would be like to . . . Holy hell! Why was she thinking about that?

"I gotta go," she said, realizing they were just standing there staring at each other's mouths like in some stupid movie. She only got a few feet away when she heard, "See you tonight." Anticipation sounded in his deep voice and she got a distinct feeling it wasn't just about the case.

The words "it's not happening" rested on the tip of her tongue, but she'd already told him that. She'd told herself that, too, but for safety's sake, she repeated it in her head. Then she took off.

She got out of the woods, and all three girls were waiting in an aura of curiosity. Miranda, being Miranda, dropped the question first. "Did you do it?"

Scowling at the witch, she muttered, "Hell, no."

"Told you she wouldn't do it," Kylie said.

Della glanced at Kylie. "So she told you guys the advice she gave me? Where does she get this shit?"

"I think it's a great idea," Miranda said.

"I see why it could work," Jenny added her two cents to the subject, "but it could also be dangerous. What if she likes kissing Chase? What would that mean for her and Steve?"

"I wouldn't," Della said. "Because . . . I just wouldn't." She glanced from Jenny to Kylie and hoped both the chameleons didn't have their vampire powers on and didn't hear her heart skip a beat.

"I don't know. He's hot." Kylie's grin said she was teasing.

Too bad Della wasn't in a teasing mood. "Then you kiss him. Go on. Lay one on him!" She waved back to the woods.

"Nope, I got the man I want." Kylie gave Jenny a quick glance.

"Hey," Miranda chimed in. "All I'm saying is that it worked for Perry and me. And you should at least give it a shot."

Della rolled her eyes. "I'll do that just as soon as hell opens up a free Popsicle stand. Now stop talking about me kissing Chase. It's making me think crazy thoughts."

"What kind of thoughts," Miranda asked with an arched eyebrow, then wiggled her shoulders like a dog wagging its tail.

Della growled right as her phone rang. She suspected it was Chase, leaving his number. She pulled her phone out to check.

She was wrong.

"Who is it?" asked Miranda.

"No one," Della snapped, wishing the witch would stop being so damn nosy.

"So, Steve, huh?" Miranda said.

Della growled again and started walking faster, wanting to outrun thoughts of Steve, Chase, and her prying friends.

But when her phone dinged with a voicemail, she knew sooner or later she was going to have to deal with Steve. But how?

It's amazing how many PI and police cases are solved using social media. Derek's words started sounding in her head during English, her last class. Yeah, maybe it was an avoidance tactic, to not think about all her other crap, but it worked in her favor. Because the idea just plopped into her brain, and it felt like a good one.

Facebook, here I come.

She might not know how to handle the old schoolmates of her dad and his siblings, but she knew how to handle teen girls. And maybe, just maybe, something they might say could give her a lead on Lorraine's murder. Yeah, it was a long shot. Vampire killings were a different animal from your normal everyday murder. But how could it hurt to try?

How?

Easy. She found out all too quickly.

The more she learned about Lorraine, the more it hurt. The more she realized what a waste it was that someone so decent, with so much life, had been yanked from this world.

Della had started searching for any info on Facebook and Twitter, even hit a few local online papers. She learned Lorraine had attended a New York dance school back in the summer. She even ran across several tweets with images of Lorraine's new puppy. One of those smooshed-nosed dogs with big ears that was so ugly only a mother would love it.

Or love it until the dang puppy got turned into vampire, a cynical voice whispered in her head.

Chasing that thought from her mind, Della friended about six people who claimed to know Lorraine. Thankfully, most people will friend anyone, so that worked in Della's favor. Within a couple of hours, Della was Facebook friends with four of Lorraine's school buddies, too.

Della messaged them, saying she'd met Lorraine in New York last year and had just heard she'd died. There was a chance one of these people went to New York with Lorraine, and her cover would be blown. But that didn't seem to be the case.

Three of the girls replied back over the next hour, and Della was messaging all three separately. She had three accounts of what happened to Lorraine right before the murder. Della also knew everything from Lorraine's favorite color to the argument she'd had with her mom the night she died.

Lots of info, but nothing that helped with the case.

"What are you doing?" Kylie asked, walking into the cabin.

"Research on the case."

"That couple?"

"Yeah," Della said, and wondered why her curiosity didn't extend so much for Lorraine's boyfriend. Maybe, just being a girl, she related more with her.

"You going to dinner?" Kylie asked.

"Nah, I have some blood here."

"Okay, but if you get lonely come on down. Some of us are going to light a campfire by the lake and roast marshmallows."

"Sorry. I'm working the case again tonight."

Concern flashed in Kylie's light blue eyes. "I wish Burnett would let me go to have your back."

Della shook her head. "You're a protector, not an agent."

"I thought we did pretty good at the funeral home." Kylie started out.

"We did." Della smiled and waved good-bye, then refocused on the screen.

Lindsey, one of the girls, finally wrote something interesting. *When I first heard about the accident, I swear, I suspected Phillip did it. You know, ran them off the road or something.*

Not unless he's vampire, Della thought, and she recalled someone at the funeral talking about Phillip being Lorraine's old boyfriend. Della typed back. *Yeah, I heard they broke up. But he wasn't that bad, was he?*

Lindsey replied. *Not at first he wasn't, but once he got in that band, he got effed up. I don't know if it was drugs or what?*

Hmm, so Phillip played in a band? And got effed up. Getting turned vampire could really eff someone up. Della's fingers hovered over the keyboard, typing one friend and then the next. *What was Phillip's last name? I forgot,* she asked Lindsey and the other two.

Lance, Lindsey replied, being the most eager to answer questions.

Oh, yeah, now I remember, Della typed. *Did you ever hear him play in his band? What was the name of that band?* She messaged the same question to two of the girls, thinking it would be a place to start researching him.

Lindsey came back again. *They kept changing it, but the last name before the group broke up was the Crimson Blood.*

Crimson Blood? The name of the gang Chan was involved in. Chills ran down Della's back. Could that just be a coincidence? Della recalled Burnett saying he didn't believe in coincidences.

But how could she get to the bottom of this one? Her fingers suddenly itched from the need for more information. *I never understood why Lorraine loved him so much. I think I saw a picture of Phillip once. He wasn't even good-looking. Didn't he have red hair?*

No one answered for a few minutes. Finally, Lindsey came through again.

No, brown. Kind of hot. Had a tattoo of a skull on his neck.

Shit! Glancing up, she saw the time. She didn't have time to get to the bottom of anything. She had to go meet Chase at the office. She considered telling Burnett what she'd learned but decided against it. She could hear Burnett scolding her that she wasn't keeping her emotional distance from the case and reminding her how unlikely it was that a vampire killing had any direct ties to the life of the victim. But not if the victim had an ex who was a vampire.

Gotta go, Della wrote all three girls, and then headed out. She decided to Google-search the Crimson Blood band when she got back in. And then she realized, Kevin, Chan's friend—the one who'd led her to his body—knew some of the Crimson Blood gang. She had to talk to Kevin. Maybe he could tell her if there was a Phillip Lance in the gang.

Long shot, her gut echoed back. But long or not, it was a shot, and she'd be damned if she wasn't going to take it.

The boisterous voices seeping out of the bar stopped when she and Chase landed. Della spotted a couple, limbs wrapped around each other, behind a group of trees. Two lovers? Or was it one of the girls selling her body? The idea knotted Della's stomach.

"The gang's here," Chase said in a low whisper.

She nodded.

"Stay close," he said.

She made a face and they continued toward the door. The room seemed darker, as if the crowd of vampires had sucked the light out of the room. *All the dark auras,* Della thought, and inhaled, trying to see if her sense of smell had returned. Nope.

"Over there," Chase said, pointing to an empty table.

Della felt all twenty pairs of eyes on her. Jeepers, if things went wrong, she and Chase would be pushing up daisies. A chill moved under her sweater, telling her that her temperature still wasn't right. But now wasn't the time to worry about that.

The bartender, the same one from the night before, came strolling over. "What's your liking tonight? I got some B positive. It goes down good with a splash of Jack."

"We'll take the blood straight up," Della said, not wanting alcohol involved. They were going to need all their wits about them tonight.

The bartender nodded and walked off. She took a glance around the room and discovered not all the patrons were vampires. She picked out a few werewolves and warlocks sitting among them. So, not everyone here was part of the gang. When Della came to one table of four, she recognized three of them.

Agents from the FRU—one of them the female agent who'd come to help clean up the kangaroo mess. And that was just the three she recognized. Who knew how many of the other patrons were agents?

Della didn't know whether to be relieved that they weren't alone, or offended that Burnett thought they might need help. But after another quick glance at the undesirable characters here, she decided Burnett might have been right to send them.

"You okay?" Chase asked.

"Dandy," she answered.

A couple of glasses of blood landed on their table. The server was a young female vamp. She gave Chase a good look up and down, and the swipe of her tongue over her lips said she liked what she saw. Panty perv smiled at her, and Della had no doubt that under different circumstances he and server would have ended up bumping uglies. Then again, Chase didn't look like the type who had to pay for it, and Della would bet the girl's services didn't come free.

"I think she likes you," Della said, when the girl walked away.

He looked up at Della, beneath his dark lashes. "She's not my type."

"You have a type?" she asked, and holy shit if she didn't wish she could swallow the words back into her mouth.

"I like a challenge. Or so it seems lately." The corners of his eyes crinkled ever so slightly with a smile, leaving no doubt of what he meant. "Dark hair is nice, too. Someone who speaks her mind. I don't even mind someone a bit stubborn. A good argument every now and then just gets the blood flowing. And making up is fun."

Damn, she'd started this, but how could she squash it? "Well, there's a lot of girls out there like that."

"I'm not so sure," he said, and arched one brow. "You got a type?" He turned his glass in his hands.

"No." She looked down at her blood.

"Liar," he said.

She lifted her gaze. "Stop acting as if you know me, you don't."

He shrugged. "You like dark hair. Someone strong enough to stand up to you, but not too headstrong. Tall, a little muscular. The good-looking type."

"You really have an ego the size of Texas, don't you."

He smiled. "I was describing Steve. But thank you."

She growled.

His grin didn't waver. "I might be a little too headstrong for you."

"You got that right."

"But you could probably convince me to work on it."

She rolled her eyes. Another couple of bar customers walked through the door. Chase causally looked around, and she saw his shoulders stiffen ever so slightly. Then he started a conversation about some of the places he'd visited. Paris, Germany, China. Della knew he was just making conversation so they wouldn't stand out. Knew he suspected someone was eavesdropping.

She still listened with interest, and forgot to study his face to see if he was lying.

"What part of China?" she asked, her gaze now on his left eye.

"Shanghai, Beijing, Wuhan," he said, and it didn't sound like a lie.

"You've obviously been, right?"

"A couple of times."

Chase glanced slightly to the right as if telling her something. Only then did she hear the footsteps.

A guy—a big guy, about twenty-one, shaved head, tattooed up, with enough piercings that a refrigerator magnet could take him out—came to a stop at their table.

"I hear you're asking questions about one of mine?" The guy posed his question to Della. From his words, she supposed he was the leader of the gang. She couldn't help but wonder if the one with the most piercings got to be the leader. She counted eight pieces of metal just on his face.

"Yes," Della said, trying not to stare at the ring that dangled off his nose. Man, wouldn't that be a hazard when fighting? "I heard you had a fresh turn recently join. I'm looking for a guy with short dark hair."

"And just why are you looking for him?" he asked, his tone abrupt.

Time to lie or skip around the truth. "Actually, I had a brief encounter with him." That was true. He'd flown over her at a low range.

"But you don't have a name? Isn't that kind of strange?"

"Not really all that strange," Chase, with his lying abilities, spoke up. "She met him right after he turned, and you know how overwrought a vamp can be during that first forty-eight hours. Anyway, she never got his name. Crazy, right?"

Mr. Piercing didn't look convinced. "I thought she was your girl. I heard you nearly choked a guy to death for touching her."

Chase shrugged. "Well, let's just say I'm trying to convince her to be my girl. She thinks she might have something with this other guy. Chance meeting and all that—one night with someone doesn't mean crap. I don't care how good he was in the sack."

Say what? Had Chase just basically called her a ho? He might as well have when he'd said she'd had a one-night stand and done the hump-and-bump with a crazed stranger. He couldn't think of a better cover story than that?

"And," Chase continued, still eyeing the vamp, "I think as soon as she sees him, she'll realize I'm the better choice."

The pierced gang leader stared at Chase. "Maybe you're interested in joining up with us?"

"I'm not much of a joiner," Della put her two cents in.

The gang leader looked at Della. "Actually, we're more interested in your friend here. But if you're willing to put out that easy, you might convince me."

She growled.

"Hey," Chase intervened; sounding a little perturbed, but how could he? He'd started this.

"She hasn't given it up to me," Chase said. "That's why I'm sort of curious to meet this guy and see what he has that I don't."

The gang leader seemed to buy it. Della didn't know whether to be happy or pissed off. "Well, I'm curious to see what kind of muscle you got. See if you're as strong and quick as rumor has it."

Chase leaned back in his chair. "Tell you what. You hook us up with a meeting with your new kid on the block, and you and I'll go for a little innocent one-on-one in the alley."

"How about we do that right now?" The pierced vamp extended his fangs, and Della sensed that his idea of a one-on-one sparring match wasn't all that innocent.

Oh, double damn! This wasn't going to end well.

Chapter Twenty-eight

Della cut her eyes to the table of agents. At least they wouldn't be alone.

"Nah," Chase said, keeping his cool, but his eyes grew brighter. "I like my idea better."

"And I don't." The gang leader glared at Chase. "What does it take to get you in a fighting mood? Touching your little slut here?"

"No," Della snapped, not fond of being called a slut or being used as bait, but more furious at being seen as someone who couldn't fight her own battles. "That would put *me* in a fighting mood. Then you'd be embarrassed at having your ass whooped by a girl." She let her fangs down and glared at the hand he held out.

"No trouble, Luis!" the bartender called out. "That's our deal. You still haven't paid for the last tussle your guys started in here."

The jerk shot the bartender a third-finger salute, then focused back on Chase. "I see why you like this chick. Spunk and not a bad looker either."

"Do we have a deal or not?" Chase seethed, no longer playing nice. "Bring the guy in for a chat and we'll take it outside so the bartender won't have an issue."

"We'll see," he said. "I'll make a few calls and see if my new member is interested in coming to see a lost love." Luis, obviously that was his name, looked back at Della. "But you know, considering he was freshly turned, there's a good chance he won't even remember you. Now wouldn't that just break your little heart?"

"I'm hoping that's not the case." Della tried to keep the venom from her voice.

Three minutes after he left, Chase went back to talking about traveling. He stopped when Della's phone dinged with a new text. She looked at it, hoping it wasn't from Steve again. It wasn't.

Get out of the bar! Now! Burnett wrote.

She passed her phone to Chase.

He didn't look happy, but when she got up, he followed. From the corner of her eye, she saw the agents watching. What the hell was going on?

"What about our plans?" called Luis from the bar.

"We'll be right back," Chase said. "Just going to drain the lizard."

"Is she gonna hold it for you?" someone in the crowd asked. Laughter exploded.

Della sent the crowd her own third-finger salute.

They walked out into the dark night. Chase darted around the back of the building to the edge of the woods. He raised his nose in the air, checking for any nearby company.

He must have found it clear, because he asked, "What the hell is this all about?"

"Don't know," Della said. "But Burnett always has his reasons."

"He can't send us in to do a job and then pull us!"

"He just did," she said. "And—"

Chase pressed two fingers over her lips and nodded to the woods, pulling her closer to the building, away from the moon's glow.

Della tried to catch a scent, but couldn't. But when she tuned her hearing, she heard voices. Close voices. And they were coming from two different directions. There was no place to hide. They could run, but it might be too late.

She saw a group of four guys walking from the line of trees on her left. Another two came from the right. They had their faces held up, as if they'd already picked up on their scents. Yup, it was too late. And if they were with the gang, it could mean trouble. Della's only idea was to look inconspicuous. And the only way to make it appear believable was to . . .

She swung around, wrapped her arms around Chase, and kissed him. Hard and heavy. His lips felt cold, but soft and moist. He tasted like mint, as if he'd only recently brushed his teeth. And something about that taste had her almost forgetting why she started this.

If there was any hesitation on his part, it lasted a fraction of a second. His arms wrapped around her, the palm of his hands landing at the curves of her waist, then slipping to her back. In his embrace, and somehow entranced, he turned her so his back would be facing the oncoming vamps.

Della heard laughter and one of the guys said, "Those whores are always busy."

Fury filled her heart but quickly faded as sweet hot desire spread to her belly. She realized her hands were on his chest; the feel of his hard body had her heart picking up pace. Chase's hands glided up and down her ribs, softly caressing the sides of her breasts. Then his thumb brushed across her taut nipple. She almost moaned. And she was certain she heard a soft murmur from deep in his chest.

It was all an act, she told herself, but her body responded to his touch and to every delicious inch of his firmness so close to hers.

Stop it. Stop it! she told herself, and tried to fight the passion swelling inside her.

With what little brain cells she owned that weren't drunk on the kiss, she listened to the footfalls as the group of vamps walked away. They were just past the building when Chase pulled back. His gaze met hers, and she saw the heat in his bright eyes. Bright from danger, or from their kiss, she didn't know. Then, breathless, he uttered, "Wow."

Okay, so it was probably the kiss.

Another voice sounded in the distance, and without a word he gripped her hand and lit out in a dead run. Pulling her beside him. She had no warning when his feet rose and he went into full flight, taking her with him.

Not that the soles of her boots missed the ground; she felt as if she'd been floating since his mouth had found hers. Finally the sense of danger built and the passion, as great as it had been, got swept away with the wind. And her first thought was how bad an idea that kiss had been.

They weren't past the first line of trees when she heard someone call out, "Where the hell did they go?" She recognized the gang leader's voice.

And he was too close.

Chase moved faster, still holding her hand. She tried to keep up, tried to pull her own weight, but she simply wasn't that fast. She heard the distinct sound of the vampires behind them.

Chase darted in and out of the trees as if to lose their scents. She still heard voices in the distance. The next thing she knew, Chase swung her around in his arms, holding her against him, and flew like the wind. The trees became a blur. She was no longer sure what was sky or terrain. Up, down, over this, under that, he moved faster than she'd known possible.

Her skin stung as they cut through the air. She had to bury her face in his chest to keep her eyes from burning.

She might not be able to pick up any traces, but this close, held against him, she could smell him again. The same spicy scent of male soap and the natural aroma of male skin that had surrounded her when they kissed was again filling her senses and messing with her head. Fresh. Clean. Wonderful. He had to have showered shortly before coming here.

She felt his face press down to her head. Was that his lips against her temple?

His words came against her ear. "I'm going to fly around to make sure they can't follow our scents back to Shadow Falls."

She didn't answer. Didn't think he expected her to.

A minute later, maybe two, or hell, maybe five minutes—she lost track of time—he landed. Her heart thumped in her chest, or was that his heart she felt? He held her off the ground and close. She opened her eyes and saw they were by a lake. No, not just any lake, but the lake at Shadow Falls.

He lifted his face in the air as if to see if they'd been followed. Only then did he look at her. His bright green eyes smiled. He looked happy with himself. He should be. Where the hell did he learn to fly like that?

"You okay?" he asked.

She nodded, having to swallow before she could speak. "Put me down."

He slowly lowered her, but before his hand left the curves of her waist, he drew her against him. His mouth met hers. Soft. Moist.

This time, he tasted different. Even better.

He tasted like danger. He tasted like something she'd never tasted before.

He tasted . . . forbidden.

Oh, hell! He was forbidden. Giving herself a swift and firm mental kick in the ass, she yanked away from him. Slapped both her palms on his chest and shoved him down. He landed on his ass.

"Stop that."

"You started it," he said, and smiled.

Smiled. How dare he smile when . . . ? She growled. "I only did it so they would think . . ."

"That we were about to get naked."

"So they wouldn't think . . ."

Plant one on that Chase guy. She heard Miranda's voice.

"I only did it because . . ." *Maybe because that freaking witch put it in my mind.* Had she put a curse on her? No, she wouldn't have done that, but it didn't matter, just planting the idea had caused havoc. Bad havoc. She didn't want to like Chase's kisses. Didn't want to want. . . . That was it, she was killing Miranda.

She swung around and took off. Chase followed her. His footsteps filled the night.

"Hey, we need to talk."

"No," she snapped, and followed the lake. But she was so confused she wasn't even sure which way it was to her cabin.

"Don't run away," he accused.

"I'm not running," she seethed. "I'm walking."

"Della?" Chase called out.

Walking away from you. She looked down at her feet to confirm it was true, and before she looked back up, she'd walked right into a solid chest. Damn him and his speed! Without thinking, blind with fury, she put her hands on his chest. She gave one big shove and knocked him on his ass again.

Then she heard it. Heard Chase's footsteps behind her. But if he was behind her . . . Whose ass was it she'd just bruised?

"Why the hell did you do that?" Burnett asked, getting to his feet, scowling at her with bright angry eyes.

Unable to talk, she just stared.

Then she swore the camp leader lifted his face to sniff the air. Friggin' frack! He probably smelled pheromones. And yes, she was probably putting out a few.

Damn it to hell and back, but she wanted to deny that she enjoyed the kiss. Wanted to claim it was just . . . the danger, the situation.

She couldn't deny it.

She'd enjoyed it.

"What the hell is wrong?" Burnett asked again.

"Nothing. . . . I didn't realize it was you."

"How could you not know?"

"Because . . ." She heard Chase step beside her. *I was just kissed senseless. Because my senses are on hiatus.* Taking a deep sobering breath, she shoved the kiss to the bottom of her mental problem tank and yanked up her big-girl panties to think about the case. "Because I'm pissed. Why did you pull us out?"

"As soon as the gang leader left your table, he called someone and told them to summon the whole gang there. They had plans to overtake you."

"How do you know this?" Chase asked, now standing so close she felt his hip next to hers.

"He had agents there," Della answered, staring at Burnett, not willing to look at Chase. Not yet. She needed just a few more seconds to put the kiss from her mind. Unfortunately, the damn memory buried its claws and hung on, refusing to be pushed aside. The way he'd felt. The way he'd smelt. The way his lips had . . .

"What?" Chase asked. "And neither of you felt I needed to know that?"

"I didn't know. I only knew when I saw them there," Della said, offering him a quick glance. Her gaze went to his mouth, still wet. She looked away.

"Why didn't you tell us?" Chase asked Burnett.

The camp leader didn't react to Chase's attitude. He answered calmly. "I never send new agents out alone if there's a chance it could be dangerous."

"I could have handled it," Chase said.

Della hated to agree with Chase, but after seeing how fast he could fly, and after seeing him handle the creep last night, she wasn't sure it was an exaggeration. Was there anything he couldn't handle? Fighting? Flying? Kissing?

"Maybe," Burnett said. "But it was a chance I wasn't willing to take. What matters is we got him. The fresh turn, a Billy Jennings, showed up seconds after you two left. The gang leader asked him about his rendezvous with Della." Burnett looked at her. "When he left with only a couple of other vampires, my agents followed, and I just got word that they were able to detain him. They're taking him to . . ."

Della stopped listening. *They got him!* Relief fell over her like a soft rain. *We got him, Lorraine.* Della wasn't sure why she felt like the girl could hear her thoughts—hell, she really hoped she couldn't—but she said it anyway. *We caught the creep who did that to you.*

"I'll need you two to come confirm it was his trace you got that night."

Shit! A slow burn of panic started to build in her gut. If her sense of smell was still on sabbatical, how was she going to know for sure if it was him? But if she told Burnett she'd accepted this mission without having all her senses in full operating order, he'd have her head on a chopping block.

If not her head, for sure her career.

Burnett opened a door and motioned for Della and Chase to walk inside a small room. Painted a dull gray, the room felt gloomy. Sad. One wall was made of glass, where you could see in another room. An empty room.

"They'll place the suspect in there in a few minutes," Burnett said. "You can see him, but he can't see you. And there are air vents so you two should be able to get his trace."

Should *be able to,* Della thought.

"I'll be right back." Burnett walked out. The sound of the door clicking shut played on one of her last nerves. Or maybe it was her last.

"You okay?" Chase asked, as if reading her every emotion.

She nodded and tried to stop what felt like chatter in her head. Inhaling, she tested the air, hoping her sense of smell was back. Nothing. She couldn't even pick up Chase.

A sound came from the other side of the glass. An agent, the female agent, led a boy into the room and pointed to the chair. Not just a boy, she reminded herself, but Billy Jennings, the suspect. Very possibly the person who'd viciously killed Lorraine and her boyfriend.

Della inhaled again, hoping to catch a scent. Still nothing. Her gut knotted.

She looked at Billy's face. She recalled trying to pick out a killer earlier, but not in a million years would she have picked him out. Sure, he had short dark hair, but he looked younger than her, and clean-cut enough to belong in a high-school band—a trumpet player, or maybe the clarinet.

He exuded innocence. His cheeks were even rosy like some portrait of a straight-A model kid. The kind of kid who'd never even tasted beer, much less blood.

She felt Chase staring at her and knew the question he was about to pose.

She'd already decided she wouldn't lie. She couldn't. She might not tell Burnett that her sense of smell was on the fritz, but she wouldn't condemn anyone without proof.

"What do you think?" he asked.

She looked back at Billy. He looked scared, really scared. She remembered how it felt a week out from being turned. Her life as she'd known it had been yanked from her. She hated herself, hated what she'd become.

Innocent. Innocent. Innocent. The word played over and over in her head.

In spite of being cold, the room suddenly felt stuffy, as if the gray walls were closing in on her. Blood rushed to her ears and she started getting dizzy. She had to get out of there.

She swung around, yanked open the door, and walked down the hall until she saw a door leading outside. She didn't breathe until she cleared it—until she stood in the parking lot, the moon and stars flickering down on her from above.

"Hey." Chase came up behind her. "Calm down." He put his

hands on her shoulders. His touch was cold, but comforting. She almost wanted to fall against him. Then she remembered their kiss. "It's going to be okay."

"No, it's not." She shook her head. "I can't . . . I can't do this. My . . . I don't know if that's him. I'm not that sure." Then it hit: She didn't have to be sure. She swung around and looked at Chase. "You got his trace, too. Is it him? Is he the one who killed that couple?"

He paused, then slowly nodded his head. "Yeah." But even in the darkness she noted his left brow twitched.

Della shook her head. "You're lying. You don't know for sure."

"I may not be a hundred percent sure, but I'm sure enough."

Innocent. Innocent. Innocent. The word started playing in her head again.

"No, if you aren't sure, then you can't put that on the kid."

"Della, stop and think." He took her by the shoulders. "Listen to me, okay?" Only when she looked up did he start talking. "I know it's hard to be sure, but he fits the description and MO of the person the FRU thinks did this. Before they condemn the kid, they'll get the DNA, so if we're wrong, he won't go down."

"He might not go down, but until it comes back, he's going to be accused of murder. And he'll think he did it, because he won't be able to remember." She felt emotion tighten in her chest as she recalled being brought to this very place and being tested to see if she'd killed someone when she'd been turned. Never had she felt more like a monster than that day.

Was that how Billy was feeling now?

"This isn't right," she said, trying to control the shakiness of her voice. "We can't accuse him if we're not certain he did it."

"What's not right is if they let him go and then find out he's guilty and he's gone. And he will be gone. Do you think if he walks out of here, he won't skip out? He will. He'd be nuts not to get the hell out of Dodge, guilty or otherwise. He won't want the FRU on his ass. The gang won't take him back now that the FRU are looking at him for something. It would bring the FRU down on their butts. And, statistically, when a fresh turn kills, the odds of them doing it again are twice as great as those who don't."

"You don't know that."

"I do. It's been proven. Trust me on this."

"How? Who has it been proven by? Why do you claim to know so damn much?"

"It doesn't matter." His jaw muscle clenched as if he'd said something he shouldn't have.

It did matter. Everything mattered. Lorraine and John mattered. Billy Jennings mattered.

Chase took her chin in his hand and forced her to look at him again. "Della, I really believe it was his trace. Trust me."

She shook her head. "But you're not a hundred percent sure."

"Is anyone a hundred percent sure?" He exhaled pure frustration. "Look, if he's innocent, all this will cost him is another day in jail. That might not be easy, but if he's guilty, it will cost someone their life. Do you want to be responsible for him killing again? Hasn't he hurt enough people?"

Della's mind went back to the vision of Lorraine and John, throats gaping open. Did she owe her loyalty to the dead, or to a scared kid who might not be guilty of anything other than being turned?

Innocent. Innocent. Innocent.

"I can't be sure," Della told Burnett ten minutes later. All three of them sat at a table back in the adjoining room. Della stared at the two of them, trying not to look at Billy.

Burnett didn't look happy. Neither did Chase. But why was he so upset?

Burnett leaned on his elbows and came forward on the table. "I thought you got his trace?"

"I thought I did, too. But something isn't right. I . . . I'm sorry, I can't be sure." She kept her eyes cut away from the two-way mirror.

"I know it's hard, Della," Burnett said, "but if this kid did this . . ."

Innocent. Innocent. Innocent. "Yes, it's hard, but that's the problem. I don't know if he did it. I can't . . . I'm not sure."

Burnett let go of a deep gulp of air and looked at Chase. "Please tell me you got something," he said.

Chase nodded. "It's him."

Della watched him blink. Unwillingly, she glanced at Billy. Billy had tears in his eyes, eyes that expressed self-loathing. Her breath expanded in her chest and she stood up. Stood up so fast, her chair hit the tile floor behind her.

Innocent. Innocent. Innocent.

"Chase isn't being completely truthful," she told Burnett. "He's not sure. You can't blame the kid for this." She personally knew how it felt to consider yourself a murderer. The pain, the shame could cripple you.

Burnett looked shocked. He glanced at Chase. "Is this true?"

"No," he said.

Della couldn't believe Chase's nerve, his gall. "Look at him, Chase!" she insisted, and pointed to the glass wall. "He's nothing but a kid. You're going to let him go through this when you're not sure?"

Chase didn't look at Della. He looked at Burnett. "The kid did it."

Chapter Twenty-nine

"Della!" Burnett called her back as she jumped out of his car and hotfooted toward her cabin when they returned from the FRU offices. She jogged through the gate and debated ignoring his call. But knowing Burnett, he'd come find her.

So she turned around and saw the camp leader wave Chase on his merry way. She hoped he went straight to hell, too. Or she did if Billy Jennings was innocent. *But what if he isn't?* It wasn't that she didn't consider the possibility. She did, but . . . everything inside her said he was innocent.

Everything. Including that stupid voice.

When Chase walked past her he said, "I'm sorry. I did what I thought was right."

Della scowled at him. He was lying. So how could it have been right?

Burnett walked up beside her and motioned her to walk to the office. Oh, hell, on top of being pissed, she was going to get read the riot act. She was in no mood.

She needed to be alone. Midnight had come and gone over an hour ago, and with every toss and turn her mind landed on one of her issues. She'd kissed the panty perv. And even worse, she'd enjoyed it. She was secretly worried she had the same virus that had killed her cousin. She'd discovered how inadequate she was as a vampire. And she'd assisted in ruining the life of a kid who very well could be innocent.

Holiday met them in the entrance of the office. From the look on her face, Burnett had already spoken to her and warned her of what went down.

"I know that was hard," Holiday said as she got Della positioned on her sofa. Holiday sat beside her, resting one hand on her ever-growing baby bulge. Burnett leaned against the office desk. He looked upset, but not nearly as upset as Della felt. *Or Billy,* she thought, only guessing what the kid was going through right now.

"What's hard is that he would take Chase's word over mine!" she said to Holiday, but glared at Burnett. "Even after he told me he knows Chase's not being honest."

"I didn't take his word over yours," Burnett said.

"You kept the kid."

"I kept him because he's a murder suspect."

"Wow, and here I thought you were innocent until proven guilty."

"I said *suspect,* not murderer. I haven't proven him guilty."

"You might as well have if you're locking him up. He knows you think he committed murder. And because he can't remember, he probably believes he did it, too. He's a fresh turn, he already thinks he's a monster and now you're confirming it for him."

Burnett shook his head. "What happened to the Della who came to me a few days ago? All you talked about was wanting justice for the victims. You even went to the girl's funeral. You insisted you wanted to catch the bastard who did it. And now—"

"Nothing has changed!" she spit out. "I want justice," she insisted. "And if the kid's guilty then throw the book at him, but not until you know he did it. You don't have enough evidence to hold him—neither Chase or I are absolutely certain, despite what he said."

Holiday reached over and touched Della's arm. "Let's stay calm."

Della felt the tension in her chest ease, but it wasn't enough. *Innocent. Innocent. Innocent.*

Burnett ran a hand over his face and then met her gaze. "Even without Chase recognizing the boy's trace, I would have held him until I got the DNA evidence back."

"And if he's innocent, he's suffering for no reason." Della paused. "Why didn't you just check his bite marks like you did with me when you brought me in? At least speed things up so he's not suffering unnecessarily."

Burnett flinched as if he didn't like that memory any more than she did. "The bite marks weren't clear, the wounds were too bad." He exhaled loudly. "Look, Della, even if this kid didn't commit the murders, he joined a rogue gang. Getting scared may straighten him out."

She felt emotion rise in her throat. "When you talk like that it shows that you were born with the live virus. You don't have any idea how it feels to be turned."

"I know that—"

"No, you don't know. You've never had to see yourself as a monster. I'll bet more fresh turns join gangs so they don't have to commit murder than those who join them to do terrible things. Chan told me that the gangs promise to provide blood and that they only kill when necessary."

"I know that, Della, but my job—"

"Your job is to provide justice, and tonight I'm not so sure that happened for Billy."

"Why are you so sure he's innocent?" Burnett asked.

His question gave her another pause. She'd asked herself the same thing and came up empty. "I don't know, but my gut says he is." Her gut and the stupid voice in her head.

Della flinched as the image of the couple flashed in her head.

She looked at Holiday. "Has Lorraine come back to see you? You could ask her, maybe she could tell you."

Holiday shook her head. "She hasn't appeared again. I don't know if she's crossed over or just hasn't wanted to communicate yet."

Della refocused on Burnett. "Are you going to continue to work on the case? Investigate other leads?"

"We don't have any other leads," Burnett said.

I do. She thought about the Facebook message she'd received from Lindsey, Lorraine's friend, about the Crimson Blood band. "Lorraine had an old boyfriend and her friends think he could have done this."

Burnett stared at her as if she'd completely lost it. "This was a vampire kill."

"I know, and maybe he's—"

"We don't follow maybes. We follow leads and it looks as if this lead is good."

"The name of his band—"

"You're grasping at straws."

Della gritted her teeth. Burnett had his mind made up. She had to talk to Kevin. "Can I leave now?"

Burnett grimaced and looked at Holiday.

"It's late," Holiday said, and again rubbed her belly.

"Fine," Burnett said. "We'll talk tomorrow."

Yes, they would, Della thought, and she hoped she had something to tell him about Phillip Lance. Something that would help Billy Jennings.

Della was only halfway to her cabin when she pulled out her phone and searched for Kevin's text message.

U still n Houston? I need to c u.

She stopped walking and closed her eyes as the message sent. Would he see it? Answer it?

Staring at her phone, she saw the little icon that told her she had voicemail. From Steve.

Biting at her lip, maybe because she thought she couldn't feel more than she was feeling now, she clicked it open and put the phone to her ear.

"I know you're not speaking to me, but I just want you to know that I'm sorry. And while I wasn't the one who initiated the kiss, I know I'd be pissed if someone kissed you. So get mad at me. I deserve it, but . . . damn it, Della, I care about you. I don't care about her. It's you I want. Please, call me."

Emotion tugged at her heart. What she wouldn't give for him to be here now—to just hold her, to help her understand all the craziness that was going on.

She had her finger over REDIAL, and hesitated. What was she going to say to him?

Her phone dinged with an incoming text.

From Kevin.

C me about what? Another favor? U really r going to owe me. We're talking getting naked.

He put a smiley face beside it. She hoped that meant he was joking. But what the hell? She'd already been accused of being a prostitute. She wouldn't do it, but he didn't know that.

Whatever. Where r u?

Close to ur camp. Where do u want to meet?

Della considered jumping the fence—meeting him somewhere in Fallen. Burnett would have a fit. She'd have hell to pay. Then it hit her, why not do what Chase did with whoever the hell he was in cahoots with, and have Kevin meet her at the fence? As long as he didn't touch the fence they should be fine. No reason to break a rule when one could just bend it a little.

She texted Kevin back and gave him the exact location where to meet her. *Do not jump or touch the fence.*

. . .

Ten minutes later, Della waited by the fence line where the creek ran through. Sitting on a fallen tree, she hugged her knees close. The cold air found its way under her shirt and brought goose bumps to her skin, which probably meant her temperature wasn't right. The night noises echoed in the distance. A chorus of frogs, insects, and a few small critters scurrying in the brush trying to stay warm.

Feeling alone, she pulled her phone out to keep her company. She remembered Steve's voicemail. She checked her text messages and found one from him she hadn't read.

Miss u.

She missed him, too. Closing her eyes, feeling the lack of sleep, she dropped her forehead on her knees. She envisioned his face. His smile. The soft way he kissed and how that kiss slowly became hotter and hotter.

Guilt whispered over her for kissing Chase. She'd done it to keep their cover. Hadn't she? Or had the seed the little witch planted in her head sprouted and led her down that path?

Right then it occurred to her that she was no longer so angry at Steve for . . . for letting Jessie kiss him. Hurt maybe, but not angry. She couldn't even be mad that he'd enjoyed it. She had enjoyed Chase's kiss, hadn't she?

Could Miranda's idea have worked? No, she told herself. Two wrongs still didn't make a right, but maybe walking in his shoes, she realized the kiss didn't mean he didn't care about her, or that he would necessarily do it again.

She wouldn't kiss Chase again. Wouldn't let him kiss her again, either.

Would she?

No.

Sitting up, she looked back at her phone and Steve's text, and typed in: *Let's talk this weekend, ok?* It took her longer to hit the SEND button than it did to type it.

Within thirty seconds she got a text back: *Ok. Miss you.*

Her heart gripped. He had to be awake, watching his phone. Hoping she'd text or call him. The memory of the pain she'd seen in his eyes when they'd argued had her lungs releasing air. She typed back. *Miss u too.*

A few seconds later, another ding came in: *Want to talk now? I'll call Burnett and come.*

Panic stirred inside her. Not just because she was waiting on Kevin, but because she wasn't altogether ready to talk to Steve. Was she going to tell him about Chase? Was she going to agree to . . . make this thing between them real? Or was she simply going to expect things to go on like they were? Nope, she wasn't ready to talk to him yet.

No. This weekend. Ok?

Ok.

She heard a distant noise and slipped her phone in her pocket. Tilting her head, she focused on the slight sound. Footsteps, soft, came treading her way. They came from the other side of the fence. Filling her nose with air, she hoped her sense of smell had returned and that she'd recognize Kevin's scent. She got nothing.

While the sound of steps continued, the forest noises stopped. No birds, no insects, even the trees stood silently against the wind.

It had to be Kevin, she told herself. But remembering how she got clobbered on the head not too long ago, she rose and stood behind a tree. Leaning slightly around the trunk, she fixed her eyes in the direction the sound came from.

Chapter Thirty

Della spotted Kevin moving through the brush. He lifted his nose in the air, testing it to find her.

"I'm here." She stepped out from the tree and started toward the fence.

He walked closer, and was about to latch on to the fence post when she said, "Stop. I told you not to touch the fence."

He pulled his hands back. "So it's true that there really are alarms set?"

"Afraid so," she said.

"And you can't just fly over it?"

"Not without setting it off."

"Damn! I could never live like that."

"It's to keep people out, not us in."

"Right," he said.

Della frowned. "Look, I was hoping you might be able to help me out. I'm looking for someone who I think belongs to the Crimson Blood."

"Why?" he asked.

"He was the old boyfriend of the girl I sort of ran across." The fact that the girl was dead didn't have to come up.

"I don't think I met all of them. I just hung out with them a couple of days."

"His name is Phillip Lance. He used to be in a band. Has brown hair. A tattoo on his neck of a skull."

"This ain't gonna come back and bite me in the ass, is it?"

"No," she said.

"And what do I get for doing all these favors for you?" He smiled.

"I'll owe you."

"You already owe me," he said.

"I'll owe you more."

He shrugged. "I don't know why I like you." He sighed and hesitated before finally talking. "There is a Phillip. Don't know his last name, but he has brown hair. I don't know if he played in a band." He glanced up as if debating saying more, and then he blurted out, "He has a tattoo, but I'm not sure what it is."

It had to be him. She nodded and a feeling of success filled her chest. "Thank you." Now to get one more thing. "Where do they hang out? So I can go see him."

Kevin held up his hands. "Now you're asking too much."

"Please." It didn't bother her nearly as much to beg when it was for someone else. And this was for Billy.

He hesitated. "Look, I can't tell you where they call home, but there's a supernatural bar on the north side of Houston called Hot Stuff."

"Chan took me there," Della said, remembering bits and pieces of the first week she'd been turned. If she had to, she thought she could find it again.

"Well, a lot of the Crimson Blood hang out there. You go there and you should run into one of them eventually."

She nodded. "Thanks."

He studied her a second, up and down, checking her out. "You got a boyfriend?" he asked, his blue eyes sparkling with interest.

"Yeah." When her heart didn't skip a beat, she realized it was true. Steve was her boyfriend. She didn't know how things would be after this weekend, but . . .

"A shame." He paused. "So, did you get Chan a proper burial?"

"Not yet. The FRU are doing an autopsy to confirm cause of death."

"They should," he said. "I was told it was freaky the way he got sick."

Della remembered that niggling concern that she could actually have the same virus Chan did. "What . . . I mean, how was it freaky?"

"They said, he wasn't feeling right for a while. I mean, he wasn't feeling great when he left for Texas, and they said he got a nasty rash."

Della inhaled, with a tiny bit of relief. She didn't have a rash.

Kevin shook his head. "You know he's the first vampire I ever heard of that died of illness. I mean, I've lost several friends to gang fights and all, but I didn't know we could get sick."

"There's viruses and such," Della said, thinking she'd just had one. Was still dealing with one, minus the headache. And the sooner it all went away and she had her sense of smell back the better.

"Yeah, but they are like tiny colds, nothing that could kill you. I mean . . ." Kevin leaned his head back. "Company coming. Later!" He lit out.

Della inhaled, but still got nothing. Then she heard it, a rush of air. It was fast. Fast enough that she knew it was one of two people. Burnett or Chase.

The panty perv landed beside her. He took a sniff of the air. "Who was here?"

"Just someone I wanted to chat with," Della said.

He glanced away. "Why are you meeting someone this late?"

"None of your business." She started walking then turned back around, deciding she didn't have to mention Jenny, but she could still say what she knew. "Unless you want to tell me who you've been meeting out here late at night."

Surprise widened his eyes. "I don't know what you mean." His brow twitched.

"The hell you don't."

He looked puzzled. "How do you . . . Okay, fine, it was an old friend." His brow didn't shift; neither did his eyes. He told the truth.

"Why the secrecy?" she asked.

"He's not registered." Nothing wiggled on his face this time either. She believed him.

"And now it's your turn," he said. "Why are you meeting someone at this time of night?" He looked concerned. Why?

"Let's just say I'm trying to fix your mess. I'm following another lead on the murder."

She saw him tilt his head to the side to listen to her heart rate. "True, but vague," he said.

"You only deserve vague. You lied to Burnett about Billy."

"I believe the kid is guilty, and I'm almost positive it was his trace I got, so that's not really a lie."

"And I believe he's innocent," Della countered.

He didn't say a word.

"I'm leaving." She only got a few feet.

"Wait," he said.

She paused, but didn't look back. And in spite of not wanting to go there, her mind took her back to the kiss. To the way it felt to be held close by him.

"Why?" she asked.

"To talk."

"You have nothing to say I'm interested in hearing." She got almost to the line of trees when she heard him.

"How about I tell you where I know you from?"

Of all the things he could say, that was the one that would stop her. She slowed down and heard him walking up beside her.

When he got to her side and didn't say anything, she spoke. "I'm waiting."

"One run, and then I'll tell you." He studied her face, as if looking for something. What? What could her expression give him? He could read her heartbeat and know if she told the truth.

"No," she said, and went back to walking. "I'm not playing games with you."

"It's not a game. One run. You want to know, admit it." This time she studied his face and there wasn't a twitch or a blink. Giving in felt wrong. But curiosity bit.

Bit hard.

He flashed in front of her. Stood close. This close, she could smell him. . . . Again she remembered his scent when he'd held her and flown like the wind. When his arms had held her so tight.

"One run, one lap around the property . . . and if you answer one question I'll tell you."

She took a step back. "First it was just a run, now it's a run and a question."

"It's an easy question." He moved in an inch. "I want to know if you enjoyed the kiss. I mean, I think you did. I know I did."

She tilted her chin up and wished like hell she could tell him no. "So you can kiss, it doesn't mean shit."

He smiled. "It could mean I might get lucky and sneak another one."

"Not on your life."

The smile vanished from his eyes. "So you're really into the shape-shifter, huh?"

"You said one question," she growled.

"And one run." He took off.

She actually debated not going, but she wanted to know where she'd met him. She took off, pushing herself until she almost caught up with him. He sped up. She pushed harder, but not to the point of puking. She'd done that two too many times.

When he realized she wasn't going to push herself faster, he slowed down. And amazingly true to his word, when they had made one lap, he started down.

She landed beside him, a little winded, but not embarrassingly so.

He studied her. "You could have gone faster."

"It's late," she said.

He nodded. "It is."

Della's phone dinged with an incoming text. She ignored it, thinking it was from Steve. And she didn't want to text him back in front of Chase.

"Okay spill it," she said. "Where did we meet?"

Chase moved over to the fallen tree where Della had been sitting earlier and dropped down, motioning for her to join him.

"Just tell me," she said.

"I am, but it's going to require some explanation. So sit down."

She did, but she made sure there was plenty of space between them. "I'm sitting!" she said, losing her patience. "Start talking!"

Chapter Thirty-one

"I belonged to the Blades."

The Blades? Della's gut tightened and the spot where she carried a scar from being knifed started to ache. Chase had belonged to the the Blades. A different gang than the Crimson Blood, but outlaws just the same. She and Steve had gone on a mission to see if this gang were the ones killing humans as initiation. They had been. And she'd gotten knifed during the investigation and could have died if Steve hadn't gotten her blood.

"You're rogue," she said with accusation and scooted a little farther away on the downed tree.

"No, I . . . joined the group for a reason."

"What do you mean?"

He exhaled. "If I tell you, do you give me your word that you won't repeat it? To anyone? That includes Burnett."

Della decided to be honest. "If it endangers anyone, I can't keep silent."

"It doesn't endanger anyone." He paused. "I was sent on a mission, looking for someone. I was working undercover for the Vampire Council."

Now she knew he was up to no good. "The Vampire Council are rogues who oppose the FRU."

"The council isn't rogue. They don't agree with all the FRU rules, but they aren't the bad guys."

Then something else dawned on her. Something personal.

"You were going to let the Blades kill me. And they would have—"

"No!" he insisted. "I stopped them from following you and Steve out that night. The fire Steve started just slowed them down."

Was he telling the truth? It appeared so, but . . . "Why are you here? Is the Vampire Council trying to bring down the school?"

"No. They see this place as a good thing."

"Then *why* are you here?"

He hesitated again. "I'm still looking for someone."

"Who?"

"That I can't tell you."

"If you find this person are you going to cause them harm?" She studied his light green eyes.

"No, I'm trying to help them."

Honesty rang deep in his voice. "Are they here?"

"I can't answer that either." He leaned back.

Suddenly another question hit. "Why are you telling me this?"

His expression changed and something told her he was going to lie.

"The truth. Tell me the truth."

His hand, resting on his thigh, tightened. "Because chances are, you are going to find out."

"How?"

He shook his head. "I can't say any more." A strand of dark hair swept across his brow and she had a strange urge to brush it away. She folded her hand to resist.

She sighed in frustration. Had she actually given her word she wouldn't tell Burnett any of this?

She needed more information before deciding if this was something Burnett needed to know. "Why are you trying to get into the FRU?"

"I wasn't. Burnett actually came to me. He was impressed with my strength and speed, and I thought I might help catch the killer."

"You thought wrong," she said. "It's your fault we're holding Billy. Billy didn't do it."

"It's not all on me, Della. Think about it. Burnett doesn't trust me anymore—which means he wouldn't have held the kid solely on my word if he didn't believe it himself."

"So you both are wrong."

Chase leaned over, and his shoulder almost touched hers. "Okay, if I'm wrong, give me a chance to make it right. Tell me who you think did it. I'll help look into it."

She shifted away. His closeness made her edgy. "Why would I tell you anything now?" "

He frowned as if offended. "So I tell you the truth and now you don't trust me?"

"Yeah, you're just now telling me the truth. You've been keeping things from me all along."

He shook his head. "You're harsh."

"I'm honest," she said. "Something you should have tried in the very beginning." She stood up from the tree, dusted the flaking tree bark off her butt, and started walking.

"Hey." Something in his voice had her turning around.

He stood right behind her. So close their breath mingled in the night air. It brought back memories of the kiss.

"Keep running, okay? Once or twice a day."

What was it with this guy and running? Then again, maybe if she could run/fly as fast as he could, she might be all about it, too. She tilted her head back, realizing his tone and words sounded like parting advice.

"You're leaving?" she asked.

"I don't have a choice." He half smiled. It sparkled in his eyes, but didn't touch his lips. "I guess I don't trust you either. You're going to tell Burnett."

She hadn't made that decision yet. "I'm debating. But yes, my loyalty lies with the school."

He chuckled. "You are honest, aren't you?"

"You should try it sometime." Sarcasm sounded in her voice.

"I did try. Just now, and it didn't work out so well." He stared at her as a few slow seconds passed. "Don't worry, I don't blame you." He brushed a strand of hair from her cheek. She almost swatted his hand, but didn't.

"Steve's a lucky guy." His fingers lingered on her cheek, and something that looked like regret filled his green gaze.

Before she knew what he intended to do, he kissed her. Not like before. Not a sexy, let's-get-it-on kind of kiss.

This one was short, sweet. His soft lips on hers ever so briefly.

This one was good-bye.

He turned and left. She watched his wide shoulders disappear between the trees.

She didn't like him, she told herself. So why was her heart hurting? Why did she want to call him back?

Okay, she liked him. A crazy kind of like. Part admiration, part . . . she couldn't define it. But it wasn't like what she felt for Steve. Maybe she felt sorry for Chase losing his family so young. Or maybe it was how protective he'd been of her at the bar.

Or maybe. . . . Oh, hell, why was she trying to analyze this? He was leaving. He'd barely left a footprint in her life's path.

Then she realized his recent footprints hadn't headed toward the fence, but back to the camp. Was he leaving for good, or had he lied hoping to score a kiss?

She wouldn't put it past him. Damn panty perv!

She checked her phone to see who'd texted her. It was Kevin.

She called him. It rang twice. "Hello," he answered.

"It's me, Della."

"How do you . . ." His line started going in and out. He must've had poor cell service.

"Call me back." The line went dead.

Confused about Chase, she turned to leave. Something brushed against her face. She reached up thinking some bird had just crapped on her, but nope. When she pulled her hand back, she saw it was a feather.

She stopped in the middle of the dark woods, feeling the night air grow colder. Looking into the thick line of trees, she searched for a skinny Asian ghost. Turning in a full circle, she studied all the shadows.

No ghost.

Maybe it wasn't a sign from Chan. She glanced up to the black sky with stars blinking back at her. The moon, two nights away from being full, hung heavy in the sky. Another feather spiraled down in front of her face. It spun in circles—round and round—and landed at her feet.

Chan was still here. Why? Could Chan being here be about Lorraine's killer? Since they were part of the same gang, it would make sense. "Is that what you want?" she blurted out in the cold wind. "Stop sending dad-blasted feathers and just tell me!"

It was past three in the morning when Della got to her cabin. Even exhausted, she barely slept that night, thinking about Chan, worrying about Billy, and wondering how to go about investigating Phillip Lance. And even though she wished it weren't true, she thought about Chase. Had he really left? And why the hell did she care?

When the sun finally crept into her bedroom, she longed to pull the covers up and sleep in. Putting her hand over her eyes, she realized her headache was back. Yet having missed the vampire morning ritual too many times, she forced herself out of bed. Forced herself to get dressed. But too tired to even brush her hair, she put it up in a clip. It hung down in a semi-Medusa type of style. What the hell. No one would dare say anything.

She walked up to the clearing where they always met. The blood sat on the tables and all the vamps stood around chattering. The noise had her head hurting more. Chris came toward her—even his footsteps sounded loud. He stopped at her side. "You look like shit."

Okay, some would dare say something, yet she was too busy glancing around to see if Chase was among the crowd to give Chris crap. She did manage to offer him a halfhearted growl.

The blond vamp laughed. She cut him a pissed-off glare, and he laughed harder, but the humor left his eyes when Burnett landed beside him. No doubt, the camp leader's expression was more pissed off than hers.

"Let's take a walk." Burnett's tone came with an abundance of grump.

Della waited for Chris to reply, when all of a sudden she realized Burnett wasn't talking to Chris. Friggin' hell. What now?

Before they got out of earshot of the other vampires, Della had a good idea of what it was all about. Chase.

"Did you see Chase after you left the office last night?"

Sometimes being right wasn't all it was cracked up to be.

"Yeah." It was decision time. To tell or not to tell. She wasn't sure why she felt an ounce of loyalty to the panty perv, but she did. It hung in her chest like an unwanted emotion.

"Did he mention he was leaving Shadow Falls?"

"Sort of," she said.

"And you didn't think you should inform me about that?"

"I wasn't sure if I believed him. I thought I'd find him here this morning."

The worry line between Burnett's brows deepened. "Did he say where he was going?"

"No."

"What did he say?"

It was a direct question and one she felt obligated to answer. "He told me where we met. He was part of the Blades gang when Steve and I went undercover." When Burnett didn't say anything, she decided it was time to drop the bomb. "He said he works for the Vampire Council."

"I already knew that," Burnett said.

Della stared up at him and threw his words right back at him. "And you didn't think you should've informed me about that?"

"That's different," he said.

"Yeah. The difference being, you expect me to be completely forthcoming with you, while you do just the opposite."

His scowl deepened. "But since you weren't forthcoming with me, your argument doesn't amount to a hill of beans." He ran a hand over his face.

"If he was gone, I'd planned on telling you."

"Which was too late to do anything," he seethed.

Della couldn't argue with that. "How did he leave without setting off the alarm?"

"He didn't. He called in the middle of the night and said he had to go see an old friend who was in trouble. I believed him. But . . . considering my suspicions, I had someone follow him."

"So you didn't lose him. What's the issue?" Della asked.

"He got away."

"He's fast," Della said.

Burnett nodded. "When I went to his cabin this morning, his stuff was all gone." Burnett hesitated. "Did he say anything else?"

"Only that he was looking for someone," she told him.

"Who?"

"He wouldn't say," Della exhaled. "But considering he left, I'm assuming he didn't find him or her here."

"Then why stay as long as he did? And why agree to help work this case?"

"I asked that. He said you're the one who suggested it. And since he was good at what he did, he thought he'd help find a killer. So maybe that was why he stayed."

"Do you believe him, or do you think he had some ulterior motive for being here?"

She mentally chewed on the question for a couple of seconds. "I'm not a hundred percent sure, but I think I believe him." She rubbed her temple, which still throbbed. Not sharp shooting pains, but just enough of a dull ache to make her take notice.

When she looked up, Burnett stared at her. "What?" she asked.

"Chris is right, you don't look well. Are you feeling okay?"

She grinned. "Chris said I looked like shit."

Burnett arched an eyebrow. "Holiday is on to me about my language. She said too many of the students are cursing, especially the vampires. She says I'm a bad influence on them." He cut her a direct look as if accusing her of having a potty mouth.

"Well, damn!" Della grinned, finding it funny that the badass vampire got called out for his language. When he didn't respond to her humor, she sobered. "I'll watch what I say when I'm around her so you won't get in trouble." She paused. "How is she doing?"

"Like you. She looks tired, worn out. But she has a reason. You . . . I'm not so sure."

"I'm not pregnant, if that's what you're asking."

He looked appalled. "I wasn't asking."

"It was a late night," Della said. "I'll be fine." She dropped her hand from her temple. Out of the blue, an image of Billy filled her head. "I'd bet I'm doing better than Billy."

"I'd have to agree with you on that. The DNA came back on the hair."

"And?" Della asked, wanting to rub it in a little that she'd been right. She deserved that. Then she'd tell him about Phillip Lance.

"It's a match," Burnett said. "They officially arrested him about five this morning."

"No!" Doubt reared its head in her chest. "He didn't . . . I still don't—"

"He's guilty, Della. I know you didn't want to believe that." He rested his hand on her shoulder. "And if it makes you feel any better, we'll go easy on him because . . . fresh turns don't always have control. But he'll spend some time in jail, and hopefully in the next few years we'll have him rehabilitated."

"But I have another—"

"It's a done deal. The report came back positive. I'm supposed to go and finalize the paperwork and set up sentencing. Now go get some breakfast, and if you're still tired, skip your first classes and take a nap."

"You don't understand," Della demanded. "I tried to tell you, but you wouldn't listen. I think I've found another suspect."

"You are the one not listening," he said. "The DNA is a match." He frowned but with empathy. "In this job, second to seeing the victims, the hardest thing is sometimes arresting the guilty—especially the fresh turns. It hurts like hell . . . heck . . . to realize that sometimes good people can do terrible things."

Della swallowed and tried to accept it, but that stupid voice started chanting again in her head, and it came in rhythm with the throb in her temple.

Innocent. Innocent. Innocent.

Chapter Thirty-two

Della skipped campmate hour and went back to her cabin to do an Internet search on Billy Jennings. She was right: He belonged to the school band. And to the chess club. The guy was an honor student. And not even a cool honor student. He was a geek. How could someone so . . . so perfectly geeky kill Lorraine and John?

Feeling as if she couldn't do a damn thing to help Billy, she cut the computer off and went to her first class—science. But by the time she sat down, her head pounded so hard it felt as if her eyes were going to pop out.

Mr. Yates, Jenny's brother as well as their teacher, stood up in front of the class talking about how cell phones and signals worked.

Della didn't give a rat's ass. All she could think about was her headache and then Billy. Playing the flute one week, being arrested for murder the next.

"There's one a couple of miles from here." Perry spoke up, but his voice sounded distant, as if he were far away. "I never get service there."

All of a sudden, Mr. Yates's phone rang. "Well, someone isn't in the dead zone." He answered the call. Then the teacher looked right at Della, his gaze almost angry. "Innocent." His voice echoed like they were in a cave. "Innocent!" he yelled.

"What?" Della asked. But when she blinked Mr. Yates wasn't looking at her and was back talking into his cell. What in hell's bells was going on? Had she just imagined . . . ?

She blinked again and the fogginess in her brain increased. The air suddenly changed, and she smelled wet dirt. It had turned night. Her gaze shot around, expecting to see the classroom, but she saw only woods, the trees stared down at her. Sh glanced down at her hands. A diamond ring, an engagement ring, sparkled up at her from her left hand. Engagement ring? *What the hell?*

All of a sudden, her hands didn't look like her hands. She shook her head, feeling as if her reality had been yanked away. Nothing made sense. Nothing mattered but getting that damn ring off. She started to yank at it, but her hands were covered in blood. Lots and lots of blood. But the blood didn't seem to matter as much as the ring. She tried again to pull it off, but no matter how hard she tried she couldn't move. She felt paralyzed or . . . dead.

Her heart jolted. She wasn't dead. The smell of dirt vanished, but the blood on her hands hadn't. She felt the hard school desk against her back. She started to jump up, but then the blood disappeared.

The ring disappeared.

Her breath caught.

"Della? Della?"

In the distance someone called her name. But she didn't care about that either. She kept staring at her hands, turning them one way and then other.

Damn it! What had just happened?

She closed her eyes. *Innocent. Innocent. Innocent.* The words echoed around the schoolroom, as if everyone was chanting them. Della jumped up from her seat and looked around. Everyone was staring at her, but no one was speaking, or chanting.

"Della? Della?"

Her name echoed again. This time Della recognized Mr. Yates's voice.

She forced herself to glance at him. He stared at her, looking puzzled. Della moved her gaze around, seeing everyone gawking at her as if she was nuts. And hell, maybe they were right.

"Della?" Mr. Yates said again.

"Yeah," she managed to answer, but only after she growled at the gawkers.

"Are you okay?" He walked to her desk.

No. I'm losing my mind. She nodded.

"Did you hear me?" he asked.

She stared at him blankly, and he must have gotten the message that she hadn't heard a damn thing.

"Holiday wants to see you. In the office."

Feeling her insides tremble, she grabbed her book and went to find Holiday. Find her and tell her to call the people who came in with those tight white coats and carted off crazy people. Because Della was pretty certain she was on the path to needing a padded cell.

By the time she got to the office, she'd convinced herself that living in a padded cell wasn't her calling.

Holiday rose from her desk. Concern pulled at her brows.

"What's wrong?" Della envisioned the worst—a worst that didn't have anything to do with visions of blood or engagement rings. Had something happened to someone in her family?

Holiday motioned for her to sit down. Ignoring the motion, Della stood in the middle of the office, still feeling dazed.

"What is it?" Della insisted.

"Lorraine Baker stopped in this morning. Briefly." The camp leader rubbed her belly.

"And?" Della asked, trying to convince herself that this was good news. She thought of Billy. Maybe now they'd get a break in the case.

"When I tried to get her to talk to me, she informed me that she was already communicating with someone. But they weren't a good listener."

Della's mind spun. "Then she's lying, because Kylie is good at that. Did you ask her? Maybe Lorraine told Kylie something." Something that would help Billy. Something that would keep a flute-playing chess lover out of prison.

Holiday pulled her hair over one shoulder and twisted it. Worry brightened her eyes. "It's not Kylie," Holiday said. "She said she's talking to you."

Okay, sitting down suddenly sounded like a good idea. Della took two steps to the sofa and dropped. The sofa sighed with her weight as if complaining. But not as loud as Della wanted to complain.

"But I'm vampire." A shiver ran down Della's spine and she realized she did connect with *a* ghost. Chan. But what was it Kylie had said? Oh yeah, that some spirits with a strong connection can attach themselves to normal, non-ghost-whispering people. She thought she was just one of those. Not so much normal, but someone who didn't go around talking to dead people. "Vampires don't do ghosts," Della said.

"Yeah, that has always been what I believed, too. But then Burnett . . . and now this. I'll admit, I'm puzzled. I always thought since we don't really know Burnett's heritage that he could have been a descendant of the American tribe and that was the reason he had a connection to the falls and the spirit world."

"I'm Chinese, not—"

"You're half Chinese," Holiday said. "I subscribed to ancestry. com trying to find Burnett's family history, so before I called you down here I went on and put in your mother's maiden name to see if there's any evidence that your mom might be a descendant."

"And?" Della asked.

"Nothing popped up." The camp leader exhaled at the same time Della did, but Holiday's release seemed to extend from disappointment, Della's from relief. She didn't want to be part of any bloodline that tied her to ghosts.

"But," Holiday continued, "let's worry about that later. Right now, we need to help Lorraine. What has she told you?"

"She hasn't told me shit. I haven't seen her. She must have lied to you about . . ." Della remembered the voice she'd been hearing.

"What?" Holiday asked.

"I've been hearing a voice. I thought . . . It sounded like me thinking it. Like a song when it gets stuck in your head."

"What does it say?" Holiday asked.

"All it says is . . . *innocent*. Repeatedly." The realization that she had not one, but two ghosts communicating with her scared the living crap out of her. However, Della decided to freak out later. "Lorraine must be trying to tell me that Billy is innocent. That has to be what this means."

Holiday frowned. "Burnett said the DNA came back positive on the suspect. He's there now to present the case to the FRU board to get Billy sentenced."

"All in one day?" Della asked.

Holiday nodded.

"What happened to having a trial and being judged by twelve of your peers?"

"It doesn't work that way with the FRU. When someone is arrested, their case goes before an FRU board and they are sentenced almost immediately. And . . . the bad news for Billy is that getting a sentence overturned is practically impossible."

"Then we have to stop it." Della snatched her phone from her back pocket. Seeing her hands, she recalled the vision she'd had.

"The ring?" Della said.

"What?" Holiday asked.

"In class, I . . ." Jeepers, would Holiday think she was crazy? Then Della remembered Kylie had those types of visions all the time. Oh, fracking hell, Della didn't want to go down this road. But she'd worry about that later, too. "I had this vision, I . . ."

"What vision?"

"I saw my hands with blood on them and I was wearing a ring.

An engagement ring. I was . . . repulsed by it. I wanted to take it off, but I couldn't."

Holiday stood there rubbing her stomach.

"Do you think that means anything?" Della asked. "Is she trying to tell me something?"

"It always means something. The tough part is figuring it out. The dead suck at communicating." The fae reached to the back of her chair to get her purse and slung it over her shoulder. "Let's go."

"Go where?" Della asked.

"To see Burnett. You're right, we have to stop this."

"We can't just call?" Della held up her phone.

"Nope. Love that man, but he never listens to reason on the phone. Frankly, he doesn't excel at listening to reason in person. Not when he thinks he's right. And he's pretty certain Billy is guilty."

"Then what are we going to do?" Della asked, following Holiday out.

"Convince him that he's wrong."

"How?" Della asked.

"I'm hoping to figure that out on the ride there."

They came up empty, but that didn't stop them from charging into the FRU building. Well, Della charged. Holiday, wearing a long-sleeved yellow dress that hugged her round belly, wobbled in. She reminded Della of a pudgy duck. A beautiful pudgy duck with red hair. If this weren't so serious, Della would have found it funny.

"Hi, Mr. Adkins," Holiday said to the man at the front desk, granting him a big smile. "I need to speak to my husband."

Mr. Adkins, who didn't smile back, probably because he was a werewolf—Della had checked out his pattern—stared at Holiday. "I'm sorry, Mr. James is in a meeting with the Judging Committee."

Holiday made a pleading face. "It's important."

"So is the meeting," he said.

Holiday reached out to touch the were, but he backed up. "Fae influence isn't allowed in this building."

Holiday shot Della a quick glance and cut her eyes toward the hall that led to the back. Della couldn't be a hundred percent sure, but her gut said Holiday meant for Della to make a run for it.

Della didn't need to be told twice.

"Now, you wouldn't want Burnett upset with you for not informing him that his pregnant wife is here, would you?" Holiday asked, drawing the man's attention.

"Sorry, the rules are the rules." The voices echoed behind Della as she hotfooted it down the corridor.

She tuned her ears off them and listened for voices coming from a room at the end of the hall.

Unfortunately, she heard the were yelling out for her to stop. Which meant she ran faster. Hearing footsteps, she hit the doors a little hard. The heavy oak panels slammed against the wall and one fell from its hinges.

Oops.

One swift glance around, and Della counted fourteen figures in the room. All men. But she knew she was in the right room when she recognized one of those figures as her badass camp leader. But wow, all men! She knew the FRU was chauvinistic, but damn, what century was this?

Thirteen of those men shot up from their seats.

The one who remained seated was another she recognized. Billy. Shoulders slumped, he held his head down, staring at his lap, as if his fate had been sealed, as if not one person in the world cared.

Della cared. Burnett cared. If she could just make him see reason.

Heavy breathing sounded behind her. "I'm sorry, I'll remove her immediately." The were came storming into the room.

"No," Burnett demanded. "Let me handle this. She's harmless."

Just in case the dirty dog didn't listen to Burnett, Della shot around and gave him a peek at her canines. When he took another step forward, she added, "Touch me and I'll hit you so hard in the balls you'll wish you'd been neutered as a pup."

Burnett cleared his throat. "Okay, she doesn't sound harmless, but she is." Burnett's glare said he'd be the one doing the harming if she didn't behave. "Della, this is not a good time!"

"Yes, it is," a voice came from behind her. Holiday's voice.

Della loved it when things came together so perfectly.

Burnett's eyes widened at the sight of his wife. He looked at the others in the room, then back at Holiday waddling up the center of the room. "I think you all have met my wife," Burnett said, not looking happy.

"Yes," one man said, sounding annoyed.

That was all it took for Burnett to give him a scowling look. "Is something wrong?" Burnett asked, his harsh look fleeting as he watched his wife.

"Yes," Holiday said. Burnett looked ready to run to her, no doubt fearing for his child. "Billy Jennings is innocent."

Burnett's shoulders sank with relief, but Billy's posture finally showed a backbone and he glanced up. The boy looked condemned, lost, and he had tears in his eyes, but for one second there was a flash of hope.

"And how have you come to this conclusion?" one of the Judging Committee, a blond vampire, asked Holiday.

"Lorraine Baker has proclaimed him innocent," Holiday stated with pride.

"I didn't think I did it," Billy said. "I told them I didn't think I could do it. I just didn't remember everything. It's all a blur."

"I'm afraid you are mistaken," said the older vampire in the room with a holier-than-thou attitude. "Lorraine Baker is one of our victims. She could not proclaim anything."

Burnett's shoulders flexed. "My wife is seldom wrong. She's a gifted ghost whisperer."

Della wondered why Burnett hadn't shared this information with his agency.

But in the next few seconds, she knew why. All twelve men of the committee looked a bit shocked, or maybe scared was a better word.

What a bunch of wimps, Della thought. Sure, ghosts scared the crap out of her, but she wasn't some bigwig on the FRU judge-and-jury committee. And how strange was it that they were on a committee to judge others, but feared the dead and the death angels judging them?

Another of the men, this one a warlock, spoke up and directed it to Burnett. "And you expect us to take the word of your . . . very pregnant wife, over a DNA test? No offense, but pregnancy tends to lower a female's IQ."

Burnett turned to the warlock, but before he could add his two cents—which didn't look as if it would be pleasant—Holiday added her own. "That's funny," she said, but without humor. "I've heard it also makes us vicious if provoked. And for your information, I'd be happy to put my IQ up against yours, pregnant or not."

"And I'd have to agree," Burnett seethed, glaring daggers at the warlock. "I would also add, she's helped me solve several cases. Before and after she was pregnant."

Go Burnett! The way he defended his wife was the most romantic thing Della had ever seen. There was no question where his loyalty lay.

"So, if my wife says Lorraine Baker told her Billy wasn't her murderer, then I recommend we take another look at the case." Burnett turned back to Holiday. "Exactly what did Lorraine Baker tell you?"

Oh, shit, Della thought. It was time to come out of the I-talk-to-dead-people closet. She stepped forward. "Lorraine didn't tell Holiday. She told me."

"Enough of this," said another man, this one a redheaded fae. "You're vampire. We all know that ghost whispering isn't a gift given to your species. This is ridiculous."

"I sort of feel the same way," Della said, realizing that Burnett hadn't informed them of his own abilities. But if she had to work with these jerks, she wouldn't tell them shit either. "I don't understand it, perhaps she just attached herself to me because I was at the crime scene." She said it honestly, hoping it was true.

Another one of the twelve, a were with graying temples, shook his head. "We simply can't take the word of some misfit vamp to decide the fate of a murderer."

"She's not a misfit," Burnett spit out the same time as Holiday. Warmth spread through Della knowing they were both in her corner. But that thought led her back to Billy, who felt he had no one. And Della knew his main champion wasn't her or even Holiday, but Lorraine. Della's respect for the girl grew.

Burnett focused on Della. "Do you have anything to offer us in the way of evidence?" And she could tell from his expression that he was hoping she'd come through.

But Burnett wasn't the only one hoping—nor the one with the most to lose. A storm of emotion filled her chest as she looked at Billy, his pale blue eyes staring at her with faith. And she'd give up her best bra if she had something to offer.

But she had nothing.

Chapter Thirty-three

Della's stomach clutched. "I'm sorry. I . . ." Lorraine's voice echoed in her head and she felt a chill tiptoe down her spine. *The engagement ring.* "The engagement ring," Della said, not knowing what it meant, but praying it was the answer.

"What engagement ring?" the warlock of the bunch asked.

"This is ridiculous," another man, a shape-shifter, said.

"Maybe not so ridiculous," said another vampire, standing beside Burnett. "I received a call from the family this morning. I didn't mention it because it seemed irrelevant. However, the parents went through Lorraine's belongings and said there was a ring in the box of items that didn't belong to her. Or rather, didn't belong to her anymore. It was the ring given to her by her prior fiancé. They wanted to know how it had gotten in with her belongings." He hesitated a second. "The report said she was wearing it."

Della felt a wave of relief. "His name is Phillip Lance," Della added. "He's her old fiancé. I believe you'll find he belongs to the Crimson Blood gang. From what I heard, they hang out at a bar called the Hot Stuff."

"I think I met him," Billy said, hope resonating in his voice. "I was with that gang at the bar. I almost joined them, but . . . I don't know what happened. Most of it is all a blur. But I remember a Phillip. I think we fought."

"Which would explain how the DNA evidence got transferred," the gray-haired were, who looked to be the leader of the committee, said. He glanced around at the others. "It appears this whole case needs to be reviewed again. And I won't deny . . ." His gaze locked on Burnett. ". . . that I'm disappointed in this investigation."

Burnett didn't blink. "Actually, sir, the only thing I'm disappointed in is that we almost convicted an innocent boy. And frankly, while I can take no credit for it myself, this *is* the investigation at work." He motioned to Della. "I'd like to introduce you to Della Tsang. She was the undercover agent you approved to help us on the case. As well as the one who led us to the arrest of Craig Anthony whom we sentenced yesterday. I think she's done an excellent job here."

"Agreed," said the older were. "We'll be using her for future projects."

Della wanted to smile, but contained it. Face it, weres didn't do "happy" often.

The were glanced back at the door. "However, would Miss Tsang and your . . . lovely wife . . ." He nodded at Holiday. ". . . be so kind as to leave while we close out this case? As pleasant as they both are, they are disrupting our meeting."

"We'll go." Holiday winked at Burnett, and oddly her gaze shifted up toward the ceiling.

As Della walked out, Billy smiled at her. She saw gratitude written all over his face. Waiting until they were out of earshot, she looked at Holiday. "Does it take a degree in asshole-ism to be considered for the Judging Committee?"

Holiday laughed.

"And not one woman in the bunch," Della said.

"I think you might change that someday," Holiday said.

"I'm tempted." Their footsteps echoed down the marble tile.

Della reached up to rub her temple, noticing the headache again, but too happy to care. She'd practically been told she had a future in the FRU. "We did good, didn't we?"

"Yup," Holiday said. "Especially for one misfit vamp and an IQ-impaired pregnant woman." She laughed and then flinched, putting her hand on her huge belly. "And if that kick was any indication, I think my daughter agrees."

As they got to the car, Holiday clicked the locks open and then glanced up. "You do realize that you saved Billy?"

"No, Lorraine saved him." As Della crawled into the passenger seat, she remembered the second person she'd seen when she'd found Chan's body. Had it been Lorraine?

Della bit down on her lip. "But please tell me she's going to leave now."

Holiday's smile looked almost angelic. "She did. I saw her cross over in the courtroom. She's at peace."

The fae squeezed behind the wheel, then moved the seat back. She paused as if in thought, then focused on Della. "Chan was there, too. At least, I'm assuming it was Chan. Thin Asian guy. But he didn't follow her."

Della swallowed. "You saw him?"

Puzzlement creased the fae's brow. "Yes. Not that he was there for me. He stood next to you. Has he spoken with you?"

"No," Della confessed. "But I've seen him." She closed her eyes a second.

"How long have you been aware of him?" Holiday asked.

"Since around the time he died. Kylie felt him, but didn't see him. Then I started feeling him, then . . . he started dropping feathers," she said.

"Feathers?" Holiday asked.

"It started when I accidentally ripped a pillow and they started swirling around, but then I could be outside or in a car and feathers would drop."

"Did Chan have a thing for feathers?"

"No. Not that I knew of. Why?"

"Well, ghosts are usually trying to tell us something. They use symbols or clues. Sometimes they aren't good clues."

Della shook her head. "Why is this happening to me? I'm vampire."

"Like I said earlier, I don't know," Holiday said. "Burnett feels the dead, too. But try not to see it as something bad. It's a gift. Look what good has come from it already. You were able to help Billy and catch Lorraine and her boyfriend's killer." Holiday started the car.

Della finally brought herself to ask. "Did Chan say anything to you? Is he mad at me for not . . . for not calling him back?"

"He didn't speak. But . . ." She hesitated as if debating whether to say it. "But I felt his emotions." Holiday's worry line appeared again in her brow. "He wasn't mad or upset. He seemed concerned . . . about you. And that concerns me." Before driving off, she sighed. "You need to talk to him. Sometimes the dead need us to help them, like Lorraine, but other times they are here to help us. I think Chan's trying to warn you about something. Something that he feels is serious."

While Holiday drove, Della pondered what it could be Chan wanted to warn her about. She'd sort of hoped since he was in the same gang as Phillip Lance, he wanted to tell her about the murders. But if he was still here, and Holiday was right about him being concerned about her, could he know something about her uncle and aunt that he wanted to tell her? But would that be a warning? Surely her uncle and aunt weren't . . . bad. Or could they be?

Or was this about something completely different?

Della's phone rang. She pulled it out of her pocket and saw the number. Kevin. Remembering Kevin brought to mind their conversation about how Chan had died from some strange sickness. And that brought back her niggling concern about her experiencing some weird side effects of some bug. Could that be what Chan was trying to warn her about?

No, Kevin had said Chan had gotten really sick and had a rash. Della wasn't really sick. What was a little headache? Her phone rang again.

Looking at Holiday, she asked, "Do you mind if I take this?"

"No."

"Hey, beautiful," Kevin said as soon as she answered.

Della rolled her eyes, hoping Holiday couldn't hear Kevin. "I couldn't understand a word you were saying last night when you called. You were cutting in and out."

"I was asking about Chase," he said.

Della cut her eyes over to Holiday, who was busy driving with one hand, but rubbed her belly with the other. "How do you know him?"

"He came to see Chan."

Della's heart raced. "He knew Chan?"

"Yeah. He stayed here with him for a couple of days before Chan left for Texas. I caught his scent, but didn't realize it was him until I took off. I was going to come back, but I picked up another scent—another vampire. Someone else was hanging outside your fence last night."

Della didn't care about who was hanging out, she wanted to know why the hell Chase wouldn't have told her he knew Chan. What else was the panty perv hiding?

"What did he want with Chan?" she asked.

Kevin answered, but her phone was cutting him on and off.

Holiday looked at Della. "You're about to lose service any minute now."

"Look, I'm coming up on a dead zone, can I call you back later?"

The line went dead. Della, confused and furious, stuck her phone in her pocket.

"Something wrong?" Holiday asked, probably picking up on all of Della's emotions.

"Yeah," she said.

"You want to share?" Holiday asked.

"Chase knew Chan and he never told me," Della said. "Something's up with him, Holiday."

Holiday let out a deep moan and yanked the car to the side of the road.

Della didn't understand Holiday's strong reaction. But when she looked at the fae, she saw she had her hands white-knuckling the steering wheel.

Holiday's moan hadn't been about Chase.

"Are you okay?"

"No," Holiday said through tight lips. "Something's . . . the baby." She moaned again.

Della grabbed her phone out of her pocket to call Burnett, only to remember the dead zone.

Holiday let out another deep groan. A whooshing sound filled the car. The skirt of Holiday's yellow dress, tucked between her legs, grew dark. "My water." Holiday dropped her head on the steering wheel, looking to be in extreme pain.

"Okay. Okay." Della told herself to say calm, but calm was the last thing she felt. "Let me drive. I'll take you to Dr. Whitman."

Holiday nodded, but it seemed to take effort for her to release the wheel.

Della jumped out of her side and ran around. By the time she got to Holiday, she was lying in a heap on the side of the road.

"Holiday!" Della dropped down beside her. "Holiday, talk to me. Please talk to me."

She held up one hand. "I . . . the . . . baby's coming."

"I'll go get help."

"Don't you dare leave me! I'll send death angels after you if you do." Holiday grasped Della's hand so hard, it might have cracked a bone.

Threats weren't Holiday's style, so Della knew this was serious.

"I won't leave." She watched Holiday reach down with her other hand and hug her bulge. That's when Della saw the blood. Lots of blood now stained the front of Holiday's dress.

Tears filled Della eyes. Was something wrong? She remembered the show she'd seen of the woman giving birth. There had been blood, but she didn't recall this much.

"Get me in the backseat," Holiday cried.

Della inhaled. She opened the car's back door, gently picked up Holiday, and placed her in the seat.

As soon as she got Holiday down, Holiday screamed. And loud. "My panties," Holiday yelled. "Take them off."

"You sure you don't want me to drive you to the doctor? I can drive fast."

"No time," she said. "Baby's coming!"

Della mentally pulled her big-girl panties up and physically pulled Holiday's big-girl panties down. The blood was already pooled between her legs. Fear clutched Della's belly.

If something happened to Holiday or the baby, Della couldn't live with herself. Then again, she wouldn't have to: Burnett would kill her.

Holiday reared her head back on the seat and started grunting. Della saw what looked like the baby's head between Holiday's legs.

If someone had asked her what she would be doing today, not in a million years would she have said "delivering a baby." Swallowing a ton of insecurities, she snagged Holiday's purse. Finding the alcohol cleanser that Holiday always carried, Della squirted it all over her hands.

"What are you doing?" Holiday seethed.

"It's okay," Della lied. "I saw a show once on how to deliver a baby." She tried to sound confident, but she had about as much confidence as an ant taking a stroll among a crowd of joggers.

Holiday, too busy gasping for air to answer, nodded.

"I see the baby's head," Della said. "I think this is when you're supposed to push. As soon as the baby is born, I'm driving you to the doctor."

Holiday did what looked like an ab crunch and let out another ear-piercing scream. The baby slipped out so fast, Della almost didn't catch it. It . . . no, she, it was a girl. "It's a girl" Della said aloud. But the baby was slimy and bloody, reminding Della of a wet puppy. Panic shot straight to Della's heart when she realized that the tiny infant wasn't breathing.

Again remembering the show, she reached into the baby's mouth and used her fingers to dip out any fluid. Then, fitting her palm over the baby's chest, she turned her over. She patted her back. One. Twice. "Breathe!"

She didn't breathe.

"No," Della muttered. She turned the baby back over, massaged her little chest, then turned her over again and gave her another pat, only stronger.

The baby jerked, gurgled, and took her first breath. Della, not even realizing she hadn't taken in air, took in a breath of her own. Only when the child let out a cry did Della look up at Holiday.

"She's okay." Della's relief vanished. The baby wasn't the only one in trouble. Holiday lay unconscious.

"No," Della said. "Holiday?"

When the camp leader didn't answer, Della tuned her hearing, ignored the cries of the baby, and finally heard an erratic heartbeat still pumping in Holiday's chest.

She looked at the cord still connecting the baby to Holiday. She remembered how they'd cut the cord in the show she'd watched. Grabbing Holiday's purse again, she found some floss and used it to tie the cord. Then she used another piece and twisted it so tight it severed the cord. When Holiday still wasn't moving, Della knew she had to get her help. And fast.

She tucked the crying baby beside her unconscious mom and shut the door. Racing around the car, she got in the front seat and drove like a bat out of hell straight to Dr. Whitman's office.

As the tires hummed against the street, and with Holiday's blood on her hands and making the steering wheel sticky, Della's breaths shuddered in her chest and she prayed aloud, "Look, God, let's make a deal. If you're missing your weekly quota of souls, take me. But don't take Holiday. Please."

Della sat in the vet's office, feet tapping on the floor, wringing her hands. She'd called Burnett as soon as the doctor and Steve took mother and child to the back. When Burnett answered, Della's throat was so tight from emotion, she could hardly explain. The only thing she got out was "Dr. Whitman's office."

"Holiday?" he asked.

"Yes," she muttered.

"Is everything okay?"

"No," Della said. "Not okay at all."

Then she called Kylie, thinking her healing powers might be needed. Della hissed. Of all the times for Kylie not to pick up. She left a message: "Holiday needs you," she said. "We're at Dr. Whitman's office."

The office door swung open less than two minutes later. Pain filled Burnett's expression. And all she could think about was how romantic it had been when he stood up for Holiday in front of the FRU committee. The love he had for his wife was so much a part of him that if he lost her, it would no doubt be like losing a limb.

Or maybe even worse, his heart.

The tears Della held at bay fell then. Big fat tears, rolling one after another. Burnett didn't ask for details. No doubt he saw the gravity of the situation in her expression. He took off for the back of the office.

Voices ordering him to get out echoed from behind the door. Orders Della knew wouldn't be heeded. Burnett would never leave. He'd never leave Holiday.

But dear God, did Holiday have a choice not to leave him?

Della pulled her knees to her chest, hugged them, and continued to cry. "Take me instead. Take me instead," she kept muttering.

"Hey," a voice said. Steve's voice. She'd seen him briefly when they took Holiday and the baby, but they hadn't spoken yet.

Della wiped the tears from her face and looked up. "Are they okay?"

"The baby is going to be fine."

"And Holiday?" she asked, her breath a big bubble of pain in her lungs.

Steve's expression didn't look promising, and more tears slipped from her lashes.

Chapter Thirty-four

"She's still unconscious," Steve said. "She's lost a lot of blood. But Dr. Whitman has given her some now and he's hoping she responds."

"Hoping? He's hoping." Her voice shook. "Isn't there something else he can do? She can't die," Della said. "She can't! You go back in there and tell him to do something!"

Steve dropped down beside her and put his arm around her. She buried her face in his shoulder.

"You did an amazing job delivering the baby and getting them here so quickly. They are both still alive because of you," he said. "Maybe your parents are right about you becoming a doctor."

"No, I hated every second of it. If she dies, it's my fault. Oh, God. It's my fault."

"No it's not." His words came so close to her ear, she could feel his breath. "Don't give up on Holiday yet."

Della choked on a sob.

"Shh," Steve said. "Holiday is a fighter. She's going to pull through."

"What if she doesn't?" Della asked, her chest a big knot of pain. "Do you know how excited she was about this baby? Now there's a chance the baby will never know her! And Burnett . . . Holiday is his life." Della buried her head in Steve's chest so he couldn't see her cry, but she couldn't stop the sobs that racked her body.

Steve stroked her hair and kissed the top of her head. "We just have to hope and pray—and trust that Holiday's going to wake up. Like you said, she wants this baby so badly and she adores Burnett. So she has a lot to live for."

Della closed her eyes against Steve's shoulder, her sobs subsiding. Her breath evened out and she let his warmth surround her.

In the back of her mind, she knew they needed to talk about their own issues, but that seemed so trivial with Holiday's life hanging on the line. Closing her eyes, she prayed again for Holiday. Harder than she'd ever prayed for anything in her life. Dear God, she'd already lost Chan; she couldn't lose Holiday.

Della wasn't sure how much time had passed—ten minutes or thirty—when Dr. Whitman walked out. She sat up. The smile on his face put her instantly at ease.

"Everything is going to be fine," he said. "Thanks to you." He focused on Della.

She nearly collapsed in relief, and Steve put his arm around her for support.

Right then, the front door swung open and Kylie stormed in, her eyes bright with emotion. "Where is she?" Her voice rang deep, the way it got when she was in protective mode.

"She's in the back," Dr. Whitman said. "But she's going to be fine."

"What happened?" Kylie asked.

Dr. Whitman answered, "It looks like she had a minor placental abruption."

"Minor?" Della repeated with snark. Nothing felt minor about what had happened this last hour.

"Minor doesn't mean it wasn't serious, but if the abruption had been severe, the baby definitely would have died, and Holiday could have bled to death, too. As it is, she's lost a lot of blood. If she'd lost any more . . ."

"I need to see her," Kylie insisted. "I can help. I'm a healer."

"She's asking to see Della," Dr. Whitman said. "I think you both can come in, but only for a few minutes. She needs her rest. And first you both need to go wash up." He looked at Steve. "Do you have a shirt Della could borrow?"

Della hadn't realized it until then, but she wore Holiday's blood. Tears stung her eyes.

Steve led Della and Kylie to the bathroom in the back, then left, and returned with a navy T-shirt. He handed it to Della and walked out. Kylie shut the door.

"Are you okay?" Kylie asked.

"Yeah," Della lied, and then slipped off her shirt, stiff with Holiday's blood, and slid Steve's shirt on. The feel of the cotton on her skin felt soft and cool. Della pulled it to her nose. Steve's scent clung to the piece of clothing.

She'd missed that smell.

She'd missed Steve.

When Della walked in and saw Burnett holding his little girl in his arms, tears almost formed in her eyes again. Holiday still looked pale, but she smiled. "Thank you," she said to Della, then nodded at Kylie.

"We were undecided on a middle name," Burnett said. "But we decided to go with your middle name, Rose."

Kylie chuckled and looked at Della. "Your middle name is Rose?"

Della frowned at Kylie and then looked back at Holiday. "Don't give her that," Della said. "I hate that name. It sounds like a porn star!"

"It does not!" Burnett said. "I like it. She's Hannah Rose James. Named after Holiday's sister and you. The doctor said you saved them both. Looks like I'm going to have to be nice to you from now on."

"I won't hold my breath," Della said, hoping humor would ease her need for more tears.

"You actually delivered the baby?" Kylie asked.

Della nodded. "It's not like I had a choice. Holiday threatened to send death angels after my ass if I left."

Everyone laughed.

"I'm sorry," Holiday said, but she was still smiling.

"Don't be," Della said.

"That must have been amazing," Kylie chimed in.

Della looked back at the proud mom and dad. "Yeah. And if you two ever decide to have another one, I'm getting the hell out of town. I'm not doing that again. And the minute I'm eighteen, I'm getting my tubes tied. I was too young to see that."

Laughter filled the small room again. And it felt good.

The baby made a cooing sound. Burnett gazed down at the little bundle in his arms. Della's heart melted at the love in the big bad vampire's eyes. She couldn't help but think of her own father; if at her own birth, he had loved her so much. But not wanting to get caught up in her own problems, she pushed that thought aside and studied the baby that, unfortunately, would carry her middle name.

All cleaned up now, she looked less like a wet puppy, and more like a little person. A beautiful little person. Della studied the infant's pattern. Her pattern marked her as half fae and half vampire, but with the vampire pattern larger. She was definitely vampire dominant. With Burnett as her father, it wasn't surprising. Neither was the fact that Hannah Rose James already looked like a daddy's girl.

The infant held the tip of Burnett's pinkie in her fist—his smallest finger larger than his daughter's whole hand. Her thick dark hair looked like Burnett's, but her fine feminine features were surely from her mother.

"She's beautiful." Kylie looked at Holiday. "Can I offer you a healing touch?"

"I think I'm fine," Holiday said.

"Just to make sure, let her do it," Burnett said.

"She shouldn't waste her energy if I'm fine," Holiday insisted.

"You weren't the one who had to see you lying there lifeless less than an hour ago," Burnett growled at his wife before looking back at Kylie. "Do it. I'll hold her down if I have to."

"Do the baby, too," Della said, looking at the fragile infant, remembering her not breathing.

All of a sudden, Della felt her eyes grow moist. Tears of relief. But damn, it had been a tough day. But a day of miracles.

Billy wasn't going to jail, and Holiday and the baby had survived.

Take me instead. Della recalled her prayer. It even appeared God didn't need an extra soul after all.

A few minutes later, Dr. Whitman chased all of them out except for Burnett. And since the doctor wanted to keep Holiday and the baby there for a few days, Della hoped the doctor didn't mind company, because she would bet her canines that Burnett wouldn't leave his wife's side.

As they turned to leave, Burnett asked Della to ride back with Kylie and leave Holiday's car, since it had the baby carrier in the trunk. She agreed and stepped out of Holiday's room. Steve was waiting there. Della met his eyes and remembered how good it felt when he'd held her.

"I'll give Della a ride back," he said, as if he'd heard Burnett's plans.

Kylie looked at Della as if waiting for her to argue. No argument left her mouth. She and Steve needed to talk . . . if only she knew what to say. Or what not to say. *Hey, I kissed Chase.* Or, *Hey, I think I forgive you.*

And just like that, she remembered what she learned from Kevin right before the whole baby thing happened. Chase had known Chan. She considered going back and telling Burnett, but that seemed selfish. He deserved to celebrate his daughter's birth without worrying about anything.

Later, Della thought. She'd tell him later.

"You riding with me?" Kylie asked.

Realizing she'd been lost in thought, she looked back at the shape-shifter who'd held her so tenderly when she needed him. "No, uh, Steve will take me," she answered Kylie.

Relief filled Steve's eyes.

Surprise filled Kylie's baby's blues. "I'll see you back at the cabin. With Diet Cokes ready."

Della smiled and watched her leave.

Steve drove her back to Shadow Falls in a new Honda Civic. "Nice car," she said ten minutes into the silent drive, wondering if it was Jessie's. Were they such good friends now that she just loaned him her new car?

"Thanks, my parents bought it for my birthday."

"Birthday?" she asked.

He nodded.

Della swallowed a lump of regret. "That's why they were down to take you to dinner?"

"Yeah."

She exhaled. "I didn't know it was . . . your birthday."

"I know," he said.

"I wish you would have told me." She stared out the window, not wanting to see anything like disappointment in his eyes.

"You had already planned to go to Kylie's and the funeral home. It's okay."

It didn't feel okay. She felt terrible. He'd invited her to go out with him and his parents on his birthday and she'd totally flipped like he'd asked her to get engaged or something. She hadn't even said happy birthday. Not that she'd known when his birthday was, but she still felt like the world's largest disappointment.

Damn she was a terrible girlfriend. Or a terrible "almost" girlfriend.

She finally glanced at him. "Do you know when my birthday is?"

"November eighteenth," he said.

"How did you know?" she asked.

"I peeked at your license one time."

Great. Now she only felt worse.

"I'm sorry," she said.

"For what?"

"For not knowing when your birthday was. For being a bitch." For kissing Chase.

"You're not a bitch. You're scared," he said. "Too many people have disappointed you. And then I became one of them. I'm the one who should be apologizing for letting . . . Jessie kiss me. I was feeling sorry for myself, I guess, and maybe I was a little upset. And she really was the one who kissed me, but I wasn't blameless. I knew she had a thing for me, and I should have told her earlier that it wouldn't happen, but . . ."

Della looked at him. "But it felt good her paying attention to you when I wasn't. And you were disappointed in me." Was that why she'd kissed Chase, too? Maybe.

He pulled up and parked in front of Shadow Falls and looked at her. "Yeah, but that doesn't make it right. And I feel terrible."

"You shouldn't." But didn't she feel terrible as well?

"I made a mistake, Della. I'm big enough to admit it."

She owed him the same, didn't she? She studied her boots on the floorboard. "I kissed Chase," she said. There. It was out there, now Steve could be mad at her instead of himself.

She wasn't sure what she expected him to say, but when he said nothing, it scared her. She looked up. "See, you don't have to feel so bad."

He didn't look relieved. He looked angry. Wasn't that her plan? To take some of the blame off him? But maybe it hadn't been such a good plan after all.

"You did it to get back at me?" he asked, his tone tight.

"No, I . . . I don't think so. Maybe a little. It was complicated, but I'd be lying if I said a part of me didn't want to get back at you. I was hurt, a lot." She paused and tried to figure out how to explain; then she decided to just tell him the truth. "Miranda put it in my head that if I kissed someone I would be able to forgive you, because that's what Perry did after she kissed someone a while back."

"That's the stupidest thing I've ever heard."

"I know. I told her that, too."

"But you still did it," he said, his tone filled with hurt.

"No, I mean . . . that's not why I did it. Okay, maybe in a small way her advice was lodged in my brain, but that wasn't really what happened. We were on a mission, and we were supposed to have already been left. Some gang members arrived and I was trying to make them believe we were . . ." *A prostitute and a John* didn't sound good, so she said, "That we were just part of the crowd."

He looked out the window and stared at the trees for a minute. The trees swayed in the wind, and Della realized that like the trees, things between her and Steve could go either way. She knew which way she wanted them to go, but for the life of her she couldn't say it was the right way.

Because if she'd been a bad "almost" girlfriend, would she do any better trying to be the real thing?

"Did it work?" he asked.

"Yeah, they didn't know who we were."

He looked back at her. "I mean Miranda's plan?"

She hated admitting it, but . . . "As crazy as it is, it might have."

He inhaled. "Did you like kissing him?"

Too much. She almost lied, but then . . . "Probably no more than you enjoyed kissing Jessie." And she knew he'd enjoyed it because he'd looked so guilty the day she'd called him on it.

He stared out the window again. "You could have lied on that one."

"I'm becoming a big advocate of the truth, lately." Especially after learning how many people had lied to her. Her ex-boyfriend. Her parents—they'd never told her about her uncle and aunt. Chase—what was his connection to Chan?

And yet, as angry as those lies made her, she continued to lie, didn't she? She wasn't telling her parents she was vampire—for good reasons, but it was still a lie. And she hadn't told Burnett about her uncle and aunt, and she didn't think she would. But right now, at least with Steve, she wanted to be honest.

"I'm sorry I kissed him. There was danger involved and everything was intense, but it was . . . It wasn't you. And afterwards," Della continued, "I wished it was you." Besides, Chase was gone now.

"That's exactly how I feel," he said. They sat in the front seat of the car, just staring at each other. "So what does this mean?" he asked.

"I know what I want it to mean. I want there to be an *us*, but I'm still scared."

"Then we just take it slow."

She looked at him and her heart felt half filled with promise and half filled with fear. "Wasn't that what we were doing and it didn't work out?"

"Then we don't take it that slow. We let it move faster," he said it with caution and with hope.

She bit down on her lip. "I didn't even know your birthday. I don't know how good I'll be at . . . being an us." She waved a hand between them. "You probably deserve better."

"It doesn't get better than you." The gold and green flecks in his eyes flickered as he smiled. He leaned in and, fitting his hand behind her head, pulled her closer. "You're beautiful, and funny. And smart." His words came against her mouth. His lips finally brushed hers. "Did I say beautiful? I love you wearing my shirt." Their mouths met. His palm slipped to her neck, and emotion radiated from his touch. He shifted closer to the center console, trying to get close to her.

She did the same.

Their tongues met and the kiss went from romantic to something more. Her heart raced, her skin felt supersensitive. All she could think about was getting closer.

She wanted to rip out the console between them; instead, she climbed over the dang thing. But when her ass hit the steering wheel the horn blew.

They both laughed, and dipped down in case anyone looked. Steve reached below and reclined his seat several inches, making room for her in his lap. Not really fitting, she tried to readjust. He scooted up, and she slipped legs around his waist. The position was tight, but ultra sexy. Della's heart raced and she could feel Steve's follow suit.

She pulled back just an inch, looking at his wet mouth. "You do know it's the middle of the day and someone could be watching."

"So?" He pulled her back against him. His hands slipped under her shirt. His palms fit around her waist, so warm, so right. Slowly, his touch traveled up from her waist to her edge of her breasts. She wanted his hands there. She wanted his hands everywhere.

Steve ended the kiss way before she wanted him to. His breath came hard and fast, and his eyes glittered with the same thing she felt, desire. Need. Longing.

His eyes told one story, but his facial expression told another.

"What's wrong?" she asked.

Chapter Thirty-five

"You're hot, Della," Steve said.

"So are you," she answered.

"No!" He pulled his hand out of her shirt and passed it over his face. "Not *hot*." He shook his head. "You are sexier than hell, but what I mean is that you still have a fever. What's going on?"

"Oh. I . . . I'm sure it's not a big deal." She told him what she'd been telling herself for the last few weeks. "I don't think I have a fever, I'm just not as cold." And not wanting to think about being sick, she knew what would distract her. She tried to kiss him again.

He put his hand between her mouth and his. "It could be a big deal. And if you aren't as cold, then it means you have a fever. Now get back in your seat."

"Why?"

"I'm driving you back to the office so Dr. Whitman can check you out."

"No." Della rested her forehead against his.

"Why the hell not?" He leaned his head back and studied her face.

"Because . . . I'm fine. And I don't want to worry Burnett and Holiday right now. If I'm not back to normal in a few days I'll come in. Okay? Or better yet, I'll have Kylie do some of her healing-hands stuff on me."

His expression filled with disappointment. "Healers can't cure everything." He studied her. "What are your symptoms?"

I don't have a rash. Wasn't that what was important? "Steve, I'm fine. And for your information, Kylie cured her friend's cancer. I'm sure she can take care of a little virus." She felt better saying that, too. But if she told Steve she suspected she had the same thing as Chan, he'd freak. A freaking Steve she couldn't handle.

"What are your symptoms?" he repeated adamantly. "Are you hurting anywhere?"

"No . . . well, I had a headache for a while, but it's gone now." She wasn't going to lie, just downplay it a bit.

"And?" he asked.

She hadn't said "and," but Steve had always been able to read her. "This stays between us," she said. "Doctor-patient privilege, right?"

He glared at her. "You're sitting on my lap. I had my hand up your shirt."

"It's your shirt," she corrected, and smiled.

"Whatever, my point is that I'm talking to you as your boyfriend." She smiled. "I like the sound of that."

His stern expression softened. "Me, too." But then he frowned again. "Now tell me your symptoms."

She could maybe tell him some of it. "Do I have your promise you won't say anything?" She touched his mouth. It was as soft to her fingers as it had been on her lips.

"Fine. I promise," he cratered.

"My hearing, vampire hearing, and scent, it goes in and out. It's crazy. They come and go."

His expression hardened, and his brown eyes, which had looked all sexy seconds ago, now looked fretful.

"You're beginning to look more like a doctor," she accused.

He groaned. "Let me take you now to see Dr. Whitman, Della. Please. Have him check you out, do some blood work. I'll feel so much better."

"No. Like I said, in a few days when Holiday is home and everything is okay with the baby, I'll go, but not now."

"But . . ."

"Stop making this into something more than it is." She was fine, she told herself. Vampires seldom got sick. *And yet some that do get sick, die.*

The voice echoed inside her head, and damn if it didn't sound a lot like Chan.

But right then Della heard other voices. Voices and laughter. These came from outside the car. Steve lifted his head and looked out the window.

Through a few strands of hair, she stared at Steve, hoping, praying, she was wrong. He finally glanced back at her.

She bit down on her lip before asking. "Please tell me someone hasn't seen us making out like a couple of horny teenagers in the front seat of a car."

He brushed her hair from her face. "Does it matter anymore?"

"How many?" she asked.

"How many what?"

"How many am I going to have to kill?"

A smile lit up his eyes, and he glanced back to the right and then to the left. "Six. No seven. Wait. Eight. That's a lot of people to kill." His grin widened.

She felt her face grow hot, wondering how long everyone had been watching. "I guess I should get off your lap."

He arched his eyebrows in a teasing manner. "I don't know. I kind of like it."

She started to pull one leg from behind him. "If my ass hits the horn again, I'm going to die of embarrassment right here and now."

His smiled faded and she knew exactly where his thoughts had gone. "No one's dying. "

She had started to focus on getting her leg free when he touched her face and tilted her chin up to meet his face again. "Two days,

Della. If you don't come in to see Dr. Whitman, I'm bringing him to you."

"I'm sorry, but it was funny." Miranda laughed and pulled out three Diet Cokes from the fridge. "And we didn't know it was you. All we saw were two people making out in the driver's seat." She sat the drinks on the table. "And we didn't recognize the car."

"It's not funny!" Della growled.

Miranda, Kylie, Perry, and five other students had all been standing out by the entrance watching her and Steve. Della had no idea how she could have not seen them when Steve pulled up, but then again, all her attention had been on the driver of the car.

All her attention had been on Steve's touch; on how it felt to be kissed by him. On how it felt to be understood by him. Was that what made him so special? He accepted her the way she was. He liked her the way she was.

"Hey . . . all you did was kiss." Kylie tried to assure her, but even the chameleon was smiling on the inside, Della could see it in her eyes.

"I don't know," Miranda said. "His hand was in her shirt and we couldn't tell where her hands were."

Della shot the witch a cold glare. "Drop it before I drop you!"

"Right, let's change the subject," Kylie said. "We're happy. Holiday and Hannah are going to be fine. Thanks to you, by the way. You and Steve have made up."

"Thanks to me," Miranda said. "I told you to kiss Chase. And that's what fixed this."

"Kissing Chase was a mistake." Della's mind went to him knowing Chan again, and she needed to call Kevin to see what else he knew about the panty perv, but she didn't want to think about him right now. Kylie was right. Things were too good to worry. And if that meant ignoring that she now had a little headache, so be it.

"All in all," Kylie said, and popped the top on her soda, "it's been a hell of a good day."

And I saved Billy, Della thought, and opened her own drink.

When Della looked up, Miranda stared, eyes tight, frown tighter. "What?"

The witch set her soda down. "You're happy, but . . ."

"But what?" Della asked.

"Your aura is still dark. Even darker than before."

"Well, then your aura detector is broke," Della said.

Miranda shook her head. "Tomorrow, you're going bird watching. I don't care if I have to drag the birds to you."

By eight that night, Della sat alone at the kitchen table—feeling lonely. And feeling like shit. Her headache had increased. The throb came not only at her temples, but at the base of her neck. Maybe she should have let Steve drive her back to Dr. Whitman's office after all. Or perhaps she should have asked Kylie to do her magic before leaving.

Yup, Della's two best friends had abandoned her over an hour ago to be with their boyfriends. She couldn't be pissed. If Steve was here, she'd be with him.

Staring down at her phone, she willed it to ring. She'd called Kevin back twice, hoping they could finish their conversation about Chase, but his phone went to voicemail and he hadn't returned her calls. The question weighing on her mind grew heavier. Why hadn't Chase told her he knew Chan? What could that mean?

The cabin walls seemed to moan. Was it her imagination, or had the room's temperature dropped a few degrees? She folded her arms around herself and looked around. Was Chan here? She shouldn't be afraid of him if he was. But the tickle of unease in the pit of her stomach didn't go away. What did her cousin want with her? Was it about Chase?

She recalled Chase telling her he'd been looking for someone. Had he been lying?

All at once, the skin at the base of her neck prickled. She turned her head, half expecting to see someone standing there, staring at her.

The room was empty. Or at least empty of anyone she could see.

"Is it you, Chan?" she whispered.

Only silence answered her. Picking up her phone, she considered calling Steve, but she'd called earlier and he said he had patients and he'd call her as soon as he had a few minutes. Thoughts of Jessie being with him did a lap around her already antsy mood. Trusting Steve was one thing, trusting Jessie was another. Her head throbbed harder.

When another chill ran down her spine, she stood up and decided to go take a warm shower. She moved to the bathroom, started the water, and stripped off her clothes. The sound of the shower seemed to echo, and for some reason she remembered the falls. She looked at the shower curtain. Steam billowed out. She set a towel on the counter. Rubbing her temple, she glanced up in the mirror and saw her naked reflection. Then she saw him.

"Shit! Get out of here, Chan!" Being scared of her dead cousin she maybe could have handled; being scared and naked was too much. She grabbed the towel and swung around to face him. She expected him to be gone, but he wasn't. He stood there in puff of steam.

"Look behind you," he said.

"Get out of here," she repeated, still adjusting her towel and fighting the pain.

"Look behind you," he said again, and now he was the one who looked afraid.

She glanced over her shoulder, breath held, not knowing what she would see. Nothing stood behind her, just her reflection, and the reflection of her dead cousin, staring at her with sad eyes.

She turned and faced him again, and slight movement sent her world spinning. She waited for it to stop. "Look at what?" she managed to ask, gripping the counter for fear she'd fall.

He raised his arm and pointed behind her. She glanced back again and again saw nothing. But then, in the midst of the fog, Chan's image faded.

She slowly turned her head to the front again. He was gone.

Look behind you. His words echoed in her head. *Do it!*

Shaking on the inside, she didn't know which was worse. Seeing him, or hearing him in her head.

Still, she did as he requested and looked over her shoulder again. "What am I supposed to see?" she asked, her words seeming to be sucked up by the steam. The pain in her head seemed to spread to her shoulders.

"What am I supposed to see?" she said again, her patience thin.

Only a deadly silence answered. She couldn't hear the water running anymore. She couldn't hear herself breathe.

She blinked and was just about to turn around when an arrow was drawn in the steamed-up mirror. Pointing to her reflection. She followed the arrow. And she saw it.

"Shit!" She dropped the towel. All dread of ghosts, dread of being naked in front of ghosts, vanished. A different kind of fear built in her chest.

Her heart raced and simultaneously the pain in her head and shoulders pounded harder. Standing naked in the foggy bathroom, she heard Kevin's words echo in her head. *They said he got sicker and then he got a weird rash on his back and then he died. Just died.*

Della stared at the splotchy red markings starting at the back of her neck and running down her spine. They kind of looked like feathers.

Reality set in. She had the same thing Chan had. She had the same thing that killed him.

The bathroom door opened. She expected Kylie or Miranda.

She reached to get her towel. Using all her energy, she stood, and her head swam, black dots appeared in her vision, but she focused on the door. Her breath caught when she realized she'd been wrong. It wasn't Kylie or Miranda.

"What the hell are you doing here?"

Chapter Thirty-six

"You lied," Della accused, eyeing Chase, shocked he was in her bathroom. "You were never looking for anyone."

"I was," he said. "I was looking for you."

She had to work to focus around the pain. "You knew Chan, my cousin."

"Yeah." His gaze moved over her.

Realizing she was only wearing a towel, she said, "Leave."

"I tried to. Couldn't do it. A conscience is a terrible thing to acquire. Like it or not, you and I are going to be bonded."

"Bonded?" She shook her head, only to realize that any kind of movement made the pain worse.

His gaze swept over her towel-covered body. "It could be worse. You could be ugly."

"Get out of my bathroom!"

He walked out, but didn't shut the door. She slumped against the counter, dizzy again. The fog in the bathroom seemed to seep into her mind. Had he really been here? Had she just imagined him? Had she imagined Chan and the rash, too?

"Here." The panty perv, real, not imagined, walked back in as if he had every right to be in her bathroom. He had some of her clothes in one hand, her phone in the other.

He set the clothes on the counter. "Get dressed."

"Get out!" A chill, this one coming from inside her, raced down her spine. Her insides trembled. Her head throbbed.

"Get dressed or your shape-shifter friend is going to be pissed when he sees us together and you're naked. Not that he won't be pissed anyhow." He said the second part almost to himself. "But it's too late to try and find someone else."

"What?" she asked, not understanding.

"Get dressed."

"With you standing there? Not likely!" Her voice trembled and she had to clench her jaw to stop it.

He gave her his back. "Get your clothes on. We don't have a lot of time."

"Time for what?" She spit the question out between gritted teeth. An odd kind of déjà vu hit. She remembered feeling this way once before. The chills. The pain.

Chan had been with her.

Staring at Chase's back, she dropped her towel and reached for her clothes. In the mirror she saw him turn around.

His gaze swept up her naked body.

She growled. His focus went to the mirror, to her eyes.

"Sorry. I thought you were dressed."

Sorry, his ass! Or hers, because it was her ass that was bare. She showed him her canines, then continued dressing.

He continued to watch.

"Why were you at Chan's?" she asked, managing to slip on the sweats and pull the T-shirt over her head. But each move cost her. Her head pounded. Harder.

Chase looked at her phone. "Let's get your shape-shifter here." He pushed a button.

Pain shot from her neck down her spine. Unwilling to let him start more trouble between her and Steve, she grabbed for her phone. Chase caught her hand. Her pain intensified. She didn't have the strength to pull away. Her knees gave, and she fell against him. He wrapped his arm around her and held her there. Why did he feel so warm, and her so cold?

"It's okay," he whispered in her ear. "We're going to make it through this." She felt his hand move gently against her back.

It was not okay!

She managed to push away, caught herself on the counter, but her whole body ached. Muscles she didn't know she had clenched. Tears filled her eyes. Yup, this was how it had felt to be turned.

"Hey, Steve," the panty perv said into the phone, while looking at her. "This is Chase."

Della could swear she heard Steve's voice angry.

She tried to get the phone again. Chase caught her with one hand, gently, nothing rough about his touch. He didn't have to be rough. She didn't have the strength to fight him. But she resented that his touched came so tender.

She fell back against the counter again. Breathing hurt.

"Shut up and listen," Chase seethed into the phone and studied her with empathy. "Della's running out of time. I'm taking her to Holiday's cabin. Meet us there. I know what I've got to do to save her, but I'm going to need your help." Chase hung up.

Della stared up at him. "What's happening?"

"Do you remember being turned into a vampire?" he asked.

The fact that he knew what she felt scared her, confused her. "Yeah. Why?"

"There are a few lucky, or in most cases, unlucky vampires, who get to do it twice."

She shook her head. "I've never heard of that."

"You wouldn't have. It's rare." He reached for her. "Let's go."

"No!" She held up her hand. "Not until you explain."

He frowned. "Okay, fast version. Of the hundred bloodlines proven to carry the virus, there are six who are prone to rebirthing."

She tried to think around the pounding in her head, the pain clenching at her shoulders. She thought of the rash. "The same thing happened to Chan?"

Chase nodded.

"You did it," Della accused. "You poisoned us or something."

"No."

She had just enough clarity to notice he didn't blink. So was he telling the truth? Did she even have enough wits about her to judge that?

"Here's the thing," he continued. "Less than three percent of Reborns survive. But the few who do, have tenfold the power. Thankfully, a study done by a doctor associated with the Vampire Council found a way to up the survival odds."

"What way?" she asked.

"You bond with another Reborn."

"Bond? Bond how?"

"A complete transfusion. You take the antibodies of someone who survived. It's the same premise used to create vaccinations. But in this situation, it links the two vampires. They become almost a part of each other. It has been compared to the relationship shared by identical twins or perhaps soul mates."

She tried to wrap her head around everything he said. She stared at him. "You are a Reborn?"

He nodded. "Good thing we like each other, huh?"

"I don't," she snapped. "I don't like you."

He leaned in. "Your heart doesn't lie, Della Tsang."

So maybe she liked him, but . . . "I don't want to be bonded with you." Her heart didn't jump this time. She wasn't sure she wanted to be bonded to anyone, but if she did, there was a shape-shifter she had her eye on.

Chase sighed. "Honestly, at first I wasn't all that crazy about it myself, but let's make the best of it." He held out his hand. "Come on, let's get this done. The sooner we do this the less we'll suffer."

"We?" she asked. What was this "we" crap? He obviously wasn't hurting.

"I'll go through the process with you. When I get your blood."

Her mind raced. He was going to suffer . . . willingly? He had to be lying.

She didn't take his hand. "I'll get Kylie to heal me. I don't need you to. . . . Call her." She motioned to her phone.

"Healers are wonderful," he said, "but they won't work on this. For the past five hundred years, the few Reborns who survived had to sit back and watch their entire families die. Being as powerful as they were, they brought in witches, wizards, and the most talented healers. With zero success I'm afraid."

"How do you know so much?" A charley horse latched on to her chest, and she could barely breathe. Her knees started to give.

"After going through it myself, I took an interest in finding out what it was all about." He moved in and swept her up in his arms. "Time to go."

She put her hands on his chest as he started out. "I don't want this."

"You'd rather die?" He stepped out on the porch. The cold wind stirred her hair. She shivered in his arms.

"Maybe I won't die. Maybe I'll be one of the three percent." Just like that she remembered, *Take me instead*.

Maybe God had needed that extra soul after all.

"Those are really bad odds." Chase lit out, full flight, and without ever running.

He flew faster than the wind, holding her to his chest as if she was something he treasured. She wasn't his to treasure.

He landed in front of Holiday's cabin and walked in as if he owned the place. He laid her down on the sofa. There was a table with some medical stuff set out, as if he'd already been there.

Another pain hit; this one shot from her neck down her back. It felt as if her spine were breaking. She gritted her teeth to keep from crying.

When it passed, she gasped for air. He brushed a hand over her forehead. "You don't have to be brave. I know it hurts like hell."

A second later, she felt a damp cloth move over her forehead. The gentle touch reminded her of Chan. He'd been there for her. The first time. That's when something occurred to her. "It doesn't work," she said.

"What doesn't work?" Chase asked.

"The bond thing. You were with Chan. You couldn't save him."

Chase's expression tightened. "I didn't do it."

The grief she felt for her cousin bubbled up inside her along with the pain. "You let him die?"

Guilt came and left Chase's eyes. "I tried to save him, but he wasn't like you." He looked at the door as if impatient. "How long does it take to get from the vet's office?"

She didn't answer. "What do you mean he wasn't like me? He was my cousin. We're from the same bloodline."

"Same bloodline, yes, but he was weak. No spirit. No fire in his belly. You push yourself. You're a fighter. He had no fight in him."

"Chan fought for me. He pulled me through the first turn. He didn't owe me anything, but he stayed with me. He cared. If not for him, I don't know what would have happened."

"I didn't say he wasn't a good person. I said he was weak. I tried to get to him to run, tried to help prepare him for what he was going to endure. He wouldn't even try. He lay there and let himself get sicker. Even if I'd bonded with him, the chances of him surviving were so damn low. And I'd have . . ."

"You'd have what?" she asked, finding it hard to breathe.

"He wouldn't have survived. He had no fight in him. And if I'd tried, I wouldn't have been able to . . ."

"To what? And how do you know he wouldn't have survived if you didn't even try? You let him die."

Chase exhaled. "I wanted to save him, I couldn't."

Her head pounded; her heart ached. "I don't want your blood in me."

The front door swung open and slammed against the wall. Della could barely sit up, but she did enough to see Steve storm in. He growled, a low ominous sound, aimed at Chase; then he rushed between them and dropped to his knees beside her.

She felt his hand on her brow. "You're burning up." He slid one arm under her. "I'm taking you to Dr. Whitman's office."

"No, you're not," Chase said behind him. "Put her down!"

Steve pulled away.

Pain gripped her midsection and she curled up in the fetal position. Through tear-filled eyes, she watched Steve charge Chase. Magical bubbles spilled from the shape-shifter, no doubt his plan to change into something fierce.

Chase grabbed Steve before he completed the change and pushed him against the wall.

"Listen to me before you morph yourself into something that can't reason. If you don't want Della to die, you're going to have to do exactly what I say. I know what I'm talking about. It's why I came here." Chase looked back over his shoulder at her. "And we're running out of time."

Out of time. Out of time.

She closed her eyes, and when she opened them, Chan stood beside her. He smiled that crooked silly grin of his. And this time it felt different. He wasn't here with her. She was with him. Clouds floated past.

It was okay, she thought. Death didn't suck nearly as bad as she thought it would. And Holiday was alive.

Chapter Thirty-seven

Della must have passed out. Or maybe not completely out. She heard Chase explaining things to Steve, but it sounded like they were walking away, getting farther and farther from her. Or maybe she was the one leaving. And it was okay. She let herself be swept away.

Something woke her up, or brought her back. She felt a prick in the center of both her arms. Something warm flowing through one of the needles into her vein.

Tightening her eyes, she longed for something. What was it?

Then she knew. It was that place. A place of lightness, and light. Soft breezes and calm. She remembered Chan. Being with him.

Instinctively, she knew she wasn't with him now. Vaguely, she re-called him waving to her through the clouds. Good-bye. It had been good-bye. She'd pleaded for him to stop moving away, but then real-ized he wasn't the one leaving. She was. "No," she said, realizing what it all meant. Worried about the consequences. It had been her deal with God—to save Holiday and the baby. But something, maybe gravity, had pulled her back. . . . No, not gravity. It had been figures. Two of them, wearing long robes, and as they brought her back the one with light blue eyes had whispered, "Not your time." Then she heard it. The water. The falls.

Death angels.

Right then she realized she wasn't so cold anymore.

"Hey." Steve's voice had her opening her eyes. He knelt beside her, checking the needle taped to her arm. His brow bore deep worry lines, and his eyes were filled with concern.

She blinked. More awake, she realized that pain still gripped her chest, but not nearly as bad. She saw the catheter in her arm and realized what was happening.

"Stop it," she said, her voice nothing more than a whisper, and she tried to pull the needle out of her arm.

"No." Steve caught her hand. "What Chase said makes sense, Della. You're getting his antibodies. Your fever's dropping."

She wet her lips. They felt so dry. "He said I'd be . . . bonded to him."

Steve's grimace deepened as if Chase had told him this, too. "I won't let that happen." He brushed her hair from her sweaty brow.

She heard a moan, and turning her head, she saw Chase. Stretched out on the table, he looked unconscious. "What's happening?" she asked.

"Your blood is going into him, he's going through what you were."

She continued to stare at Chase. His back arched in pain. Her pain. He shouldn't have to . . . "Stop it," she said, and again tried to pull the needle from her arm.

"We can't stop it." Steve caught her hand. "He made that very clear. If I stop it now, he'll die. He has to go through with it to survive."

She closed her eyes, but hearing Chase's moans sent a memory of the severest pain coursing through her body. Tears filled her eyes. Why had he done this?

She swallowed, her throat raw. He had saved her, but why hadn't he done it for Chan?

He was too weak. She heard Chase's words, but it still hurt.

Steve touched a moist cloth to her lips as if he knew how thirsty she was. "You're still running a fever, but it's coming down. You should be fine soon. Just rest now."

He pressed a kiss to her brow. "I'll take care of you. I'm right here." But even as he said it, she felt the blood being pumped into her veins. Chase's blood.

Bonded.

The smell, it was hideous. Something touched her nose, and she went to wipe it away and heard a loud crash. She tried to open her eyes; they felt dry, raw. Her tongue felt stuck to the roof of her mouth.

"I told you the garlic wasn't a good idea," a voice said. "She didn't mean to knock you down. Now can you please take it out of here?"

She recognized the voice, but it wasn't Steve's. Was it . . . Chase's?

She remembered hearing him moan. Remembered thinking he might die. That wouldn't have been right.

Forcing her eyelids open, she realized she wasn't on the sofa any longer, but in a bed. She looked around, having to squint to focus. Holiday's bedroom.

Burnett sat in a chair beside the bed. Something moved on the floor. She lifted her head slightly and saw it was Dr. Whitman. *She didn't mean to knock you down.* Burnett's words echoed in her head.

Had she done that?

Burnett leaned in and studied her. "She's awake," he said to the doctor. "Can you leave us?"

"You sure it's safe?" the doctor asked as he got to his feet.

"I'll be fine." Burnett looked at her.

Della ran her dry tongue over her parched lips. "Where's Chase?"

Burnett frowned. "He's gone."

She lifted her head off the pillow as emotion filled her chest. He'd died saving her. Grief, real and deep, took over her lungs and made it almost impossible to breathe. "He died?" It felt as if her heart had been yanked out. An empty hole left in her chest where it had once beat.

"No," Burnett said. "He left. Probably didn't want to face me."

The sense of loss didn't go away. Less grief and more . . . anger. He left her? Saved her life and then ran off? What kind of person did that?

Burnett held out some water. "Drink. I know you're thirsty."

She reached for it but quickly he pulled it back.

"Easy," he said, "or you'll break it."

She made a face and caught the glass in her hand. It shattered in her grasp. "Crap," she muttered, and stared down at the glass and water on her chest.

Burnett grimaced. "I warned you." He stood up. "Don't move, I'll get it."

He pulled a trash can over and, using a towel, carefully removed the glass. "It will take some time to get used to it." He dropped back in the chair and reached for her hand to check for injuries. There were none, or if there had been, they had already healed.

"Used to what?" Her head still spun in a fog. Her heart still ached with abandonment.

"Your new powers."

She closed her eyes and recalled Chase saying something about that, but so much of what happened was a blur. Normally, the idea of more powers would have had her jumping up and down, but not now.

It seemed somehow insignificant. Chase was gone.

She sat up. Maybe she could find him. "Where did he go?"

"Who, Steve?"

"No. Chase. Do you know where he went?"

"No." Burnett stared at her as if something was wrong.

"What?" she asked.

"Nothing. I just . . . I don't understand this part."

What part was he talking about? She shook her head. "Would

you mind explaining what part you *do* understand? Because I'm pretty much in the dark here. And a little damn light would be appreciated."

He leaned forward, his elbows resting on his knees. "I was fourteen. I got sick. The pain was excruciating. My foster parents took me to a doctor, but I don't even remember that. They said I almost died. When I woke up, I was a hell of a lot stronger than I used to be. That's most of what I remember."

He paused and took a deep breath. "All supernatural doctors are registered. And when my report came across the FRU table, I got my first visit from an agent."

Bits and pieces of what Chase had told her started coming back, and suddenly she realized what Burnett was saying. "You're a Reborn."

He nodded.

"But I don't understand. Why wouldn't you have said anything? I know you are strong, but I've never seen you do what . . . Chase can do."

"You can't tell anyone either, Della. The vampire society—mainly the rogue society, but even some of the good guys—maintain an Old West mentality. The fastest gun in town is nothing but a challenge. Someone's always looking to best you."

He glanced down at his folded hands and then back up. "Look what happened when Chase showed too much of his power at the bar. The gang leader called him out. Your powers are a gift, but one you should downplay constantly and only use in dire emergencies. You don't have to pretend to be weak, but you never show all your cards. To do otherwise puts your life, and those you love, in jeopardy. It's worse than being a protector, which is seen as something honorable. This is viewed as someone being a badass. It makes you fair game."

She shut her eyes a minute, hearing what he was saying, but it didn't seem to be the thing she needed to worry about. She willed herself to remember everything that had happened and tried to put the pieces together. "You knew Chase was a Reborn," she said. "How?"

Burnett nodded. "I saw him flying the first day he showed up here—which he shouldn't have done in a place anyone could have seen him. I immediately started investigating him. I worried there was a reason he was here. Then I was hoping it was just to get involved with the FRU. I didn't know he was here because of you."

"He was here because of me?" Her voice came out raspy, dry. The question had just left her lips when she remembered. He said he'd been looking for someone and then he'd admitted it was her.

"Yes." He picked up the water pitcher and poured another glass. He handed it to her. "He told Steve he'd been sent here to make sure you survived."

She took the glass carefully. Her mind spun. She took a small sip. It actually burned her throat, and so did her next thought. Chase had suffered for her. Endured the pain. Then it hit: He'd done it for her, but not for Chan. "Chase could have saved Chan?"

Burnett nodded. "I don't think it was his fault, Della. Chase told Steve that Chan was too weak. His odds of survival were very low. That it only works if the Reborn is strong enough. I don't know if all of this is true, this transfusion procedure is new, but at this point it makes sense."

Della's heart gripped. She didn't know whether to be grateful or angry. Maybe both.

"Perhaps Chase could only save one of you. And he chose the one he knew would have the best chance of survival."

A new emotion crowded Della's chest. She knew this one well. Guilt. Chase could only save one and he'd chosen her. She'd lived and Chan had died.

"That said," Burnett continued, "I think the bigger question is who sent him?"

My uncle and aunt. That's was the only thing that made sense.

And maybe when she had a chance to process this, she'd tell Burnett. But not now.

"It was reported a few years back that a doctor, not one working with the FRU, was researching Reborns to see if he could offer a better survival rate. In the report, it stated the condition was thought to be hereditary."

Burnett paused. "I took a personal interest in discovering all I could about it when Holiday got pregnant. If my own child fell prey to this, I'd go to the end of the earth to save her. But all I could dig up was vague reports."

For the first time, Della thought of Holiday and Hannah and she felt selfish for it. "How are they?"

"They are fine. Beautiful," he said, his eyes lighting up with love. He paused. "The truth is, I've learned more about this process today than was in any of our files. I'm sorry you had to go through it, but it's given us a lot of information. So you may have saved my daughter's life twice. And for that I'm eternally grateful. If Holiday wasn't so set on the name Hannah, I'd give her your first name, too."

Della offered him a weak smile and swallowed another sip of water.

A few minutes of silence passed. "Phillip Lance was arrested. He confessed to killing Lorraine and her boyfriend. You did an excellent job, Della. You are going to make one hell of an agent someday."

She nodded and tried to draw pleasure from it, but no pleasure came. Her thoughts shot back to Chase. And she asked the question that for some reason concerned her the most. "The bonding thing, do you know about that?"

Burnett sighed. "I'm sorry. Steve mentioned this, but I haven't heard of it before." He paused a minute. "Does it concern you? Do you feel any differently about Chase now than you did before?"

"No." She heard and felt her heart jump.

And so did Burnett.

She wanted to deny it. "He saved me. He gave up some of his power and endured the pain for me. It's understandable that I'd be grateful, right?"

"I'd believe so," Burnett said, but he didn't sound convinced.

She swallowed, her throat still parched. Her thoughts shot back to her cousin. "He should have tried to save Chan." Tears filled her eyes. "It only makes me feel worse. Chan helped me through the first turn, and because of me, because I was a little stronger than he was, he was passed over." She wiped the tears from her eyes. "Is that fair? I lived, and he died."

"No," Burnett said. "But life is seldom fair." He dropped a hand to her arm. "But I can tell you what *is* fair. You are still with us. And . . ." He pointed to the door. "In the living room are several very concerned friends of yours who are also grateful that you are alive. Kylie and Miranda haven't left this cabin for two days."

"Two days?" she asked. "I've been out for two days?" Her next thought was how long ago Chase had left, but she didn't want to ask it. Didn't want to think about him, but she couldn't seem to help it. What did that mean? Or did it mean anything at all?

Burnett nodded. "We were all getting worried. And, I know they are all ready to see you, but are you ready to see them?"

No, she thought, but nodded. If it were Kylie or Miranda in here, she'd be freaking out.

"Remember, Steve knows all of this. The doctor knows some of it. And I'm aware you share everything with Kylie and Miranda, and even though I can't tell you not to, in this case, I'll suggest you don't."

Keep secrets from her two best friends? She didn't think so.

After freshening up, Della nodded to Burnett, who stood in the back of the room and opened the bedroom door. They all came barreling in. Kylie, looking panicked, came in first. Miranda, a close second, with tears in her eyes, followed. Perry stood at her side. Steve moved in behind them, and then Jenny and Derek. She even saw Lucas hanging in the back.

Friends. She had a butt-load of them.

Miranda, the perpetual hugger, dropped on the bed, and when she tried to do her thing, Della held up her hand. "I'm fine." Right then, she looked up and met Steve's gaze. He winked at her, but she saw something else there. Fear. And she knew exactly what he feared.

Bits of their conversation from when she'd been feverish sounded in her head. *He said I'd be . . . bonded to him.* She had told Steve about Chase.

I won't let that happen, Steve had answered. But he had to have known he might not be able to stop it. Yet, he'd done it. Emotion squeezed her chest. Chase had risked his life, endured pain to save her, and Steve helped him do it, knowing he might lose her.

"Don't you ever do that again!" Miranda snapped.

"I'll try not to." Della met Kylie's eyes. "I'm fine, so get that worried look off your face."

"I tried to heal you," Kylie said, and her eyes brightened with unshed tears. "I couldn't. My hands wouldn't get warm and you wouldn't wake up."

Della recalled Chase saying healers wouldn't work.

"But I'm better now. So no emotional outpouring okay?"

"Oh, my God! Oh, my God!" Miranda started chirping and bouncing her butt on the bed.

"What about no emotional outpouring did you not understand?" Della asked.

The witch rolled her green eyes. "You better be glad your pissy pass hasn't expired."

"Her what?" Lucas asked.

Della exhaled.

"I'm just happy," Miranda said. "It's your aura. It's not dark anymore. I mean, it's still vampire dark, but it's not ugly dark."

"Nothing about Della could be ugly." Steve moved in and sat down beside her. He still looked worried. His hand eased over close and touched her wrist. Almost testing her.

She wished she could tell him not to worry.

But she could, couldn't she?

No one controlled her. It was her choice. She had to believe that. Turning her hand over, she laced her fingers with his. She held on tight, but her heart still hurt. Hurt from missing Chase.

An hour later, Della was back at her cabin—alone in her bedroom. Pacing. Left to right. The tiny room made pacing difficult.

Steve had walked her back with Miranda and Kylie. When he saw that her two friends weren't going to give them any alone time, he kissed her on her cheek—in front of them—and told her to call him the minute she could talk.

She hadn't called him yet. He was going to ask her. Ask her if she felt different about Chase. What was she going to tell him? He deserved the truth. And yet . . .

She hadn't even told Miranda or Kylie anything about what really went down. Della could tell they were waiting for her to explain things. They'd gotten out the Diet Cokes. But Della had played the "tired" card and come to her bedroom.

Okay, fine, she was being a terrible friend and worse girlfriend. But give her a freaking break! How was someone to explain something they didn't understand? Or tell the truth when they didn't know the truth.

Bonded? What the hell did that even mean?

She didn't want to believe it could mean anything.

And yet she hadn't stopped thinking about him. Her emotions spun like a roller coaster jacked up on coffee that had been laced with speed.

Angry.

Confused.

Beholden.

All of them targeting the same guy.

Almost as frustrating—almost—were her newfound powers. Which she understood even less than the word "bonded." Of course, it could be because she hadn't checked them out yet. And when would she get that opportunity?

She had a feeling Burnett was going to be watching her like a hawk to make sure she didn't expose herself—the way Chase had.

Frankly, she didn't blame Chase. What good was having powers if she could never use them?

Or, as in this case, almost never use them. Burnett *had* said they could be used in dire emergencies. *Define "dire emergency."*

Della picked up her phone. Her mom had left a message. She needed to call her. But it must not be a dire need, because she didn't want to do it. Or maybe she just didn't know what to say to her any more than she did to anyone else?

Oh, she knew what she wanted to say: *Hey, Mom. Did you know Chan's dead? I know you thought he was dead a while back, but he wasn't. And guess what, now I'm not just a vampire, but a really badass one. And, oh yeah, I've supposedly bonded with a guy. Though I don't have a fracking idea what it means. So could you stop being ridiculous and tell me about my dad's sister and brother who I'm pretty sure sent this guy here to bond with me?*

Oh yeah, that would go over about as well as a fart in church.

She heard someone walking up to the cabin. Lifting her face, she inhaled, wanting it to be a certain scent. Chase's scent.

But what did she want with him?

Answers, she told herself. Chase had some explaining to do. And not just about this bond thing, but about who sent him looking for her.

It wasn't Chase.

She heard Derek ask where she was, and then Miranda said, "You're going to tell her now?"

She swung the door open. "Tell me what?"

Both Kylie and Miranda looked concerned.

Derek walked over to the sofa and dropped down.

"Just tell me," Della said. "It's about Chase, isn't it?"

"No," Derek said.

"Then what?" she asked.

"A couple of days ago, I finally got someone from your father's school to chat with me about your aunt and uncle."

"And?"

"Your aunt is . . . dead."

Della heard him, but didn't want to accept it. "So you found her obituary. She could have faked it, just like my uncle."

"I don't think so," he said.

"Why not? Just because she wasn't in the same funeral home. There could be others who—"

"It's not that," he said. "She was murdered."

"Murdered?" Della's gut tightened. Someone had killed her aunt? "When? How?"

"It was about a year after your uncle was supposedly killed in the car accident."

"Who killed her?" She thought about her father, the pain he must have endured after first losing his twin and then his sister. No wonder he didn't talk about the past. "Did they catch the bastard?"

His eyes filled with regret. "When I found this out, I went to my PI buddy and asked him to look into it. He has a lot of friends who are detectives." Derek cupped his hands and paused.

"And?"

"He got someone to pull the file. It's listed as a cold case. They never arrested anyone because they never had enough evidence."

"So they had no suspects? None? Someone kills my dad's sister and just gets away with it?"

He paused, and she could tell he didn't want to tell her. "Spill it!"

"There was only one suspect."

She waited for him to tell her more. Her patience snapped. "Good Lord, do I have to reach in your mouth and pull out the words? Who was it?"

He still hesitated. "Your father."

Della swallowed. "They thought. . . . That can't be right. My father would never—"

"I didn't say he did it, I just said that he was their only suspect."

Della saw the way Miranda and Kylie looked at her. Empathy. And the little witch was about to try and hug her again. "He didn't do it," Della seethed. "I'm telling you he didn't do it!"

"We believe you," Kylie said. "We just feel bad that you have to hear it. And you've been sick and—"

Wanting to scream, no, wanting to run, she took off. At first, she forgot not to run too fast. But she slowed down just enough that she wouldn't have Burnett after her. She made seven laps, pretty damn fast, and never even got tired. Finally, she landed. There wasn't one noise. Silence.

Then her phone dinged with a text.

She pulled it out. Her breath caught. It was from Chase.

Worried about u. We need to talk.

"No shit, Sherlock!" she said, and started to type a response, but she heard and smelled someone coming.

Kylie, with Miranda on her back, landed beside her. Della slipped her phone back in her pocket.

"Are you okay?" Kylie asked.

"No," Della said, miles past trying to pretend. "I'm not."

"Do you need a hug?" Miranda asked.

Della stared at the little witch and thought of about ten over-the-top pissy things she could say, but when she opened her mouth, not one came out.

"Yeah," Della said, and a few tears slipped from her lashes. "I think I do." Confusion to the point of pain swelled inside her. Her dad was suspected of killing his sister. She was bonded to some guy she barely knew, and didn't know what that meant. But as much as she wanted to deny it, it felt like it meant something.

Standing in the midst of a group hug, without a friggin' clue what she was going to do, she found a moment of clarity. She had a shitload of questions that needed answering and big decisions she had to make, but one thing she knew. She had two of the best friends ever.

And if she could just remember that, she'd survive all of this. Survive and find answers. She had to.

After all, she was a reborn. That had to mean something.

Della's journey continues!

Don't miss *Eternal*, coming Fall 2014.

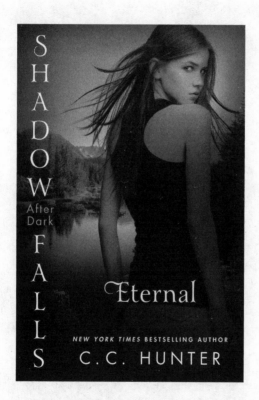

Read the series that started it all

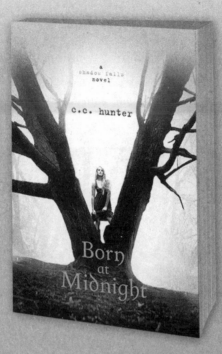

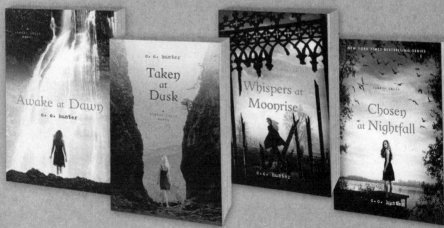

Available now.